Cover Up

Karen Woods

EMPIRE
PUBLICATIONS

First published in 2013

EMPIRE PUBLICATIONS
1 Newton Street, Manchester M1 1HW
© Karen Woods 2013

ISBN 978-1-909360-17-4

Printed in Great Britain.

In memory of Lee Finnighan and Linda Bradshaw

ACKNOWLEDGEMENTS

Once again I would like to thank all my family and friends from Facebook and Twitter. My children; Ashley, Blake, Declan, Darcy thanks for all your support. To James as always, thanks for being my rock. My Mother Margaret and My father Alan, thanks for always believing in me. I have also won The National Award and regional award for Adult learners and I will be so proud to represent a nation of learners and people like me when I pick up my award.

Big thanks to Niace for all the hard work they do in helping people get back into education. I can't thank my tutor Christine Ansell for all her hard work and support throughout my learning journey, a friend always. Thanks to All the actors who are performing in the play of my first novel Broken Youth based on my first novel. You guys are so talented and deserve to shine.

A big mention to Kirsty Milne, keep smiling and never stop believing in yourself, your stronger than you think girl, I'm so proud of you. Hugs and kisses to the cast of Broken Youth Lisa Carey, Ray Driver, Samantha Jones, Kelly Hughes, Emma and Lydia, Clarie O'Rourke, Daniel Jackson, Jack Nolan, Fraser Williams Seb, Jack Willis, Bev, Danny Baker, Regina, Gino, and Baz, Lewis and Darcy. A big thanks to Lauren Warwick for helping me bring Broken Youth to the stage at the Lowry. Also Louis Beckett from Moston Miners club and Paula, and not forgetting Racheal Crosby and Gail from Harpurhey neighbourhood project for all their help and support.

At the moment I'm working on my next novel called "Riding Solo" so watch out for it folks.

Finally a big thanks to Ashley Shaw and John Ireland from Empire, thanks for believing in me. Thanks to Dean Duffy for his input into the cover design and all his hard work and Delennyk Richardson for proofing the book.

As always I would like to say thanks to my son Dale, without you none of this would have happened. Goodnight Godbless son, always in my heart.

"Never stop believing"

Love Karen Woods
www.karenwoods.net
@karenwoods69 Twitter

CHAPTER ONE

Mary Wilson was shopping in the superstore when her waters broke; she had no warning - it was trickling down her legs. Her mother was on another aisle searching for some new product that she'd seen advertised on the TV. Nelly was always the same once she got it into her head that some new diet on the market would help her drop a few dress sizes - she really thought they worked. Nelly was at her biggest and she hated that her clothes didn't fit her anymore. Her belly hung low underneath her knickers and she was forever prodding at it with her fat fingers.

In shock, Mary dropped her head down between her legs; she could see a large puddle of water forming around her feet. Her face was beetroot as she tried to hide from the other shoppers. The smell from the bakery filled her nose and the aroma from the freshly baked bread made her puke into her cupped hands. This baby was early; Mary wasn't due until the following month. She'd woken up that morning with pains in her back and just thought she had another water infection. Over the last few months she was always nursing a water infection and thought today was no different.

A teenage boy walked past her and his eyes shot down between her legs. The corner of his mouth started to rise and he couldn't wait to shout his mates over to make them aware that this woman had pissed her knickers. "Norman, get over here, and check this dirty bitch out, she's pissed her knickers," he waved his hand about in the air frantically enjoying every minute of the woman's misfortune. Mary

7

pressed her body up against the wall and sank her fingers deep into her waist as the next contraction surged through her body. Growling at the group of youths gathering in front of her she tried to walk away from the mess on the floor. An elderly woman walking past clocked that the woman was in distress. Quickly walking to her side, she took hold of Mary's clenched fist and waited until the contraction had passed. Mary's face was on fire and she was panting like a dog on a hot summer's day. "Somebody get a bleeding ambulance," the woman screeched. "This woman's in labour." The other shoppers hurried towards the drama. They all stood gawping, their trolleys full of shopping in front of them, watching the woman's face crease with pain, whispering to one another. Mary let out a scream like an injured animal and squatted down. The contractions were coming fast now and there seemed no way of stopping them. Her cheeks looked on fire; small beads of sweat were dropping from her brow. "I want my Mam," she yelled at the top of her voice. The shoppers parted as a voice from behind them filled the air. An older woman with bright red hair looked frantic as she pushed her way through the crowd.

"What's up Mary?" she ranted as she came to her side. "Is it the baby?" Mary nodded; this girl could only have been seventeen years of age and she still looked like a child. "You lot move out of the bleeding way. Can't you see what's happening?" Mary's mother took control of the situation, she was waving the crowd away but they weren't budging. Nothing like this had ever happened in the store before and they were making sure they didn't miss a single moment of the drama.

The supermarket manager ran towards them looking traumatised, she was stuttering and her mouth was dry as she tried to get her words out. "An ambulance is on its way." Her eyes shot down to the girl on the floor and her face frowned. She was thinking the same as everyone else who was stood there. Her words leapt out of her mouth without any thought. "Is she having a baby? I mean, is she even old enough?"

Nelly sprang to her feet and gripped the manager by the arm; there was no way she was putting up with this kind of talk. "Listen, you stuck up bitch, that's my daughter you're talking about. Who gives a toss how old she is, she needs help, so just sort it out will you, before I shove my foot right up your arse." Whispering from the gathered crowd filled the air; this was a show not to be missed. Nelly snarled at the onlookers and shot her eyes to another woman who was stood at the front of the crowd and appeared to be the ringleader of the mob. "And, if you've got anything to say love, let's hear it; otherwise keep your big trap shut." The shopper smirked; she was a right cocky cow, she never replied. The manager led Mary down the shopping aisle and tried to get her out of public view but she could only manage a couple of steps before she collapsed to the floor again. Her legs were parting – this baby was coming now.

The baby's father was nowhere to be seen. He'd disappeared the moment he'd found out she was pregnant. He was an older man who had taken advantage of Mary, well that's what Nelly was led to believe. Mary held so many secrets about her baby's father and she was happy that her mother bought the story regarding him. She could never breathe a word of his true identity; he'd told her straight that if she told a soul about him he would make sure she ended up in a body bag. Mary believed every word he said. He was a force not to be messed with.

Covering Up

Suddenly medics appeared on the scene, charging through the store to the pregnant woman's side. By now Mary was flat on her back and shrieking at the top of her voice. "Get it out of me now. I can't do this anymore; get the bastard out of me." Her eyes looked like they were going to pop out of her head as she bore down for the next contraction, her face creased with the pain and her knuckles turned white as she gripped her bare knees. Nelly screamed out as her daughter pinched her arm. "Turn it in, bloody hell you're going to make me bleed if you carry on doing that."

The manager looked mortified; she'd never seen anything like this in her life. She'd dealt with a few angry customers before and the odd shoplifter, but this was in a league of its own. She shouted to some of her staff stood in the distance talking. "Right get this mess cleaned up, and get a warning sign around it. That's all we need is another claim coming in," her finger pointed behind her at the wet floor. The two workers looked at her with frowned faces, slowly they trudged away to get a mop and bucket. They kept turning their heads back over their shoulders continuing to watch the drama.

The medic knelt by Mary's side, he placed a pair of Latex gloves on his hands. Using some silver scissors from his bag he quickly cut her pink nylon knickers off and tossed them to the side of him. His face was white; he could see the top of the baby's head. Mary's face was boiling hot and this time she brought her knees up to her chest. "It's here again, please make it stop," she screamed. Nelly hid her face away behind her hands; this was all too much for her to take. Mary hadn't been to one birthing class and this was all a big shock to her, she just thought the baby would just fall out without any fuss. How wrong

10

could she have been? The area was closed off and Mary's screams echoed throughout the store. The sound of a baby crying made the onlookers' part; the drama was over.

Nelly held her Granddaughter in her arms for the first time. Tears filled her eyes as she stroked the infant's delicate pink fingers. This was her first Grandchild and she was cherishing every minute of the new member to her family. Mary frowned as the medic got her ready to go to the hospital; she was relieved it was all over. She was never giving birth again, no way, it was way too painful. She could see her baby in her mother's arms and snarled as she got a glimpse of her child for the first time. This baby had a lot to answer for. Without it, she would have just been a normal teenager, free to go wherever she pleased. She hated it and knew she could never be the loving mother that everyone expected her to be. Nelly stood to her feet and passed the baby to the ambulance man. As they walked out of the store she could see she had the full attention of the shoppers. Ramming her two fingers in the air she made sure they could hear every word she spoke. "Show's over now folks, get back to your shopping, you nosey bleeders."

CHAPTER TWO

"Mam, I'm going out will you watch Kendal for a few hours, while I nip to see Debbie?" Nelly dragged her plump body out from the chair and nearly lost her balance. She was raging and ready to attack. Mary hadn't spent any time alone with her child; she was always passing her about to anyone who would give the child the attention she needed. Even late in the night Nelly would have to crawl out of her bed to feed the baby. Mary would just roll over and drag the covers over her head, she hated that she was a mother. Nelly thought that her daughter had post-natal depression at first, but as the months ticked away, it was there for everyone to see, Mary didn't care about her child.

"No Mary, you can stay in for a bleeding change. It's every night you want to go out. I'm not doing it anymore. She's your baby, not mine; so start acting like her mother."

Above the silence you could hear Mary's heavy breathing; steam was coming out of her ears. Pacing about the front room she let rip, she'd had enough. "I hate the little bastard; there you go, I've said it. I never wanted her anyway, mother," her bony finger pointed in Nelly's direction. "It was you who made me have her. I wanted an abortion, but, oh no, you and your Catholic faith was against all that, wasn't you, you Bible-basher?"

Nelly stood frozen for a second and swung her arm back. Before it reached her daughter's cheek she screamed out. "You should have kept your bloody knickers on then and none of this would have happened. You've always been the same you Mary, you're one selfish bitch. She's your child, now, you look after her." The sound of a slap landing on Mary's face filled the room.

Mary stood shivering and her nostrils were flaring, her chest was rising with speed. "Get her adopted for all I care. I'm leaving mother, I've had enough. That kid is not ruining my life. I've got plans and they don't include her," she pointed her finger towards Kendal who was sitting in her bouncy chair in the corner of the room. Nelly ragged her fingers through her daughter's long hair, making sure she had a firm grip. She swung her about the front room like a rag doll.

"Selfish, selfish, cow. How can you say that about your own flesh and blood? God forgive you."

Mary wriggled free; standing with her hands on her hips she opened fire. "I hate her, she just reminds me of how fucked up this family really is?"

Nelly ran at her again and pinned her up against the wall, her hot breath was in her face. "What do you mean by that? Come on; say what you've got to say. Spit it out." Mary was gasping for breath, she was turning blue. Her mouth was open but no words were coming out, Nelly had hold of her windpipe. You could see the evil look in Mary's eyes as she smirked; she definitely had something to say.

The baby's piercing screams stopped the action. Nelly paused for a second and walked away to tend to her needs. Kendal was teething and she was constantly craving attention. Nelly growled and turned her head back over her shoulder. "You're lucky I've not knocked you to Kingdom come Lady." Mary plonked down on the sofa; she was as white as a sheet. Her mother had a short temper and she knew she'd pushed her too far this time. Nelly was a battle-axe and was more than capable of looking after herself.

The living room was depressing, clothes were all over the place and it stunk of cheesy feet. The black fungus creeping across the ceiling told you just how unhealthy the abode really was. The family lived from hand to mouth most of the time and money was tight. Mary knew she wanted more from life than being a single parent; she had plans, big plans of changing her life. Watching her mother tend to her baby's needs she gritted her teeth tightly together. Her eyes focused on a brass candlestick sitting on the wooden cabinet next to her, just one swipe across her mother's head that was all it would have taken to knock that cocky smile right off her face. Mary sat on her hands to control her temper, she was shaking inside. Nelly picked Kendal up in her arms and nursed her; she was rocking her slowly in her arms. Mary listened to the lullaby her mother was singing and shook her head. Motherhood was the pits and the sooner she could get away from her child the better. Standing to her feet she halted, she wasn't sure of her next move. After a few seconds she left the room. Nelly was shouting after her to come and get the baby but she blanked her completely and went upstairs to her bedroom.

Mary sat on the edge of her bed, chewing the skin on the side of her thumb. The walls seemed to be closing in on her and she looked pale, her skin was grey. Quickly, diving into her wardrobe, she knew she didn't have long to pack her stuff. Grabbing all her belongings she snatched a sports bag from under her bed and shoved her clothes inside it, she was frantic. The sound of footsteps coming along the landing made her jump; she froze and held her ear to the door, there was someone there. The bedroom door creaked open and there stood her mother with Kendal in her arms, she wasn't happy. "Here, get hold of her. I'm off to bingo, so you need to sort her out. I think her nappy needs changing, so take a look." She forced the baby into her daughter's arms. Mary snarled and hung her head low. "I don't know why you're looking at me like that young lady; she's your child, not mine, so start acting like her bleeding mother. I don't know what's come over you lately, you're a right pain in the arse." Nelly left the screaming child and started to walk out of the room, turning her head back over her shoulder she growled at Mary. "Make sure, you change her arse, because if I come back home later and she's still wet, you'll have me to answer to." Nelly was gone.

Mary plonked the baby on the bed. Kendal was crying hysterically. She gripped her fat legs and shook her lower body with force. "Shut up, you mard arse, that's all you do is cry. I hate you, I hate you."

Mary's younger sister marched into the bedroom, her face was like thunder. "Will you shut her up, why she's crying all the time?"

Mary sighed and stood to her feet. Glimpsing in the mirror on the wall she replied to her sister. "Why don't you take her for a bit, she likes you? Just let me have a break from her for half an hour and I'll come and get her back." Molly stood looking at Kendal crying; slowly she made her way to the edge of the bed, her legs bent slightly as she opened the pink fluffy blanket. Mary was watching her actions through the mirror with a cunning look on her face.

Molly picked Kendal up in her arms and kissed the side of her face. "Now, now, come on, stop all that crying. Auntie Molly's here with you now, not your nasty mother." Molly was sixteen years old and acted much older than she really was. She also had bright red hair just like her mother, and her temper was explosive. Her skin was pale and she was covered in freckles, you couldn't put a pin between them. Mary often took advantage of her younger sister and today was no different. "Right, half an hour, that's all. You'd better come and get her back Mary because I'm going out soon. I swear if you don't, I'm going to tell my Mam."

"Stop stressing will you? Go on, take her. I'll come and get her in a bit." Molly left the bedroom and you could hear her talking to the baby in an animated voice. She was always jealous of her elder sister and the fights between them were constant. Mary held her ear to the door; she knew she didn't have long. Running about the bedroom she grabbed the rest of her belongings, ramming them into the bag. With one last look in the mirror she gripped her black leather bomber jacket from the side of the bed and sneaked down the stairs like a German sniper. Quickly checking her wristwatch she opened the front door. She was gone.

Mary sprinted down Rochdale Road towards the Milan Pub. It wasn't far from where she lived in Harpurhey. The sound of passing traffic rushed past her ears, she kept her head low, she didn't want anyone to see her. The bag on her shoulder was heavy and she kept stopping to try and get a better grip on it. The pub was in sight; her heart was pumping at twice its normal speed. The cold Manchester air was circling her body and it seemed to be holding her back, she was struggling to walk against the chilling wind.

Popping her head inside the pub vault she scanned the area, her eyes were all over the place. She could see a gang of men sat bickering around a small wooden table playing cards, they were shouting and bawling at each other. They looked like they were ready to fight too. One man was dragging another towards him by his shirt and his teeth were clenched together tightly as he ranted into his face. Stretching her neck further inside she could see him, her face looked relieved. Mary placed her two fingers inside her mouth and whistled. All heads turned and faced her and her cheeks were blushing, she didn't think anyone would have heard her. "John, can I have a quick word with you?" she mouthed. A tall man stood up from the table and stomped towards her. He was a big guy and had the build of a rugby player. His pearly white teeth gritted tightly together as he neared her side, he was angry.

"What the fuck are you doing here?" he whispered. "I don't want people talking. Get outside, you daft bitch." A blonde woman who was stood close to the exit was watching them from afar, her face seemed anxious as she chugged on her cigarette. Mary was dragged out of the pub by her arm and she was wriggling to break free. They were alone.

"I had to come John, I had no other choice. I've left home." The man gripped her by the throat; he was nose to nose with her outside the boozer.

"So, what's that got to do with me? I hope you don't think I'm going to look after you?"

Mary's eyes welled up and she was pleading with him, her hands were pulling at his clothes in desperation. "John, you said you would always be there for me. I need you, and I'm homeless." Gripping her by the arm he dragged her behind the pub, she lost her balance. The light was low and you could see the white of his eyes.

"Listen bitch, you've had more than enough from me.

You're not getting another bleeding penny." Mary broke free and stood in front of him with a cocky look on her face; she was bouncing about waving her hands out in front of her.

"Well, we'll see about that if that's how you want to play it. I think it's about time everyone knew about the true John Daley, especially your wife," her eyes were wide open. "Oh, what about my Dad too," her manner was confident. "He'll skin you alive when he finds out," she chuckled and took a few steps towards him, bending into his face. "Let's see what Jackie has to say as well when she finds out her husband is a kiddy-fiddler, a fucking pervert. Because that's what you are John. I was only sixteen, a child who didn't know any better. You took advantage of me."

John knocked her to the floor, Mary could feel warm liquid running down the side of her mouth, she was bleeding. He stood over her with a menacing look in his eye, he had half a brick in his hand; he was ready to finish her off, she could see it in his eyes. A noise behind him made him stop, he hesitated. Mary gripped his legs and that seemed enough to make him realise what he was doing. Bending to his knees, he held her trembling chin in his hands; he squeezed at it with force, it was turning white. "Look at what you've made me do now, you little slag. I swear, you breathe one word of this to anyone and you'll go missing. Do you hear me?"

Mary snivelled and nodded her head slowly. She knew he meant business. John stood up and paced the floor; he ragged his fingers through his hair as he held his eyes up to the night sky, he let out a laboured breath. Quickly flicking his lighter, John lit a cig up and blew a cloud of smoke out in front of him. His eyes were all over the area.

Licking his dry cracked lips he walked back to her side. "You can go and stay with the girls at the brass gaff, but just one week tops, and then you need to be gone."

Mary scrambled to her feet. "I can't stay there, somebody will tell my Dad". John held his hands around his throat, the girl was right. If Paddy Wilson ever found out he'd been dabbling with his daughter he would have had his guts for garters. Paddy was a man's man. He was well known in the area and held the respect of a lot of the men. John was a good friend to Paddy and often put business his way. This was such a mess, John knew he shouldn't have gone near Mary, but she was such a prick teaser. Every night she sat waiting outside the pub's door for him, hoping he would talk to her. Mary knew she wanted John from the minute she saw him at her family home, he'd made her heart beat faster than normal. The smell of his aftershave told her he was rolling in cash and he was drop dead gorgeous, she just had to have him.

Paddy Wilson should have been a rich man too but his cash was always spent on gambling and beer and not his family, he was a selfish old git. His wife Nelly never saw a penny of his money. She had to beg, borrow and steal to keep her head above water to feed her family.

John always showed Mary the attention she craved from the second he met her, she was always flirting with him, and he couldn't help himself. Her sister Molly was the same but Mary always made sure she was out of the picture whenever he came to their house. Mary wanted his complete attention; there was no way she was sharing. John was always bunging her money on the quiet, and he loved that he controlled her. The night Mary conceived with his child he was pissed out of his head. He was staggering out of the boozer and could barely walk. Mary was like a preying lioness waiting for him, she knew the time was right to capture her heart's desire. Sitting near the pub with a few of her mates, drinking and smoking, she sat wishing for some adventure. Her friends had just gone home and she was ready to leave herself. The minute she saw John on the street her heart missed a beat, the time was right to make her move. Mary had long blonde hair, and her eyes were as blue as the sea, they were enchanting, she looked a lot older than her age with the help of make-up. That night, she knew she would get the man of her dreams and made sure John knew exactly what she wanted from him.

John Daley took Mary back to his house and treated her like a woman. He made love to her all night long and didn't think for one minute she would ever get pregnant. His own wife was away visiting her sick mother, and he knew he had the run of the house. He was lonely and craved some female attention. Mary was in love with him for sure, she would have done anything for him. John told her she was like a drug to him and he was addicted. Well, that was until she told him she was pregnant, and then he was off like a shot, he wanted nothing more to do with her once the shit had hit the fan. Mary was big trouble and he knew that more than anyone. His own wife Jackie was barren and he never expected to father a child, especially to a teenage girl.

Mary had been fleecing John for months to hold his secret, but he'd had enough of her now and was planning to get rid of her for good. John dragged his hands through his thick greasy black hair; it was scooped back from his forehead. Stomping up and down the cobbled alleyway he never took his eyes from the girl, she was dangerous and he knew it. "Just wait here for me, I'm just going back inside to tell Jackie I've been called away on business, and then I'll be back with you to sort this mess out." Mary raised her eyes to the sky and screwed her face up. Why he was even informing his wife of his whereabouts was beyond her, he'd never given a toss about her in the past, so why now? The sound of his footsteps crunching along the ground sent a chill down the back of her neck. A black cat hissed at him as he walked by, its back was arched and it was ready to attack him. Launching his foot back he kicked the feline out of his way and watched it scarper from the dark alleyway. Mary held her head to the red brick wall and tried to steady herself, she was dizzy. Wiping her hand across her face she could see the dark red blood on her hands. She knew John was a violent man, but he'd never showed her this side before, until now, and she was frightened.

The roads were quiet as Mary trudged towards Queen's Park on Rochdale Road. John had told her to meet him there. He said it was better that way and he would follow her shortly. Mary's face was covered in blood on one side; the bastard had split her lip open and it was still bleeding. She was picking the dried blood from her face as she walked along the deserted road. Mary's eyes were all over the place and she was constantly looking over her shoulder, she seemed edgy. Queen's Park was daunting. It was pitch black and she couldn't see a thing as she sneaked through the black iron gates to get inside. The place was eerie. Owls hooting in the distance made her panic, and at one point she was going to turn back. Mary made her way to the old museum set deep inside the park; they'd arranged to meet there. She kept twisting her head over her shoulder as she quickly marched to the meeting place. Someone was following her, she was sure of it. "Hello, is that you John?" she shouted behind her. There was no reply. Mary was running and heading to the big building not far from where she was. Her breathing was rapid. She was scared; her eyes were wide open and she regretted ever agreeing to meet him here.

Reaching her destination she sat on the top of the steps to the entrance of the museum, she could see everything from here. Her knees were held up tightly to her chest as she pulled her pink woollen jumper over them. Mary was shivering and her teeth were chattering together. Rustling behind her made twist her body quickly, she couldn't see anything. It must have been a cat. She was petrified and sucked on the cuff of her coat. A loud noise at the side of her made her stand to her feet. As her eyes focused she could see John, the smell of the beer on his breath was overwhelming. His face looked strange and she was unsure of his next move. Mary walked down the steps towards him and smirked. "I thought you weren't coming, I've been crapping my knickers sat here waiting for you. It's really spooky." John pushed her away with a flat palm; he was constantly looking over his shoulder. The moon was shining brightly and she could see a shiny metal object concealed in his hand. He had a knife. Mary swallowed hard; she clocked it straight away and backed off slowly. Her feet crunched on some broken twigs as she stepped back with caution. John dived on her and ragged her to the floor. His large hand covered her mouth and she was frantic, trying to break free. A warm feeling in her waist filled her body, he'd stabbed her. The knife surged deep into her stomach; he was twisting it around with a demented look on his face. With the last bit of strength inside her, she brought her knees up to her chest and managed to move him from on top of her, she kicked him in the nuts. John rolled off her in pain. The knife was still in his hand and he was getting ready to use it again, she was sure of it.

Stumbling into the park she could hear his laboured breath behind her, he was hot on her trail. A large oak tree was nearby and Mary made her way behind it, she couldn't see a thing as she squatted down. John's voice in the distance was chilling, it echoed around the park. "Mary, I'll find you. If it takes me all bleeding night, I'll find you," he ranted. Sinking her head onto her lap, she remained still. Her breathing was fast and she found it hard to swallow, she was shaking from head to toe. The pain in her waist was rising and she knew she had to make a getaway. Mary's feet sank into the thick black mud and she was swaying from side to side. John's voice faded into the distance and she wasn't sure if he was still there. Her body was weak and she was trying hard to focus. Placing her hand onto her side she could see blood all over her fingers, it was pumping from her. Gripping the tree she heaved her body up and stood shaking with shock. Taking a few steps forward, she knew she didn't have long left to find help, she was barely conscious. Mary fell to the ground with a loud thud; she'd been hit over the head. Her chest was rising slowly and you could see her clenched fingers sinking into the ground. "Help," she whispered with her final breath. The shadow of her attacker ran into the night.

CHAPTER THREE

Mary Wilson's body was found at eight thirty-five the next morning. The birds were chirping loudly and they were jumping about from branch to branch watching the commotion below. A dog walker had raised the alarm and the police were now at the scene. DCI Callan stood clocking his surroundings with a serious face. He was chewing frantically on the end of his black pen. He'd been on the force for over twenty years and knew his job well, he smelt a rat. This was a murder case for sure. The female's body had suffered a single stab wound to the stomach area, but that wasn't the cause of death. The jagged brick that had been plunged into her head had finally ended the young victim's life. The forensic team were still with the body and the DCI was working on any scrap of evidence they had to go on.

Daniel Callan had witnessed some of the worst murder cases in Manchester and this was right up there with the rest of them. Danny was forty-five years old and he was used to the sights that lay beyond the white tent where the body was lying. Chewing hard on his bottom lip he inhaled deeply, this was going to be a long day. Police officers swarmed the area around Queen's Park. Onlookers were gathering as word spread that a young girl's body had been found. The police had found what they thought was the murder weapon. The red jagged brick had traces of the victim's blood splattered all over it and it was already bagged up ready for forensic inspection. The police were still waiting to find out the identity of the young girl, all they had to go on was a necklace with the name "Mary" on it. Daniel was a father himself and knew some family out there would be missing this pretty young girl right now.

Nelly sat nursing Kendal in her arms; she'd been up with her all night long. Her eyes were tired and dark black circles were present underneath her eyelids. Paddy walked into the front room in a strop. "Does that kid ever fucking shut up? All night long she's been at it, is she ill or something?" He was hungover and looked rough; his hair was stuck up all over the place. It looked like someone had rubbed a balloon all over his head. Nelly took a deep breath as her eyes flicked to the clock on the wall; she knew her husband would go off his head once she told him that Mary hadn't been home all night. Paddy sat down in his armchair searching for the remote for the TV. Nelly raised her eyes to the ceiling; she knew she'd have to tell him the truth; she was waiting for the right moment. Molly would be up out of bed soon and she wouldn't hesitate in filling her father in, she was a daddy's girl and loved getting her elder sister in trouble.

"Mary's not been home all night Paddy." Nelly closed her eyes and her face cringed as she waited for his reaction, it was coming, and she prepared herself for the onslaught.

"What do you mean? She's not been home all fucking night. Where the bleeding hell is she then?" Nelly knew somehow this would be all her fault. Paddy was always the same, and he'd showed her with his fist on more than one occasion, he was a violent man.

"I don't know Paddy, we had an argument last night and she said she didn't want Kendal anymore. She said she wished she was dead." He sat twisting his fat banana- like fingers; his nostrils were pumping at the sides.

Throwing his slipper across the room at his wife he snapped. "Get our Molly out of bed, and tell her to go and find her." His clenched fist smashed on the table and the loud bang let his wife know he meant business.

Nelly ran to the hallway with Kendal hanging on her waist. There was no way in this world she was putting the child down when her husband was like this; she was her only protection from his violence. She yelled up the stairs, eyes always looking back behind her. "Molly, get your arse down here, now." Nelly stood looking up the stairs until she saw her daughter stood by the top banister. "Get ready quick, I need you to go and find our Mary. Go to Beverley's, and Debbie's, she's most probably there. She'll still be pissed up if I know her."

Molly rubbed her knuckles into her eyes. "Mam, why do I have to go? Just leave her there, she'll come back when she's ready, she always does." Paddy raced into the hallway, he was livid. Stretching his neck to see his daughter's face he growled as he yanked his denim jeans up. Paddy's yellow tobacco-stained teeth ground tightly together.

"Get ready, and go and find her, now! Or do I have to come up there and make you go myself?" Molly's face dropped, her jaw was swinging low. She didn't know he was the one who'd given the order.

"No Dad, I'm going to get ready now."

"I thought so," he hissed as he stomped back to the front room. Molly stood still for a minute, she was hungover herself and hadn't got in until the early hours, she was still drunk. She trudged back into her bedroom to get ready.

Nelly stood looking out of the living room window; her eyes were all over the place. Her wrinkled hand held the corner of the grey net curtain up from the dirty windowpane. The street was busy today and the neighbours were stood talking to each other over their fences. Nelly loved to gossip too, but when her husband was at home she had no chance of joining them, he hated women gossiping. Nelly sighed and turned her head back towards her husband. "You need to have a word with our Mary when she gets in; she's been nothing but trouble lately you know."

He dropped the packet of tobacco from his hands and growled. "I'll knock her head off as soon as the little tart walks in through that door. She doesn't seem to care that she's brought shame on this family already. I mean, pregnant at sixteen, I should have sorted her out then. She got off too lightly, if you ask me."

Nelly knew he was on one and she was sorry she'd even opened her mouth. Her head spun back to the window. "Ay Paddy, the police are swarming outside. I wonder what's going on, they're bloody everywhere, come and have a peep." Paddy bolted up from his armchair. His fat hairy belly was hanging over his jeans. Grabbing a t-shirt from the side he hung it over his shoulders and crept towards the window trying to stay well out of view, he was ducking and diving. This was all he needed, the dibble on his case. He pushed his wife from her place near the window and nearly sent her flying. A cig hung from the corner of his mouth and he was fidgeting.

"Oh, fucking hell, they're coming over here; get your head down woman." Nelly sank to her knees, Paddy was white in the face and he was chewing hard on his bottom lip. "Fucking hell, what do these bastards want now?" he cursed. "Quick, get all that paperwork out of our Mary's room before they find it," Nelly ran upstairs. Kendal was moaning, he gripped her fat pink arm and shook it vigorously. "Sssshhhh." Even from an early age the child seemed to know when to keep quiet, she sucked on her fingers trying to comfort herself. Molly opened the living room door unaware of what was going on. Her father jumped up from his hide-out and dragged her down to the floor with him. "Keep it shut, the pigs are at the door." Molly looked flustered. This behaviour was second nature to her, and she was used to the police raiding the house for her father, she didn't seem too bothered by the commotion. The letterbox was rapping in the hallway. The family all stared at each other and Paddy was debating getting on his toes, he was creeping about the front room. Nelly came back into the room and tried her best to keep Kendal entertained, but she was struggling.

"Fuck, fuck, fuck," Paddy cursed as he dragged his hands through his hair. "Right Nelly, go and see what they want. We can't sit here forever, there's fuck all in here for them to arrest me for anyway. Did you get rid of all that shit out of Mary's room?" Nelly nodded. "Yeah, I've hid it away." Paddy sighed. "Go and see what the nosey bastards want." His wife stood to her feet; just before she walked away he dragged her back by her pink cardigan. His face was fierce. "Don't let them in here, keep them at the door. Do you hear me? Keep them at the fucking door." Nelly nodded and left the room. Molly peeped through the window and the colour drained from her face. The police were team handed and she could see them swarming all about the street.

Peering through the glass pane on the front door, Nelly spotted two uniformed officers stood there. Her heart was pounding in her chest and she tried to look casual as she opened the front door. In her heart she was praying that they'd come for Paddy, she couldn't take much more of his drunken abuse; he was making her life a misery. A bit of time would do him good. Pulling her sleeves down over her arms she tried to hide the purple bruises all over her skin. Paddy had been at it again and this batch of bruises was from his recent reign of terror. The front door opened slowly and Nelly peeped out, she left a small gap in the door. Kendal was chewing on her fingers and she was chuckling as her Nana opened the front door. Mrs Wilson stood with a stern face waiting for the officers to speak. There was no way she was speaking first; her heart was in her mouth. "Hello Nelly, can we come in?" The officer knew Nelly from all the times she'd been down to the police station to bail her husband out. Nelly swallowed hard and remembered what Paddy had told her. She placed a firm hand on the door frame and it was obvious to them that she didn't want them to come inside. "Mrs Wilson, it's about your daughter Mary." Nelly sighed and screwed her face up; she shook her head from side to side.

"I knew it; I just bleeding knew it. If she's in the police station she can bloody well stay there. I don't have time for this. I mean, look, she's left her baby with me all night long and didn't have the decency to come back home," she was closing the front door too as she spoke. "No officer, let her stay where she is for all I care, I've had enough."

The policeman cleared his throat as he took his hat from his head. The other officer did the same. "We've found a body in Queen's Park, and we believe it's your daughter Mary." Nelly looked confused; twisting her head over her shoulder she looked anxious, she wasn't sure if she'd heard them right.

"Come in," she stuttered. Paddy was sat in his armchair when she came back inside, seeing the officers walking in behind her, he prepared himself to be arrested. His face was bright red as he bolted up from his chair; he was in two minds to make a run for it, but his exit was blocked.

"What the fuck do you want?" he ranted at the officers. The vein in the side of his neck was pumping and he was sweating. "I've done nothing wrong, so you've got Jack shit on me." Nelly walked to his side and rubbed softly at his arm.

"It's our Mary, Paddy. They're not here for you." His eyes danced from Nelly to the officers. Molly was sat on the edge of her chair holding Kendal in her arms, her jaw dropped and she swallowed hard.

"Can we sit down for a minute," the officer asked. Paddy was marching about the front room, he looked relieved that they hadn't come for him and stuck his chest out firmly.

"What's she done now then?" he chuckled. "I hope you're not stitching her up, like you do with me? I know what you lot are like, are you're forgetting that?" He raised his eyes at Nelly and sucked on his teeth.

The police officer sat forward in his chair and cupped his hands together, his palms were sweating. Everyone was hanging on his every word. "We've found a body in Queen's Park, and we believe it's the body of your daughter Mary." Silenced filled the room. Nelly rubbed at her arms and the hair on the back of her neck stood on end.

Paddy smirked. "Is this some kind of joke? Come on, stop pulling my leg, you're here for me aren't you?" Nelly sobbed in the corner of the room and collapsed to her knees. Paddy was unsure, and grabbed the officer's arm in desperation. "Stop fucking about now will you. Look at the state of my wife. Come on, if you're here for me I'm ready to come with you, put the cuffs on me, let's have it?"

"Paddy we're not lying, this is serious. We think Mary is dead." Paddy folded in two on the floor; his head sank to the threadbare carpet. Molly came to his side and rubbed his back with a flat palm, her bottom lip was trembling.

"Dad, they said they think it's our Mary they've found; they haven't said that it's definitely her." Nelly shook her head in her hands, she knew it was her daughter they'd found, she had a gut feeling deep inside her. The officer asked Paddy to come with them to identify the body. His face collapsed and tears streamed down his cheeks. No one had ever seen this side of him before, not even his wife, they were all shocked.

"I need a cig first, just sit down for a minute and let me take this in," he pointed his finger towards the door. "Molly, go in the kitchen and pour me a whisky. Make sure it's a large one." She obeyed her father and left the room. Once she was inside the kitchen she gripped the whisky bottle and necked a few mouthfuls herself, she was shaking. Wiping her mouth with her sleeve she headed back. Nelly sat staring out of the living room window, her chin was shaking and she was sucking on her lips. Kendal was crawling towards Nelly seeking some attention; she was ignored and left to cry.

★

Paddy walked into the mortuary, it was cold and he was shivering. The hairs on his arms were stood on end and he was hesitating. The place smelt of death and he was gagging as he waited to see the body. The grey walls seemed to be closing in on him and he asked for a seat before his legs buckled from under him. The officer stayed with him and tried to calm him down, Paddy was a walking wreck. The corpse of a young girl was brought before him and he didn't know if he had the strength to continue. The body bag was unzipped, Paddy's head was low. He couldn't look. As his head slowly lifted, he could smell the scent of his daughter's perfume, he breathed in deeply and his chest expanded. His fingers gripped the side of his cheeks. The fragrance was the one that his brother had bought Mary for her birthday the month before. He knew the smell of it because it smelt of vanilla, and he'd often commented on the aroma of it saying it made him feel hungry.

Paddy's face creased as he saw the body for the first time, he was blowing frantically and he was unsteady. Mary's father sprinted from the room as if his life depended on it, he was retching violently. His daughter was dead.

CHAPTER FOUR

The streets of Harpurhey were full of mourners on the day Mary Wilson was laid to rest. All the dead-legs and grafters were stood on the street paying their respect to Paddy Wilson's eldest daughter. Standing, huddled together they whispered quietly. They too knew that Mary's death was suspicious but none of them breathed a word of what they thought, they kept schtum. The code of the area wouldn't allow them to grass, nobody liked a snitch and they knew more than anyone what would happen to them if they ever put someone's name into the picture. The grey clouds hanging in the Manchester sky looked angry, they were ready to burst. Drops of rain started to fall and you could hear the moaning from the mourners as they covered their heads.

The black hearse pulled up outside the Wilson home and you could see a light pine coffin in the back of it. The family had done her proud. Nobody could believe that Mary Wilson lay inside the casket. She had always been so full of life, and never deserved death, even though she was a handful. John Daley was the one to thank for Mary's send off, he'd had a whip round amongst the lads in the pub and there was more than enough money to cover all the cost of the funeral. Flowers from friends and family were handed to the funeral director and he was carefully placing them next to the coffin. The smell from the wreaths was overpowering, they smelt of death and deceit. Debbie and Beverley stood near the back gate of Mary's house; they were trying to keep a low profile.

They had been Mary's best friends. Nelly asked them to come inside the house with the family but Paddy was pissed out of his head and they couldn't stand yet another interrogation from him. Every day since Mary's death he had summoned them to the house and constantly asked them questions about the night his daughter died, he was a nightmare. They didn't know a thing

Paddy didn't believe them, he thought they were covering up for someone. He'd had them both in tears and threatened to end their lives if they didn't spill the beans, they didn't know anything to tell him. The police had questioned the girls too, but they told them the same thing as they told Paddy, they didn't have a clue about what had happened to their best friend. Mary Wilson's death was a mystery.

DCI Callan stood in the shadows watching the funeral from afar, he seemed edgy. He didn't have a speck of evidence to pin the murder on anybody; he kept hitting a brick wall every time he thought he had a lead. Watching Mary's family and friends was a chance to pick up on the body language of her nearest and dearest, perhaps there'd be a clue that could provide a breakthrough in the case. He stood smoking, examining everyone who was there. He had a gut feeling that the murderer was right there before him.

"Paddy, the cars are here," Nelly whispered as she patted her husband's arm softly, she was treading on eggshells. He was pissed out of his head, his eyes were glazed over and he seemed in a deep trance. The doctor had given him some sleeping tablets to help him get through the trauma, but nothing was working, he still wasn't sleeping. Sat in his black suit he shook his head, he was devastated. John Daley came inside the room and helped him up from his chair, everyone was watching him and they knew at any time soon Paddy Wilson was going to blow. John approached him with caution.

"Come on lad, it's time to go." Paddy lifted his head up and stared at him, spit was hanging from the corner of his mouth. John had been with the family every day since they'd lost their daughter and Nelly had told him that she would never forget all his help and support he'd given to the family. John's wife Jackie stood at the back door smoking; she seemed in a world of her own and very rarely spoke to anyone. Molly came into the front room holding Kendal in her arms, her face looked thinner and her cheekbones were more prominent on her face. The two of them had been inseparably since Mary's death. Jackie stared at the child and chugged harder on her cigarette.

The family closed the front door and walked towards the back of the house where the cars were parked. As they appeared on the car park you could have heard a pin drop. Once Nelly saw the coffin she crumbled, she looked like she was having a heart attack. Tears streamed down the side of her face and her legs buckled. John was by her side in a flash and helped her inside the car. "Come on love; just take it easy, it will all be over soon." Paddy stood looking at the crowds of people who'd gathered. His face hadn't seen a razor for days and he looked ill.

Taking a deep breath he poked his finger at them all. "One of you bastards knows what happened to my Mary, and once I find out who you are, you'll be six foot under. Do you hear me? Six foot under!" John pulled him away by his arm; Paddy was fighting to break free, he was as strong as an ox.

"Come on mate, this isn't the time or the place to be

saying things like this. The law will find out who's done it, they always do, but for now, let's give Mary the send off she deserves."

DCI Callan stood on his tiptoes in the alleyway, he was listening carefully and his eyes darted at Paddy Wilson. He was still cursing as his head went into the car. John was struggling to get him inside. Molly looked anxious, she paused. "Orr, I've forgot Kendal's pink teddy, she won't settle without it. Just hold her a minute John while I run back inside the house to get it." Before he knew it he was holding the baby in his arms. This was the first time he'd seen the child properly, his face was paralysed. A single bulky tear formed in the corner of his eyes, and he swallowed hard. Kendal was his own flesh and blood and he couldn't tell a living soul about her. Her eyes were blue just the same as Mary's, they were beautiful. In the baby's eyes he could see his betrayal and he looked anxious. His wife came to his side; she loved children and quickly gripped Kendal from his arms. He shot a look at her and passed the child over without saying a single word.

DCI Callan stood out from his hide-out and squeezed his eyes tightly together; he was scribbling in his notepad. He knew John Daley of old and wondered why he was being so nice to everyone. Usually he was a vicious bastard who wouldn't have given anyone the time of day; he was acting strange and completely out of character. Daniel threw his cig to the floor and stamped firmly on it, he was watching with eagle eyes. He could smell a rat but he knew he would never solve this case; there wasn't one scrap of evidence to make an arrest.

St Patrick's in Collyhurst was packed out. It was a lovely church and everything inside it seemed mystical. The highly polished wooden benches looked new. Nelly

Wilson had sat on these exact benches nearly every Sunday for the last twenty five years. She believed that if she prayed for long enough, her life would change, but of course it never did. She only had her faith left to keep her going and she pleaded with the Lord every day to make her life better, normal. Molly's eyes focused on the coffin at the front of the church. Her shoulders were shaking as the organist played the last few notes of "Day by day," a song her sister loved when she was younger. Whispering into her niece's ear she spoke softly making sure nobody could hear her. "Say goodbye to your mummy baby. I'm going to look after you from now on. Your mother didn't deserve you; she was a nasty selfish bitch who only ever cared about herself, you've got me now, don't you worry." Kendal looked at Molly and smiled, she didn't have a clue what she was saying but she was glad that someone was entertaining her for a change.

Paddy Wilson sobbed his heart out; you could feel his pain from the back of the church. He held his head in his hands and never looked at the coffin beside him. As the Priest read out the details of Mary's life Paddy kept stopping him to add more things about his daughter, he was annoying everybody in the church and Nelly had to tell him to keep quiet, he was making a show of himself. Nelly cast her eyes around the church, the words of the Priest just seemed to float past her and she wasn't taking anything in. She was numb.

The funeral headed to Moston cemetery, where Mary was laid to rest. A long row of black cars headed up Rochdale Road, the traffic was at a standstill. Nelly gazed out of the window and shook her head slowly. "I still can't believe she's gone Paddy." She turned her head and watched her husband slurp the last bit of whisky from the

bottle he pulled out of his jacket. He snarled at her and
gritted his teeth tightly together, his fists were clenched
into two round balls and he leant into her face.

"If you would have kept your big gob shut she would
have come home, it's your fault. You killed her." Nelly
choked back the tears as Molly rubbed her arm.

"Dad, just leave my mam alone will you. You know
what our Mary was like she was a," before she could finish
her sentence she was rubbing the side of her face. The
sound of the slap caused the driver to twist his head back,
he was watching with an anxious face through the rear-
view mirror. Nelly kicked at her husband's leg, she knew
he wouldn't beat her in public, that wasn't his style; he
would keep that until they were alone.

"Turn it in, you drunken bastard. What are you
hitting Molly for; she was only telling the truth. Mary was
a handful, and if you would have spent a bit more time at
home instead of in the boozer every bleeding night you
would have seen that." Paddy snarled and leant forward in
his seat, he was ready to pounce. Fortunately the driver
slammed his brakes on hard at that moment, they were at
the cemetery.

The thick brown mud was caked over everyone's
shoes as they walked to Mary's resting place. John came
to Paddy's side and draped his arm around his shoulder
to offer support. Molly smiled at John and blushed as
she walked behind him down to the plot. Around sixty
people stood around the graveside; there wasn't a peep
out of anyone. A black bird sat on the wall nearby and
he seemed to be watching the family with cunning eyes.
Every now and then it's squawked and jumped closer
to the graveside, it was as if it was trying to tell them
something. Nelly picked up a handful of soil and threw

it down onto the coffin. The earth landed on it and everyone else copied her. Paddy stood tall and watched the faces of the mourners; he was ready to strike again. Nelly whispered into John's ear to sort him out. John Daley knew what made Paddy tick and when he pulled out a small bottle of brandy from his jacket pocket he knew Paddy wouldn't cause anymore fuss.

The family went back to the Wilson's household. Nelly cracked open a bottle of gin, she was more than ready for a drink, her nerves were shattered. Kendal was tired and Molly took her upstairs to bed for a while. John Daley stood watching Molly tend to the child from afar; he was licking his lips slowly. His hands gripped the doorframe and he was aching to go and see the child again. Molly turned her head from inside the bedroom and clocked him watching her, her heart missed a beat; she was alone with him at last. Molly was smitten and she couldn't keep her eyes off him. She was just a kid though; surely John would never look at her twice, well that's if he knew what was good for him anyway. Smiling softly she waved her hand at him for him to come inside the room. "Just come and have a look at how she sleeps," she whispered.

John crept across the landing towards the bedroom, he was nervous. His eyes dipped into the cot and his face melted with love for her. Kendal was lying on her stomach sleeping; this was just the way he slept. His lips trembled and he looked like he was going to fold in two. "She's beautiful, isn't she?" Molly said as she stroked the side of the baby's face. John's hand seemed to have a mind of its own and before he knew it, his hand was on top of Molly's sliding across Kendal's pink soft skin. Her cheeks blushed, but she remained still, she wanted this moment to last forever.

Nelly's shrieking tones filled the room. "Molly, get your arse downstairs and make sure your father isn't causing any more trouble. I've just had to apologise to legless Lenny from down the street, your Dad wanted to fight him in the garden. I mean, the man is disabled, what is he thinking, he's a goddamn bully." Molly scarpered from the room and left John looking gobsmacked. Nelly marched to his side with a screwed up face. "What are you doing up here? More importantly, why are you in the bedroom with our Molly?" His tongue was twisted and he was struggling to get his words out. Nelly had heard rumours about him having eyes for the younger girls but she always took it with a pinch of salt. "Well," she hissed.

"I was just looking at little Kendal sleeping in her cot. It's such a crying shame that she will never know her mother." Nelly trudged inside the room and plonked herself down on the end of the bed, she sat twisting her fingers. John stood quivering in his boots waiting for her to reply.

"Never mind her bloody mother; she'll never know her father either." His eyes were wide open and his chest was rising faster than normal. He wanted to turn and run but he knew he had to remain calm; he stood fidgeting with the collar of his shirt.

"Who's the father? I heard it was some lad from the Mannings Estate?" Nelly lifted her head up and played with the hem of her black dress, she snapped off a dangling piece of cotton.

"Yeah, that's what she told me, but I know there was more to it. Our Mary was a dark horse and nothing would surprise me about her. I think he was a married man or something, because why else wouldn't she tell me his name?" She paused and looked at him a bit longer than necessary. "I mean, our Mary was a right gob-shite and couldn't hold her own piss. If you ask me, the guy was married. I suppose I'll never know now will I?" John pulled at his jacket and swallowed hard, his cheeks were going bright red. Someone stomping up the stairs made them look at each other. Nelly held her ear to the door. "Oh, fucking hell, that's all I need him starting again." Standing to her feet, she made her way to the bedroom door. John stood frozen and he was trying to digest all that she'd said.

Paddy barged past the door and in his hands he was holding some black bin-liners. Nelly sprinted after him with a distressed look on her face. "Paddy what the hell are you doing, wait there will you." John stood looking at Kendal asleep in her cot for the last time. The curtains had been pulled together and there was barely enough light inside the room for him to see. Quickly making sure no one could see him he kissed his fingertips and placed them on the child's cheeks, he was gone.

Paddy was like a bull in a china shop. He emptied all Mary's clothes from her drawers and he was throwing them inside the bin bags, he'd lost the plot. Nelly stood watching him; she was scared of his next move, he was off his head. "Paddy, just leave them for now, we can do this some other time, when we both feel ready." He ignored her completely and carried on regardless. Nelly walked away crying. Emptying Mary's bedside cabinet Paddy could see a diary sticking up at the back of the drawer. His fat fingers pushed inside and he grabbed at it with his fingertips. Placing it on his lap, he opened the first page. His eyes squeezed together as he tried to focus on the words, his head wasn't with it. He could hear his wife in the toilet and she was still shouting at him to stop. The diary held Mary's full name on the front of it. He stroked his hand softly across it.

Paddy was illiterate. Schooling had never taken a place in his life and he'd hidden it away for most of his life. He had his hands for work and that was all he needed to get by in life, well, that's what his father had told him when he was growing up. Closing the book shut he rammed it deep inside the bin liners and tied it tightly shut. Nelly was back at his side and tears were streaming down her face. "Right woman, get these bags into the loft. I don't want to see anything left of our Mary's inside this house, do you hear me?" She blew a laboured breath; he was waiting on her reply, and threw a pillow at her to remind her.

"Right, I'll do it, but for now, come on, let's go downstairs and try and be normal." Paddy wobbled, and grabbed the wall as he stood up, his jaw was swinging. His warm stale breath was in her face as he spoke in a low tone.

"Fucking normal, how can we ever be normal again when my baby's dead? She had her life set out in front of her and now she's gone." Nelly cradled him in her arms as he sobbed.

"Come on Paddy, I know I know." Molly stood listening to them at the bottom of the stairs. Her heart missed a beat as she heard her father's voice coming down the stairs, she scarpered.

CHAPTER FIVE

Nelly looked old and wrinkled, her skin was grey and she didn't look well. You could hear her chest crackling as she sat twiddling her thumbs in her chair. Kendal was fifteen now and she was stunning, she looked like a supermodel. Her long apple blonde hair tickled her shoulders and she could have had her pick of any of the lads from the estate. Nelly started coughing, she sounded like she was choking. Her face was turning blue. With a clenched fist she banged it on her chest and tried to regain her breath. Kendal stood watching her from the corner of the room with one hand placed firmly on her hip. "Nana, why don't you turn it in with them fags, your chest is rattling again. Surely, it's time to give up?" Nelly held a flat palm towards her and tried to speak, she was gasping for air. Resting her hands on her knees she blew her breath.

"It's not the cigs love, I've smoked for years. It's this bleeding chest infection. I can't seem to move it, three weeks I've had it now, and it's not shifting." Kendal was by her side and she looked frustrated.

"Are you right in the head, the chest infection is caused because you smoke, when are you ever going to learn?" Paddy walked into the front room, he looked ancient. There was a strange silence as he made his way to his chair. He was half the size he used to be and he looked yellow, even his eyeballs did. Kendal dipped her head low; this was her moment to get off, he snarled at her and he was ready to give her a mouthful. Ever since her mother's death Paddy had made her life unbearable. Over the years

43

he'd made her life hell, he treated her like a slave and very rarely showed her any affection. The only person who gave her the love she craved was her grandmother Nelly. Paddy flopped into his armchair and opened a small bottle of whisky, they both watched as he gulped a large mouthful, his hand wiped away the bit that dribbled on his chin. Nelly shook her head and urged Kendal to follow her into the kitchen. Kendal walked behind her but kept looking over her shoulder to make sure Paddy wasn't following them. Her granddad was crafty like that, he was paranoid. Many a time she'd caught him listening outside her bedroom, to her conversations with her best friend Jane.

Nelly closed the kitchen door and walked towards her "Here, get this fiver in your pocket and get something for your tea. Don't tell him in there though, you know what he's like if he finds out I've been bunging you money, keep it to yourself," she placed a single finger over her lips. Nelly pushed the crumpled note into her hands and smiled. "Where you off to anyway? I hope you're not with that Scott Green from the estate?" Kendal blushed, she stood swinging her body. She couldn't look Nelly in the eyes, she kept her head low.

"Am I 'eck. I don't know who's been filling your head with crap, but don't listen to them, because it's all lies." Nelly turned the cold water tap on and held her glass underneath it, turning her head she watched Kendal leave the room. Nelly's health had gone downhill rapidly over the years and without Kendal looking after her she would have been dead. Her daughter Molly had helped her out, but she was a lost soul these days and Nelly very rarely saw her due to her lifestyle. Molly was a heroin addict. After Mary's death, she'd got mixed up with the wrong kind of people and before she knew it she had a habit. Molly had been banished from the house for years and every now and then she would turn up on her hands and knees begging for some money to score her next fix. Paddy had disowned his daughter from the start and warned Nelly that if she ever stepped foot in his house again he would not be responsible for his actions. Kendal had seen so much heartache in this house, it was a wonder she was still alive. Paddy had threatened to end her life on more than one occasion, and she knew he meant it; he always stuck by his word. Nelly's illness affected all the household; they were falling apart without her to turn to for help. Kendal very rarely attended school. Nobody batted an eyelid about her education and it was just brushed under the carpet, just like all the other problems in the household. Kendal had quit school at the age of thirteen without a single qualification.

Kendal walked through the estate to meet her friend Jane. The two of them came from the same kind of background and they were both out for some fun. Jane Murray lived a few minutes' walk from Kendal's house. It was cold and a chill wind was picking up, Kendal zipped her coat up and snuggled inside it. Kids were running about the estate and they were all shouting and screaming at each other, they were up to no good. Rapping on the silver letterbox Kendal shouted through it in a loud voice, she had her mouth right inside it, nobody was answering. Music was pumping inside and the walls were thudding with the bass. Kendal walked to the kitchen window and banged her clenched fists onto the window. As she pressed her face up to the dirty windowpane she could see someone inside stood at the sink, they were singing. Sinking her face onto the glass she shouted again. "Jane, it's me Kendal, open the door will you?" She walked back to the front door in a strop. Jane was stood there smiling, she had a grey bath towel hung above her head and she looked like she'd just got out of the bath. "Bloody hell, I've been knocking for ages; turn that music down, I can't hear a thing?" Jane marched into the front room and twisted the volume button down. Her brother Mike was sat there chilling. She poked her finger into his head with force.

"Keep the music down you muppet, Kendal's been stood at the front door for ages because of you, you nob-head." Mike bounced out of his chair and headed back towards the stereo system.

"Hard luck, I'm listening to my tunes, so get your hands off it. I'm turning it back up." Jane gritted her teeth tightly together and stood in front of him, her face was on fire, she was ready to rumble. Her brother was younger than her and she knew she could kick his arse. She'd done it before, and today would be no different. Grabbing him by the scruff of the neck she swung him back onto the sofa, she leant into his face.

"I've told you once you dick-head, keep the noise down. If you turn it up when I've gone, trust me, I'll waste you." Mike snarled and rammed his two fingers up behind her back as she left the room, there was nothing he could do, and he knew she meant business. Kendal smiled at Mike and left with her friend. Jane Murray was as hard as nails and this girl could fight. Kendal had seen her in action and knew what she was capable of, she was ruthless. The two of them had met in Primary school years before and they both were in the bottom sets of each class that they attended. None of them took any interest in the lessons and most of the time they bunked off school to escape the humiliation of not knowing the answers to any of the questions the teachers asked them. Jane was always the class clown and she had Kendal in stitches laughing in most lessons. The teachers hated her with a vengeance; she always disrupted the class and made sure nobody else could learn while she was in the room. Most days the girls were slung out and nobody seemed to care that the two girls could barely read or write.

Jane's bedroom stunk of weed. She was always smoking it and loved getting stoned to escape the realities of her life. Kendal smoked it too, but she didn't really like it, she just did it to impress her best friend. The bedroom was a shit-tip. Clothes were all over the floor and the bed sheets looked crusty. Wallpaper hung from the walls and black fungus grew all across the ceiling. Kendal moved the clothes from the bed with her arm and sat down. Jane was in the mirror applying black mascara to her eyelashes. "So are we getting wrecked tonight or what? There should be loads of guys there tonight at Regina's party, it will be rocking. She said she's invited all the top dogs," she turned her head from the mirror. "Ay, Scott Green might even be there." Kendal blushed as she flicked her hair back from her face.

She'd been seeing Scott on and off now for over six months, and she really liked him. Scott was well known around the area and he was one of the top lads from the estate. He sold drugs to earn his cash and he was very rarely short of money, he was wadded. Kendal first met him at a party, and from the moment she set her eyes on him she was smitten, he was everything she wanted from a man. He made her feel safe. "Are you going to let him bang you tonight or what? You must be ready to lose your virginity now; it's been ages since you've been seeing him."

Kendal looked stressed as she answered her, she licked her dry lips. "Stop pressurising me will you? I'll sleep with him when I'm ready. I'm not like you Jane." Jane snarled as she twisted her face away from the mirror, she was fuming.

"What do you mean by that, are you saying I'm a slapper?" Kendal knew she needed to think fast; she stood up and dug her fingers into the make-up bag at the side of her.

"Nar, you know what I mean. You're more confident than me. You've got the gift of the gab and all that. I'm crap where lads are concerned." Jane carried on applying her make-up, Kendal was off the hook.

"You just need to relax a bit more, you're always to uptight." Kendal looked serious as she slid the candy pink lip gloss over her lips, she was pouting. Her confidence was low and her friend was right, she didn't know how to act around lads. Paddy had made sure of that, she wasn't allowed a boyfriend, or to talk about boys, he made that quite clear from the moment she started school. He was always drilling it into her head that her mother wouldn't have died if she had respected herself more. Paddy dressed Kendal like a nun, long skirts and jumpers that covered her body shape; he never wanted anyone to be attracted to her. Jane was right though, she did need to relax more.

Kendal spoke in a low voice. "I know what you mean Jane; perhaps I might do it tonight. Scott's always gagging for it anyway and he did say that he loves me, so I suppose I may as well sleep with him."

Jane raised her eyes to the ceiling. "Scott Green loves anything with a pulse, don't let him fool you. He's a right player; don't swallow any of his bullshit. He's having you over," her face was serious as she continued. "Can't you see he's only after getting into your knickers when he tells you he loves you. Come on, you're not that daft are you?"

Kendal looked hurt by her words, but kept her mouth shut, she didn't want to get into an argument. Jane made sure the bedroom door was closed and started to roll a joint, she sat on the floor with her legs folded out in front of her. Her toenails were painted in bright red nail polish; she was trying her best not to smudge them. Her fingers sprinkled the marijuana into the Rizla paper with expertise, she was concentrating. "Let's gets wrecked before we go out, this shit will help you relax, it's pucka bud, trust me," she shot her eyes to her hands and wafted the finished spliff about in the air. Jane twisted the end of the joint and passed it to Kendal with a cheesy grin across her face. Searching for a lighter she threw it across the bedroom towards her. "Go on then, spark it up." Thick grey smoke covered Kendal's face as she took a long deep drag from the joint.

Jane's head was dug deep inside the wardrobe searching through her clothes. She pulled out a black mini skirt and a bright pink belly top; she quickly turned her head back to Kendal. "Here, why don't you wear these tonight? You look like a right prude dressed in that long skirt, it looks depressing, live a little." Kendal stroked her hand across her clothing with a disheartened smile. Jane was right though; it was covering her knees and looked anything but sexy. Paddy wouldn't allow her to wear short skirts in a million years, when she'd come home once wearing one he'd gripped her by the throat and told her how much of a tart she looked in it, she never wore it again. He would have had kittens if he could have seen her now.

"Here, try it on," Jane urged. Kendal handed the joint

back over to her and slid her own skirt down over her waist. She was all skin and bones, and her knickers looked saggy on her bum cheeks. Jane rolled about the bedroom floor laughing her head off. "Oh, my God, what the hell are them moth balls?" she pointed her fingers at Kendal's underwear. Kendal screwed her face up, and pulled at them trying to cover them up, she was embarrassed.

"What's wrong with them?"

Jane chuckled, "You mean what's right with them, they're rancid. They're passion killers for sure," Jane looked serious as she continued, her eyebrows were raised and her eyes were wide open. "Don't tell me you're thinking of having sex for the first time with them big bloomers on?"

Kendal snapped, she'd heard enough of her banter. "Will you turn it in putting me down all the time? You know money's tight in our house. How do you expect me to have all the top gear on when we don't have a pot to piss in?"

Jane lay flat on the floor and chugged hard on the joint, blowing the smoke out from her mouth in hoops she answered her. "Don't give me all that shit, our house is just as fucked up as yours is. I shoplift all my underwear, no one buys it for me. If it was left up to my family to provide for me I would have to go commando, trust me. The last time my Mam bought me any knickers I was about ten years old."

Kendal ragged the skirt up over her thighs and her face creased at the sides. "Well, the next time you're going to get any new knickers, tell me, and I'll come with you, I'm desperate too you know," she stamped her feet on the floor. "Orr.... fucking hell, lend me a pair of knickers for tonight, like you said, I can't lose my virginity in these rags, can I?" Jane giggled and held the bottom of her stomach.

The bedroom door creaked open slowly and Jane's brother was stood there smiling like a Cheshire cat, he leant on the doorframe with a cocky look on his face, he smirked. "What are you two laughing at?" he chuckled, trying to get in on the joke. Jane sprang to her feet and gripped him by the arm.

"We're laughing about boys with little nobs, so get out of here, before I tell Kendal all about your little screw dick." Mike was lost for words, he was stuttering as she pushed him out of the bedroom. He ran back into the room trying to have the last word.

"It might be little Kendal, but it would make your legs shake. Take no notice of her; she's not seen it since I was a kid. The last time she saw it I was about four years old, trust me, it's grown a lot since then, it's massive. It's a python."

"Out," Jane screamed into his face. Mike ran from the room.

Kendal stood admiring herself in the mirror. She was turning from side to the side and glancing at her slender figure. "You're right Jane; this skirt does looks miles better than the one I was wearing. Hold on, let me try the top on too." She yanked her own jumper over her head, and Jane had the other one ready to hand to her. Kendal's bra was old and tattered too and it didn't even fit her properly, her breasts were popping out from it. Jane clocked it straight away but kept her mouth shut, she didn't want to offend her mate any more than she had already. Kendal looked stunning; she looked completely different to the girl who'd walked into the bedroom earlier. Jane stood back against the wall and admired her with her head held to the side.

"Right, just let me do something with your hair and then we're ready to go, it's a ball of fluff."

"Pass me some knickers first," Kendal stressed. "Like you said before, I can't wear these ones, can I?" Jane searched her bedside cabinet and passed her friend a pair of red and black lacy knickers. Kendal's eyes lit up, she'd never seen anything like them in her life. They were so sexy. "Wow, is this what everyone's wearing now, what happened to nylon knickers?" She held the briefs up in front of her and stretched them out fully. "I'm so out of date aren't I? I'm definitely going to have to start wearing these from now on, they're mint." Sliding her old ones down her legs, she kicked them to the side of her. Jane picked them up and shoved them inside her drawer, she was laughing.

"Don't leave them lying about, our Mike will be sniffing them, he's a right pervert lately. Trust me, he'd have them away if he knew they were yours, he's a sex case." The new knickers were on now and Kendal was smiling from ear to ear, she was parading about the bedroom.

"Scott is going to burst when he gets a look at these sexy babies. Orr.....Thanks Jane, what would I do without you ay, you're a true friend?"

They both headed down the stairs into the front room. Mike was sat there listening to his tunes. His mate was with him and he was sprawled across the sofa. His head nearly fell off when he clocked the two girls entering the room, his jaw dropped. Mike sat humming the song that was playing on the stereo and he smiled when he caught Kendal's eye. He had a crush on her for sure and his hand was constantly tugging at his crotch. Jane checked her hair in the mirror on the wall one last time and flicked her brother's ear as she walked past him. He tried retaliating but she just pushed him away with a quick movement. Mike stood up with a newspaper in his hands. "Ay, Kendal, have a read of your horoscope today, you might be meeting the man of your dreams tonight, he shouted," He placed the newspaper in her hands pointing at the words. Kendal was going red in the face; she looked hot and out of her comfort zone. He was shouting at the side of her, "Go on then, read it out loud so we can all hear it too." She was going under, her eyes tried to focus on the words and her mouth was moving but no words were coming out. Mike was getting inpatient and tried grabbing the paper back from her. Kendal gripped it tightly and started to speak. There was no way this little shit was making a fool out of her.

"It says, be aware of a friend's brother and his mate, it says they are both no-hopers and they sit masturbating all day long." Mike looked confused, and ragged the paper back from her hands. He'd already read her star sign and knew she was lying. He started to read it to himself.

"You liar Kendal, it doesn't say that at all, stop messing about." Jane smacked him around his head with a flat palm.

"Yeah, but it's true though isn't it? You both sit wanking all day, don't you?" Mike looked at his mate in shock, but his pal was white as a sheet and never spoke a word. It was obvious; there was some truth in what Kendal had just said to him. Jane dragged Kendal by her arm. "Come on then, let's go and party, girl. See you later sad sacks," she shouted to her brother and his mate.

It was eight o'clock at night and the roads were busy with traffic. Jane and Kendal walked up the main road towards the party on the Two Hundred Estate in

Harpurhey. Kendal was forever pulling at her skirt, she didn't feel comfortable. Her legs looked cold and goose-pimples were visible on her pale skin. Jane linked her arm and whispered into her ear, she was excited. "Right, if Scott's here tonight, make sure you get bonding with him straight away. Don't let him just blag you at the end of the night like he always does, make him work for it."

Kendal rubbed her hands together with excitement. "I know what you're saying; he always waits until the night's over before he makes his move on me, doesn't he? Well, tonight's going to be different," her face was serious as she continued. "If I'm going to be his girlfriend he better start showing it to everyone else, he's not treating me like any old slapper." Jane giggled as they walked across the road. The heels clicked along the pavement.

The music pumped inside the house. All the lights were on in every room and it looked like Blackpool Illuminations. People stood about in the garden and they were dancing and screaming at each other. Jane pulled out a bottle of brandy from her bag and necked a large mouthful of it; she passed it over to Kendal. "Here, get some of that knocked back. You need some Dutch courage." Kendal gulped two large mouthfuls of the brandy, and passed it back to Jane. They opened the back gate to the house and walked inside. Scott Green was stood at the other end of the garden and he was definitely watching Kendal, his eyes were all over her like a rash. Jane clocked him straight away and dragged Kendal by the arm over to where he stood. "Alright lads? It's hammered in here isn't it?" Scott's eyes were fixed on Kendal and he seemed hypnotised by her, the corners of his mouth started to rise. Licking his lips slowly he pulled her closer.

"You look hot tonight babes." Kendal smirked and

her cheeks blushed. Jane was darting her eyes at her for her to respond, she was missing her chance.

"Thanks, you look good yourself," she said. Jane screwed her face up and shook her head. Her eyes were wide open as she came and stood by Kendal's side.

"Ay, she's got a surprise for you tonight Scott, well, that's if you're a good boy. Haven't you Kendal?" All eyes were on her now and she was stuttering, Jane had put her on the spot for sure. Scott gripped her face in his hands and kissed her firmly on the lips.

"Oh, has she now, I look forward to it Jane. I hope it's something wet and warm?" Jane chuckled and punched him softly in his arm.

"Just wait and see. I'm sure you won't be disappointed." Shouting from inside the house stopped the conversation. Jane turned her head and scanned the area; it was her man, Jack. "One minute, get me a drink," she shouted back at him. Jack nodded his head and walked inside the house. He was well built and looked handsome. Jane had been going out with Jack for months, and he was the one who'd taken her virginity. She didn't love him though; she'd made that quite clear from the start. He was just someone to help her pass the time until her Prince Charming came along. Well, that's what she told everyone anyway.

Scott passed Kendal a bottle of beer; he'd already opened it for her with his teeth. She stood looking uneasy until he pulled her nearer and placed his arm around her shoulder. She looked at Jane and smiled. Everyone around them seemed to be watching them, especially Natalie Patterson; Jane could see her growling from the other side of the garden. Natalie was Scott's ex-girlfriend and she always made sure she was never far from his side, she was a stalker. She was still in love with Scott and you could see it written all over her face. Jane made eye contact with Natalie and nodded her head slowly; she was ready for anything the hussy had to throw at her. Natalie went and joined her friends and you could see her whispering to them with her hand covering her mouth. Jane leant into Kendal with her eyes still fixed on Natalie. "Watch that tart, I don't trust her as far as I could throw her." Scott looked uneasy and scratched his head, he was aware of what was going on.

Finally twigging he chirped up, "Just ignore the slag; she's always the same when she sees me with someone new. If she comes within an inch of you Kendal I'll floor the scrubber, trust me." Jane started to relax, Scott had their backs. She kissed her friend on the cheek and started to walk off with a bounce in her step.

"See you in a bit, just going to see Jack." Kendal looked sheepish as she snuggled inside Scott's jacket. The party was swinging and Kendal was wrecked, she looked half asleep. Her words were slurred and she was finding it difficult to stand up straight. Scott held her up by her waist and kissed her cheek. His voice was low. "Are you ready to get off or what? You can come back to my sister's gaff if you want? I'm getting my head down there tonight."

Kendal smiled. "Yeah, if you want too, just let me find Jane before we go so I can word her up. I've told my Nana that I'm staying at her house tonight so I better make sure she'll cover for me if it comes on top." Scott patted her bum cheeks as she left his side. He rubbed his hands together and stood chatting to his mates at the side of him, he was on a promise.

Natalie Patterson was like shit from a shovel and ran after Scott's new girlfriend. Kendal staggered into the house and her eyes scanned the area for her friend, she was swaying. The music was loud and she covered her ears as she made her way through the crowds of people there. Kendal's head was yanked back by her hair and she looked confused as she tried to turn around. As she struggled to break free she could feel Natalie's warm breath in her face. "Do you think you're smart ay? You know me and Scott have history, are you taking the piss or what?"

Kendal tried to speak but before she could open her mouth Natalie's clenched fist connected with her cheek. Everyone was gathering around now trying to break up the fight but Natalie wasn't stopping for love nor money. You could see it in her eyes she wanted to hurt this girl bad. Shouting from behind made the crowd part. Jane's face was on fire, she was ready for action, she quickly pulled her silver hooped earrings from her ears. She gripped Natalie by the hair and swung her about the room like a rag doll. Kendal was on the floor and she could only watch her friend attack the trouble causer. Jane squatted over Natalie and let rip, her fists pounded into her face with speed. She was livid.

"Who do you think you are? Scott's not been with you for moons, so get over it, he's been seeing Kendal for months." Scott Green stood over them both and the vein in the side of his neck was pumping with rage. Jane could see his Nike trainers stood near her face as she lifted her head up.

He pulled at her arm as he spoke. "Jane, leave her now. Let her get up." Natalie stood to her feet and tried to straighten her clothes, she smiled thinking Scott was saving her. His large hand gripped her by the throat and he dragged her outside away from the public view. Everyone was shocked and a few of the people stood there were ready to follow him outside to see what he was going to do. Jane helped Kendal up from the floor, and studied her injuries.

Scott head-butted Natalie before anyone could see him, he was a violent man and he was never afraid to let his woman know who was boss. Blood trickled down the side of her face and she was screaming out in pain. He growled as he went nose to nose with her. "It's over; do you hear me, over?"

Natalie stopped wriggling and looked directly into his eyes, she knew he was serious. "I hate you; you said it would be me and you forever, what happened to that ay? Was it all lies?" Scott let out a menacing laugh and threw her to the ground; he could see people watching him and put on a performance any leading actor would have been proud of.

"I'm done with you, just stay well away from me. You make me feel sick, you runt." The sound of his feet crunching along the gravel was the only noise you could hear. He walked to Kendal's side and grabbed her by the hand. "Come on. Let's get off." Kendal quickly told Jane where she was going and told her to cover up for her if Nelly phoned her house. The two of them left the party.

Kendal was nursing a thick lip; it was swollen. Scott placed his arm over her shoulder and dragged her closer. "She's mental she is," he moaned. "I swear, if she gives you anymore shit, let me know and I'll have her dealt with good and proper, she's a crank." Kendal had never felt as safe in all her life, his arms felt like steel bars wrapped around her body, nobody could hurt her now he was in her life, he was her protector. Scott's mobile phone started ringing, he searched deep in his tracksuit pockets rummaging for it. He was panicking. Looking at the screen he let go of Kendal's hand and walked in front of her, he was being secretive. Kendal could hear him speaking. "Yeah John, I'm just on my way home from a party. You can come and pick it up now if you want? It's all there, every penny. Okay," he paused. "I'll make my way there now then. See you in a minute pal." The call ended and he bounced back to her side. "I've just got to go and meet somebody, I won't be long. Do you want to come with me or what?" Kendal really wanted to go home, but this man looked like he'd cast an invisible spell over her and she seemed to be controlled by him.

"Yeah I'll come, but we won't be long will we? I'm freezing." He pulled his coat off his shoulders and draped it over her.

"There you go princess, you can have my coat," he was proud of his actions. This was right out of character for him, but he was out to impress. Kendal put the jacket on and zipped it up fully, you could see her inhaling his body odour from the collar. They both started to walk onto the main road, he was dragging her by the arm, he was in a rush.

"Where are we going anyway?" Scott's head was all over the place and he seemed to be looking for someone. After they walked a few steps further he started to run off in front of her towards a black car parked in a side street. "What about me?" she shouted after him.

"Nar, just wait there," he snapped. Scott was talking to an older man sat in the car. Kendal could see him from where she stood, she stretched her neck to try and get a closer look at the driver, but her view was restricted. Rubbing her arms she tried to keep warm. You could see the mist from her breath as she blew it onto her hands.

Scott watched eagerly as John Daley counted the

money out in front of him, he licked his finger and flicked through the notes counting them one by one. Scott knew if it was one penny short his life would be in danger, he seemed edgy. He'd been selling drugs for John for as long as he could remember and he respected this man like a father. John stretched his neck over to the wing mirror and clocked the young girl waiting for Scott in the distance; his hand twisted at it the mirror so he could get a better look. "Who's that with you?" Scott swallowed hard and small beads of sweat formed on his forehead.

"It's my new bird Kendal, she's hot isn't she?" John looked at him and snarled. He looked a lot older these days and his face was full of deep wrinkles. His once pearly white teeth now looked yellow and tobacco- stained.

John's voice was stressed. "Do you mean Paddy's granddaughter, Kendal Wilson?"

Scott looked uneasy. "I'm not sure John; I don't know who Paddy is." John stared a lot longer than necessary in the wing mirror; his fingers were tapping rapidly on the corner of it. You could see his fist clenching at his side. "Is the money right then?" Scott asked, his voice unsure. John turned his head quickly and nodded.

"Yes, thanks for that. I'll drop you some more shit off tomorrow." The car door opened and Scott was about to get out when John dragged him back inside by the back of his pants. "Be warned lad, if that's Paddy Wilson's girl, make sure you treat her right, because he's a good pal of mine and I wouldn't want to have to deal with you if you ever hurt her."

Scott gave a nervous giggle. "Me, John, I wouldn't hurt a hair on her head, I'm no wife beater. I look after my women me. I treat them like princesses I do." John's nostrils flared as he looked deep into Scott's eyes.

"I hope so, for your sake lad, I hope so." The car door slammed shut and John watched Scott run off back to the girl in his rear-view mirror. Slowly his hand turned the key for the ignition. John gripped the steering wheel tightly and rested his head on it.

Scott looked over his shoulders as he ran back to Kendal; John had spooked him for sure. His body was still trembling. Why was John so concerned about his new girlfriend, because he'd never taken any interest before, even if it was his mate's granddaughter, he was still overreacting.

"Come on then lovely, let's get out of this cold, I'm freezing my balls off," Scott said. John's car went screeching past and honked its horn. He raised one hand in the air and blew a laboured breath as it drove past.

"Who was that?" Kendal asked.

"Stop being nosey," he giggled. "The less you know the less the police will know," he was playfully pushing her now. Kendal was in a strop. She didn't know if he was joking or not, there was no way in the world she wanted him to think she was a grass, she defended herself.

"Ay, I'm no midnight mass, ask Jane. I know loads about people and never breathe a word."

"I'm joking, you muppet, chill your beans, you stress head. Can't you take a joke?" Kendal turned her head away from him, he'd hurt her feelings and she was thinking about going home on her own. "Give us a kiss then," he chuckled. Kendal tried not to smile but he was tickling her and he was aware of her strop. Their lips connected as he pushed her up against a wall at the side of them. Kendal seemed lost in the moment, and nothing else seemed to matter to her anymore, she was in love.

Scott flicked on the letterbox of the maisonette. He stood
back and held his head up to window looking for any
sign of life. Searching the ground he found a small grey
pebble and chucked it at the window. A distressed face
appeared. It was a woman. Lights being switched on
inside the house could be seen. Scott looked at Kendal
and urged her to come and stand next to him. "She's not
going to bite you, you know. Our Pat's bang on, you'll
love her. The door opened and Scott's sister stood there
scratching her head. Her discoloured t-shirt just covered
her bum-cheeks.

"Bleeding hell, you should have told me earlier you
were coming back and I would have left the key under
the mat." Scott started to walk inside the house and pulled
Kendal along with him.

"Sorry, Pat. I just lost track of time, have you got
anything in to eat, 'I'm Hank Marvin'?" Pat's eyes were
all over Kendal like a rash, she was making her feel
uncomfortable. Her face was stern as she sparked up a
cigarette.

"So who's this then, aren't you going to introduce me
or what, ignorant?" Kendal blushed, she was crumbling.

"Yeah, give me a chance, this is Kendal." Scott linked
her arm and kissed her cheek. "She's my new bitch," he
giggled. Pat playfully slapped him on the arm.

"Don't speak about her like that. It does my head
in when you talk like that, treat her with respect." Scott
dipped his head inside the fridge.

"Fucking hell, I'm joking, what's it to do with you?
Are you on the blob or something, you hormonal cow?"
Pat kicked the bottom of his leg.

"Come on love, come and sit in here with me," she opened the kitchen door and twisted her head back over her shoulder beckoning Kendal to join her.

"Make me a butty or something will you?" Pat shouted to her brother. Then, turning to Kendal she said, "Are you having one as well? If he's making something, you might as well fill your face, there's some nice ham to throw on a butty too. Get some before the greedy bastard eats the lot."

Kendal nodded her head slowly, she was hungry. Pat was in her early thirties, she had bright red hair and her figure was plump. You could see two tattoos on her arms; Kendal was trying hard not to stare at them but she couldn't help herself. To buy herself time Kendal asked "Can I use your toilet?"

"Yeah, knock yourself out, up the stairs second on the right." Kendal just started walking off when Pat's shrieking voice shouted after her. "Watch that toilet seat, it's loose. The kids have broken it, so be careful you don't fall down it," she was holding the bottom of her stomach as she giggled. "I fell down it the other day, you should have seen me. It took my ages to pull my fat arse out of it."

Scott frowned, "Shut up you minger. Oh my God, fancy telling Kendal stuff like that, too much information if you ask me. Keep it to yourself."

Pat chuckled, "Since when have you been arsed what I speak about!" She smiled at Kendal who was edging her way up the stairs; she was bursting for the loo. "Tell you what love; he must think a lot about you. He's never bothered before." Kendal ran up the stairs, she was in a hurry and holding it in between her legs. As she walked along the landing her heart was beating faster than normal, her chest was rising. Fumbling about she found the light switch on the wall outside the toilet. The bathroom was full of stale smelling washing scattered all about the floor. Treading carefully she locked the door behind her. The toilet bowl was brown inside and it didn't look healthy, it stunk of piss. It was dirty and skid marks were visible at the bottom of the bowl. Kendal's face creased as she peeled her knickers down her thighs to squat on the toilet, she was trying to make sure her bum-cheeks never touched the bowl. Reaching over she searched for some toilet roll, all that was left was an empty grey roll swinging on the toilet roll holder. Panicking, she stood up and scurried across the bathroom floor looking for something to wipe herself with. On the window-sill she clocked some baby wipes. With her finger tips she pulled a couple from the packet and hurried back to the toilet.

Kendal stood up and looked at the mirror hung from the wall. It was old and the metal around it was all rusty. With a quick glance she straightened her hair and headed back down the stairs to the living room.

There was some music on low and Kendal smiled when she heard her favourite track "I won't let you go," by James Morrison. She paused and sat down next to Scott. Pat passed her a sandwich with raised eyebrows. "Here, get that down your neck before greedy balls scrans it all, he's had his eyes on it you know." Kendal reached over and took the small plate from Pat's hands. Scott sat munching at the side of her. She devoured the sandwich like she hadn't been fed for days. Pat sat chuckling. "Mind your fingers love, bloody hell. Are you hungry?"

Kendal lifted her head up and smiled, she was embarrassed. Pat was right though, she was more than hungry. "Skin up then," Pat shouted over to her brother.

"You've woke me up now and there's no way I'm getting back to sleep without getting stoned. I don't know what's up with me lately I just can't get any shut-eye no matter how hard I try." Scott started to build a joint on the small table in front of him; he turned his head to face her.

"You won't sleep will you? I bet your still thinking about that dick-head aren't you?" he looked her straight in the eyes and continued. "Don't even try lying Pat, because I've been told by a good source that you still want him back," he ranted. Pat was chomping at the bit and her face was angry.

"Scott, will you fuck off getting on my case about Paul. You have to understand I was with him for ten years, and he's the father of my children."

"He treated you like a slave, and what, after him shagging your best mate you still want him back, get a grip, surely you're not that desperate for a man?" Pat was sulking, her brother was right though, Paul was a womaniser and she'd caught him bang to rights with her best friend in bed.

"We all make mistakes and he's told me he loves me and he will change."

Scott snapped and whacked his flat palm on the arm of the chair. "He'll never change, the sooner you get that into your thick head the better." Kendal looked like she wanted the floor to open up and swallow her, they were both bang at it and none of them were backing down.

Pat spoke in a low voice. "I still love him Scott, what can I do to change that? Don't you think I want to get over him? It's been four months now and I'm getting worse, not better. I've not had a decent night's sleep for months. I need him."

Scott could see she was at breaking point and backed

off, he took a couple of puffs from the weed and passed it over to his sister, she needed it more than him. Kendal placed her plate on the table and sat back in her chair, you could have cut the atmosphere with a knife.

"You've got a top house Pat," Kendal lied; she needed to change the conversation quick.

"Orr, thanks love. I try my best you know, but the kids wreck it all the time. Look at the wallpaper over there in the corner," she pointed behind the sofa. "Our Bradley just sat there picking it off the wall and eating it the other day. I've only had it decorated a few weeks ago," she was shaking her head. "Oh, I smacked his arse red raw though, the little bastard didn't know what hit him." Kendal's face dropped, this woman was being serious.

"What, he eats wallpaper?"

"Yeah, I tell you what I'm worried about him; he eats stones, mud and anything else he can get his hands on. His latest craze is cig dimps, so make sure you don't leave any lying about, or he'll have them." Pat's face was wreathed in smoke as she passed the joint over to Kendal. "Here, get a chong on that, it will chill you out." Kendal could feel Scott's eyes on her, she was hesitating. Bringing the weed up to her mouth she took a long hard drag of it and sat back in her chair. Scott reached over and took it out of her hand after she'd had a few more blasts of it. Kendal looked like she was melting into her chair. Her fingers unfolded slowly and her bottom jaw dropped, she was stoned. Pat stood up and grabbed the crust from the butty Scott had left on the plate. "Fucking hell, I've got the munchies now. No wonder I'm overweight. I will have to stop smoking the weed because it always makes me hungry. I think I've got a few snacks upstairs though, so goodnight you two, see you in the morning." Scott nodded his head slowly. Kendal tried raising her hand, but her body had a mind of its own and it wouldn't budge.

Scott moved back on the sofa next to Kendal, he stroked the side of her face. Her eyes had changed, they were glazed over. She could feel his lips on hers and all his words seemed slurred. Kendal sat up and tried to snap out of it, but she was a prisoner to the marijuana. "So, Jane tells me we are getting it on tonight, is that what you want?"

Kendal nodded her head slowly. Scott stood up and she could see him pulling his t-shirt over his head, and stripping down to his boxers. "Just hang on there, while I run upstairs and get the duvet from the bed, it's freezing in this house isn't it?" Kendal smiled, he was right though, it was cold. "Get your kit off then, I'll be back in a minute." Scott was gone and you could hear his feet pounding up the stairs. Kendal took her shoes off slowly, she was thinking. Sliding her skirt down her legs she could see her underwear. Before she pulled her top off she looked around the house. Was this the place where she going to lose her virginity? She never expected it to be like this. She wanted it to be like she'd seen on the TV, candles burning, soft lighting and romantic songs playing in the background. This wasn't what she'd dreamt about.

Scott was back, his eyes were all over her and he liked what he saw, jumping onto the sofa, he urged her to join him. "Quick, get under the quilt; you'll freeze if you stand there any longer. Kendal bent her body down and joined him. Giggling noises filled the room. Their lips connected. The quilt was falling off their bodies and you could see Scott's hand entering her knickers. Kendal's face changed, her cheeks were going red and her eyes were wide open, you could hear her groaning. Scott was toned and slightly tanned compared to her pale body. You could see goose pimples all over her thighs as his hand caressed her legs. Looking into her eyes he spoke. "Have you ever done this before?" Scott could sense this because she was just lying there like a sack of spuds. The women he'd been with before were more experienced and it was very rare he had to take control.

"This is my first time," she whispered. Scott ran his finger over her bottom lip.

"Well, I'll take it easy; you're going to love it." His hand fumbled under the quilt and you could see him on top of her thrusting slowly. "Fuck me, you're tight," he moaned. His hand took hold of his penis and he directed it inside her, it was in. Kendal's fingernails gripped his shoulders and you could see his skin turning white, she was groaning as each thrust went deeper inside her. Scott was excited and you could tell he wasn't going to be long. Kendal's legs were held up in the air and she could feel his speed picking up. Scott's face changed and you could see small beads of sweat forming on his brow. "I'm going to shoot my load, are you going to come or what?" Kendal didn't have a clue what he was going on about but nodded her head just to please him. His face creased and his movement slowed down. He'd ejaculated.

Scott rolled off from her and stood up, his legs were shaking slightly. He was searching for his cigarettes. Sitting back down he patted the side of her leg. "Ay, that was bang on that, especially seeing as it's your first time. Next time I'll show you how to ride me, you'll like that." Kendal pulled the duvet up and tucked it under her neck. She looked white. He sparked two cigs up and passed one to her. "Move over then, let me back in, it's like the Antarctic out here." Kendal shuffled over and her back was against the sofa. Scott was facing her. "So, come on then, did you like it or what?" She was gobsmacked, this lad was so open. Her family didn't speak about sex and her face was beetroot.

"I think so," she smiled.

"What do you mean, you think? How would you know anyway, if you're a virgin?" She could see he was annoyed and back-pedalled.

"Yeah, it was good, but I'm sore though underneath, is that normal?" Scott's head was swelling and he looked proud.

"That's because I've got a big nob, don't worry you'll be fine. Just give it a few days and you'll be walking properly again."

Kendal looked devastated. "What, won't I be able to walk properly?"

He chuckled loudly and pulled her closer towards his chest. "Yeah, I'm just joking with you, you're so vulnerable you are. I will have to give you some lessons in life." Kendal looked relieved. Stubbing his cig out in the ashtray he lay back and cuddled up to her, she lay on his chest. This was the first time in her life she'd ever felt love. She closed her eyes and snuggled into his body. Her fingers tickled his chest as they both drifted off to sleep.

CHAPTER SIX

Paddy Wilson sat in his chair watching the TV, he looked agitated. It was early in the day and not time for him to go out to the boozer yet. He'd already had his hands down the side of the sofa searching for any bits of change. He'd found a couple of quid up to now and that was enough to get him into the pub. Hopefully, he could nurse a pint until one of his pals came in, and then he could bum some drinks from them as he'd always done. Somebody was at the door, Paddy shot his eyes over to Kendal, "Go and see who that is."

She got up from her seat and left the room, there was no way Paddy would have moved, he never did. He was a lazy old fart and treated everyone like they were his slaves. Nelly was coughing in the bedroom, Kendal heard her as she entered the hallway. Her eyes shot up the stairs and you could see the fear in her eyes as she waited for the coughing to stop. Nelly was in bed most days now and she very rarely came downstairs, she was too weak.

Kendal opened the front door and a man stood there with a smile across his face. She looked at him closely; he was a good looking man and right up her street. She flicked her hair back over her shoulder and pushed her perky breasts out in front of her. "Is your Granddad in, love?" he asked, his voice was husky.

Kendal nodded, "Who shall I say wants him?"

"Just tell him it's John Daley, he'll know who I am." John Daley hadn't been to Paddy's house for years. He'd seen him in the pubs on lots of occasions, but he tried to distance himself from him as he was always pissed and trying to sponge money from him. At first John had bunged him a few quid, but that had stopped a long time ago. The man had no pride in his eyes and he was the lowest of the low. John watched Kendal walking back into the house, his head dipped low. Kendal shouted to John from the living room door.

"He said come in. Will you close the front door after you?" John walked into the house and you could see him inhaling, he could smell sweaty feet, his face creased. Once the front door was closed Kendal sat back down in the front room and watched John enter the room. Paddy remained in his seat, and held his hand out for John to shake once he'd seen who it was.

"Are you alright pal? What do I owe the pleasure of the mighty John Daley coming to my humble abode," he sniggered. John sat in the chair facing him, but his eyes kept wandering looking at Kendal. Paddy clicked his fingers to get his granddaughter's attention. "Go and get John a drink, where have your manners gone girl. Since when do we ignore our guest? Get up from your arse and sort it out."

Kendal stood to her feet; she started to trudge out of the room. "Do you want a cup of tea or coffee John?" she asked.

Paddy was angry and waved his hand about in the air to get her attention, he was showing off. "Don't insult me by offering him tea and bloody coffee, get him a glass of whisky, and get me one too while you're there." Kendal left the room. Paddy raised his eyes to the ceiling; he was planning on saving the last drop of whisky for bedtime, he was gutted.

"So John, what can I do for you mate? Like I said, it

must be something serious, because you've not been to my house for some time. Well, in fact not since our Mary died." Just the mention of Mary's name sent shivers down John's spine and you could see him rubbing his arms as if someone had walked over his grave.

"It's nothing serious mate, I've just come to see you how you are. I've heard that Nelly isn't her usual self, and well," he paused. "I'm here to give you some support." John was lying through his back teeth, the only reason he was there was to see his daughter. Paddy sat forward in his seat and rubbed his palms together. He knew that support meant money from John, and you could see him getting excited. Kendal walked back into the room, she looked tired. She'd been sneaking out from her house most nights to see Scott and it was taking its toll on her, she was knackered.

"Thanks sweetheart," John said as she passed him his drink. Paddy was more than ready for his drink and he was licking his dry cracked lips. As he held his hand out for the drink you could see his fingers trembling. John watched Kendal, he was mesmerised by her. She turned her head quickly and caught him checking her out, she smiled softly. Sitting down in her chair she looked at him in more detail, he had a look of George Clooney. The stubble on his chin made him look sexy. She pretended to read the free local newspaper on the table. Turning the pages slowly, she just looked at the pictures and tried to work out the storyline, she loved this game and it kept her occupied for a while.

Paddy coughed to clear his throat; he was ready to give his speech about how much he was on his arse, the man had no pride. John knew him of old and prepared himself for a sob story. "It's been hard you know John. My

Nelly's been bedridden for weeks and it's left me looking after the house and our Kendal." Kendal growled as her eyes shot over to her granddad. He was such a liar, no way in this world had he ever looked after her; it was the other way around. She wanted to pipe up and tell John the truth but she kept silent to keep the peace. Her fingers tapped on the table rapidly, and John turned his head towards her.

"You have a good granddad here love, not many men would do what he's done for this family." John was playing with Paddy; he knew the truth more than anyone. There was no way in this world the old bastard was getting his hands on a penny of his money. John reached into his pocket and pulled out a black leather wallet. Paddy sat forward in his seat and stretched his neck out trying to see the amount of money he had stashed inside it. "Here you go girl, you go and treat yourself, get some new clothes and that." Paddy was on the edge of his seat and his hands were cupped together, his jaw dropped and he was fidgeting.

"Oh, she's alright for clothes John, aren't you Kendal?" She lifted her head up and her words seemed to be stuck on her lips. Paddy was growling at her and she could see him from the corner of her eyes.

"You must be joking Granddad, I haven't had any new clothes for ages. My Nana got me this skirt from the charity shops ages ago. I do need clothes." John stood to his feet and walked over to where she was sat. His heart melted for her, you could see it in his eyes. Paddy stood up too so he could see what was going on; his eyes were squinting together trying to focus.

"Here, go and splash out. Get a few new rig-outs, I'm sure there's enough there to sort you out." Kendal smiled from ear to ear, there were more twenty pound notes there than she'd ever seen in her life, and they were all hers. She could see Paddy heading towards her at speed. Quickly she shoved the cash in her pocket.

Paddy was up in arms, "John don't be giving her all that money," he gritted his teeth as he darted his eyes at his granddaughter. "Kendal we need food more than clothes, tell John, you're alright." Kendal kept her mouth shut and dipped her head low, there was no way she was parting with the cash, not a chance.

"Here Paddy, here's a few quid for some shopping, I'll give it to Kendal so she can go to Asda. You don't want to be doing the shopping do you; it's a woman's job isn't it?" Paddy was snookered, his mouth was moving but no words were coming out. He was marching around the front room like a headless chicken. John gave a cheeky wink to Kendal, and sat back down. Paddy was in a strop, and he kept snarling at Kendal but she wouldn't look at him. She stood to her feet and spoke.

"Thanks John, I'm going to get ready now and nip into town. I'll get some shopping on my way back."

John looked anxious. "If you wait for five minutes I'll give you a lift, I'm heading down that way anyway." Kendal nodded, this was the perfect opportunity to get away from Paddy before he got his grubby hands on her cash because that's what he would have done as soon as John had left the house, he was an evil old bastard.

"I'm just going to go and see my Nana before I go John, give me a shout when you're ready to leave."

"No worries, ay, tell Nelly I hope she gets better soon. She's a tough old dog that one, she won't be long in that bed, she's a fighter," he winked at her again.

"I will," Kendal said as she left the room. She stood at

the bottom of the stairs, her heart was beating ten to the dozen, this man was having an effect on her, he excited her. Taking a few seconds to compose herself she ran up the stairs to see Nelly.

The door handle moved slowly as Kendal entered the bedroom. The room was dark and it smelt of misery. Kendal walked over to the window and opened the curtains slightly. Nelly covered her eyes with her hand and her face creased with the light. "Turn it in love; close those curtains a bit more, the light's blinding me eyes." Daylight filled the room and Nelly was still struggling to adjust to the light. Kendal sat on the edge of the bed. She studied Nelly's face, it had definitely changed. Deep seated wrinkles now looked like they'd doubled overnight and her eyes held so much sadness. Kendal reached over and stroked her cold pale hands.

"Why don't you come downstairs for a bit, you've been banged up in this bedroom for weeks, it will do you good, a change of scenery." Nelly blew her breath and prepared to talk, spit hung from the corner of her mouth.

"What, and sit down there with that miserable cunt, you must be joking. He moans when I start coughing and he told me straight the other day that I would be better off dead."

Kendal snapped, "What, he said he wanted you dead?"

Nelly shuffled her body about on the bed. "Well, he may as well have. The cheeky old fart, asked me when I would be well enough to start making his tea again."

Kendal shook her head. "He's going worse you know, he's the same with me, he thinks I'm his personal slave. If he could have me wiping his arse I'm sure he would." Nelly chuckled, as she tried to get comfortable in the bed, her body was weak. Kendal stood up and moved the pillows up behind her back to make her more comfortable.

"Who's downstairs?" she said as she held her ear to the door.

"John Daley has just come to see my Granddad." Nelly looked concerned as she reached over for her fags off her bedside cabinet. Kendal shook her head. "Keep off the cigs, will you. Bloody hell, have you heard your breathing?"

Nelly frowned, "Oh piss off will you. Who are you, the smoke police?" Kendal looked deflated and stroked her hand across the bed. Nelly sparked her cig up and inhaled deeply, she was gasping for her nicotine intake. "What's he here for, did he say?" Kendal pulled the money from her pocket and spread it across the bed. Nelly looked at it and was puzzled. "Where's that from?"

Kendal smiled. "It's from John, he's given me the money to go and get some new clothes, and look," she paused at she pulled fifty pound from the spread of money. "He gave me money for shopping as well." Nelly chewed on her bottom lip, she was thinking.

"That's odd; he's not been near this house since our Mary died," Nelly thought. She tapped her finger on her top lip before saying "Erm... Funny that is, I bet that sponging bastard downstairs has asked him to come around, he has no shame you know." Kendal giggled as she picked up the money from the bed.

"Who cares why he's here. We've got some shopping money now, so don't stress about it," Kendal folded the cash and shoved it into her back pocket. "He's giving me a lift into town in a minute, he offered me a lift. I didn't even have to ask him. I'll get you some of them soups you like from Asda, if you want? You know the ones with the chunky vegetables in it."

Nelly was staring into space; she seemed in a deep trance. John Daley's voice was shouting up the stairs. Kendal stood to her feet. "Right Nana, try and get up ay. I'll be back soon. Ay," she giggled as she turned her head back. "My Granddad's got a face like a smacked arse. He's gutted John gave me the money instead of him. Imagine, if he'd have got his mitts on it, he would have been straight down to the pub like a blue-arsed fly, partying like it was his birthday."

Nelly agreed. "Oh, don't we know it. Just make sure he doesn't try to tap you on the way out. You know what he's like; he'll give you some story, so you'll feel sorry for him."

Kendal smirked. "Not a chance Nana, he's getting Jack-shit from me, don't you worry about that." Nelly wriggled about in the bed; her feet were sticking out of the bottom of it.

"You're right, I'm going to get up for a bit, with a bit of luck he might piss off out and give me some peace."

"That's the spirit, Nana. Ay, when I get back, I'll blow-dry your hair for you, if you want?" Nelly covered her face with her hands.

"That's if I'm still alive by then." Laughter filled the room as John Daley shouted again. Kendal popped her head out of the bedroom door and answered him.

"One minute, I'm just saying goodbye to my Nana." Kendal walked to the top end of the bed and leant down to kiss Nelly's cheek. "Right I won't be long, Get up, and I'll cook us a nice tea when I get back."

"Okay, I'll try," Nelly said as she left the room.

Kendal could see John's hand resting on the wall as she came to the bottom of the stairs, it was hairy and his hands looked like bunches of bananas. Paddy was there hovering, he was trying to catch her attention. Kendal blanked him completely and opened the front door. "See you later Granddad," she shouted over her shoulder. Paddy stood at the front door and watched them head to the silver car parked at the end of his garden.

"Little bastard." He muttered under his breath.

Kendal clicked her seat belt into the socket; she could feel John's eyes all over her like a rash. Turning to face him she smiled. "Can we pick my mate up first, she's coming with me?" John asked for directions. Music was playing inside the car and she was surprised he was listening to all the latest tunes. "I thought you would have been into some other kind of music, not N-Dubz," she giggled. "Don't you think that's a bit young for you?"

John flicked his fingers on the steering wheel. He knew she was right. The CD didn't belong to him; it was his latest leg-over, a sixteen year old girl from Collyhurst. He tried to sing along to the song but his words were mixed up, he didn't have a clue. Kendal was folded in two laughing her head off. "Orr sort it out, you can't rap. You need to start listening to the Bee Gees or something like that. These tunes are our era, not yours."

John was laughing. "Ay, I'm not dead yet, I'm still up with the times I am." Kendal turned her head and looked out of the window; she'd missed the fact that she never had a Dad. Is this the way she would have been with her own father if she would ever have known him? The sound of the horn honking made her turn her head to the road. Scott was waving his hand in the air in the distance. His face was like thunder when he saw Kendal sat in the passenger side and she knew he wasn't happy, she gave him a half-hearted wave. John turned the music down. "Is that your boyfriend?"

"Mind your own business," Kendal giggled.

"I know everything that goes on around here, and I believe you and Scott are an item." His voice was husky and she couldn't help but stare at his biceps that were bulging out from his t-shirt.

"Who's told you that? Ignore them because they're chatting shit, me and Scott are just good friends that's all." There was no way she was telling her granddad's friend all about her love life, no way in this world, she kept her trap firmly shut.

Jane was stood waiting outside her house for Kendal to arrive, when she saw her pulling up in the smart car her face lit up, she thought they were travelling by bus into Manchester. Jane opened the back door with haste. She caught John's eyes as she sat down and introduced herself without giving it a second thought, she was so confident. "Check you out Kendal in this mint car," she patted John's shoulder. "I'm Jane by the way." he smiled back at her through the rear-view mirror.

"I know Kendal had told me all about you, she said you're a right man-eater." John was grooming her for sure; his tongue was tickling his top lip as he spoke. "So, is it true or what then, are you a man-eater or what?" Jane remained calm; she knew he was winding her up. Leaning forward she rested her hand on the back of his chair.

"Why are you so interested anyway, do you fancy your chances with a bit of young stuff or something?" John was stuck for words; he wasn't used to anyone having a quicker wit than he had. As the traffic came to a standstill he sat up straight in his seat and made sure Jane could see his full face through the rear-view mirror.

"Cheeky aren't you? I would show you a good time, believe me, one kiss from me and you would be hooked."

"Fuck off, you're a fossil," she shouted. Realising what she'd said she covered her hand over her mouth. "Orr I'm sorry. I was only joking, I forgot where I was?"

John shook his head. "I might be older, but believe me, I'm a lot wiser. There's always a good tune played on an old piano, or so they say."

Kendal jumped into the conversation, she was jealous her friend was getting more attention than she was. "Jane, will you shut up. John is a friend of my Granddad's. You don't want him thinking we're a pair of slappers do you?" Jane sat back, she was quiet now, but she kept catching John looking at her in mirror, she stuck her tongue out at him and giggled.

The car pulled up near Manchester city centre. Kendal was looking proud as she stepped from it; she wanted everyone to see her. She bent back down and placed her head back inside the car. "Thanks John for the lift, and for the money."

"No worries, if you ever get short of money or need some help come and see me. I'll make sure I look after you." His eyes looked enchanting. Kendal stood back up and her face look flustered. Jane was taking her time getting out from the passenger seat. As she was about to leave, John handed her a business card. "And, cheeky chops, if you need an older man in your life, you just give me a ring," she snatched the white card from his hand and slid it inside her back pocket, she was acting cocky.

"I doubt it mate, but who knows, this could be your lucky day." The car door slammed shut, and he watched carefully as the two girls ran across the road in front of him. Jane turned her head back and gave him a wave; he started to drive off and blew a kiss at her. Jane looked at him and smiled, he'd definitely impressed her.

"What you laughing at?" Kendal asked as she linked Jane's arm.

"He's mint, Oh my God, I'm in love. Did you see the way he looked at me, he wanted me. I could see it in his eyes." Kendal pulled her along by the sleeve of her coat.

"Does he 'eck, he was trying to come onto me too, so get a grip. He was just joking with you." Jane pulled away and rummaged into her back pocket, she pulled out the card.

"Did you get his number though," her voice was sarcastic. "It doesn't look like a joke to me, he wants me for sure?" she was rubbing her hands together with excitement. Kendal spat her dummy out and tried not to show her disappointment. John had been flirting with her too, she was sure if it, but if that was the case, why hadn't he given her his phone number too. Jane playfully punched her in the arm. "Ay, you've got a boyfriend, so what good would his phone number have been to you anyway. I'm young free and single me, so I can do whatever I want; you're on lock down, so deal with it."

Kendal gritted her teeth together, Jane was right, her relationship with Scott had been going on now for over five months and they were classed as a couple. Scott had been acting strange lately though; he was trying to control her life. She kept her mouth shut though, and didn't tell a soul, she didn't want anyone to know about her private business. If Jane would have got a sniff of what Scott was saying about her she would have had kittens, he wanted Kendal to cart her as a friend saying she was a dirty trollop.

Kendal dropped the subject as they entered the Arndale shopping centre. Jane looked at Kendal with a concerned face. "Where have you got your cash from anyway, Miss Moneypenny? Don't tell me old Paddy has treated you? Has he had a windfall or something on the gee-gees? Usually he wouldn't give a door a bang the tight old git." Kendal held a proud look on her face; this was going to wipe the smile right from her friend's face for sure.

"John treated me, he bunged me two-ton before, he said for me to go and treat myself, and," she paused. "He gave me fifty quid for some food shopping too." Jane stood still and gawped at her.

"So, he's minted as well? Why didn't you tell me that before, he's definitely getting a phone call off me now? He can be my sugar daddy." Kendal looked deflated her plan had backfired on her again, she couldn't hold her tongue.

"He won't just give anyone money you know, he knows our family, that's all." Jane was bouncing about.

"I don't care who he knows, if he wants to pamper me, then who am I to step in his way. I'm ringing him later. I'm going to fleece the tosser. I have to take my chances while I can, don't I?" Kendal was lost for words; she tried ignoring her and carried on walking, but she was narked. They both walked into New Look looking at the latest fashion. You could see Jane's hand stroking the top of the business card sticking out from her pocket, she was plotting something.

The girls spent hours in town getting Kendal a new wardrobe. She purchased new underwear, earrings, shoes; she got herself the full shebang. Waiting at the bus stop she held her bags at her side with pride. So many times in the past she'd seen young girls shopping in town and always wished she was like them, this was the first time ever that Kendal had really tasted any money. She liked it, you could see that in her face and she wanted more, no matter what she had to do to get it.

★

Nelly sat in her chair and she looked a lot healthier than earlier. She'd combed her hair and had a wash and the colour had returned to her cheeks, she looked perky. Paddy sat watching the TV. The sound of the front door closing made him sit up straight in his chair. As soon as Kendal came into the room he was like shit from a shovel, he was up on his feet marching towards her. "I hope you haven't spent all that bleeding money John gave you? Come on, hand it over, "his flat palm was in front of her face touching the end of her nose. Kendal looked at Nelly for help; she could see his fingers curling into a ball at the side of his legs. He was ready for hitting her; she could see it in his eyes.

"I haven't got any money left. John told me to go shopping with the money he gave me, and that's what I've done. You can check on the side in the kitchen, the receipts are there for everything I've bought, so don't start accusing me of having any money away." Paddy ran at her with a face of fury, all she could do was cover her head with her hands. He was beating her bad. Nelly nearly had a heart attack as she tried to get up from her chair, her legs were shaking.

"Leave her alone Paddy, get your hands off her." Nelly was on the floor and his foot swung back before he surged it deep into her waist. Her piercing screams filled the room. Kendal lifted her head up and clocked the brass ornament at the side of her. Jumping up to her feet she grabbed it and launched it at her Granddad's head. He felt the blow; you could see it in his eyes. Bright red claret dribbled down the side of his cheek. Touching it with his fingers he brought it towards his face.

"You dirty little slag; after all we've done for you. You should have been put in care, like I told her there," he rammed his finger into the side of Nelly's head. Kendal was crying and her hands were trembling, years of abuse had final surfaced and she was ready to put the record straight, she jumped to her feet and ran at him.

"You old cunt, you should have put me in care then, perhaps then, I would have felt part of a family, because, let's face it Granddad, you've always treated me like an outcast." He snapped and grabbed her face in his hands; you could see her skin turning white.

"You are a bleeding outcast that's why. You remind me of my Mary. Every day I look at your face, and hate you with a passion. She would have been alive today and happy at home if it wasn't for you." Nelly crawled up onto her feet, she was panting like a dog. There was no way she was letting him speak to Kendal like that.

"You keep your evil mouth closed, Paddy Wilson. Mary wasn't all you make her out to be. She was selfish and only thought about herself, don't kid yourself, she was a handful, so don't keep putting her up on a pedestal all the bleeding time." Paddy sank to his knees and covered his ears with his hands.

"Shut up, shut up. My Mary was a good girl." Nelly walked to Kendal's side and placed her arm around her shoulder.

"Come on love, ignore him, he's been at the whisky again, he's drunk. Kendal pulled away from her and bent her knees down towards Paddy's red face.

"I wish you were dead, my mother was just like you. Selfish and controlling. I'm glad she died, because if she was anything like you, I would have hated her, just like I despise you. There you go, I've said it," she kicked her foot into the side of his stomach. "I hate you with a passion. I'm leaving here; see what you're like when I'm gone. You've drove me away just like you do with everyone else who's loved you." She made her way to Nelly and helped her back to her feet. "Come on Nana, leave him to wallow in his own self pity, he deserves it, the drunken bastard." Nelly followed Kendal out of the living room, she was a nervous wreck and her legs were buckling from underneath her. Kendal caught her just in time and helped her back up the stairs to bed. Once she'd got her to the top, she opened her bedroom door and guided her back into bed. Kendal fell to her knees and sobbed her heart out, her shoulders were shaking.

Nelly spoke in a low voice as she hung her head over the side of the bed. "Come here love, come and sit down here." Kendal wiped her tears on her sleeve and lay next to her grandmother. Nelly placed a flat palm on her head and slowly stroked her hair back from her face. "He's mental isn't he? I tell you what love, if I could move out of this bed at this moment I would stab the bastard right through his heart." Kendal lifted her head up and her eyes were wide open, her face was serious.

"I'll stab him Nana, I'll finish him off," she grabbed hold of her hands and moved them towards her face. "Nobody would ever know. I will go back downstairs and just stick a knife into him; we can say it was self-defence." Nelly looked at her with a concerned face, she knew she was serious.

"What, and we both go to prison for him, no love, leave him be, he'll get his comeuppance one of these days, trust me." The room was filled with an eerie silence.

"Tell me about my mother Nana, I don't know anything about her. Nobody has ever told anything, it's like she never existed. I have a right to know don't I," she was squeezing Nelly's hand. "I mean, who's my father?" Nelly clammed up, her chest was rising and her heart was pumping inside her ribcage. She knew this day would come, but she never expected it to be today. "Will you tell me please," Kendal urged. Nelly closed her eyes as if she was visualising her daughter's face, the corners of her mouth began to rise slowly.

"Oh, your mother was a pretty girl, and she knew it too. She had all the young lads eating right out of her hand. She was the life and soul of the party, so full of confidence you know, our Molly never got a sniff," Nelly rolled her eyes. "Mary was a feisty one too, she had a really bad temper and when she was upset everyone else would know about it too, she was a nightmare," Nelly's face lost its colour and you could see the painful memories of her dead daughter right across her face. "Many a night I had to peel her off our Molly, she would have killed her if I wouldn't have stopped her you know, seriously, I could see it in her eyes, there was no stopping her once she snapped."

Kendal sat up on the bed and brought her knees up to her chest. "What, Molly was scared of my Mam?" She tilted her head to the side and tried to digest the information she'd just been given, Kendal continued. "Our Molly can fight too, she's as hard as nails." she sank her head into her thighs. "Tell me more about her please."

As Nelly sat talking of her dead daughter, you could see a lump forming in her throat and she was struggling to hold it together, she was cracking her knuckles as she tried to control her breathing. What Kendal asked her next knocked her for six, she wasn't ready for it. "Who's my father?" Nelly started choking and pointed to a glass of water at the side of her bed. Kendal jumped up and passed it to her with haste. "Sit up proper and drink it, drink it slowly though, try and catch your breath first." Water dribbled down Nelly's chin as she slurped the cold water. Her coughing fit had subsided but she kept on coughing hoping Kendal would forget her last question.

"I'm hungry," Nelly said as she wiped her mouth with her hand. Kendal was ready to ask the question again, but backed down seeing the stress Nelly was under.

"I'll go and make us both something to eat. He's getting nothing though Nana," she stood up from the bed and placed her hands on her hips. "So, don't even ask me to make him anything. He can starve for all I care." Nelly looked down at her wrinkled hands on the bed, they were still shaking vigorously. Even though Paddy was a bastard he was still her husband and she still felt the need to care for him, it was just in her nature.

"Please Kendal; just make him something to eat. He'll probably go asleep after it anyway, please, for me." Kendal blew a laboured breath and gritted her teeth together.

"Right, okay, but I'm doing this for you, not him. I'm going to spit all over it though," she growled. Nelly chuckled and waved her away with her hand, she was starting coughing again.

Kendal crept down the stairs. Her face looked worried. As soon as she stepped into the kitchen she grabbed one of the big silver bread knives from the drawer. She placed it on the worktop at the side of her, if Paddy walked in; he was getting it rammed into his body for sure, she was ready for him. Kendal set about making the tea. The sound of pots and pans clashing filled the room. She checked the time, and panicked. It was nearly time to go and meet Scott; he'd go mad if she wasn't there on time, he hated waiting about for her. She buttered the bread quickly, and set the plates out on the side.

Paddy passed the kitchen door and headed up the stairs, he was carrying the stepladders in his hands. A shiver went down her spine as Kendal prepared for round two. Clashing and banging noises could be heard on the landing. She stepped out into the hallway, but she couldn't see him, she carried on cooking.

Carrying a black tray up the stairs she looked at the meal she'd prepared for her Nana. It was chunky vegetable soup, Nelly loved it. As she reached the top of the stairs she could see Paddy going into her bedroom, she froze and her nostrils were flaring. After a few seconds she took the food into Nelly. Kendal stood at the end of her bed with a face like thunder. "What's he up to? He's in my bedroom."

Nelly hunched her shoulders and leant forward as she whispered. "Just stay in here until he goes back downstairs. If he's got anything to say, he'll come in here."

They could hear noise outside the bedroom. Kendal tiptoed across the threadbare carpet and slowly pulled the door open; she could see Paddy walking down the stairs. Kendal disappeared. Stepping into her bedroom, her eyes were all over the place trying to work out why her grandfather had been in her bedroom. Her eyes shot to two black bin-liners at the side of her bed. Slowly she walked towards them with caution. Opening them slowly, her face dropped, she looked surprised. She pulled a coat out of the bag. Looking at it in more detail, she was confused. Her head dug into the black bag again and she pulled out more clothing. She placed them on her bed in a pile. The next bag contained more bulky objects. Kendal put her hand in and pulled out a book, it was a diary and across it read the name of Mary Wilson. Kendal sounded the first word out; she knew the second word was Wilson because she could recognise her own surname. Her lips came together as she sounded out the name Mary. A single bulky tear fell onto her cheek. This was all her mother's belongings, why hadn't she ever seen them before? Nelly had told her about this stuff years ago, but she didn't believe it existed. Kendal held the diary to her nose and inhaled deeply. Her eyes closed and you could see the pain in her face.

Opening the diary for the first time, she could see her mother's handwriting. The words on the pages didn't mean anything to her; it was all gibberish. At that moment she wished she could read. Hearing Nelly coughing again from the other room, she slammed the diary shut and placed it under her mattress. When she finally learned to read she would read the last words of her mother and try to understand why she was murdered, but for now, she put it in a safe place away from prying eyes. Kendal grabbed a few of the clothes in her hands and headed back to see Nelly.

"Nana, are these my mother's clothes?" Nelly sat up in the bed and her eyes tried to focus properly. Kendal walked to the end of the bed and passed the small bundle over to her. Nelly held the clothes out in front of her eyes and then she inhaled.

"Yes, they are love." Kendal looked like she was going to collapse where she stood, her face drained of any colour. Nelly chewed on her bottom lip and tried to fight back the tears. "This was one of her favourite tops you know; she never had it off her back." The pink top looked old now and the colour had faded. "Bloody hell, what else did he give you?"

Kendal was on the verge of speaking but held back, she didn't want anyone else to know about the diary she'd found. That was her secret, hers and her mothers.

"Just two bags of clothes and a few bits and bobs. I will check them out properly later, when I get back in. What time is it anyway, I need to go and meet Scott?"

Nelly growled. "Why are you still seeing him, I've heard he's a bit of a Jack the lad. For fucks sake don't let your Granddad get a whiff of you having a boyfriend, he'll have your guts for garters if he does." Kendal took the pink top from the bed and headed to the bedroom door, before she left she turned back.

"He does love me Nana, just ignore all the rumours about him, people are just chatting shit about Scott because they are jealous."

Nelly fidgeted about in her bed, "Well, just be careful love, if he lays one finger on you, let me know and I'll have the bastard put in a body bag before you can say a word."

Kendal smirked, "You're such a mad-head you are. Right, see you later." Nelly was alone with her thoughts, her face looked sad as she gazed out of the window. She missed Mary.

Kendal walked to Scott's sister's house. She was wearing her mother's old top. Every now and then you could see her pulling it up through her coat, sniffing at it. She felt she had a piece of her mother with her now. Scott's sister's house stood facing her and she could see the net curtain twitching. As soon as she walked into the garden Scott was stood at the door, he was in a mood, his face was like thunder. "Why are you late? You should have been here ages ago." Kendal walked into the house and she could feel his hot breath at the back of her neck as he walked behind her.

"Oh, don't start going on, I was arguing with my Granddad again, he's a crank, look at my arms where he grabbed me." Scott wasn't looking at her arms when she rolled her sleeves up revealing the red marks, something else was on his mind and he couldn't wait to get it off his chest. Grabbing two cans of Foster's lager from the fridge he passed one to her and they both went into the front room. "Where's Pat?" she asked him in a low voice. She was always in the house and it was strange that she wasn't sat in her usual seat.

"I'm babysitting, she's gone to bingo. She should be back home about ten o'clock." Kendal sat down and pulled the ring from her can, taking a drink she placed it at the side of her legs. Scott seemed edgy; he kept staring at her and grinding his teeth. "What were you doing in John Daley's car today?"

Kendal knew this moment would come and stuttered. "He was giving me a lift into town; he gave me some money for clothes as well. He's a good friend of the family," before she could finish her sentence he threw a newspaper at her. Scott bolted up from his seat and leant into her face, he was on the verge of ramming his fists down her throat.

"He's a pervert, he's well known for shagging young girls. I hope he didn't come onto you, because if he did," he pulled her towards him by her coat. "I swear, I'll waste the both of you." Kendal was petrified.

"What are you going on about? I've just told you before; he's a friend of the family. What, can't I even get a lift anymore? Just stop being paranoid will you," she wriggled free. Kendal's head smashed to the side of the sofa, he dragged her by the hair and pulled her head to face him.

"You cheeky bitch, don't you ever tell me to stop being paranoid. You're my fucking girlfriend not his, I know what he's like are you forgetting that? He starts by giving you little gifts, and before you know it, your knickers are off and he's banging you. I've seen him do it a million times before, so don't tell me anything about John Daley as if you know him." Kendal pulled away from him; she didn't want to add fuel to the fire. Scott was short-tempered and this wasn't the first time he's raised his hands to her, she never told anyone though, that was her business and she wanted to keep it that way.

Silence filled the room. Kendal was trying to straighten her hair. Scott sat back down and you could see a large vein at the side of his neck pumping with rage, his face was on fire. "Come and sit over here," he growled. Kendal knew if she didn't go and sit with him the place would go up; slowly she stood to her feet and moved to sit next to him. Looking at her face he stroked her red cheeks slowly. "See, what you've made me do now, it's your fault why I snapped. Fucking hell, why do I even let that prick wind me up?"

Kendal dropped her head; she knew what was coming next. It was always the same after any big argument. Scott lay on the sofa and nudged her in the waist. "Come on then, get your kit off. Pat will be back soon, so we need to make the most of it, don't we?" Her face looked sad as she peeled her clothes off. Slowly she lifted her mother's top over her head. Kendal felt like her mother had witnessed what had just happened and she was ashamed that she wasn't strong enough to walk away from her abusive boyfriend.

Kendal had been having unprotected sex now for months and she was playing with fire every time. Scott told her straight that there was no way he was wearing a condom, he said it was like eating a toffee with the wrapper still on and refused point-blank to wear one, she had no choice. His naked body lay on the sofa; you could see his toned stomach muscles as he sat up slightly. Kendal was naked now and slid next to him. Scott wasted no time in entering her, he was like a bull in a china shop. Any affection she once felt for him had disappeared months ago, he was just out to empty his sack and he never thought about the way his girlfriend was feeling during sex. Kendal's eyes were staring into space as his body pounded on top of hers. He was biting her body as he thrust deep inside her. Scott's face changed and he was ready to ejaculate, he lifted his head up so he could see her, quickly she closed her eyes and pretended she was enjoying it. She was groaning.

Scott lay on his back, his face was hot. "Spark two cigs up then," he prompted her. Kendal stood up quickly and got her clothes back on, she was cold and her teeth were chattering together. Sitting down she passed him a cigarette. Taking a long hard drag from his cig, he spoke. "I think we should get our own gaff you know. What do you think?" Kendal's face dropped and she kept her head low. She wasn't ready for this but he was pressing her for an answer, she could see it in his eyes that if she didn't agree with him he would go off his head, he always did.

"Yeah, but not yet, we can't afford it can we?" Scott sat up and dragged her by the arm closer to him.

"I earn a good crust; we can just rent a small flat or something, are you up for it or what?" Kendal nodded her head slowly, how was she ever going to get out of this one? Life at home was bad, but living with Scott twenty-four-seven would be pure hell, he was a control freak. The sound of keys rattling in the door made them both jump. Scott quickly found his jeans and put them on, his eyes checked the clock on the wall, he looked confused. "What the fuck is she doing back so early, she said she was going to bingo, and that doesn't finish for ages yet." Kendal looked relieved that he was off her back, Pat had saved her bacon. The living room door opened slowly and Scott's sister stood there looking apprehensive, she had something to say but she was hesitating. Pat turned her head back and shouted over her shoulder.

"Make sure that front door closes properly Paul, the lock keeps sticking on it, give it a good bang."

Scott sprang to his feet, "Why have you brought that dickhead back here?" She shook her head, as he marched towards her. Pat had been drinking; you could smell it on her breath.

"Listen you, just keep your beak out of my business, don't you start going on or else you can get out." Paul was at her side and he smirked at Scott with a cocky face, he knew he was winding him up but he didn't care, he was ready for anything he had to throw at him.

"Alright pal, good to be back home, ay."

Scott gave Kendal the eye. "I'm going to bed," he said pushing past his sister. "You're a nob if you ask me Pat." He shoved Paul out of the way with his shoulder. You could hear him stomping up the stairs to bed.

Kendal raised her eyes at Pat, "Just ignore him, you just do whatever makes you happy, you know what he's like. He'll come around without water, just leave him to it the mard arse." Pat patted her arm as she walked passed.

"Thanks' love, see you in the morning." Kendal followed Scott up the stairs. The bedroom was dark and Scott was lying on the double bed with his hands looped behind his head, he was feeling sorry for himself.

"That's sorted then, I'm going to start looking for somewhere for us to live, there's no way I'm staying here with that prick, he just makes my blood boil and I'll end up doing the cunt in." Kendal didn't reply. She lay next to him on the bed and watched the moonlight shining through the window, it looked so calming and peaceful, and she started to relax. As she closed her eyes she could see John Daley's face, he could solve all her problems and make her life so different. He could be the answer to all her prayers. Snuggling into the duvet the corners of her mouth started to rise; she had a cunning plan.

CHAPTER SEVEN

Jane sniggered as she sat on her bed; her legs were folded out in front of her. She was talking to Kendal as she played with her fingers. "It's my birthday next week; I wonder what John will buy me, it will be something expensive, because he doesn't buy crap presents?" Kendal shrugged her shoulders; she had a face like a smacked arse, she was never good at hiding her feelings.

"How the hell should I know, you are a right grabbing bitch, is that all you're with him for, the money?" The jealously was written all over her face she couldn't hide it no matter how hard she tried. In the last few months Jane had been having an affair with John Daley. He was always buying her presents and bunging her money, her appearance seemed to have changed overnight.

"I think we're going to go out for something to eat tonight. He said we can drive out into the countryside and have a romantic meal together."

Kendal giggled and shook her head. "Yeah, it has to be far out because if his wife finds out she'll do you in. I've heard Jackie is a crank. You need to be careful you know, because she'll make your life unbearable if she ever gets a whiff of you sleeping with her husband." Jane lay flat on the bed, her legs were kicking out behind her; she was watching Kendal's reaction from the corner of her eye.

"He's told me he loves me you know. At first, I thought he was lying, but I think I'm falling in love with him too. He said he might even leave Jackie for me."

Kendal sprang up from the bed. "He's having you over you muppet, Scott said he's like that with all the young girls. You just watch in a few months, he'll kick you to the kerb like he's done with all the others. He's an old man, what do you even see in him anyway?" Jane was angry and she went nose to nose with Kendal, she was fuming.

"You can tell Scott to fuck off. What does that twat know about John anyway, he just sells drugs for him? He doesn't know shit about him. Anyway," she rolled her eyes and pointed her finger at Kendal. "Scott wants to concentrate on his own relationship before he sticks his nose into mine." Kendal's face creased with embarrassment. Did her friend know something about Scott that she wasn't saying?

"What do you mean by that, come on then, if you know something about him, just tell me?" Jane sighed, she couldn't back down now, it was too late.

"I mean, don't think I haven't noticed all the bruises on your body lately. Don't start covering up for him because I know what he's like, he's a controlling prick, and those marks are from him no matter what you say. Go on admit it, he's hitting you isn't he?" Kendal grabbed her coat from the bed, she was burning up, her cheeks were beetroot.

"You know nothing about my life, Scott treats me well, you're just jealous because you're sharing a man. Don't come crying to me, when the shit hits the fan and he goes running back to his wife as per usual, because, he will you know." Jane ran after her as she left the room, she wanted the last word, there was no way she was winning this argument.

"Don't worry, I won't come anywhere near you again. Go on, fuck off out of my house, you horrible bitch. You've always been jealous of me and John anyway, what's up ay? Is it because he never fancied you?" Kendal was halfway down the stairs, she wanted to shout back but when she saw Jane's head hanging over the banister she could tell she would have ran down the stairs after her and throttled her, she kept her trap shut and left the house.

Kendal walked along the pavement with her head hung low, she was crying. Jane had been her best friend for as long as she could remember and now she was gone, she was alone and scared. With nowhere else left to go she decided to go to Pat's house, she knew Scott wouldn't be in at this time but she needed someone to talk to and Pat was always helpful when she'd spoken to her in the past.

The traffic was flying by on the road and Kendal seemed in a daze as she stood waiting to cross at the zebra crossing. A car honking its horn brought her back to reality. "Come on love, I've not got all bleeding day," the driver ranted out from his car window. Kendal crossed the road quickly, her feet were moving at twice the speed as normal.

"Okay, okay, take a chill pill you nob-head," she ranted back at the driver as she rammed her two fingers out towards him.

"Hi ya love," Pat said as she opened the front door. "Come on get inside it's bleeding freezing out there." Kendal walked inside the house and as soon as the door closed all her emotions came flying out, she couldn't control them, she was blubbering. "Come and sit in here," Pat pleaded. "What's up, come on, it can't be that bad to make you this upset. Is it our Scott?" Kendal snivelled as she sat down with her head held in her hands.

"No, it's not Scott. I've just fallen out with Jane." Pat

looked relieved.

"Bloody hell, is that it, I thought somebody had died the way you were going on?" Kendal lifted her head up slowly and nodded.

"Yeah, we've never fell out before, she's my best friend, what am I going to do without her?" Pat giggled and sat down beside her; she reached over and took her hand in hers.

"Well, if you're best friends, you won't be fallen out for long, stop getting upset. You'll be back mates before you know it." Kendal raised a small smile, and at that point she realised Pat was talking sense. Pat lit a cig up and passed Kendal one. "Come on; get a blast of nicotine down your neck it will calm you down". Kendal inhaled hard on the fag and her face turned green, this was her first cig of the day. She covered her mouth with her hand and her cheeks filled up at both sides, she looked petrified. Kendal stood up and her eyes were all over the place in a panic. Running into the kitchen she plonked her head inside the sink, she was retching. Pat was behind her now rubbing her back; she turned the tap on and watched as the thick yellow bile ran down the plug hole. "Are you not feeling well love?" Pat asked with a concerned voice. Kendal lifted her head up and moved her hair from near her mouth.

"Yeah, it just came on me all at once. I think it was the cig." Pat studied her face, it looked grey. She poked her fat fingers into her waist.

"Ay, you're not pregnant are you?"

Kendal looked shocked; she stood fidgeting. "No, am I eck, I don't think so anyway." Pat chuckled with the cig still hanging from the corner of her mouth.

"What do you mean, you don't think so? You need to

be sure about stuff like that."

Kendal walked about the kitchen and she was thinking. Her face was serious. "I'm not sure when my period is due. Oh, fucking hell, why can't I think straight?" Pat grabbed her arm and spoke into her face.

"Well there's only one way to find out, I've got a spare pregnancy test upstairs, do you want me to go and get it?"

Kendal was apprehensive. "Yeah, if you think I need to do one." Pat disappeared out of the room and left her alone. Kendal sat down and played with the cuff from her sleeve, she was concentrating. The sound of Pat coming back down the stairs filled the room; she was a right noisy cow.

"Here, go and piss on that bit," she shoved the white stick under her nose. "It only takes a few minutes and then you'll know one way or the other. Go on, get to the toilet and piss on it." Kendal trudged out of the room, her face was red and her cheeks seemed like they were on fire, she was definitely burning up.

Closing the bathroom door behind her she held her nose as the smell of urine hit the back of her throat. Pat was a scruffy cow and her house was forever in need of a good clean. Sliding her knickers down her legs she held the pregnancy test between them. Once it was done she placed the plastic stick on the windowsill while she wiped herself. Her hands were shaking as she picked it back up. Standing looking at it her heart was beating ten to a dozen. She headed down the stairs, she was still examining it, but nothing made sense to her. "Well, are you tubbed or what?" Pat joked.

"I don't know, I've just done what you told me to do, but I don't know how to read the results, it doesn't say," she lied. Pat rubbed her hands together, and took the test from her hands. Her face was studying the little square box where the results would appear any minute now. Kendal was by her side as Pat held it in her fingers.

"Hold on, it will be here in a minute." As they watched the results, one bright pink line started to form. Pat grabbed the box from the side and started to read the instructions. Her face dropped. "Fuck me, you're pregnant love." Kendal grabbed the box from her hand and looked at the picture on the back of it, she couldn't read the words. Her legs melted into the ground and this time she really was crying her eyes out.

"What am I going to do Pat? My Granddad will kill me stone dead. He'll throw me out for sure. Oh Pat, what the fuck am I going to do?" Scott's sister knelt beside her and she gripped her chin in her hands, she just stared at her at first.

"You don't have to have it, you can get an abortion. No one would ever know." Kendal looked her straight in the eyes.

"How do I get one of them, I don't have any money." Pat stood up and she was anxious.

"You could get one done on the NHS, but that could take months before they get you in." Pat was pacing the kitchen floor. "Can't you borrow any money from anyone?" Kendal shook her head.

"I don't know, how much do I need?"

"About three ton love. If you can't get that, you'll have to go on the waiting list for the NHS." Kendal was desperate and she pulled at Pat's jumper.

"I need it doing as soon as possible, I can't be pregnant, my life's fucked up enough without me having a baby in it." The kitchen door flung open and there was Scott looking like a man of steel, he'd heard everything that was going on, he must have sneaked in and been listening at the door. He was always doing that, he was so paranoid.

"You won't be getting no abortion, and what the fuck are saying that for anyway Pat? This is my baby, your niece or nephew, are you forgetting that?" Pat hung her head low; she was ashamed and tried to make him see sense.

"Scott it's only an option. At this moment in time you two don't have a penny to your name. How can you look after a baby?" He knew she was right but bounced about the kitchen in a fury.

"I do have money; you don't know shit about my finances. I'm raking it in," he growled into Kendal's face, his teeth were clenched tightly together, spit hung from the corner of his mouth. "Is that what you want to do, kill my baby?" She stood shaking and her arm came up to cover her face, she knew he could lash out at any moment.

"No Scott, but your sister is right. I'm too young to have a baby." His stale breath was in her face.

"You're my girlfriend, and I said, I'll look after you. Are you listening you daft bitch," He grabbed her hair and started to rag her about, he'd lost the plot for sure. Pat jumped in and tried her best to pull him off her. She knew Scott had been beating her in the past, she'd heard him through the paper-thin walls and she hated herself because she never stepped in. This time it was different though, there was no way she was standing for it.

"Get your fucking hands off her you bully, why are you hurting her, I thought you said you loved her?" Scott's saw red, his eyes looked menacing.

"Pat, get out of my face now before I deal with you too." He held her back with one hand around her throat. He was squeezing her windpipe and she was turning blue.

Pat was stood on her tiptoes and she was barely breathing, her eyes were bulging from the sockets. Kendal wriggled free and pulled as hard as she could on Scott's hands, he was killing his sister. She was prising his fingers from his sister's throat. Pat freed herself and sank to the floor, she was gagging for breath. She held two trembling hands around her throat trying to catch her breath, she was coughing.

Scott paced the floor; he was ragging his fingers through his hair. "See what you two have made me do now. Fuck, fuck, fuck." He ran at the kitchen door and punched his clenched fist into it; a hole appeared in it straight away. Kendal covered her eyes as she heard his fists connecting with the door. Sitting down next to Pat she placed her hand over her shoulders.

"Are you okay?" Pat was finding it hard to talk and her words were low. "He's a fucking psycho; you need to get well rid of him if he's treating you like that." Scott turned his head slowly, his eyes were rolling, you could see he'd been on drugs.

"She'll never get rid of me Pat, she loves me too much, don't you Kendal?" His girlfriend's nerves were getting the better of her now and her lips were trembling, they looked purple. His voice was loud as he repeated his words. "Tell her you still love me." Pat whispered under her breath so he couldn't hear her.

"Just say you still love him and shut the mad bastard up."

Kendal's chest was rising; it looked like her heart was going to burst out of her ribcage. "Yes, I do." He nodded his head and smirked; he walked to her side and held his hand out to her.

"Come on, get up off the floor, we're getting out of

this shit-hole." He looked at his sister and spat into her face. "I'll never forgive you for trying to kill my baby, do you hear me, never!"

Pat dropped her head onto her knees, there was no way she was winding him up. She just wanted him out of her house, he was a ticking bomb and she was scared of his next move. Kendal stood next to Scott and you could see the fear in her eyes as he pulled her out of the room, she had no choice other than to go with him. Kendal had seen him being violent in the past, but never to this extreme, he was scaring her, he was like a man possessed. "We can go to Duggy's house; he said if I ever needed to get my head down I could always go there. First thing in the morning I'm going to sort us a gaff out. You better start packing your stuff, do you hear me?" Kendal didn't reply, she just followed him like a lost puppy. Her heart was low and you could see the pain in her eyes, she had no choice other than to go with him, nobody was going to save her.

Scott gripped her hand tightly and pulled her along the busy road. Dragging her into a bus shelter he pushed her body up against the wall with force, he was in her face. "Tell me you weren't going to get rid of our baby, please tell me you weren't going to do it." She spoke in a low voice; there was no way she was admitting to it, he would have killed her stone dead.

"It was just an option that's all. My Granddad will go mad when he knows, I was just trying to come up with another option," He covered her mouth with his hand.

"I'll go and tell the old cunt, he won't lay one finger on you, because if he does," he paused and his nostrils flared as he held his head back. "I'll pop a cap in his old wrinkly arse, trust me, he'll be a goner." Kendal sighed, she could tell by his tone of voice that he meant every word. He was more than capable of killing Paddy. She grabbed his hands and pulled him closer, she needed to calm him down, he was frightening her.

"I will tell him myself, you don't need to do anything Scott. And, if we're moving in together, then fine. I'll pack my stuff as soon as we find somewhere." Scott chuckled; he was like Jekyll and Hyde.

"Me, a Dad, who'd have thought it," he snuggled his head into the nape of her neck and started to kiss her. Kendal cringed and she felt relieved that he'd controlled his temper. It was like history repeating itself. She was going to be a young mother at an early age, just like her own mother had been. At that moment she closed her eyes and tears streamed down her face. Her Granddad was right; like mother, like daughter.

Kendal sat on the edge of her bed. All her belongings were packed and she was ready to leave. She kept standing up and sitting back down. There was no way she could go without seeing Nelly first; she just needed to find the courage. Her nana's coughing echoed throughout the bedroom walls. Kendal stood to her feet and opened her door; her eyes were all over the landing. She could see Paddy in the bathroom; he was brushing his teeth with his body bent over the sink. Her feet crept along the landing; she was as quiet as a mouse. Nelly's bedroom door was opened slightly, she pushed it open and she could see her lying on the bed reading a magazine. Quickly she went inside and closed the door behind her. Kendal stood with her back held up against the wooden door, her legs were shaking.

Nelly sat up, and looked at her. "What are you doing love?" She bit hard on her bottom lip; this was going to be so hard to tell her she was leaving. Her legs didn't look like they had enough strength to take her the short distance to the bottom of the bed. Nelly was agitated, "Is it him again? What's the old bastard done now?" She was trying to get out of the bed and her face was like thunder. "He never learns does he? Well, not this time, he's getting a mouthful from me, I'm sick of him having a go at you all the time." Kendal walked to the bed and placed her hand on Nelly's shoulder, her eyes held so much sadness.

"It's not him Nana, he's not said anything. I'm leaving." Nelly looked at her face and realised something serious had happened.

"You're not going anywhere lady, this is your home and no matter what's gone on, we can sort it out."

"I'm pregnant," Kendal whispered under her breath. Nelly's mouth was wide open, and she was lost for words, she was blowing her breath slowly. Kendal sat on the edge of the bed and all her heartache came flooding out at once. "I'm sorry, I've let you down, it just happened." Nelly gripped the duvet in her hand and you could see her squeezing at it with all her might, this was the last thing she wanted to hear.

"How many times do you need telling, are you tapped in the head or something?" She could have coped with anything else, but this was her worst nightmare. "Oh Kendal, anything, but being pregnant, are you trying to kill me or what? How could you have been so stupid? Your Granddad's going to hit the fucking roof when he finds out," she shook her head and let out a laboured breath. "I warned you about that Scott didn't I? You're just like your bleeding mother, you think you know it all, and you know fuck all. Do you hear me, fuck all?" Kendal stood up and her eyes were on the floor, she didn't have the courage to face Nelly, she was ashamed.

"I'm leaving Nana, Scott's found us somewhere to stay and we are going to have this baby together." Nelly sprang to her feet, she was holding onto the side of the bed to steady herself.

"Oh, lover boy has got this all worked out hasn't he? He knew exactly what he was doing when he got you pregnant that one, mark my words." Kendal tried to stick up for Scott but the more she listened to what her nana was saying the more she believed her.

"You're fifteen, you're still a kid, he should have known better. He's a kiddy fiddler, he's groomed you. Get me the phone I'm reporting him to the police, he's a bleeding sex-case." Kendal wiped her eyes and turned her head back to Nelly.

"Please don't make things any worse than what they are Nana, I love him, he's all I've got." Nelly choked up and at that moment she realised she was right, Kendal didn't have anyone else. Anyone who'd ever loved her was gone and her heart sank.

"I love you sweetheart, I've always loved you. You don't need him, he's a scally."

"Yeah, I know Nana, but this a different kind of love. He loves me proper, he shows me affection, and I've never had that in my life before." Tears streamed down Nelly's face, Kendal was right. Her lips were quivering. Paddy had always made sure Kendal wasn't nursed or showed any love and even from being a baby her granddaughter had to learn to live without love.

The door opened with a bang and Paddy stood there watching them both, his face was on fire. "What's going on here then," he clocked Nelly was crying and shot his eyes to Kendal. He ran at her and gripped her by the throat. "What have you done again, you cheeky bitch. Don't you think she's been through enough without you adding to it, your Nana isn't well?" Nelly shrieked from behind him.

"Oh, says you, who has me run ragged twenty four hours a day. She's done nothing wrong Paddy, so get your hands from her you barmy bastard, you could hurt the baby." Silence, eyes locked together, Paddy's head swivelling around the room, he wanted answers.

"What did you just say?" Nelly realised that she couldn't hold her own piss and prepared for World War Three, she'd dropped a bollock this time. Taking a deep breath she spoke in a calm voice hoping to calm him down.

"She's pregnant Paddy, and she's leaving, I've told her she's can still stay here, we will help her won't we?" Paddy's face was white, his nostrils flared and you could see his fist curling into tight balls at the side of his leg.

"You dirty bitch, like mother like daughter. How dare you bring more shame on this family? Don't you think your mother has already done that?" Kendal wanted out of there as soon as possible, her eyes shot to the door, it was now or never, she had to make her move quick. Scampering, she managed to open the door, but he was behind her, his breath was on her neck, she could feel it. Running straight down the stairs she opened the front door and ran outside, there was no way the old cunt could catch her now, he was like a slug. She turned around as she ran out of the gate.

"I need my clothes," she ranted. Paddy stood at the front door with his hands resting on his knees, he was knackered and he was trying to catch his breath.

"You're getting nothing from this house; I'm going to burn them, just like I should have done with all your mother's stuff." Kendal knew she was fighting a losing battle and started to walk off, she kept twisting her head back over her shoulder though because she knew at any second he could come running after her. Half a brick hurled through the air in her direction, it just missed the side of her head. Standing looking at Paddy she shook her head.

"That nearly hit me that."

"It should have taken your bleeding head off, it was meant for you," he screamed as he stood at the gate. He was searching for more objects to launch at her, he'd definitely lost the plot. Kendal started running as fast as she could.

Once she was away from the house she sat on a red brick wall, gasping for breath, she was so unfit. Digging her hand inside her jacket pocket she pulled out her mother's diary. Stroking her hand across the front of it, she spoke in a low voice so no one could hear her. "Well, he always said I would end up like you mother," her words were stuck in her throat and she was stuttering. "What the hell am I going to do now?"

CHAPTER EIGHT

Kendal sat in her new home. Her belly was stuck out in front of her, she was heavily pregnant. With her hand she stroked the life growing inside her. Jane was due around any minute now and she'd done her best to make the place look half decent, but it still looked like a shit tip. Jane and Kendal had made friends not long after they'd fallen out. Kendal was the one who made the first move though, because she knew Jane was a stubborn bitch and she would never have backed down, no matter what. The noise of someone rapping on the letterbox filled the room. Kendal sat up and listened again, she could hear Jane shouting.

"Right, I'm coming, hold your horses will you." She made her way to the front door and she could see her friend's face squashed up against the glass.

"Fucking hell, you knock like the dibble, I shit myself then, why are you knocking like that?" Jane paraded past her, she was strutting her stuff. She was still sleeping with John Daley and her style had changed from the scruffy fifteen year old she used to know. Jane's hair was pinned back from her face and it looked like she'd spent hours styling it.

"I hope that prick isn't at home?"

Kendal shut the door and followed her inside into the front room. "No, he's out. I've told you before, he's never in anymore."

"Good job, because I can't stand him. I wish you would cart him and find someone else; he's a dead beat."

Kendal hung her head low, she knew what Jane was saying was right, but she just didn't have the courage to leave her boyfriend. Scott had told her more than once that if she ever left him he would hunt her down and do her in, he'd even threatened to shave all her hair off and she knew he would do it, he was more than capable. No, she was staying put, she couldn't be doing with all the hassle. "Put the kettle on then, I'm gagging for a brew; I hope you've got some decent coffee in, not that snide shit you gave me last time." Kendal made her way to the kitchen and she could feel Jane's eyes all over her, she prepared herself for the usual abuse she got from Jane. "Your arse is massive; do you think you're going to lose all that weight when you've dropped the baby?"

Kendal was inside the kitchen and shouted back to her. "Yeah, course I will. I would like to see what you look like when you're pregnant then we'd see who has a fat arse." Kendal was giggling to herself, she knew Jane had issues about the size of her backside, and she hated anyone mentioning it. She held her ear to the door and waited for a reply, she knew Jane wouldn't take her last comment on the chin, and here it was, just like she expected.

"Ay, I'm not having any kids. Why, would I want any little ankle biters in my life." Jane was stood at the kitchen door now. "I mean, can you see these nails wiping a shitty arse," her talons were fanned out in front of her as she picked a bit of fluff from beneath her fingernail. "No love, motherhood is not for me. I'm concentrating on me and my life." Kendal poured the hot water from the kettle into the cup; you could see her raising her eyes to the ceiling.

"Oh you're right up your own arse these days aren't you, what happened to the Jane that I used to know, the rough and ready Jane?"

"She's grown up Kendal," Jane said as she flicked the collar from her white shirt. "I want more from life than you. Just because I don't want kids it doesn't mean I'm stuck up." Kendal was carrying the cup into the front room.

"Grab them chocolate biscuits from the side. They're only smart price ones though, I don't think these are your usual quality now you're living the high life, are they Jane."

"Shut up you dick-head. Why're you saying I've changed? I'm still me you know." Jane was in a huff, and stomped into the front room behind her; she opened the biscuits and rammed one into her mouth. "So, when are you due now, it looks like it's going to burst out of you any moment soon?"

"Anytime now, my due date was yesterday, but the midwife said not to worry, it will come when it's ready."

Jane looked confused; she wasn't into talking about pregnancy anymore and changed the conversation quickly. "John's leaving Jackie; he told me last night." Kendal reached over and grabbed a biscuit. She'd heard this for last few months but John never budged from his wife's side, she wanted to hear what bull shit he'd fed her this time. Nibbling on her biscuits Kendal giggled, she loved winding her up. If Jane could give it out she wanted to see if she could take it back.

"I thought you said that last month, he's always chatting shit to you, he'll never leave Jackie."

Jane slammed her cup on the coffee table. "Yeah he will. The last time he told me he was leaving her he was all up for it, but Jackie got ill at the time so he had to wait until she got better. This time it will be different though, you just wait and see." Kendal knew she was fighting a losing battle and brought her legs up onto the sofa. She placed her hand on her stomach as a pain surged through her body.

"I hope he does leave her Jane, I just can't see it though. Anyway, where will you live if he does, because there is no way his wife will budge from that house is there?"

Jane took her time to answer; she chewed on her bottom lip, you could tell she hadn't thought about this before. "We'll just cross that bridge when we come to it, I'm not arsed as long as we're together." Jane was in love for sure, it was written right across her face.

Kendal backed down, she hated that she'd given her a hard time about her true love. "Yeah, John will sort it out won't he?" she added hopefully.

Jane kicked her shoes off and threw her legs over the arm of the chair. "Yeah, he better had, otherwise I'm off. So, come on then, what's that ball bag been up too again, because everyone's talking about it you know." Kendal reached for her cigs from the table, every time she was stressed it was always the same, she must have been blazing at least fifteen cigs a day.

"What are you going on about?" Kendal asked casually.

Jane threw the cushion at her and chuckled. "Scott's had a big earner, don't tell me you don't know?" she tapped her fingers on the arm of the chair. "Well, that's what Duggy told me anyway. He said he got a few grand, he had some safe off from a warehouse in Cheetham Hill."

Kendal looked at her and frowned. Scott hadn't mentioned any of this to her, she played it by ear. "Oh, yeah, that. There was only a few hundred quid in it. You know what people are like round here for chatting shit." Jane backed off, and slurped her cup of coffee.

"Did he bung you a few quid then, or what?" Kendal wasn't ready for the question and sat fidgeting, she'd put her right on the spot. Scott hadn't given her a penny out of his graft and he'd not even told her he had any money, according to him he was on his arse, or that's what he'd said.

"Yeah, he's given me some money to buy baby stuff," she lied, "I've spent loads on this kid you know, absolutely loads, it's not going to want for anything." She was lying through her teeth, and the shit was rolling from her tongue.

"You want to try spending some money on this house never mind the baby; it's a right dump in here, I don't know how you live here, I couldn't do it." Jane was at it again, she just couldn't help herself. Kendal hung her head low and hated that she was poor and she didn't have any money. All her plans of getting a good job had gone out of the window forever. Scott had told her point blank that she was looking after the baby and to get any ideas of working right out of her head. Jane looked surprised.

"Ay, I was down at the brass gaff the other day, you know the one that John owns," she couldn't get the words out fast enough. "Lady Jane's, do you know where I mean?" Kendal nodded her head, everyone in the area knew about the brothel. Jane continued, "Have a guess who I saw?" Kendal hunched her shoulders and waited for her to continue. "I saw your Molly, I swear it was her, I shouted after her but she just ran off, she looked as rough as a bear's arse you know." Kendal's face dropped, no one had seen Molly for years.

"Stop lying Jane, it's not funny. Why would our Molly be at the brass gaff?"

"Well, that's what I thought. I swear Kendal, it was

definitely her." Kendal looked uncomfortable and her face was filled with sadness. She'd missed Molly so much and often thought about trying to find her but she didn't have a clue where to start looking. Molly was an addict and never stayed long in one place, she was always on the move. She didn't even go to see her mother any more, her life revolved around the drug scene.

At that moment the front door slammed shut and Kendal and Jane shot a look to each other. Scott was home. Jane rolled her eyes and searched for her coat. "Fucking hell, I thought you said he's never at home. Well, that's me gone for sure, there's no way I'm staying here with him at home. I can't stand the sight of him." Kendal grabbed her back to the seat.

"Just stay where you are, he might be going back out. I bet he's forgotten something." Scott opened the living room door, his eyes danced about the room and once he clocked Jane his nostrils flared.

"What is she doing here?" he snarled. Jane stood to her feet and her face was on fire, there was no way she was letting this prick talk to her like that.

"I'm not here to see you, so don't you worry about that. I'm getting off now anyway, so wind your neck in." Kendal was scared and she sat playing with her fingers, her master was home. Standing to her feet she followed Jane to the front door, she could feel his stare as she walked past him. As she turned her head back she could see Scott watching her with a look that could kill on his face, she knew she was in deep trouble. "Right Kendal, you come and see me next time, I'm not coming here again. Just give me a ring when you're coming and I'll make sure I'm in."

"Yeah, I will," Kendal whispered. The door closed and

she could feel Scott's eyes burning into the back of her head, she walked back to the front room slowly.

"What the fuck is she doing here? How many times have I warned you about having your mates over, especially her, she's a little slag?" Kendal cowered as she walked past him, his warm breath was in her face and she could smell alcohol.

"She wasn't here long, why can't I have friends round anyway. I'm not a prisoner you know." She knew she'd overstepped the mark but she just couldn't keep her mouth shut. Kendal crashed to the floor and he was on top of her, spit was hanging from the corner of his mouth as he opened fire.

"Oh, so you think you're a prisoner now do you. I'll tell you what shag-bag, get your stuff together and fuck off out of my house." He dragged her by the hair and pulled her to her feet and headed to the bedroom. "Come on, get your shit together. I'm not having you speaking to me like that, where's the respect?" Kendal was screaming but it fell on deaf ears, nobody was going to help her. A blow to her face sent her head crashing into the wall. As soon as she saw the blood, she pleaded with him to stop.

"Scott, stop it please. Think about the baby. Please, just leave me alone. I won't have anyone at the house again, I promise." This was music to his ears and just what he wanted to hear. Slowly he backed away from her.

"I swear to you, if this happens again, I will do you in big time." Kendal knew when to keep her trap shut. She could feel the warm blood trickling down her lips. He'd busted her nose. Again. The bed sank in as he sat down on it, he was thinking. This was normal behaviour for him; he always went quiet after he'd beaten her. She knew what was coming next and cringed inside at the thought of having sex with him. "You make me treat you like this you know. I'm not a wife beater, it's just you, you do it on purpose I'm sure of it."

Kendal sat with her legs up to her chest she kept her head down and tried to avoid any contact with her abuser. His feet trudged towards her; she could see his black trainers near her feet, she was trembling inside. "Look at me when I'm speaking to you," he snapped. Slowly she lifted her head up; the blood was streaming down her upper lip, he looked disturbed. Sliding his finger along her mouth he held a look of malice in his eyes. He was studying the bright red claret. "Get up from the floor and go and sort yourself out." As she tried to lift her body up, a sharp pain pierced her body. She paused and gasped for breath. "What's up?" he asked. Kendal couldn't talk, the pain was getting worse. "Don't ignore me Kendal, I said what's wrong?"

"I've got a pain in my back, I can't move, she groaned." Scott chuckled and dragged her up by the arm.

"Stop being a mard arse. Get in the bathroom and get cleaned up before anyone sees you. What's for tea anyway?" Kendal was bent over as she left the room, you could see the pain on her face. Scott kicked his shoes off and switched the TV on.

Kendal's breathing was rapid. She put her hand flat on the wall as she tried to clean her face up, she was a mess. The mirror in front of her showed her just what her boyfriend was capable of. Tears were falling fast and she covered her mouth with her hand so no one could hear her sobbing. If Scott would have heard her crying he would have been inside the bathroom and beat her some more, he hated crying, he said only weak people cried. The water in the sink was bright red; her nose was still pumping blood. Twisting some toilet roll together she shoved it up both her nostrils to try and stop the flow of blood. She could hear Scott shouting her from the front room. "Where the fuck are you?" he ranted.

"I'm coming," she shouted back. Her face creased with pain as she tried to stand up straight.

Scott examined every inch of her face as she stepped back into the room, he was pleased he hadn't marked her too much. Patting the sofa he looked at her with puppy dog eyes, he wanted forgiveness. "Come and sit down here." She knew she had no choice and obeyed his orders. Moving her hair from her face he smiled. "I do love you know. I just get so angry. You know me and Jane don't see eye to eye, so what did you expect?" Her lips were trembling, and she was trying her best not to break down, she opened her eyes wide to force the tears back inside, there was no way she was crying in front of him. There it was again, Kendal keeled over and this time she let out a piercing scream.

"I think it's the baby," she mumbled. Scott sprang to his feet and paced the floor.

"Don't be having the baby now; I'm going out in a minute. I've got to meet John, so sort it out yourself, fucking hell you drama queen." Kendal rolled about on the sofa her head was dug deep into the pillow and you could see her teeth clenched tightly together. A mobile phone on the side started ringing. Scott ran to it and looked at the screen. "Kendal shut up for a minute, John's on the phone and I won't be able to hear him with all this racket you're making. Shut the fuck up will you?" She rammed her fist into her mouth and you could see her knuckles turning white as her teeth sank into her skin. Small beads of sweat were visible on her forehead, she didn't look good. "Hiya mate," Scott chuckled as he pressed the button to answer the call. "Yeah I'm setting off now, give me ten minutes." Kendal let out a howling scream and he ran at her and covered her mouth with his hand. She was wriggling about but he made sure nobody could hear her. "Alright John, see you soon," the call ended. Scott stood looking down at her, he was thinking. Grabbing his coat from the side he shouted back at her. "I'm going out, see you in a bit." He was gone.

Kendal tried to stand to her feet, her legs were buckling. Reaching over she grabbed her mobile phone from the side. It was only a cheap phone and it looked ancient, but it did the job. Taking deep breaths she found the contact number in her phone, she rang Jane. The ringing tone filled the room and the call went straight to voice mail, Jane must have been with John, she always turned her phone on silence when she was with him. Kendal collapsed on the floor and you could see her hands gripping around her stomach, she lay on her back rolling about in pain.

Half an hour passed, and Kendal was bearing down every time the labour pains came, she wasn't coping. Holding her phone she tried Jane's mobile phone again for one last time, this time she answered. "Jane come quick, it's the baby. Please, I've got no one else." The call ended as her credit ran out, she was alone and scared.

John Daley was with Jane as they entered Kendal's home. His eyes were all over the place and you could see he didn't like what he saw. Jane ran to her side and tried to sit her up. "Fucking hell Kendal, why didn't you phone an ambulance?"

John stepped forward and for a minute he forgot who he was talking too. "Kendal, can you speak, are you okay sweetheart. Just hold on we'll get you to the hospital as soon as possible, just hang on in there." Kendal lifted her head up and she could see his face.

"Help me John, please help me."

"What's all the blood all over her face Jane, look she's covered in it?" Jane huffed and looked him straight in the eyes.

"Scott's probably wasted her again. I bet he did after I was here before. I've told her he was a no good bastard I don't know why she's even still with him." John stood to his feet and walked into the hallway, he was fuming. Slowly he closed the living room door and searched his pocket for his phone.

"Hi ya mate, listen up, I need someone to get a good kicking, as soon as possible. Meet me later and I'll fill you in with all the details," John listened to the other person on the phone. "Sorted mate, see you then." Licking his dry lips he walked back into the front room. Kendal's face was on fire now and she was panting like a dog on a hot summer's day. This baby was ready to be born. John knelt by her side and his face creased when another pain surged through Kendal's body, she was gripping his hand and digging her fingernails in him.

"Where's that ambulance," Jane shouted as she paced the living room floor. A single tear fell down John's face and he quickly wiped it away. This was all too much for him. Seeing his daughter in so much pain was breaking his heart in two.

★

Ella May Wilson was born at eight thirty that day, weighing seven pound five ounces. Jane ended up being her birthing partner and without her help Kendal would have been in deep trouble. You could see John pacing about outside the room through the glass panel, the nurse told him he could come in soon. The baby lay on her mother's chest, wrapped in a pink cotton blanket. Kendal was tired and her face was blood red. "I tell you what Kendal, there is no way in this world I would have a baby after seeing that. Your fanny stretched out so big I nearly fainted." The midwife turned her head from where she was stood and smiled.

"They all say that love, but in years to come you'll be lying there doing the same thing, trust me." Jane stood up and reached for her bottle of water, her mouth was dry.

"I swear, I will never have any kids, I'm honestly traumatised by it all." Jane re-iterated.

Kendal waited for her to sit down. "Did John get in touch with Scott?"

"Yeah, I think so; he said he was on the way to the hospital." Jane leant over and tickled her friend's hand. "Seriously Kendal, you need to get rid of him, what did he hit you for? Was it because of me being at the house?" Kendal placed her hand on the baby's back and patted her softly, she was her world now and nothing else seemed to matter, she covered up for Scott.

"No, I was going into the bathroom but I wasn't looking properly and I walked straight into the door."

Jane rolled her eyes. "Do you honestly expect me to believe that? Come on girl; give me a bit of credit. I'm not daft, and I know when you're lying, your right eyebrow always twitches, you can't hide it."

Kendal stuck to her guns. "I swear to you that's what happened. You know how clumsy I can be, I can fall over fresh air, me." Jane knew she was lying and dropped her head onto the bed. Kendal stroked her hand across her hair. "Thanks Jane for being here, I couldn't have done it without you." Lifting her head back up Jane chewed on her lips; this was so unlike her, she was so emotional.

"I'm a friend for life me Kendal, no matter what, I'll always be there for you. I have your back and you've got mine simple as." The door opened and Scott stood there looking as proud as punch, John was behind him.

"Let's see my little girl then, I hope she's been washed and all that, these are my new strides and I don't want any crap all over them." He bounced to the side of the bed and parked his arse, he completely ignored Jane. John was at the side of the bed and he couldn't wait to see the baby. Jane growled as Kendal passed Scott his daughter, he made her blood boil for sure, she stood up.

"Right John, are we getting off or what? I'm not staying here with that shower of shite," she was being brave knowing if Scott laid one finger on her John would have dropped him like a ton of bricks. Scott nodded his head slowly at her, you could see the hate in his eyes. Kendal sat up and held her two arms out.

"Come and give me a love then, like I said before, thanks for today, you've been my rock." Jane cuddled her friend and stood at the end of the bed, she grabbed John by the arm, he didn't look like he wanted to move.

"Make sure that prick looks after you and the baby now. Let's see if he can man up for once." Scott was ready to answer her when John stepped in and cut him short.

"She's right Scott, I know her Granddad Paddy, and if I get just one drop of shit telling me you're not treating her right, I'll be round to see you, you know what I mean don't you?" Scott dropped his head and played with his fingers, there was no way he was winding John up, after all he was his bread and butter, he never whispered a word back, he was a shit bag.

The door closed and Scott and Kendal were alone. He looked across the room to the midwife and shouted over to her. "Was my girl brave or what, or was she howling when the baby was born?" The midwife turned her head slowly, she'd met some arrogant men in her lifetime but this one was in a league of his own.

"Well, if you would have bothered to turn up for the child's birth you would have seen. And yes, she was brave, no thanks to you." The woman knew she wasn't being professional but she just couldn't help it, this man was doing her head in. Scott chuckled and picked the baby up from Kendal's chest. Holding her in his arms he held her away from his body. Studying her face for a while he looked at Kendal.

"She looks fuck all like me, I think she's like you, she's got your eye shape."

"I know I thought that, when I first saw her, she's lovely isn't she?" Scott passed the baby back over to Kendal, he was checking his watch.

"Are you coming home tonight or do you have to stay in hospital?"

Kendal looked at the midwife for the answer. "She'll stay in tonight, if everything is okay with her and the baby tomorrow she will be able to come home."

Scott huffed, "Fucking hell that's shit, who's going to make me tea?" The midwife was watching him and she couldn't make out if he was being serious or not, you could see her twisting the white cotton sheet in her hands and she looked like she was imagining it was his neck. Scott stayed for twenty minutes, he was itching to go. "You look tired Kendal. You need to get some sleep. I'm going to get off; I'll be here tomorrow morning just ring me when you're ready?"

Kendal agreed with him, and sat up in the bed. "Yeah I'm done in, I'm absolutely knackered." That was music to his ears; he stood up and pulled his jumper down over his waist.

"Right, see you tomorrow then, get some shut eye ay?" She yawned and smiled as he pecked her on the cheek; he kissed his fingers and placed it on the baby's forehead. Kendal watched him leave.

All through the night, Kendal watched her baby sleeping. She kept getting up out of the bed and stroking the side of her head. Ella May was her world now and she was going to be the best mother she could be. The night staff in the hospital pulled the curtains around her bed and all the lights were dimmed, you could hear babies crying at the other end of the ward. Kendal snuggled under her blankets and she was ready to drift off to sleep. A nurse patted her shoulder softly. "I have a woman outside the ward who wants to see you, she said she's your Nana Nelly, she's heartbroken love, do you want to see her?"

Kendal rubbed her knuckles into her eyes and tried to focus on the woman's face. She wasn't sure if she heard her right. "Did you say it's my Nana?"

The nurse nodded her head slowly and whispered, "Visiting time is over and I'm not really allowed to let anyone in, but she seems really desperate to see you." Kendal choked back the tears; of course she wanted to see Nelly. She hadn't seen her for months now and her heart was pumping inside her chest.

"Please let her in, she won't stay long, I promise." The nurse patted her arm and left her side, she quickly closed the curtain behind her.

The sound of footsteps behind the curtain made

Kendal alert. She was watching the curtain with eager eyes. Nelly stepped inside and the nurse smiled at Kendal. "Try and keep the noise down please, if the matron gets a wind of this she'll have me on a disciplinary." Nelly looked hot, her breathing was heavy and she sat down as soon as she could. Kendal got out of bed and draped her arm around her shoulder.

"Nana, what are you doing out at this time of night, look at the state of you? You're not well; you should be at home in bed." Nelly blew her breath a few times and moved the piece of hair that had fallen onto her face.

"I don't care how ill I am, I wouldn't have missed seeing my great Granddaughter for all the tea in china, let me have a hold of her, come on pass her over." Nelly blew her warm breath onto her hands and rubbed them together. As she held Ella May for the first time she choked up, a large lump appeared in her throat and she was finding it hard to talk. "She looks just like our Mary when she was born; she's the spit out of her mouth." Kendal smiled; she loved hearing her mother's name.

"Do you think so Nana, Scott said she looks like me around the eyes?"

"He's right, you and your mother are alike, she's definitely one of us." Nelly was examining the baby; she was counting her toes and playing with her fingers. She dipped her head into the pink blanket and she inhaled deeply, she smelt the baby. "So, how was the labour? I bet you won't be as quick to take your knickers off next time will you," she chuckled.

Kendal smirked, "You're off your head you are, fancy saying something like that to me when I've just given birth, there's only one of you Nana, that's for sure." Nelly passed the baby back over to Kendal, she was getting ready to have another coughing fit, her cheeks were full blown at the sides as she tried to control it.

"Pass us a drink of water love, hurry up before I start coughing, you know what I'm like, once I start, I can't stop." Kendal poured a glass of cold water and passed it to her, she was sipping at it slowly.

"Does my Granddad know I've had the baby?" Nelly nodded her head.

"Yep I told him before, but you know what he's like the stubborn bleeder. He'll come around without water, just leave him to it." Kendal looked sad, and reached over to Nelly.

"Just hold me Nana, just cuddle me. I'm a bit emotional at the moment."

Nelly saw all the bruises on her body and she knew without asking what was going on in her granddaughter's life. She kept schtum though, she couldn't bring herself to speak about it, and who was she to judge anyway, she'd lived with a violent partner for years. Nelly cradled Kendal in her arms, and she was sobbing her heart out, her shoulders were shaking up and down. "I know I've let you down, but one day Nana, I will make you proud."

Nelly patted her on the back, "I just hope I'm still alive to see it cock, I just hope and pray." The nurse must have heard the commotion around the bedside; she opened the curtain and looked at the two women. "I think it's time to go now, the Matron is on the prowl and like I said, she'll go ape if she knows I've broken the rules."

Nelly stood to her feet. "Thank you so much for letting me in, it means a lot."

Kendal stood in front of her nana and hugged her for the last time. "Come and see me when you get home, I'll let you know when it's safe to come around," she rolled her eyes meaning when Paddy wasn't home. "Look after you and that baby love, and remember if you need me, I'm only a phone call away."

Kendal smiled, "Thanks Nana, I will."

★

Kendal sat on the side of the hospital bed waiting for Scott to pick her up. She wasn't even ready yet, she was waiting for him to bring her a fresh set of clothes and all the baby stuff she needed. Her eyes shot about the room watching other couples on the beds facing her. She watched the love she saw between them and her heart sank; she knew she would never have that kind of love with Scott. The doctor did his final checks on the baby and he was pleased to announce she was a fine healthy baby girl. Kendal's eyes watched the doors constantly and every time it opened she jumped up from her bed thinking it was Scott. Two hours later he made his presence felt on the hospital ward, and he was drunk. She watched him stagger down the ward and hid her face away in shame; she could see the nurses whispering to each other. "Where the hell have you been, you should have been here hours ago, for fucks sake Scott, just for once, couldn't you put me first?" He laughed out loud and pulled her up from the bed.

"I was out celebrating last night, fucking hell I've just become a Daddy, what did you want me to do, sit in the house all night?"

"No, Scott, I just wanted a bit of support that's all. You wasn't there at the birth either, how do you think that looks like to everyone?" His face changed and he pulled her closer as he whispered into her ear, he was slavering.

"I don't give a flying fuck how it looks. I'm here now, so get your kit on and let's go home." Kendal pulled away from him and grabbed the bag he'd brought with him from the bed. She went to get changed. As she started walking off she could feel something dribbling down her legs, it was dark red blood. Her pace quickened and she ran inside the nearby toilet. Stood with her back against the door she cried, was her life ever going to get any better? Scott had even forgot to bring her some sanitary towels to the hospital and now her only option was to fold some toilet paper and place it between her legs to stop the blood rushing from her body.

Scott was laughing and joking with the nurses when Kendal came back from the toilet. He was flirting with one of the medics for sure, she could tell by the false laugh he always did when he was trying to impress someone and she saw red. "Get hold of the baby then, or are you too busy chatting up nurse fucking Nightingale here," her eyes darted at them both as she growled. He sniggered, and tried to make a joke out of it, just like he always did when he was caught bang to rights. Both the nurses left the bedside in a hurry; they knew she was a woman on a mission.

"Why are you being jealous Kendal?" he held his head back and waved his hands out in front of him. "So, I can't talk to anyone now, can I? You need to get a grip woman. I thought it was me who was the paranoid one." Kendal was white, her face was grey and she looked like she was going to burst into tears.

"Just get hold of Ella May will you, come on, I want to go home." Scott stood frozen, he gritted his teeth together, he wasn't happy and steam was coming out of his ears.

"What did you say she's called?"

"Ella May, if you would have listened to a single

word I said, you might have heard what her name was last night."

Scott picked the baby up in his arms, and snarled. "We'll see about that you cheeky bitch, she's my baby too."

Kendal walked off in front of him, she decided once she got out of the hospital doors she was taking the baby straight from his arms, he was nowhere near in a fit state to hold her baby; he was pissed as a fart. Kendal thanked the nurses for their help and said her goodbyes.

The sun was bright as Kendal walked out of the hospital's main entrance, she squeezed her eyes together tightly; the sun was blinding her eyes. Sitting on a wooden bench at the side of her she looked at Scott. "Pass her here, while you go and ring a taxi, hurry up will you, I don't feel too good. She could feel the warm blood between her legs getting ready to flow again. Scott passed the baby to her; she avoided any eye contact with him because she knew he was in a mood. Watching him stomp off in the distance she looked down on her child. "I'm so sorry I've brought you into this world, your Dad's a full time dick head you know, when will I ever learn?" The sound of a taxi honking its horn in the car park made her lift her head up. It was time to go home and start her days as a mother.

★

The health visitor came to see Kendal at home, Scott was out as per usual and he'd told her straight, he didn't have time to wait about for anybody; he needed to be out earning a crust. Kendal seemed edgy, she was sat chewing the skin at the side of her thumb. What was she going to do if the health visitor asked her to fill out any forms, she couldn't read or write properly? Scott usually did all that for her, he always filled in any paperwork, she looked desperate. Kendal told Scott she hated her own handwriting and he never questioned it, he just filled out all the forms and read any letters that were addressed to her, he liked the control. The knocking on the front door made her jump out of her skin, she was a nervous wreck lately and the slightest noise made her jump. Ella May was hung around her hips, she was four months old now and was a contented baby. Kendal opened the front door to a smiling plump lady with honey blonde hair; she looked like she'd won the lottery the way she was smiling. Kendal had met this lady before on a few occasions at the clinic, but this was the first time she'd ever been to her home. The house smelt of Dettol, Kendal had tried her best to make the house clean and tidy. Not a lot had changed in the house, it was still a dump. "Hello Kendal," the health visitor said as she reached over and tickled Ella May on her stomach. "Oh, you're such a happy baby; I wish they were all like you." Kendal opened the door wider and asked her to come inside. You could tell by the visitor's face that she wasn't impressed with her home.

"I'll just put the baby down and I'll make you a cup of tea." The lady who was in her forties plonked down on the sofa. She sneered at her client's home. She'd been to some dumps in the past, but this house was up there with the worst of them, it was rancid. Kendal walked back into the room, she looked embarrassed. "Sorry I've ran out of milk, I can make you a cold drink instead if you want?" The health visitor waved her hand about in front of her.

"No, you just come and sit down, I'm not really bothered about a drink, I just had one before I left the office. "

Kendal looked relieved, if the truth was known she didn't have any juice to offer her either. Kendal watched as the lady pulled out a pile of papers from her bag, she watched her as she read through them. "My name's Alison, and I am going to be looking after you and the adorable Ella May for some time," she reached over to the bouncy chair and pulled on the baby's pink feet. Kendal didn't look comfortable, she was fidgeting. Alison sat back and passed her a pile of leaflets. "These should help you with your baby; there are a few diets in there to show you what kind of food she should be eating, and when to start weaning her." This was going way over Kendal's head and she was like a duck out of water. Shooting her eyes down to the leaflets, she looked at the pictures of the food and tried to look like she was reading the information. She'd done this plenty of times and no one had got onto her secret so today shouldn't have been any different. Alison sat back in her chair and started writing in her red note pad. "Just have a read of the leaflets I've given you, while I just do a few assessments on this little girl here."

She picked the baby up from her bouncy chair, and started to shake a rattle at the side of her ears. Kendal watched closely, to make sure her baby responded to the sounds, she did. Head held low she pretended to be reading the pamphlets. Alison kept turning her head to her and smiling. "Oh, she's a clever baby this one, I think you might have a professor on your hands when she's older, does she get her brains from you?" Kendal's face was on fire; her words were stuck on her tongue. Nobody had ever asked her about her education before, so why now? This woman was just being nosey; Kendal was panicking and twisting her hair around her fingers. Alison was waiting for an answer and she had to think quickly.

"It must be, I was always top of the class in school," Kendal lied.

Alison was still on her and Kendal was sorry she'd opened a can of worms for herself. "Did you get good exam results in school?"

Kendal was going under, she was crumbling. "Yeah, but since Ella May has come along I've put education on the back burner for a while, I want to concentrate on being a good mother first." Alison looked at her with approving eyes, she was impressed. Kendal was off the hook and tried to change the conversation. "I think the baby is teething, she's always gnawing on anything she gets her hands on."

"Yes, she will be. I think she'll let you know when she cuts her first tooth, in fact the whole estate will know, that's when your sleepless nights will start." Kendal smiled; she was getting to like this woman. "Why don't you come along to our mother and baby clinics at the neighbourhood centre, lots of young mothers go there and it gives you a chance to talk about your different issues about your children," she started scribbling something down on a white piece of paper. "There you go, that's the address and the times of the meetings, come along, you just might even enjoy yourself." Kendal took the piece of paper from her, perhaps Alison was right, she might enjoy it. Folding the paper into a small square she shoved it into her back pocket. Kendal stared at the clock on the wall, she was supposed to be going around to see Nelly today, and she was already late.

Alison could see her getting bored and stood up. "Right, onwards and upwards then. I have to get going now. I've got another four visits before I can go home and then I can kick my shoes off and start to relax. It's a very tiring job this you know?" Kendal wasn't sure if she was being serious or not, how could going around to someone's house be tiring, she would have loved the chance to get out and meet different people every day. Some people didn't know how lucky they were. Alison walked out of the living room; in her hand she had a white card. "Here's your next appointment, so I'll see you then. Take care." The front door opened and Alison was gone. Kendal looked at her appointment card and tried to make out what day it was on. She looked frustrated and shoved it in her back pocket. With a jump in her step she started to get ready, she was eager to see Nelly; she hadn't seen her for a few weeks now.

"Nana, where are you? Are you in bed?" Kendal held her ear to the wall, there was no reply. Ella May was asleep in her pram, and she pushed her into the hallway and headed upstairs. "Nana, are you up here or what?" She pushed the bedroom door open and she could see a mound underneath the bed clothes, her face dropped as she crept further into the bedroom. "Come on you, it's nearly bleeding dinner time you should be up out of that bed," there was no reply. With caution she walked to the edge of the bed, softly she pushed her hand into her Nana's shoulder, her heart was pounding inside her ribcage. "Nana, are you awake?" Rustling noises could be heard, Nelly slowly poked her head from underneath the sheets; she looked like death warmed up, her lips looked dry and cracked. "Bloody hell, how long have you been like this?" she stressed. Nelly was at death's door for sure, she struggled to breath and you could tell by her blue face that she didn't have long left.

Kendal opened the curtains to let some light into the room. Once she did, Nelly covered her eyes with her hands and screwed her eyes tightly together. Today there was no moaning from her, she just fell back down on the bed and closed her eyes. Kendal sat on the side of the bed and gripped Nelly's hand in hers. "How long have you been in bed for Nana, don't tell me he's left you up here all on your own every day?" Nelly was breathing through her mouth; she took a few seconds before she spoke.

"I've not been well love; this is the worst I've been in a long time. I've been in bed for four days and that bastard has just left me here to rot." Kendal looked horrified, surely she was joking. There was no way in the world Paddy would have just left her in bed on her own.

"Has he been cooking for you and getting you drinks?"

Nelly shook her head slowly; you could see the sadness in her eyes that her husband had deserted her. "No love, like I just said, he's not been near me. I've heard him moving about outside the bedroom door though, but he never comes in, he just stays well away from me."

Kendal blew a laboured breath. "I'm coming home to look after you. You can't stay here on your own. No, I'm coming back to look after you. My Granddad can get to fuck if he thinks I'm just going to leave you here on your own. I've had abuse from him all my life so what's another mouthful from him going to do to me? No, I'm coming back here for a bit until you're back on your feet."

Nelly wanted to tell her to go home, but if the truth was known she wanted her back at home, she couldn't survive without her. Kendal walked out of the bedroom and searched her jacket pocket for her phone; she stood with her back resting on the wall. "Scott, it's me. Listen

I've just come around to see my Nana, and she's really ill. Do you mind if I come and stay with her for a while, just until she gets better?" She held the phone from her ears and her face creased at the sides. "Scott, you're not being fair, I don't mean forever, just a few nights." Scott was having none of it, and you could see it in her face that she had enough of his bullshit. Taking a few seconds she stood thinking. She walked back into the bedroom. "Right that's sorted, I'm staying here with you until you get back on your feet. Right, let's begin by getting some food down your neck; you look a mess you know?" Nelly smiled for the first time in weeks; she missed her granddaughter so much.

Kendal was a woman on a mission; she headed down the stairs and planned to make Nelly something to eat. As she opened the kitchen door her face dropped. The sink was stacked high with pots and pans and the rubbish bin was overloaded with rubbish, it stank. Flies were all over the place and she swung her arm to get them out of her way. Kendal pinched her nose together at the sides, the smell was rancid. Quickly opening the back door she tried to let some fresh air inside the kitchen before she spewed her ring up. This was going to take forever to clean, there was no way she was cooking a thing in here until this place was cleaned up. With a quick look inside the front room she knew her help was more than needed in the household. Scott could go and take a running jump if he thought she was coming home tonight, her Nana needed her more than anything and there was no way she was selling her out when she needed her most.

Nelly wasn't strong enough to make it out of bed, her legs were too weak. The doctor had been around earlier in the week and he'd put her on another course of stronger antibiotics, hoping they would fight off the infection that was crippling her lungs, but he wasn't hopeful. He more or less told her she was on her way out. Popping another pill from the side of the bed she made the sign of the cross across on her head and body. You could see her lips moving slowly as her eyes closed, she was praying.

Kendal cleaned the house from top to bottom and for the first time in weeks the place looked half decent. Her phone was ringing constantly until finally she answered it. "What, I've told you where I am Scott so stop being a nob with me," she paced about the floor shaking her head. "Stop lying to me, why are you saying you've been done in when it's quite obvious that you're only saying that so I come home tonight," she rested her elbows on the kitchen worktop. She listened to Scott rambling on for a few more minutes and decided he was lying. "No, I don't care. I'll see you when I come home tomorrow. Go to the hospital if you're bleeding, I have to stay with my Nana," she ended the phone call and stood staring at the kitchen wall. Scott had told her he was in a bad way, and that he'd been jumped. He was always filling her head with shit and she didn't believe a word he told her anymore, she headed upstairs with some food for Nelly. As she walked into the hallway she could see Ella May stirring, she was awake and wanted to get out of her pram, her legs were kicking out in front of her and she was babbling. "One minute baby, just let me take this up to Nana Nelly and I'll come back down and get you," as she disappeared out of the lobby Ella May started whimpering. Kendal placed the food on Nelly's lap and ran back down the stairs to get the baby.

"Say hello to Nana Nelly, Ella May," Kendal chuckled as she bounced her child about on her lap. Nelly raised a smile and stretched her hand over to hold the babies fat pink fingers. Ella May was gurgling, and she seemed contented with playing with an old ornament Kendal had passed her. Nelly looked about the room, her eyes looked vacant and she seemed in a trance.

"Kendal, you know I haven't got long left don't you?"

"Nana, shut up saying things like that, you're a soldier, you've got years left in you yet."

Nelly wriggled about and sat up with her pillows folded behind her head. "Our Mary was here last night you know, sat right over there in that corner she was," she pointed her finger to the back of the room, her face was serious. Goosebumps appeared on Kendal's skin and a shiver went down her spine, the hairs on the back of her neck stood on end.

"What are you talking about Nana, don't be daft. My mother is dead."

Nelly's face was stern and her voice suddenly changed, she was angry. "My Mary was here last night; she keeps waking me up singing." Kendal patted Nelly's hand, she was getting upset. "She was singing a song she used to sing when she was younger, I told her after about the fourth verse of it to shut the hell up, she was doing my head in, she sounded like a strangled cat." Kendal tried to raise a smile, but she was scared. Her Nana was definitely acting out of character.

"What medication are you on? Let me see the tablets because I think you might have been hallucinating." Kendal stood up with Ella May hanging on her hip and walked to the stack of the tablets at the side of the bed. Picking up a white box she looked at the tablets. They were only pain killers; she's seen them hundreds of times before. Nelly was smiling now and she seemed to be having a second wind of energy. She coughed and cleared her throat.

"I'm not going up the wall you know. I know by your face that you think I'm cuckoo, but I'm not you know. Mary was here last night and we were talking for ages. She even said how pretty you were." Kendal looked about the room, she was trembling inside. What if her mother appeared to her there and then, she would have shit herself for sure. She tried to change the conversation but Nelly was having none of it. "Ay, your Mam said you need to get rid of that Scott, she said he's nothing but trouble in her eyes. Her words not mine," Nelly chuckled. Ella May was quiet and she seemed to be laughing at something in front of her. Kendal gripped her closer to her body and tried to get her attention but the child was having none of it, she was moving her head about trying to see whatever it was in front of her. There was a chill in the air and Kendal felt it pass through her body, her mother's presence was in the room. Kendal gave her head a shake and came back to reality, she didn't believe in the afterlife.

"Right, come on you; let's get some food down your neck. You need to start getting better." Kendal sat next to Nelly and started to spoon the thick chicken soup into her mouth, it was dribbling down Nelly's chin. Both their eyes seemed to meet at the same time and Nelly's eyes started to leak tears of sadness. Kendal stretched her face out trying to hold her emotions back, but it was no good, her tears were falling. Ella May was crawling about on the floor and Kendal was watching her from the corner of her eyes. "Nana, don't leave me. I need you. You and Ella May are all that I've got." Nelly sat forward and inhaled deeply, a large lump appeared in the front of her throat.

"I'll never be far from your side, never. Be it, in this world, or another, I'll always be watching over you." That was it, Kendal broke down, her shoulders were shaking and her head was buried into Nelly's chest. Nelly just sat there staring into space stroking the top of her granddaughter's head, she'd lost the will to live, and she was more than ready to die. Groaning from down the stairs made Kendal lift her head up, her eyes opened wide. Paddy was home, it was time to face her demons.

Nelly fell asleep, she'd hardly touched the soup and just a few mouthfuls were all she could manage. The bedroom door creaked opened slowly. Kendal ran to the other side of the room and scooped the baby up in her arms. Stood quivering, she snarled at Paddy, she was ready for him. Their eyes locked together and neither of them was backing down. Ella May was stretching her arms out towards Paddy and smiling, she was such a happy baby. He walked a few steps into the room and you could smell the whisky on his breath. He looked calmer than usual. Tugging on the bottom of the bed he shook Nelly's feet softly. There was no way she was waking up though; she was dead to the world. "How's she been then?" Kendal was on her guard and knew he could change like the wind at any second.

"She's not good. No thanks to you. Why have you left her on her own? Why didn't you come and get me? Surely, you must have known how bad she was?" Paddy closed his eyes and held his head back, his chin was trembling. This was the first time she'd ever seen her grandfather upset. She approached him with caution, aware that he could flip at the touch of a coin. "She's been saying some really weird things you know. She said that my Mam has been to see her," she shook her head and looked concerned as she paced about the room. "Why is she saying things like that Granddad?" Paddy folded in two and sat on the floor, his head was resting on his knees, and he was sobbing his heart out.

"I've heard her talking to her you know. I've been sat outside the bedroom door listening to her. I never came in though, things like that scare the life out of me." Kendal pinched herself. Was this her Granddad speaking about his emotions? She'd never seen him like this before; he must be going soft in his old age. Kendal knelt next to him and lifted his head up.

"She's dying isn't she?"

Paddy looked her in the eyes and nodded slowly. "Yes, she's not got long left love."

Kendal felt a wave of emotions ride through her body; this was all too much for her take in. How would she ever live without Nelly in her life? Leading Paddy by the hand she picked Ella May up and headed downstairs.

Paddy looked around the front room and he smiled. "Thanks for sorting this place out; I just lost heart when she was in bed every day." Kendal placed her hand on his shoulder and she was finding it hard to forgive him, you could see it in her face. He'd made her life a misery for so many years, so why should she feel sorry for him now? Kendal sat down, and let out a laboured breath.

"Granddad, why are you being so nice to me after all this time? You know what?" she paused. "I promised myself that I wouldn't piss on you if you were on fire, but now you're acting all strange and being nice to me. My head's going to explode with it all, I can't cope." Paddy looked over to her as he popped a cigarette into his mouth. A thick grey cloud of smoke covered his face as he answered her.

"Things change love, I've changed. Don't you think I've had enough time sat on my own to think about what I've done? Nelly is my world, and the thought of losing her makes me shake inside," his face was creasing with emotion; there was no way he could hide it. "If my Nelly dies, then I'm going with her. I don't want to breathe another breath unless she's with me." Kendal couldn't hold her tongue; this man was such a hypocrite.

"You've made her life a misery Granddad, and mine for that fact. If you loved her, why did you treat her the way you did?" She stood up tall and darted her eyes at him, he didn't scare her anymore. "And," she growled. "Don't think I didn't hear the beatings you gave her at night when you thought I was asleep, because I did." Paddy stubbed his cigarette out in the ashtray.

"Sit down Kendal, let me try and explain." She brought Ella May closer to her feet and plonked down on the sofa, she couldn't bring herself to look at him while he was speaking, he made her skin crawl. "Our Mary was the apple of my eye. I know I had Molly, but your mother was my first born. I had so many expectations for her and she let me down." Kendal was hanging onto his every word, her mobile phone was ringing again, she just looked at it and blanked the call. "I know someone out there knows more about who killed her, but they're keeping it close to their chest. In my day I was a bastard, and they all know what I'm capable of." Kendal knew Paddy was a big name in Manchester in his day, and she'd listened to Nelly on many a night tell stories about his criminal activities.

"Why did you hate me Granddad? I was innocent, I didn't deserve the life you led me." Paddy closed his eyes tightly and you could see his chest rising rapidly. His bottom lip trembled as he tried to speak.

"You are so much like her, it killed me every day to look at you and see my daughter's eyes in yours. Why do you think I drink?" Kendal bent down to pass Ella May an old teddy from the floor. Looking at Paddy in more detail she didn't know if he was being genuine or pulling the wool over her eyes, he was a crafty old fart and she was still wary of him. Her mobile phone started ringing again and this time she answered it, Paddy was watching her with eager eyes.

"Scott, stop ringing me. Fucking hell, just leave me in peace will you?" Her face was serious and she looked anxious. "Right okay, come here then, but you're not staying, you can go back home." She ended the phone call and sat looking at the floor; she could feel Paddy's eyes burning into her.

"Is he giving you a hard time, because if he is, I'll have the fucker wiped from the face of the earth?"

Kendal sat back in her chair and cracked her knuckles. "No Granddad, he's not. He said he's been jumped and that he's in a bad way. Is it alright if he comes here for a few hours?" Paddy curled his fist and you could see his knuckles turning white.

"John Daley tells me this so called Scott is a bit of the Jack the lad. Let me find out he's giving you the run around and I'll have the bastard destroyed. I've still got the contacts to do it you know, mark my words. I can have him done in at the drop of a hat."

Kendal felt loved and cared for. Nobody had ever stuck up for her before and she smiled softly at Paddy. "Why's John Daley getting busy in my life anyway?"

Paddy chuckled and started to take his heavy black boots off his feet. "John is a friend of the family, and he watches my back like I watch his." Kendal melted at the sound of John's name, he was her knight in shining armour for sure, and he always seemed to be there when she needed him most.

Kendal stood up as she heard the letterbox rapping at speed. "That must be Scott Granddad. Is he okay to come in?" Paddy nodded his head slowly, he wasn't sure of his answer. Kendal marched to the front door. "Bleeding hell Scott, who's done this to you?" Scott gritted his teeth together and gripped her by the throat.

"I told you before, I don't know. But do yourself a favour, get your stuff ready and get your arse home now, before you see what I'm all about. I swear, if you don't come now, I'll put every window through in this fucking house." Kendal tried to break free but his grip was tight.

"My Nana is dying Scott, please, don't do this." His eyes danced with madness and he wasn't backing down.

"I said now bitch." This man meant business and she knew he would stick to his word if she stayed a moment longer in the house.

"Right Scott, just take a chill pill will you. Let me just go and get the baby first." Kendal walked away from the front door and she was holding her neck. Scott paced about in the front garden, there was no way he was moving.

"Granddad, I have to go home. I'll be back first thing in the morning, I promise."

Paddy stood up and studied her face; he could see she was agitated. "Is everything alright?"

Kendal took a deep breath; she knew she'd have to cover up. "Yeah, Scott just needs me home tonight that's all. I forgot I've got the health visitor coming around in the morning, so I need to be at home," she was lying. Paddy seemed to buy her story and walked closer to her side as she was getting the baby ready to leave.

"We can talk more tomorrow, if you want? I know I've got a lot of making up to do, and I promise you that from now on I'm going to be the Granddad I should have been." Kendal looked at him, and wished he could help her out of the dark hole she'd fallen into too. With a half-hearted smile she made her way to the hallway.

"See you tomorrow, please look after her will you?" Paddy gripped Kendal in his arms, he was holding her tightly and it looked like he was suffocating her.

"I'm going to look after the both of you from now on, trust me."

As Scott walked at the side of Kendal down the road his hot breath was down her neck with every step she took. She knew without any shadow of a doubt that as soon as she walked through the front door he was going to knock ten tons of shit out of her. She prepared herself for another beating.

CHAPTER NINE

Kendal lay in the double bed and tried to focus, dried blood was visible all over the sheets. Her eyes were bruised and her bottom lip was swelled up like a dingy. Scott had beaten her bad this time and there was no way she could go out and face the world today, she looked a mess. No amount of make-up would ever cover up these wounds, not even the tinted moisturiser she'd used so many times in the past. Turning her head to the side she could see the body of her abuser lay beside her. She hissed as she clocked his stuck up hair. He was fast asleep, spit was hanging out of the corner of his mouth and his breath stank of stale tobacco.

Slowly, Kendal crept out of the bed hoping not to wake him; she was as quiet as a mouse. As her foot touched the carpet she felt his hand grip her shoulder with force, there was no way she could escape him, he was wide awake. "Where are you going? Get your arse back in bed. I want my bollocks emptying before you go anywhere." Kendal bit down hard on her bottom lip; she couldn't show him any signs of fear. She turned her head towards him and you could see in her eyes that she feared for her life. Her body was dragged back onto the bed and within minutes he was on top of her pounding away. Kendal stared at the ceiling as he penetrated deeper into her; he made her want to puke. Scott had already made her stop taking her contraceptive pill and he was trying his best to get her pregnant again. Groans filled the room and you could see his toes curling, he was getting ready to shoot his load.

When he had finished, he rolled onto his back and looped his arms behind his head, his face was cocky. "That was just what the doctor ordered that was. I swear, if I wouldn't have had a bang soon, my gonads would have exploded." His laughter made her cringe inside and she couldn't hide the hate she felt for him. "Our Pat's calling around later, so you better get yourself sorted out hadn't you?" his eyes were on her waiting for an answer. She nodded slowly and tried to smile but her face was crumbling. Scott had made friends with his sister after their argument and this was the first time she was allowed to come to their house in months. His hand stroked the side of her face. "Look at the state of your mush again. It's only what you deserve though isn't it? You know what I'm like when I switch though, don't you?"

Kendal moved her fringe over her eyes, but no amount of hair would ever cover up the signs of a domestic violence victim. Ella May was awake and she was sobbing nearby, she wanted some attention. "Grab her for me ay?" Scott said as he pushed her body to get back out of the bed. Kendal picked the baby up and placed her on the bottom of the bed. You could see Kendal was in pain and she was struggling to make any sudden movement. Scott grabbed hold of Ella May and bounced her about on his chest, he was chuckling. "Hopefully you will have a little playmate soon, won't she Kendal? Well, that's if your Dad's spunk is still working." Her face dropped and she cowered as he pulled her back towards him. Kendal's life was set in stone now and she couldn't see a way out of the deep dark hole she'd dug herself into. She never answered him, she just lay frozen scared of saying a word.

★

When Pat walked into the front room she clocked Kendal's face straight away. Her first reaction was to say something but as she looked at her brother watching her like a hawk she ignored the abused woman and sat down keeping her head low. There was no way Pat was causing a scene, she'd only just made friends with Scott and she didn't want to put a spanner in the works so soon. Pat picked Ella May up in her arms and kissed her cheeks. "Orr she's bloody lovely, Kendal, she's a credit to you both. Come and give your Auntie Pat a big sloppy kiss then," she said in an excited voice as she puckered up to kiss Ella May. Kendal smiled and watched Scott leave the room. Pat quickly twisted her head over her shoulder and made sure he was out of the way. She kept her voice low and whispered. "Fucking hell, is that what he's done to you?" she was aware he could walk back into the room at any second and kept watching the door. "You need to leave his sorry arse, or phone the fucking police. You can't go on like this; you'll end up dead, love." Scott was back in the room and he was aware that the conversation had stopped suddenly. Walking to the chair where Kendal was sat, he perched at the side of her.

"Look at the state of her face Pat. She was pissed again and fell down the full flight of stairs." Pat sniggered, she knew he was lying through his front teeth but she played the game that she believed him.

"Orr I've been pissed like that Kendal. I fell down a hole one night when me and Paul was on our way home from a party. There I was talking to him one minute and the next thing; I was down some big dark hole. I swear, I thought my number was up." Kendal covered her mouth as she laughed; her lips were aching with pain. Scott sprang to his feet and quickly checked his wristwatch.

"Right, I've got to go and see a man about a dog, so to speak. I'll be back later tonight, so don't be going out Kendal, I haven't got a key." Kendal looked at him and sat forward in her seat, she knew she was playing with fire.

"I have to go and see My Nana today Scott, she's ill. I said I would go and help my Granddad and all that?" He stopped dead in his track and turned his head back slowly, his teeth were clenched tightly together, he meant business.

"You're going nowhere. Since when have you been arsed about your Granddad, he's never give a flying fuck about you in the past, so why are you bothered about him now?" Kendal knew she was fighting a losing battle and her head sank low. Pat was watching her from the corner of her eye and her heart went out to her. Scott gave her a look that would kill and walked out of the room. That was enough to let her know she was going nowhere. The house shook as he slammed the front door behind him.

Pat ran to Kendal's side and cradled her in her arms. She broke down and tears were falling from her eyes, she couldn't talk. Scott's sister pulled her head back and looked at the bruises in more details. "When did he do this?" Kendal couldn't get her words out; she knew she needed to tell someone exactly what was going on, she couldn't cope anymore.

"He did it last night Pat. What the hell am I going to do? How can I ever walk away from this? He's told me he'll kill me if I leave him. And, he will you know, he's fucking mental." Pat lit two cigs up and passed one to Kendal.

"If you don't do something soon, I'm scared he might hurt you proper. Mind you, he looks a mess too, so you must have had a good battle with him," Pat sniggered.

"No, I didn't lay a finger on him. He got wasted last night."

Pat's face dropped, "Who jumped him then, he must have deserved it the bullying bastard. I said to my Mam the other day that I was only making friends with him to see how you were. I've missed you loads you know. I've missed our chats." Pat sucked hard on her cig and her cheeks sank in at both sides. A phone ringing stopped Pat from continuing. Kendal searched her coat pocket on the arm of the chair and her face looked frustrated as she tried to find it.

"Hiya Jane, I know, I couldn't find my phone. It was ringing for ages." Pat was listening into the conversation, she could tell by the tone of her voice that Kendal wasn't happy. The phone call ended. "Fucking hell, that's all I need, Jane coming around here."

Pat jumped in, "You should have just told her you was going out or something."

"No, it's too late; she's on her way now." They both sat in silence for a few seconds. All you could hear was the ticking of the clock on the wall. Pat was playing on the floor with Ella May. She kept watching Kendal and knew she was at her wits end.

"I'll tell you what, get the baby ready and I'll take her to see my Mam, she's not seen her for ages and plus it will give you a bit of time to yourself. If I was you, I would go and see your Nana. Fuck our Scott; he's not your jailer is he? How would he even know anyway, you'll be back before he knows it?"

This was music to Kendal's ears, she'd never had a moment away from Ella May ever since she'd been born and she accepted her offer without any hesitation. Pat stood up and grabbed the baby's pink coat from the side.

"Right I'm going to get going. You do whatever you have to do and I'll bring her back later." Kendal thanked Pat and you could tell she couldn't wait to her get her out of there as soon as possible.

Jane sat looking at Kendal as she waited for her to get ready. "You are such a nob-head, fancy letting him do that to you again. You deserve everything he does to you. You need to grow a pair of balls and sort your shit out, once and for all." Kendal pulled her skinny jeans up over her legs and quickly shoved her shoes on, she didn't care that Jane could see the marks on her body. Jane had already agreed to go with her to see Nelly.

"It's not as easy as that Jane; he's the father of my baby. If I leave him, Ella May won't have a Dad. And I know first-hand how that feels. I would never do that to her, no way in this world."

"Well, you're a fucking crank then. One day you will learn. I just hope it's not too late."

Jane and Kendal walked down Rochdale Road. The traffic was busy and the cars were flying by at speed. "John's being a right prick with me lately you know. I'm sure he's seeing someone else," Jane moaned. Kendal was all ears, she urged her to continue.

"Why, I thought you two were all loved up. I thought you said he was leaving Jackie and all that, don't tell me he's had you over again."

Jane stopped dead in her tracks. "No one's had me over; I just think something has changed between us. He seems distant."

"Perhaps, he's met someone else then, you might be right." Kendal loved that things were falling apart between Jane and John and if she was true to herself she wouldn't have minded a piece of him herself, he was just what she needed to escape the life set out in front of her. So what, if he was older, he was still a dish in her eyes. A car honked its horn as they crossed the road near Carrisbrook Street in Harpurhey. Jane nudged Kendal in the waist.

"It's John, don't say anything about what I've just told you, he'll go mad if he knows I've been discussing his business."

"Will I 'eck, don't be daft," Kendal answered. She followed Jane to the passenger side of the door and stood back. Kendal was watching her friend sat inside the car. She could hear a bit of commotion and it sounded like they were arguing. The traffic flying by stopped her tuning into all the conversation fully. Jane's legs started to come out of the car first; she raised her eyes at Kendal.

"John wants a word with you," she looked flustered.

"What, he wants me?"

Jane snarled, "Yeah, fucking hell, hurry up. I want to get as far away from this place as possible, that prick is doing my head in." Kendal lowered her head inside the car and she could see John Daley's, she'd forgotten all about her bruised face.

"What's happened to boat-race," John asked with an eager voice.

"Oh, I fell down the stairs when I was pissed," she giggled, trying to shake his comment off. John was having none of it and raised his voice.

"Get in the fucking car now." Kendal felt confused, but obeyed his orders, she was scared. His hands gripped the steering wheel, and his nostrils were flaring, he made sure Jane couldn't hear him.

"I'll tell you what; Scott is getting it this time. Who the fuck, does this kid think he's messing with?" Kendal studied John's face, he was fuming. She found it quite attractive that somebody actually cared about her. She knew John was a friend of the family but his interest in her love life was right over the top, she was sure he fancied her. Touching his hand softly he pulled it away as if she was carrying some kind of lethal disease. Kendal looked sheepish and she didn't know where to look, he'd turned her down. "Does Paddy know what he's done to you?".

Kendal was stuttering, there was no way she could tell him the truth. "John, Scott hasn't laid a finger on me, it's like I just told you. I fell down the stairs."

"Bullshit, don't try and kid a kidder. Why are you protecting him, don't you have any pride." His words crippled her, and for the first time ever she realised exactly what she was putting up with. John checked where Jane was through his rear-view mirror, he could see her talking on her phone at the back of the car. "Let me help you Kendal. I can help you start a new life away from him," his face was sincere. Kendal folded her arms and rocked about slowly.

"Why are you helping me John?" She'd taken him by surprise and he was stuck for words, there was no way he was telling her he was her father.

"I'm helping you because I'm a good friend of your family. Why are you always asking questions, do you want my help or what?" He was getting angry and she could see the vein in the side of his neck pumping with rage.

"It's not as easy as that John, where would I go? Because, he's told me he would hunt me down and do me in," she covered her mouth with her hands when she realised she'd let the cat out of the bag. John gripped her arm and squeezed it hard, she was in pain.

"Get off me will you, go on fuck off, I don't need your help, you interfering bastard." He growled at her and his fist curled at the side of him he was ready to strike a blow but stopped at the last minute.

"Are you right in the bleeding head?" he poked his finger into the side of her skull. "I'm offering you a way out. A chance of a new life for you and your daughter, surely you must want that?" Jane bent her head into the car and she could tell something was going on.

"What's up with you Kendal?" John turned the engine over and he kept his eyes fixed on the road. Jane shot a look at him at him as she pulled Kendal out of the car by her arm. "Has he come onto you, or what?" she asked. There was no reply from her friend and Jane was livid, she rammed her bony finger across the passenger seat towards her lover. "I'll tell you what John, that's it for me and you. You're a fucking liberty taker, fancy thinking you can try and cop off with my best mate, you old wanker." John spat at Jane from across the seat. He was trying to grip her but his seat belt was restricting him from any movement.

"Yes, you're right Jane, it is over. Get your sweaty arse away from me now, before I show you what I'm all about." Jane looked pale, and her words were stuck in her throat. Kendal was walking away from the car and Jane knew she had to be quick before the old git got a grip of her.

"You're a pervert anyway. You prey on young girls. Just count yourself lucky that I'm not at your house now grassing you up to your wife." Jane shouted and got on her toes; her feet were pounding the pavement. She reached Kendal and dragged her along by the arm. "Come on; get the fuck out of here before the old cunt gets a grip of me." John was reversing the car and he was getting ready to drive onto the pavement after her. The car was burning rubber, he was trying to twist it around, and he looked frantic. A few onlookers were standing still, watching the commotion, they loved a drama.

Jane and Kendal ran through the estate, they weren't stopping for man nor beast. Gasping for breath Jane folded in two, she was so unfit, her face was bright red. Kendal rubbed her back with her hand. "What did you say to him? Fuck me Jane, he was fuming, I saw his hands on the steering wheel. He was going to kill you for sure." Jane stood up and she was watching over her shoulder all the time.

"I told him straight, that's what happened. He thinks because he's got a few quid, he can treat me like an idiot, so I just came out and said it."

"Said what?" Kendal urged.

"I told him he was an old pervert, and that I was going to tell his wife all about his antics." Kendal held her hand over her mouth, she looked shocked. Nobody messed with John Daley, well, not if they knew what was good for them anyway.

"Jane you're such a mad-head. He'll be gunning for you now you know?" Jane shoved her face in front of her and pointed at it with a cocky look.

"Does this face look like it gives a fuck? He thinks he's above everyone else anyway, it's about time someone told him some home truths." Kendal was gobsmacked; this girl was definitely playing with fire.

"You'd better watch your back from now on, because we all know John Daley doesn't let sleeping dogs lie, he'll be on you like a rash now, you need to be careful."

Jane let out a laboured breath, "Fuck it, I'll cross that bridge when I come to it. Never mind me anyway, was he coming onto you or what?" Kendal was going to tell her the truth, but something inside her made her stop, she lied.

"Yeah, he gives me the creeps. He asked if I fancied meeting him sometime, I was like, are you having a laugh or what? I couldn't believe the cheek of the guy." Jane screwed her face up and kicked an empty tin can along the pavement.

"I knew it, you just watch me now, his wife is getting a letter through the post, trust me. I'm going to tell her everything." Kendal draped a comforting arm around Jane's shoulder; she had a cunning look in her eyes, she was up to something.

"He's cheeky isn't he? It just goes to show you what men are really like, you're better off without him if you ask me." Jane stopped walking and looked at Kendal in disbelief, she'd rattled her cage.

"Since when can you give advice about men when your boyfriend knocks ten tons of shit out of you all the time? Do yourself a favour and save your advice for yourself, you need it more than me." Kendal rolled her eyes, Jane was right.

"Okay, okay, calm down will you. I was just saying that's all. Don't bite my head off." The girls linked each other and headed towards the row of houses facing them. Kendal looked at Jane and her voice was low. "She's dying you know. I just have a gut feeling she's not got long left. Ay, my Granddad has even apologised to me for all the shit he's given me over the years. He's really changed now. I couldn't get my head around it at first, it's weird." Jane sighed and twisted Kendal round to face her, she was giving her a piece of her mind and holding nothing back, she'd heard enough bullshit for one day.

"How can you be so forgiving with that old bastard? I tell you what; if he'd have been my Granddad I would have stuck a knife in him years ago. Just be careful with him. I don't trust him one little bit. A leopard never changes its spots, remember that."

"I know Jane, I will be careful, but for now my concerns are with my Nana, she's been saying some strange shit lately and it's scaring me." Kendal pushed the back gate open and walked to the door. Squashing her face up to the glass she could see Paddy sat down in his chair rolling a cigarette. Her hand pressed the silver handle down on the door. As soon as she walked inside Paddy sat up straight in his chair, he looked anxious.

"She's not well you know, the doctor has just been, he said that he doesn't think she'll make it through the night." Kendal was in shock as Jane closed the door behind her. She hurried up the stairs followed closely by Jane.

Nelly was sat up in her bed and she was talking to someone. Kendal shot her eyes about the room but she couldn't see a living soul. "Nana, it's me Kendal, who are you talking to?" Nelly chuckled and pointed to the draylon chair at the side of her.

"It's our Mary. Oh, look Mary, I told you she would be here soon." Kendal was just about to turn and run out of the room when Jane stopped her.

"Don't be scared. Come on, I've seen this before when my Gran died. She said my old dog Max was with her before she snuffed it, it's normal behaviour all this, trust me." Jane walked further into the bedroom, she urged Kendal to come with her. Paddy came into the room behind them; he was spooked.

"She's been rambling on all night Kendal; she said her Mam and Dad were here too. Do you think she's losing the plot or what?" Nelly looked at Paddy; she was smiling from cheek to cheek. Her energy seemed to have come from nowhere.

"Am I fuck losing the plot. I've never felt better in my life." Nelly's eyes had a glassy coating over them, they looked different, something wasn't right. Paddy sat by his wife's side and reached over for her hand. Kendal rested on the end of the bed with Jane who looked terrified.

The next few hours flew by and Nelly's life was coming to an end. As she gasped her final breath her family was by her side. Paddy looked like a man twice his age and you could tell he would never get over the death of his wife. Nelly sat up and smiled at her Granddaughter. "I've got to go now love. I know you will make me proud and show everyone what I already knew. You're special Kendal, and one day the world will see it too. Don't let anyone tell you any different. You're a diamond in the rough you are, and although you don't think so, you're stronger than you think." Kendal snivelled as Jane held her close to her chest. Nelly looked at Paddy, her face changed. "And you Paddy Wilson, you need to right the wrongs you've done over the years. You know what I mean don't you?" He dipped his head onto his chin; he knew exactly what she meant. Nelly's face looked towards the window; she was holding her hands out. Kendal screamed out and stretched her body out over her Nana's chest.

"No, not yet, please Nana, I need you." Jane came to her friend's side and stroked her hand across her back; she didn't know what else to do. They were all watching the dying woman.

"I'm ready now," Nelly's breathing was shallow as she closed her eyes. Her face was free from pain and she looked like she was smirking.

Paddy stood to his feet and his lips quivered. "She's gone hasn't she?"

Jane bit down on her lips and nodded her head. "She

has Paddy, she's gone." The screams of a banshee filled the room, and you could see Kendal's knuckles turning white as she gripped Nelly's lifeless body.

"Bring her back Granddad please, bring her back." He folded in two and ragged his fingers through his hair, he was a broken man.

Jane became the backbone of the family and she took care of the calls to the doctor and anything else that needed doing. Kendal sat with Nelly and you could hear her heart-breaking sobs as she poured her heart out. "I will make you proud one day Nana, I will, I will."

Nelly's body was taken to the Chapel of Rest after the doctor had pronounced her dead. Kendal was a wreck and she was swilling glasses of whisky as if it was water. Jane rang Pat and told her what had happened and it was decided that Ella May would stay the night with Scott's sister.

A little later the back door opened slowly and John Daley was stood there looking apprehensive. Jane's arse was twitching and she knew she had to make amends before he ended her life. She looked sheepish and shouted him into the kitchen. A few raised voices filled the room and minutes later Jane walked out from there still in one piece, you could see red marks around her neck. She was always a good talker and she could talk her way out of any trouble at the drop of a hat. Jane was shaking as Kendal looked at her. John's face was flustered when he came back into the front room. He walked over to Paddy and shook his hand. "She was a good woman Paddy; she'll be greatly missed by all." He reached into his jacket pocket and pulled out a half bottle of Jack Daniel's whiskey. "Here you go mate, get a swig of that down your neck."

Jane looked uncomfortable and when she got the

chance she made a quick exit, there was no way she was hanging around. John was a ticking bomb, and he could have flipped at any second. Kendal sat staring at the wall; she could feel John Daley's eyes all over her. Swigging a large gulp of whisky she lifted her eyes to him. His eyes looked sad and she couldn't bring herself to speak to him, she'd lost her bottle. Paddy was pissed and his eyes were closing, he was nodding off. Every now and then he would bolt up from his chair and start shouting out his wife's name. John rested his hands on his lap, he was thinking. He leant forward and kept his voice low. "Kendal, about before, I didn't mean to get busy in your life, but I just can't help it. You're a lovely young woman and I hate to see you wasting your life away with a dead-leg like Scott. You can have so much more you know." Kendal blew her breath; she'd been right all along. He was coming on to her.

"John, I know why you want to help me, but Jane is my best friend and I wouldn't ever stab her in the back." John thought about her words and he realised what she must have been thinking, his cheeks went beetroot.

"No, you've got it all wrong; I don't fancy you or anything like that. I'm just trying to help you." The alcohol had really kicked into Kendal's body and her words were slurred.

"So, you don't fancy me then. Why the hell not? Am I ugly or something like that?" John wanted the ground to open up and swallow him; this was his daughter for crying out loud. His face was distraught.

"You're like my family," he lied. "I've known you since you were a baby. I care for you a lot, but not in the way you're thinking." Kendal stood to her feet, there was no way she was having that he wasn't attracted to her, she was ten times prettier than Jane. She flung her hair back over her shoulder and staggered to where he was sitting; she held his chin in her hands and darted her eyes into his.

"Admit it; you know it, and so do I. You want me don't you?" He pulled his jacket open at the front, he was suffocating, he was lost for words.

"Stop it Kendal, you're drunk and upset. Please don't do this." He pushed her away. Kendal turned to face him and snapped.

"If you don't fancy me, just say it how it is, don't go around the houses. I can take it you know." John stood to his feet and pulled a cigarette from his packet, he held one out to her.

"Here, have a cig and calm down. You are beautiful yes, but you don't understand." Kendal stood with her hand on her hips her jaw was swinging.

"Go on, fuck off out of here. I don't need you here and neither does my family. It's always been the same with you, any misery in this house and you're always here, you're a fucking jinx. Now, fuck off before I stick my foot right up your arse." John chuckled to himself, this girl had balls. He grabbed his coat from the side and headed to the living room door.

"Like I said, I'm here to help, nothing else." He reached inside his coat pocket and pulled out a white card with his phone number on it. Placing it on the table he smiled at her. "The offer still stands, if you need me, I will help you. I don't want anything in return."

"I said fuck off," Kendal screamed at the top of her voice, Paddy's eyes flickered but he remained asleep. She picked up a shoe from the floor and launched it towards his head, he ducked just in time. John was gone.

Paddy sat snoring in his chair, his chest was rattling.

Kendal had never felt more alone in her life as she did now. Life without her nana was going to be hard, and the words she'd spoken to her before she passed away were still stuck in her head. If she could have written a letter to her, she would have poured her heart out and told her all about the life she was leading. She hated that she couldn't read or write properly. She'd always imagined when she was growing up that she was a best-selling author and her books were selling worldwide, but that dream had died when she quit school barely able to read and write. Kendal closed her eyes, a single salty tear rolled down her cheek; she was drifting off to sleep.

Nelly Wilson was laid to rest at Moston cemetery on the twelfth of September at ten thirty in the morning. There was a good turnout for her, and Nelly would have been impressed if she could have seen all her friends and family stood around her graveside. Scott hung his arm over Kendal as she sobbed her heart out. It was all for show and you could see by his face, that he didn't give a flying fuck about Nelly popping her clogs. He was all about himself and Nelly's death just meant he would have more control over Kendal now. The heavens opened and everyone walked away from the graveside with their heads hung low, it was a sad day. Kendal could see a head sticking out from behind a headstone in the distance, someone was hiding away. Stood looking for a few seconds the image disappeared, she carried on walking; she must have been imagining it because nobody was there now. Scott held her cold hand and squeezed it, this was his way of saying he cared about her. Kendal's face was grey and she ran to the side of the grass verge and bent over, she was gagging.

Yellow bile seeped from her mouth. Lifting her head up she could see Scott's feet at the side of her. He rubbed her back slowly. "What's up, are you okay?" Kendal wiped her mouth with her sleeve, and her face changed. She'd been waiting for her period for days now and she was late by two weeks.

The wake at the Wilson's household carried on well into the early hours. Jane didn't stick around long after the funeral, she hated the sight of Scott, and John Daley was throwing daggers at her from the other side of the room, it was only a matter of time before he dealt with her. Kendal walked about the room looking like a lost soul, her heart was heavy and she looked like she had the worries of the world on her shoulders. Scott was never far from her side, he looked agitated as he watched her talking to the other guests. Necking the last bit of brandy in his glass he stood up and swayed towards her. "Are we getting off or what? I want to get my head down; I've got some hard graft on tomorrow and I need to be fresh." Kendal looked at his face, and this time she wasn't scared of him, she opened fire.

"Listen, I'm not going anywhere. If you're tired, then go home, but I'm staying here." He gritted his teeth together and pulled her by the arm; pressing her body up against the wall he spat into her face. His eyes were all over making sure nobody saw him.

"Get your coat and do what I tell you. Since when have you grown a pair of balls, hurry the fuck up, before I start proper and smash your fucking head in." Kendal held her head against the cold wall. She was pissed and her jaw was swinging, it was now or never.

"It stops here Scott, you don't own me anymore. I was a kid when I met you and didn't know any better, but as from now, it stops, do you hear me?" Her head crashed against the wall and her legs buckled from underneath her, he'd struck the first blow.

"Get on your feet now bitch, I swear if you carry on, I'll smash this place up." Kendal was bewildered and she was trying her best to focus, behind Scott she could see a figure of a man walking towards her. Her eyes closed and she fell to the floor again.

The birds tweeting outside her window woke Kendal up; she rubbed her knuckles into her eyes. Her head was banging and her mouth was like sandpaper. Sticking one of her legs out of the bed, she could feel the cold chill on them and pulled the covers back over her head.

"Do you want a drink?"

Kendal's head appeared from under the blanket and her face froze when she saw John Daley sat in the corner of the room. He was still dressed in the black suit he had been wearing the day before. Kendal quickly looked under the covers; she was relieved when she saw she was still dressed.

"What am I doing here?" she asked in a frightened voice. John stood to his feet and sat on the edge of the bed.

"You were pissed love, you collapsed you know. Paddy asked me to put you in bed, he was worried about you." She kicked the blankets off her legs and sat with them dangling over the edge of the bed. Her eyes shot about the room and she realised she was in her old bedroom.

"Where did Scott go? Didn't he mind me staying here without him?" John sniggered, and looked at her directly in the eyes.

"Oh, don't you worry your pretty little head about him. He was off his head and went home. Drunk as a skunk he was." She felt relieved; this was a first for Scott and right out of character for him. Usually he was like a fart lingering around her body, he never gave her a moment's peace. Kendal looked at the clock on the wall and panicked.

"Bleeding hell, is that the time? I need to go and pick Ella May up. I said I would be there first thing this morning, and it's nearly twelve o'clock."

"Stop stressing, I'll drop you off there. I'm going now anyway, Jackie will be wondering where the hell I've got to. She was ringing me all last night thinking I was up to no good, she's a right paranoid bitch." Kendal was just about to add her penny's worth, but she stopped herself. John's love life was none of her business, and she didn't want to open that can of worms, she kept her trap shut. Paddy came into the bedroom, his eyes were red raw. Watching his granddaughter put her shoes on he winked at John. "It's a good job John was here last night otherwise you would have had to stay where you fell. A proper mess you was when John found you, you must have fell and banged your head." Kendal had a flashback and she shot a look to John.

"What, you carried me to bed?"

He stuck his pigeon chest out and flexed his muscles. "Ay, there's plenty of life left in this old dog yet. It's like they say Paddy isn't it. There's many a good tune played on an old piano."

Paddy tried to raise a smile but his heart was broken and he was struggling. Kendal jumped off the bed, her mind was working overtime and she was remembering what had happened the night before. She knew Scott attacked her. Paddy left the room and Kendal and John followed behind him. Kendal gripped John back before he went down the stairs.

"You sorted him out didn't you?"

He turned his head slowly and his nostrils flared. "I did what I had to, that's all."

Kendal didn't know whether to laugh or cry, her hormones were all over the place at the moment and she knew without doing any test that a new life was growing inside her.

"Thanks," she whispered.

Kendal gripped Ella May in her arms as she entered her home. "Scott," she shouted. A cloud of smoke filled her face and she took a few minutes to see him properly. Scott was stood in front of her and he looked a mess. His eyes were black and blue and he was holding his hand on top of his head with a bewildered look on his face.

"What's happened to you Scott?" His face dropped and he paced about the room.

"I'm not sure," he ranted. "Someone whacked something over my head I think. I woke up in the fields this morning. I must have been spiked or something, because I don't remember jack shit about last night."

Kendal smirked to herself, she knew exactly what had happened to him and loved that he was getting a taste of his own medicine. "I know what you mean Scott; I woke up this morning and didn't have a clue where I was either. We must have been spiked or something."

Scott looked confused, "So did you stay with Paddy," Kendal answered him quickly.

"Yeah, where else would I have stayed?" He gripped

Ella May from her mother's waist and placed her into the playpen.

"Come on, I fancy a shag before I go out, get your knickers off." Kendal obeyed his orders and took her place on the sofa for a quick knee trembler, she knew he wouldn't be long and couldn't be bothered arguing with him about sex again. Kendal had a smile on her face throughout sex, she was thinking about her hero John Daley and how he'd saved her. Scott finished in minutes; it was only a jerk and a squirt. He jumped up from her and started to get ready.

"Big job on today Kendal, if it comes off we'll be laughing all the way to the bank."

Kendal smirked, she knew more than anyone he was chatting shit again. Every day he went out he always said the same thing. "John Daley's put me and Mikey onto a right good earner. We could be talking grands if it all comes off." She was listening now she'd heard John's name mentioned her heart melted.

"I hope so Scott, because I think we've got another mouth to feed."

He looked at her and tilted his head to the side. She was waiting until the penny dropped. "What, you're pregnant?"

Kendal sniggered, "Derrr...Yeah. That's why I've been throwing up all the time. I'm going to do a pregnancy test today," she was pretending to be happy. Scott picked her up by her waist and sank his head into her breasts.

"Top one. I tell you what, if this graft comes off we can go out for a meal and celebrate, what do you say?"

Kendal tried to wriggle free from his tight grip, he was crushing her. "Yeah, put me down then, I can't breathe." He dropped her back on the floor; he was giddy and kept punching his fists into the air.

"Just call me super spunk from now on," he giggled.

★

John Daley sat in his car watching Scott and Mikey. He was out of sight and he was trying to keep a low profile, his head was dipped low as the music played softly in the background. He'd told the lads there was a grow of marijuana in the warehouse facing him and he knew they would breaking into the old mill any second now. Once he saw Scott gaining entry, he lifted his mobile phone to his ear and waited patiently with a sly look on his face. "Hello, I want to report some men breaking into a warehouse. Yes, they are in it now. I've just seen them booming the doors down, hurry up before you miss them. I'm sure there are drugs inside the place too." John gave a bit more information to the police and ended the call. He'd set Scott and Mikey up.

Meanwhile Kendal sat waiting for her pregnancy test results. She was chewing rapidly on her fingernails. There was no way she wanted another baby and she was hoping the test was negative. Someone was knocking on the front door. She stood to her feet and placed the test on the windowsill in the front room.

Opening the door Jane stood there, she looked like she'd been crying. "What's up Jane, what's happened?" Kendal closed the front door and followed her into the front room. Jane plonked herself down onto the sofa and covered her hands over her face, she was blubbering. "What's happened, if you don't tell me how can I help?" She removed her hands from her face, and blew a hard breath.

"I'm fucking up the duff aren't I?" Kendal stared at

her and went to sit down next to her.

".What, you're pregnant?"

"Derr...Yes, fucking hell I've just told you once."

"Who to?" Kendal said in a high pitched voice. Jane snapped and stood to her feet.

"Fucking John Daley, that's who. I haven't slept with anyone else since him. I knew I was late on my period but I just forgot about it hoping it would go away. I think I'm about four months gone." Kendal walked over to her test hanging over the windowsill. Taking it in her fingers she gawped at the result window. She wasn't sure what the two thick blue lines meant. Jane was a better reader than her and she walked back to her holding the box in her hands.

"Just check what two blue lines mean for me. Is it positive or negative?" Jane's eyes opened wide, he jaw dropped.

"Don't tell me you think you're pregnant too?"

"Just fucking read it for me will you, hurry up." Jane studied the box, and she was sounded some words out.

"Give me a butcher's at your test, go on hold it up next to the box." Kendal was anxious and her hands were shaking. Jane studied the test and the box; her eyes were flickering from one to the other. "Yep, you're pregnant; it shows it here, two blue lines mean you're pregnant. Fucking hell Kendal, what are the chances of that? I mean, both of us finding out on the same day." Kendal sank back onto the sofa with a heavy heart. She sat forward rubbing her hands together frantically.

"Shall we get rid of it? I won't tell if you don't. Nobody would ever know," her voice was desperate. Jane was thinking, she lit two cigs up and passed one to Kendal. Blowing the smoke out from her mouth she clicked her jaws together making smoke hoops.

"I was thinking about that already, I'm not going to lie to you, but just think of what I could get out of John Daley if he knew I was carrying his child, he could give me a good life couldn't he? His wife Jackie can't have kids, so I think I might keep it." Kendal's face creased at both sides, she waved her hands about in distress.

"You can't just keep a kid so you can get money from its Dad."

Jane bounced back at her, "Who fucking can't? Watch this space Kendal. I don't work, and let's face it," she raised her eyebrows, "who's going to employ me, I'm thick as fuck, I can barely read or write," she tapped her fingernails on her front teeth. "No, John is my only option for a better life."

Kendal's face looked like a smacked arse. "Do whatever you want, but if you ask me it's fucking snidey."

Jane stood to her feet and stubbed her cig out in the ashtray. "What is it with you and John fucking Daley? Every time I mention his name you always get defensive, is he slipping you one or something?" Kendal went bright red, and stood twisting her fingers.

"No you muppet. Is he fuck, slipping me one. I just think you're tight on him. You hated him the other week, so why would you want his baby now. Have an abortion and have done with him for once and for all. He's bad news." Jane was chomping on the bit to have her say.

"Yeah, he's bad news, you're right. But when he knows I'm having his baby he'll look after me and all that, won't he?" Kendal was lost for words; she paced the front room and held the lower part of her stomach.

"Well, I'm getting rid of this baby for sure. Scott got me pregnant on purpose. He thinks by doing that, that he will make me love him more. I'm done with him Jane, I don't love him anymore. I'm going to leave him."

Jane let out a sarcastic laugh. "I've heard all this shit from you time and time again. Why are you saying you don't love him? After all he's put you through you should have said this years ago? No, I don't believe you. You haven't got the bottle."

Kendal held her body tight and knew she would have to search deep within herself to make the break. Jane was right though, she didn't have the guts to leave him.

John Daley sat smoking his cigarette as he watched Scott and Mikey being dragged from the warehouse by a team of police officers. He could see Scott fighting with them as they tried to throw him in the back of the police van. A smirk was fixed firmly over his face and he let out a menacing laugh. "Let's see you talk your way out of this one smart arse." He flicked the engine over and crept from the alleyway where he was parked. He turned the music up loud and tapped his fingers on the steering wheel as he hit the open road.

★

Kendal walked in the house to see Paddy. Empty bottles of whiskey were scattered about near his feet. Sat in his arm chair he was just staring at the wall in a world of his own, he was in desperate need of help. She walked to his side and bent down to pick up the rubbish near his feet. He gripped her arm tightly and growled. "Leave it where it is, I can clean my own bleeding mess up, I don't need your help." Kendal backed away and stood near the door.

"What are you being like this for Granddad? I'm

here to help. Look at the state of you, you're a disgrace." Stumbling to his feet he wobbled towards her. He gripped her by the throat and pinned her up against the wall, his warm breath was in her face.

"Nelly's not here to save you no more. I don't want you in this house again, are you listening to me?" Kendal pushed him away, he was weak and she knew he was still pissed, he didn't scare her anymore.

"Oh, so you're starting all that again are you? Why did I ever think you could change? Jane was right; you're still a conniving old bastard."

Paddy launched an old brass candlestick at her head, and it skimmed past her forehead. The ornament sank into the wall leaving a large dint in it. She opened the door and stood grinding her teeth. "You'll die a lonely old man you will Granddad. I'm gone from here, you sad old bastard. Let's see what you're like when you're left on your own." Kendal banged the door shut behind her and nearly took it from its hinges. Paddy was on her trail and she was watching her back all the time. Kendal stood on the street corner, she was panicking, she didn't know which way to turn. Her feet were turning one way then the other, she was confused. Heading towards the Harpurhey Asda superstore she decided to go and pick Ella May up from Pat's. She's slept there the night before and she was due to go and pick her up anyway.

A gang of smack-heads were huddled together near the corner of the shops. Kendal could see them approaching people in the distance trying to sell their swag. This was normal behaviour for the Harpurhey area, the addicts shoplifted in the precinct and as soon as they sold their knock-off gear they would go and score some brown. Kendal kept her head low, she was in no mood to speak to them today, although in the past she'd bought cheese and bacon from them at next to nothing prices. She dodged through the crowds of people and thought she'd escaped the junkies. Kendal felt her arm being gripped from the side. "Here you go love, do you want to buy some Mach3 razors? I can do them cheap for you?" Kendal shook her head and was all set to carrying on walking when her face changed, she looked like she'd seen a ghost.

"Molly, is that you?" The addict gripped her neck and looked hot.

"Nar, I'm not Molly, you must have got me mixed up with somebody else." Kendal pulled at the woman's grimy black bubble coat; it was filthy and full of dried mud.

"Molly it is you, it's me Kendal." The junkie started to panic and covered her brown stumpy teeth with her hands. The heroin addict got on her toes and ran from her side at speed. "Molly," Kendal screamed after her. "Come back, it's me Kendal."

Kendal knocked on Pat's front door and stood waiting for her to answer. She was more than sure she'd just seen her auntie Molly at the shopping centre and her mind was doing overtime as to why she'd ran away from her. Pat opened the door and raised her eyes to the ceiling. "Have you heard then?" Kendal walked inside hunching her shoulders.

"Heard what?"

"About Scott and Mikey, they've just been nicked. Mikey's girlfriends just left here in a right state; apparently they've been caught bang to rights. Scott won't be home for a long time if he's charged with this." Kendal walked over to Ella May and picked her up. This was music to her ears. She tried to look concerned and blew her breath.

"No way have they been arrested? Scott said this morning they were on a big job. That must have been what they've been dragged in for." Pat led her into the front room, she sniggered.

"A bit of time in old chokey won't do him any harm anyway. It might sort the cocky bleeder out." Kendal tried not to laugh and dipped her head low. Her mind was working overtime; this was just what she needed to rid of Scott from her life for good. Looking at Pat, she hesitated to get it off her chest that she was pregnant, but she needed some advice.

"Pat, I'm pregnant and I need to get rid of it as soon as possible. Please don't tell Scott will you?" Pat chuckled and held the bottom of her belly.

"What? Do you think I would breathe a word after what happened last time? No love, your secret's safe with me."

"Where do I go Pat to get sorted out, will you come with me?"

Pat nodded her head and paced the floor. "If you get it done on the NHS, it could take weeks, months. You need this doing as soon as possible, well, at least before Scott gets out, don't you?" Pat placed her hand on Kendal's shoulder. "If I had the money love, I would pay for it, you know that." Kendal nodded her head.

"I know love, don't worry about it. I will sort it out myself. How much do I need?" Pat scratched the top of her head.

"About three ton should cover it, but you need to be rapid and get it done before Scott gets bail. You can just tell him you had a miscarriage, he won't know the difference," Pat raised her eyes thinking. "I think they will be up at court in a couple of days. Mikey's girlfriend told me they were caught bang to rights though, so I think they will stay on remand until the court date hopefully." Kendal was excited inside. This was the break she needed. She grabbed Ella May's coat and walked around the front room like a headless chicken.

"I'm going to see if I can get the money together. Will you book me in for tomorrow if possible?"

Pat rubbed her body as a cold chill passed over her. "I'll do my best love. Where are you going to get the cash from though; it's a lot of money just to get at the drop of a hat?"

Kendal tapped the side of her nose with her index finger, indicating that she was keeping a secret. "Just leave it with me Pat, thanks for having Ella May for me. I'll be back in touch as soon as I've sorted the money out."

Kendal sat in the front room watching Ella May playing, she was so big now and she was trying to walk by herself, she kept standing to her feet by holding the corner of the sofa and falling back to the floor. Holding her mobile phone in her hands Kendal was thinking. She was unsure of her next move. Searching deep inside her jacket pocket she pulled out the white card that had John Daley's phone number on it. Her heart was beating ten to the dozen and you could see her chest rising with speed, taking a deep breath she dialled the number. Kendal held the phone to her ear, it was ringing. Quickly she pressed the red button and ended the call, she'd lost her nerve. "Fuck, fuck fuck," she whispered under her breath as she slammed her phone on the arm of the chair. Ella May started moaning and she made her way towards her. The mobile phone on the chair started ringing behind her. Kendal froze for a split second and stood chewing on her fingernails. With quick steps she looked at the screen, it was John Daley returning her call. Kendal picked Ella May up and stood gawping at the phone, it was now or never.

"Hello," she said in a soft voice, her face cringed. "Yes John, sorry my phone cut out, it was me who rang you." Kendal was walking up and down the front room; she swallowed hard as she tried to pluck up the courage to ask him for the money. "John, you said you would help me if I needed it, didn't you? Well I'm in shit street and I desperately need you to help me. I would never ask you, but I'm desperate." She was listening to him on the other end of the phone. "Yeah, I'm at home now. Okay, see you soon." Kendal's face was bright red, she was a nervous wreck and she was shaking from head to toe. Running about the room she started to clean up the mess. There was no way she wanted John to see the state of the house, it was a disgrace.

When he arrived John sat facing Kendal, his eyes were all over her waiting for her to speak. Ella May was sat on the floor munching a biscuit Kendal had just passed her, she had chocolate all over her face. "Do you want a brew John?" Kendal asked in a nervous voice, she couldn't look him in the eyes. He shook his head and sat forward in his seat, his hands were cupped together between his legs, he wanted to get down to business.

"No chicken, I'm fine. Come and sit down here and tell me what's wrong." John was relaxed, he knew exactly where Scott was and he didn't fear being caught alone with Kendal. He patted the space next to him. Kendal sat down and her eyes were fixed on the floor. Clearing her throat, she started to speak.

"John, I need to borrow three hundred pounds for an

abortion. I would never have asked you, but I'm desperate. Scott's been arrested and I don't know when he's getting out, but all I know is that I need to get this done as soon as possible before it's too late." John looked at her in more detail, his eyes were filled with love for her and he slowly took her hand in his.

"I can do that for you, and you don't need to give it me back either…" he began but before he could finish Kendal threw her arms around his neck and hugged him tightly, he was her knight in shining armour.

"Thank you so much John, I'll never forget this. And once I get back on my feet I will pay you every penny back, I swear. I'm no charity case." John held the tears back; you could see his eyes welling up.

"No, you don't have to give me anything back. Like I said, I just want you to be happy." Kendal sat back in her chair, she felt so comfortable with John and she started to open up to him telling him about her plans for the future.

"I'm leaving Scott; I hope he stays in jail for as long as possible. I'm going to move out of the area and start a new life for me and Ella May." John smiled and nodded his head slowly; this was music to his ears.

"That's the most sensible thing I've ever heard you say. I will help you, if you let me. I've got some mates who rent houses out in all different areas across Manchester, I'm sure they can help you out." Kendal looked confident as she spoke.

"Thanks John, you're like the Dad I never had. Please don't tell anyone about our conversation though, will you? I don't want people talking behind my back. I just hope Scott gets remanded in jail, otherwise I'll never get away." John chuckled as he stood to his feet.

"I think Scott will be banged up for a long time.

My mate's just told me what he was caught doing, so if that's true, you can say goodbye to him for at least a three stretch." John's mobile phone was ringing. He dug his hands into his pocket and walked into the kitchen to answer it. Kendal was trying to listen, John was shouting. "I don't give a fuck about any baby, get fucking rid of it. I'll tell you now Jane, you won't get a penny from me." Kendal covered her mouth with her hand. It must have been Jane on the phone telling him that she was having his baby. As he walked from the kitchen he was angry and his nostrils were flaring.

"Are you okay John," she asked in a low voice. He walked to her side and rubbed his hand on the top of her head.

"I'm fine love, nothing I can't sort out. I'll call back later with the money if that's okay?" She nodded her head and walked behind him to the front door. As he was about to leave, she looked at him with endearing eyes.

"John, you've saved me you know. I'll always be thankful." Chewing on his bottom lip he held back his emotions and said goodbye.

Jane stood on the corner of Conran Street, she was watching the traffic fly by with eager eyes. Her small red jacket was zipped up to the top and she was waiting for someone. Jane was anxious and she couldn't keep still. John Daley pulled up at the side of her and she jumped into the car before he drove off again. The music in the car stopped her from talking, it was loud and she knew if she would have spoken she would never have been heard. John looked angry; his eyes never met hers until he pulled over in some alleyway not far from the main road. He turned to face her as he clicked his seat belt out of the socket. He knew he could have dealt with her there and then, fucked her up good and proper, but he held back as he watched her hands resting on her stomach protecting the seed he'd planted inside her.

"John, this is your baby too. Just think about it, we could be happy like we used to be," she placed her hand on his lap as she continued. "Jackie can't have any kids; do you want to end the life of your only flesh and blood?" John opened the car window and lit a smoke up, he was playing mind games with her and she didn't know if she was coming or going. "Are you listening to me or what John? If you want me to get rid of the baby then fine," she cleared her throat and prepared herself to deliver the next line. "But, you'll have to pay for an abortion. You know I'm penniless." Jane watched his face from the corner of her eyes. If he was paying for an abortion then at least she could earn a few quid if she got it done on the NHS without telling him. She prodded her finger into his waist, she knew she was pushing her luck with him, but she didn't care, after all she was holding all the cards, she was carrying his child.

"How do I know it's mine? It's been months since I last slung one up you."

Jane nearly choked, "You cheeky cunt, I've been upset since we split up. I don't want anyone else, I've been pining for you." He chuckled loudly and looked at himself in the rear view mirror. Stroking his grey stubble he nodded his head.

"Yep, I do take some getting over don't I? Anyway, like I said how do I know it's mine, because don't think for one minute your setting me up with some other fucker's kid." Jane spat her dummy out and folded her arms in front of her; she had to up her game. This was a lot harder than she first thought.

"Just take me home. If you think I'm that sort of girl who would do something like that to you, well, you can fuck right off. Fuck you and fuck your baby; I'll just get rid of it. Just take me home." John's face was serious; he believed every word she'd said now. At first when she'd told him she was pregnant his initial reaction was for her to get an abortion, but now, as he looked at her face, he mellowed. John was coming round to the idea of being a Dad again; he tapped his fingers on the steering wheel.

"So what do you want from me if you keep this baby?"

"Nothing," Jane lied, she kept her face straight. Of course she wanted something back from him, but there was no way she was letting this old cunt know that at this stage. John gripped her face in his large sweaty hands. Her cheeks were being squeezed together tightly.

"You're a pain in the arse, you are Jane, you're too much of a risk. Since when can you keep your big trap shut and keep a secret. The world and his wife would know in weeks, you couldn't hold your own piss could you?" Jane moved his hands from her face, he was hurting her.

"John stop fucking about. I wouldn't say jack shit to nobody. Do you want this kid or what?" She knew by his face that she had him. "Well, what's your answer?" she urged. If John would have said no she would have been devastated. She looked at him with a poker face and pressed him for an answer.

"Okay, you can keep the kid, but I swear, if I hear one little murmur on the street that the kid's mine and I'll kick the little bastard right out of you. My Jackie is a ruthless bitch," his face was serious, "and, if she got wind of any kid she'd land on you like a ton of bricks, trust me she's hardcore." Jane looked relieved, her worries were over she was back in the circle of trust with John. Touching the side of his face softly she opened her eyes fully.

"So, does that mean me and you are back on then. I know you've missed me." The corners of his mouth started to rise. He'd not filled Jane's place yet and he was dying for a shag, he grabbed at her perky tits.

"I don't know, maybe if you suck me off I might think about it." Jane stretched her hand over and placed it on his crotch. All the blood went from his brain and down to his cock. Jane and John were back together.

CHAPTER TEN

Scott stood in the dock at Manchester Crown Court awaiting sentencing. He looked like a smackhead; his clothes were crumpled and dirty. This man looked old and haggard, his face looked desperate. Dark circles lay deep underneath his eyes and you could tell he hadn't been sleeping well. Mikey, his co-accused, was fidgeting about in the dock and he didn't look arsed that he was going to get slammed. Scott's co-accused had done time in the past and he was used to the life behind prison walls, unlike Scott. Kendal's boyfriend had been in trouble with the law before, but he'd always got off by the skin of his teeth. This time was going to be different though, very different. Scott's brief had told him straight that he would be looking at a few years rammed up his arse, there was no way he was walking this time. Mikey was on a lesser charge of burglary and breaking and entering. Scott had had the book thrown at him big time. His assault on the officer who'd arrested him carried at least an extra eighteen month sentence. He was well and truly fucked.

Kendal walked inside the courtroom with Pat by her side. She kept her head low and knew this would be the last time she saw her boyfriend. John had already set the wheels in motion for her to move out of the area and it was only a matter of time before she said goodbye to the streets of Harpurhey. Scott waved his hand over his head when he saw Kendal sat in court, she could tell by his face he was petrified. He was locked behind a glass panel and she could only see the top half of his body, he looked thin and gaunt. Pat nudged her in the waist and kept her voice low. "Fuck me, he looks like he hasn't been fed for moons. I bet his arse is twitching today though; there is no way he's going to get off with this, this time. He'll get about four years shoved up his shitter, trust me. Judge Merdock is a ruthless old cunt. I know a few lads who've been up in front of him before; he takes no shit." Kendal listened to her and tried to look gutted, but she wasn't doing a good job, you could see it in her eyes that she wanted the bastard banged up for as many years as possible.

The usher made sure there was silence in court before the judge entered the courtroom. As the door opened everybody stood to their feet and kept their heads low. It was like this man was royalty. Pat was whispering under her breath. "If he broke a smile his face would crack, the miserable fucker, check him out Kendal, he looks like he's on one today." The usher darted her eyes at Pat and made sure she didn't speak again. Mikey's family were sat in front of them and you could tell by their faces this was run of the mill for them, they were so used to him being flung in and out of prison, it was his second home. The judge read through his notes and asked Mikey to stand up first. His face was smiling and he didn't have any respect for any of the people sitting in the courtroom. Scott was white in his face and you could see him licking his bottom lip.

Scott's co-accused got slammed for three years for his part in the crime. Before he was led out of the dock by the G4S security guards he shouted back at Judge Merdock, he was waving his hands about in the air. "I'll do that on my head you old wanker. You can't break me, I'm a fucking warrior." Mikey's family giggled and kept their heads low. He was as daft as a brush for sure. Kendal sat forward in her seat and she was constantly playing with her fingers, the time had come for Scott to be dealt with. Her eyes closed slowly and she looked as if she was praying. Scott's brief stood up and made his plea for a lighter sentence, everything he was saying sounded good. He was making Scott sound like a saint. Kendal was on the brink of standing up and telling the courtroom the truth. The man who was stood before them was a bully, a control freak, an out and out bastard and she wanted the world to know that too but she controlled herself. Pat could see her face and gripped her by the arm. "Don't make a show of yourself love, it all comes to those who wait." Kendal looked deflated and she was hanging on every word said inside the courtroom. The time had finally come for Scott to be sentenced. As the judge read his name out to stand up Scott wobbled, his legs were giving way, there was no way in this world he was ready for prison. His face looked angelic and he was trying his best to look as innocent as possible. Judge Merdock coughed to clear his throat. Looking at the man stood in the dock he read out his fate.

"I sentence you to five years imprisonment." Kendal's face was on fire. Did she hear him right? Was Scott finally out of her hair for the next five years? She poked Pat in her stomach. "Did he get five years?" Pat nodded her head slowly as she watched her brother being led through the doors at the back of the courtroom. She knew he was a bastard but he was still her flesh and blood. Scott was trying to wriggle free and he was doing his best to get his face back up to the glass panel.

"Kendal, get down to the cells and see me before I get shipped out, do you hear me? Get your arse down there as soon as." Kendal smirked and stood to her feet, she was smiling like a Cheshire cat. She wanted to run up to the Judge and shake his hand for getting rid of her nightmare boyfriend.

Pat linked Kendal's arm as they left the courtroom. "Are you going down to the holding cells to see him or what?"

Kendal shook her head and she knew it was time to come clean to tell Pat her plans for the future. She prepared herself. "Pat, you have been like a sister to me, and I would have been dead if it wasn't for you. I'm leaving Scott and moving out of the area. This is my only chance to get away from him and make a better life for me and Ella May. If I don't do it now, I will never do it. I'm not adding fuel to the fire by saying goodbye to him; he will go sick if he sees me. Will you tell him goodbye from me? I know I'm a coward, but I think it's the best way."

Pat looked gobsmacked, her jaw was swinging. Never in a million years had she thought Kendal would have plucked up enough courage to leave her abusive partner. Half of her was happy for Kendal, but the other half of her was scared of what lay ahead for her in the future. Her brother would never let this go; he'd search for her until his dying breath. There was no way he would take it lying down. Pat hugged Kendal and a tear trickled down the side of her face.

"So, this is goodbye then. I won't say I will keep in touch, because the less I know the better. I just want you to be happy in life, and find what you deserve." Pat kissed her on the side of the cheek. "Goodbye love, be lucky."

Kendal choked up and tried her best not to cry. She walked away from the courtroom and for the first time in her life she felt free, the shackles from her legs had been broken and she now had a new life set out in front of her. With a spring in her step she ran towards the bus stop. Jane was minding Ella May for her and she knew she would be struggling with the toddler if she was left any longer.

★

Pat sat at the wooden table waiting for Scott to come out from the other side of the doors. There was a glass partition between them both and she was relieved that he couldn't get to her once she'd broken the news to him. The rattling of keys alerted Pat and she gulped as Scott walked inside the small room.

He sat down on his chair and his eyes were all over the place. "Where's Kendal?"

Pat took a deep breath and placed her hand onto the window to comfort him. "She's gone Scott, she's not coming back." He sprang to his feet and gritted his teeth together tightly.

"What do you mean? She's not coming. Where the fuck is she?"

Pat knew it was now or never and she broke the news to her brother the best way she could. He melted onto the floor, and she was stood up watching him from the other side of the glass. "No!" he screamed at the top of his voice. He was ragging his fingers through his hair and lifted his head up slowly. "Pat, I swear to you I'm going to kill her if she doesn't get her arse back here, she needs to come and see me. I've just had five years threw at me, what the fuck, is she thinking? Is she right in the bastard head or what?"

Pat sat back down in her chair, no wonder Kendal had left him, he was such a selfish bastard he was all about himself. The guards heard the commotion from outside and stepped into the room. Seeing Scott on the floor, they brought the visit to an end; they didn't trust him, he was a danger to himself.

"Right lad, come on, times up," the two guards walked towards him with caution, they were aware that he could strike at any minute. They were ready for action. Scott sprung to his feet and stood with his back up against the wall.

"It's going to take more than you two pricks to get me out of here. I haven't finished my visit yet, so fuck off until I'm ready." The security guards looked at each other and knew this lad was a first to prison life. Within seconds he was twisted up and lay with his face pressed against the cold concrete floor. His screams rattled the walls of the holding cells and all Pat could do was sit back and watch. As they pulled him to his feet his sister stood up from her chair.

"Scott calm down will you. You're just making it worse for yourself, just chill for a minute and think about this." Scott spat at the glass before he was dragged out of the room. Pat rubbed at her arms; goose pimples were all over her skin. "Silly bastard," she whispered under her breath. "No wonder she's fucking left you. Good riddance to bad rubbish, that's all I can say anyway. Do your rip Scott, you nob-head." Pat chuckled to herself before she left the room. She knew Scott would seek his revenge, but five years was a long way away, and hopefully by then Kendal Wilson would have found her feet and found the happiness she was seeking. Pat let out a hard laboured breath and made her way out of the holding cells.

Kendal ran into the front room and punched her clenched fist into the air. "The bastard got five years. I'm free for the first time ever. I can go where I want, eat where I want, fuck who I want, get in there. It's a whole new life for me Jane as from now. Today is the first day of the new me." Jane's face was sour, she was trying to force a smile but it was half-hearted. Kendal ran to her side and snuggled up next to her on the sofa. "Trust you to be preggers when I'm young free and single. Fucking hell Jane, we could have had a ball, remember how we used to be. You should have had an abortion like I did." Jane knew she was right and hated the thought of being a mother before her time. Her life was set out in stone and her future looked grim, she'd made the biggest mistake of her life. "Has John rung you yet, he said today I should get the keys for my new house." Jane was playing on her phone and she wasn't listening. "Jane, what's up with you? Aren't you listening to a word I'm saying?" Jane had heard everything she said but she pretended she hadn't. She hated the attention John was giving her friend lately, and she thought something was going on between them.

"What? I didn't hear you," she lied.

"Derrrr… I said, 'has John been in touch with you?' He said today is the day that I will get the keys to my new house in Middleton," her face was serious. "Jane you need to promise me that you won't tell anyone where I've moved too, because if anyone finds out they will tell Scott. And you know what he's like; he'll probably send someone round there to deal with me and all that. He said he would shave my hair off if I ever left him, you know?" Kendal looked in a trance and she seemed in a world of her own as she thought about the consequences of her actions. Jane nudged her with a firm hand.

"You would suit a skinhead anyway, I don't know what you're stressing for," Jane giggled and she was back to her normal self. As she stood up you could see the weight she'd gained during her pregnancy, she was a bloater. Kendal was so glad that she'd had her child aborted; she could never have left Scott if she'd have had another baby to care for. No way in this world, it was way too much. "Make me a butty or something Kendal, I'm starving. I swear I never feel full these days. John Daley's kid is sucking every bit of life out of me." Kendal walked into the kitchen, she was happy and singing. She'd never felt so happy in all her life.

"It's a weird feeling you know. Say I don't make it on my own. Say I miss Scott?"

Jane launched an old pot towel at her head from the front room. "Will you shut the fuck up? How can you miss a beating from your boyfriend?"

Kendal reached over to the fridge and grabbed the butter and some ham. "I've only ever had Scott to love me. Now my Nana's gone too, I feel alone." Jane choked back her tears, she was feeling so emotional lately and she was crying all the time. Walking to her friend's side she touched the top of her shoulder.

"I love you; you'll always have me no matter what. Friends forever ay?" Kendal turned to face her. When she saw the tears streaming down her face she knew she meant every word she'd just said.

"Yep, friends forever me and you I promise. Come on, don't be blubbering, you'll have me at it as well if you carry on like this." Kendal went back to making the sandwich for her friend. "Do you want pickles on this or what? I know you have a craving for them."

Jane giggled,"Yeah, bang about ten on it and cover it with mayonnaise too." Kendal squashed all the contents on the butty down and passed it to Jane who devoured it in seconds; she nearly bit her own fingers off.

"Shall we go for a walk to Asda after we've dropped Ella May off at playgroup; she's there until three o'clock so we could have a walk about to kill some time?" Jane pulled a face; she hated any form of exercise these days, she was so lazy.

"Orr, do we have too? Can't we just stay here and watch repeats of Jeremy Kyle? I swear, it was mint this morning, you will piss yourself laughing when you watch it." Kendal dragged her up by the arm.

"No, come on, you can get some fresh air you lazy cow. Grab your coat we're going out."

Jane was fighting a losing battle and she knew it. Under protest she slipped her jacket on and sat waiting while Kendal nipped to the toilet. Ella May was awake now and she wanted attention. Jane watched the kid crying and sighed. She didn't have one motherly bone in her body. She turned her head pretending she couldn't see the child at the side of her.

Jane and Kendal strolled up Rochdale Road. The sun was beaming down today, although it was still quite cold. Jane seemed to be waddling, she was only a few months pregnant but she was acting like the baby could fall out of her at any minute. Kendal was relaxed, her usually stressed manner had left her, she was like a different woman. Ella May was loving playgroup and she was mixing well with all the children there. Mrs Jackson had asked for a word with Kendal after school, regarding Ella May and she was picking her brains as to what the teacher could want her for.

The Harpurhey precinct was buzzing with shoppers. The local market was on and you could hear people shouting in the distance. Young lads were on the corners selling cheap tobacco and sleeves of cigs, everyone loved a bargain. Kendal went to get a shopping trolley and she could see a woman staring at her from across the way. The woman was dressed to the nines and looked out of place in these settings. Jane came to her side and her face was bright red. "For fucks sake, Jackie's over there. Look at the tart staring at me." Kendal looked flustered.

"I thought she was looking at me. I swear to you she's not took her eyes off me." Jane kept her head low, she kept sneaking a peak at Jackie as they made their way into the shopping centre.

"Fucking hell, she's coming in here with us." Jane went white as a sheet, she was crumbling and her legs were buckling as she tried to hide away in an aisle close by. Kendal was confident for a change and stood her ground, she had nothing to hide and if this woman wanted to start any shit with her she was ready. Jane was waving her hand frantically at Kendal. "Hurry up get over here before she sees us." Kendal rammed her two fingers over at her.

"Nar, I'm soldiering it. If she's got anything to say, let her come here and say it. I'm not hiding from anybody anymore." Kendal turned to push her silver shopping trolley and Jackie Wilson was stood tall in front of her. Their eyes locked and for a split second nobody spoke. "Excuse me," Kendal snarled. Jackie was having none of it and gritted her pearly white teeth together.

"Double of your Dad aren't you."

Kendal fidgeted about, she was lost for words. "I think you've got me mixed up with somebody else love, can you move out of my way, I'm trying to do my shopping." Jane could see them talking from where she stood, she'd had enough she was ready to face her demons, she darted to Kendal's side ready for action.

"Are you alright Kendal?" Jackie looked Jane up and down and held her head back chuckling.

"Yep, you must be right; I've got you mixed you up with somebody else."

Jackie moved her foot from the trolley and headed into the store. Her Chanel perfume was still lingering in the air near them both. Jane nudged Kendal in the waist.

"What the fuck did she say to you, is she on to me or what?" Kendal looked puzzled and watched Jackie in the distance.

"She said nothing really; she thought I was somebody else."

Jane let out a hard laboured breath. "Thank fuck for that. I swear, I thought she was on to me. Why was she looking at me though, I bet it was me being paranoid wasn't it?" Kendal nodded, she was still concerned by the conversation she'd just had.

"Yeah, she's gone now anyway, let's get on with the shopping, ignore the tart."

Kendal continued shopping, when she got to the checkout she lifted her head up from packing her bags. A few tills down, Jackie was there laughing with the checkout girl. Kendal was in two minds whether to march back down to her and ask her what she meant by her comment, but she'd lost her nerve. Jackie looked as hard as nails and she didn't fancy her chances against her.

As they left the store Jane was still pecking Kendal's head. "Did you see her Kendal; she's not a patch on me. I mean, come on. I know I've not had a wash today and that but I give her a ten break don't I?"

Kendal lied, "Yeah she's an old hag. You're well nicer than her; she was like mutton dressed as lamb." Jane looked relieved and stood tall. If the truth was known, Jackie was a class act. Everything about her was neat and tidy and she looked like a glamorous model. Kendal's mobile phone started ringing. Grabbing it from her pocket she smiled at Jane. "It's John, I bet he's sorted the house out for me," Jane chewed on her bottom lip and her face creased at both sides.

"Why didn't he phone me, I could have told you what was going on?"

"Hi John, yeah I'm just out in Harpurhey at the minute. I'll be back home in about an hour," she held her ear to the phone and she was concentrating. "Okay, see you soon." Jane trudged to her side.

"Does he want to talk to me?" Kendal shook her head.

"No, he was just phoning about the house."

Jane was green with jealousy. "Well, he knows I'm always with you. I'll tell you what Kendal; if you're shagging him I'll do you in big time." Kendal's mouth dropped. Jane just couldn't hold her thoughts in any longer and opened fire. "It's not right; if John was your fella you would go sick if he was phoning me all the time. He's up your arse," her voice was sarcastic as she mimicked John. "Yeah Kendal I'll do that for you, I'll help you get a new house. I'm fucking sick to the back teeth of it. You can tell him to fuck off in future."

Kendal was shocked, she'd never thought about it from Jane's point of view, but there was no way she was backing down. "Stop being a paranoid bitch. John is a friend of the family, and he promised my Nana on her death bed that he would look after me. Are you begrudging me a bit of help to get myself sorted, because if you are, you can fuck right off now? I would never touch John, he's like the Dad I never had." Jane was calming down and realised she'd overreacted. Her hormones were all over the place.

"I'm just saying that's all. Oh, just ignore me; I'm a hormonal bitch at the moment." They stood apart and waited for the taxi to come; you could have cut the atmosphere with a knife.

Not a word was spoken between the girls in the taxi. The driver kept looking through his rear-view mirror and he could tell something had gone on. "Drop me here," Jane said to him. Kendal kept her eyes on the car window at the side of her and she'd well and truly spit her dummy out. "I'll ring you later," Jane said.

"Yeah, whatever," Kendal answered her. Once she was gone out of the car door, the driver spoke.

"Bloody hell, have you two fallen out?"

Kendal ignored him and kept her eyes low. "Nosey fucker," she whispered under her breath.

★

As Kendal stood with all the other parents in the yard waiting to pick Ella May up from school, her mind was filled with all the new exciting things that were happening in her life, she felt like a new woman. The wooden gates opened and Mrs Jackson was stood there smiling at the parents, she walked towards Kendal with her bucked teeth sticking out of the front of her mouth. "Mrs Wilson," she called out in a high pitched voice. "Can I have a quick word with you?" Kendal trudged towards her and entered the building, this woman was a jobsworth and grabbed parents in for meetings at the slightest thing. Mrs Jackson was a round fat woman. Her hair was steel grey and it looked like wire wool. The chains hanging from the side of her glasses made Kendal smile; they were so ancient and reminded her of her old teacher Mrs Buble.

The teacher escorted Kendal into a small office at the side of the corridor; there wasn't a soul about, it felt so eerie. "Don't you worry about Ella May, I've asked the teachers to keep hold of her until we've finished." Kendal was worried, this meeting seemed so corporate and nothing like the others she'd attended. White pieces of paper were stacked high on the table, and it looked like Mrs Jackson was ready to lay the law down to Kendal. She'd only been late a few times for school with her child, but nothing to bring on this big meeting. Kendal sat down on the green leather chair and watched the teacher close the door behind her. She sat cracking her knuckles. As Mrs Jackson sat down she smiled at her from over of her gold glasses. "Don't look so worried sweetheart, I don't bite. I just need to get all this paperwork signed off for Ella May. I sent this letter home about three weeks ago and you still haven't handed it back in," she raised her eyebrows with disappointment. Kendal was fidgeting, this was her worse nightmare. She was locked inside a room with a teacher. Her face was burning up and she felt suffocated.

"Can I have a drink of water please, I don't feel too good." This was just the excuse she needed to get out of the office and avoid any humiliation. Mrs Jackson walked to the side of the room, and placed a glass under the tap. Walking back she placed it down next to Kendal.

"Right, where were we? Oh, yes," she said as her hand flicked through the paperwork with her fingers. "I need you to read through these forms and fill out the questionnaire, it's simple yes or no answers." Kendal was worried, small beads of sweat were forming on her brow. At that moment she regretted falling out with Jane because her friend would have got her out of the mess for sure. Jane always saved her bacon at times like this; she knew exactly what to say to hide her secret. Kendal held the black pen in her hands and her eyes were fixed onto the pieces of paper on the table. She could feel Mrs Jackson's eyes on her from the other side of the table. Twisting the pen in her fingers she knew she had to act quickly. Dropping the pen on the floor she hung her head low, the teacher moved forward in her chair to get a better look.

"I feel so hot; can I get out of here and get some fresh air?"

Mrs Jackson sprang to her feet. "Come along with me. We can do this after you've had a few breaths of fresh air. I must admit these offices do get warm at times; they make you feel all hot and clammy. I know that first-hand, I'm stuck in them all day," she smirked. Kendal played the part of a sick woman well, she would have got an Oscar for her performance; she was the leading lady for sure. Mrs Jackson paced to the door at the side of the corridor and opened the fire exit. She made sure Kendal was getting all the air she needed. A few other office staff came outside to see what the drama was, but the teacher hurried them along telling them everything was fine. Kendal's head felt like it was going to explode, she'd never felt so vulnerable in all her life. How was she ever going to get out of this one? In the past Scott had dealt with all the paperwork, but now she was alone and felt like a piece of meat being thrown to the lions.

Being led back to the office felt like the walk of death to Kendal. Every step she took was small and she was trembling inside. Mrs Jackson sat down and pushed the paper towards her again, she was watching her like a hawk, she was sure she was hiding something. With her sausage fingers she underlined the area where she wanted her to read. Kendal tried her best to sound out the words but her mind was going blank, she was under so much pressure. Mrs Jackson spoke in a calm voice.

"Please, don't take this the wrong way Mrs Wilson, but can you read and write?" The words were stuck on Kendal's tongue and all her fears hit her at once, this was the first time she'd been uncovered for being illiterate. A single tear rolled down the side of her face and she held her hands up to cover her face, she was humiliated. The teacher jumped from her seat and walked to the window sill and grabbed a box of tissues.

"Now, now. There's no need for tears. A lot of people can't read or write. It's nothing to be ashamed about." Her words crucified Kendal, her secret was out. She lifted her head up slowly and looked the woman in the eyes. This was the first time she'd ever told anyone her secret.

"You're right, I can't read or write. I feel so ashamed. I just never learnt in school, I was always bunking off."

Mrs Jackson loved a challenge and this girl was right up her street. Clutching her hand tightly she calmed her down with a gentle voice. "My father was illiterate too. I can help you learn if you want to?" Kendal looked the teacher right into her eyes, she looked so sympathetic. Searching deep inside her soul she said the words that would change her life forever.

"Would you really, would you help me?" The woman choked back her tears and nodded her head; her heart went out to Kendal.

"Everyone has the right to education sweetie. It would be my pleasure to teach you." Kendal realised what she'd just said and was still in two minds as to whether to accept the offer or not. Could she ever face a classroom again? What if she was that thick that her mind wouldn't take in all the information, she was stuttering. "Can I think about it? I'm not sure if it's what I want?"

Mrs Jackson was selling education now and she had Kendal's full attention. "Do it for Ella May, just think you'll be able to read to her every night at bedtime, and fill out all your own forms. Learning to read and write will open so many doors for you and your family; you just need to believe in yourself."

Kendal couldn't reply. She kept her head low and wanted the ground to open up and swallow her, her heart was beating ten to the dozen. Mrs Jackson was pressing for an answer and she wasn't letting up. "I'll leave it with you, but if you want me to help you, come and see me. Ella May is in playgroup every day, so we can do it then." Kendal stood to her feet and headed towards the door, she couldn't wait to get out of the place. She'd fallen into a thousand pieces.

"Thanks Mrs Jackson, if I decide to come I'll let you know." Kendal left the room and ran to the classroom to pick up her daughter. Her face was white and she was suffocating, her windpipe was closing up and she feared she was going to collapse. She was having a full blown panic attack.

★

Kendal sat in the house waiting for John Daley to call. With a desperate look on her face she crept into her bedroom. Pulling a large box from under the bed her hands searched frantically through the jumble. Her heart stopped beating for a second as she picked up her mother's diary in her hands. Holding it to her chest she gasped for air, her eyelids flickered rapidly. Slowly her hands opened the diary. The words inside it were all a blur to her and she hated that she could never read the last few months of her mother's life. Closing her eyes, she gripped the book close to her heart and you could see her fingers digging deep into it, she was pressing it into her chest. The decision was made. Kendal was going to learn how to read and write.

CHAPTER ELEVEN

Kendal sat in her new home and smiled. This was it, a new beginning for her and Ella May. John had made sure she had a nice abode and even the furniture was top of the range. It was their little secret that he'd helped her out with the furniture and sworn her to secrecy to keep her trap shut. Jane knew of course, but she didn't know of all the cash he was bunging her behind her back. Kendal liked it that way and kept her lips sealed.

Jane sat on the chair opposite Kendal and she was watching The Jeremy Kyle Show whilst she was munching on some hot toast. She was always eating lately and you could see she'd banged on a few stones, especially around her waist. The two girls made friends not long after they'd fallen out and it was normal these days that they had cross words. Jane was ready for dropping her baby anytime soon. She looked like a beached whale that needed harpooning. Her cheeks were full and her face looked bloated, she was always hot and sweaty. Kendal looked at the clock and sighed. "Come on Ella May, let's get you to playgroup before we're late, we don't want Mrs Jackson on our case do we?" Jane kicked her feet up onto the chair and made herself comfortable, there was no way she was going out with her, it was freezing. She snuggled down into the armchair. Jane often stayed with Kendal in her new house and she'd made it quite clear to John that she needed her own house too. I mean, there she was having his kid and she was still living at home with her parents. No, she'd told him straight to pull his finger out of his arse and get her sorted as soon as possible. Kendal had already told Jane about Mrs Jackson teaching her to read and write and Jane told her blatantly that there was no way in the world she was ever going back into education, she'd had enough the first time around. Kendal loved that she was learning new skills and she seemed different in herself, she was more confident. Even when she looked at herself in the mirror she had to pinch herself because she didn't recognise the woman she'd become. Her once saddened face was full of happiness and she was on her way to better life, she was content. Jane hated that her best friend was bettering herself and if the truth was known she would have loved to have gone back to school too, but becoming a new mother soon she knew that that would never happen, she would never find the time. Kendal was getting right up her nose lately and she was so far up her own arse it was untrue, Jane hated the person Kendal was becoming.

Kendal dropped Ella May off in her classroom and stood for a minute looking at the notice boards, her eyes squinted together. She was smirking to herself and knew that one day soon she could stand there with all the parents and discuss whatever was written. It was funny how just learning to read and write would let her into so many circles that she'd been banished from in the past. Even when people discussed world events from the newspapers Kendal would have no idea what they were going on about, but that was all changing now.

Scott had tried to contact Kendal many times in the past, he was a nightmare and changing her phone number was the only way she could get rid of his nuisance calls. She'd seen his sister Pat weeks before and she'd told her just how bad Scott was without her, he'd been involved

in numerous fights inside the prison, and Pat blamed it all
on the anger he was carrying about for Kendal, he was a
ticking bomb. Scott's sister told her straight that she feared
for Kendal's life if her brother ever got his hands on her.
Kendal was scared and she had every right to be.

Kendal knocked on Mrs Jackson's office door with
a gentle tap. She'd been going to see her for months and
nobody ever questioned why she was a regular face on
the school's premises. Nothing was running smoothly at
first when she started to learn and it was only recently
that Kendal felt like she was getting to grips with things.
Books were scattered across the table when Kendal sat
down and curled the edge of the paper with her fingertip.
Mrs Jackson, who Kendal now called Betty, sat down at
the table and looked relieved that her pupil had turned up
again. She opened the books and started the lesson where
they'd left off last time. Kendal seemed distracted today,
and the constant ringing of the phone behind her was
making her lose her concentration, she kept twisting her
head over her shoulder looking at the phone.

"Just ignore it," Betty said. "It will only be one of
our suppliers at this time, they can phone back later."
Kendal pointed at the glossy book and sounded out a
word, her lips changed shape as she sounded out the
words. Betty was hanging on the finished word but when
Kendal couldn't grasp it, you could see her deflating
and shaking her head with frustration. Betty studied her
face and moved in closer. "Kendal is everything alright
today? You just don't seem your normal self." Betty rested
her elbows on the desk and waited for an answer. As a
flashback occurred in Kendal's mind, she could see herself
sat in her old classroom with all the other pupils laughing
and shouting and throwing things at her. The teacher was

stood over her waiting for her to start reading.

"Der.... thicko, Kendal doesn't know how to read. Come on Miss, let someone else have a go, she's a waste of space," John Warburton shouted out. The lad was a pupil in the same class as Kendal and he was a right gobshite, he'd made her life a misery. The words she heard in her head seemed real and she covered her ears as if she was back in her old classroom. Her face changed and she hammered her fist onto the table, her knuckles were red raw, she snapped.

"Listen Betty, I don't think this is for me. It's taking ages to learn me anything. I'm too thick for you to teach me, I can't do it." Betty gripped her by the hands and squeezed them tightly. There was no way she was giving up on this woman.

"You're not too thick at all; you're just having an off day, it happens all the time when you're learning. Take a few deep breaths and let's start again. Just try and calm down." Kendal dragged her hands away and stood to her feet, her chest was rising with speed.

"It's too hard, my mind keeps going blank and I feel," she paused and wrapped her hands around her body and rocked slowly, "I feel useless." If Kendal was true to herself Scott was lying heavily on her mind, and speaking to Pat had spooked her. She knew he would never let her go without a fight, and she hated that he was still in her head.

Betty walked to her side, "Come on let's go and have a fag break. I could do with one too," she raised a smile and knew it would calm her down, she changed the subject. "I'm trying to give up, but once a smoker always a smoker I suppose," she giggled and dipped her head into her handbag looking for her cigarettes. Kendal was ready for getting on her toes, but as she looked at Betty her feet seemed to be glued to the floor. This woman had put so much work into her and she was letting her down if she left. They both headed to a secret location for the smokers in the school. Betty looked like a naughty child as she hid away behind the corner out of sight. Kendal lit her cigarette and inhaled deeply, she more than needed this blast of nicotine.

Betty was not only a teacher to Kendal now, she was becoming a friend to her too. Kendal held lots of stuff back from her though, she hadn't told her about her ex-boyfriend or about her life in the past, she held that close to her heart. There was a time when she was going to bring her mother's diary into school for Betty to read to her but she had second thoughts and left it at home. Mary's diary was personal and she wanted to be the first person to read her mother's thoughts when she'd learnt to read.

"Sometimes it's going to be hard Kendal" Betty said as she exhaled a large white puff of smoke, "you will have up and down days and you'll feel like you want to give up. You're stronger than you think, and I know you will conquer your fears." Kendal blew smoke from her mouth hoping it would make her invisible for a minute. Her eyes were welling up and she didn't want Betty to see her. Stubbing her fag out on the floor Betty smiled softly and held her hand out towards Kendal. "Come on love, don't give up. You're doing so well."

Kendal stood as if she was in a trance; her mind was all over the place. The easiest thing to have done would have been to walk away, and carry on with her illiterate life. She'd covered up for this long; she could just carry on like she'd done before. Betty was edgy and stood cupping her hands together; she blew her warm breath onto them. "Come on, let's get back inside, it's freezing out here, you'll catch your death of cold." Kendal hesitated and followed her slowly, every step she took seemed like she was in two minds as to whether she was going to carry on. Before she knew it she was walking along the blue corridor heading back inside the office. Betty was a wise old woman and she made sure they walked past Ella May's classroom on the way back. As she peered through the small window she could see all the children on the grey carpet settling down for a story. This was just what she was hoping for.

"Come and have a look at Ella May's face. It's story time." Kendal moved forward and squashed her face up to the glass. Betty gave a cunning smile, her job was done. Kendal's heart melted as she watched her child listening to the story. The teacher's voice was soft and calming and all the toddlers' faces seemed fascinated by the characters in the story. Kendal watched her child with eager eyes and knew at that moment that if she ended her education, Ella May would suffer in the future.

Turning her head slowly she looked at Betty who was smiling from ear to ear. "Okay, I'll give it another go, but don't expect miracles. Rome wasn't built in a day."

Betty chuckled and playfully pushed Kendal along. "It would have been if I'd been the foreman." The sound of their heels clipping along the vinyl corridor echoed down the hallway, Betty was humming a song as she walked along.

★

Jane sat in the house. She appeared bored as she twisted her hair around her finger. Her favourite TV show had gone off now and she was looking for something to occupy herself. Walking into Kendal's bedroom she opened the wardrobe. Her eyes focused on all the new outfits in there. Sticking her hand inside, she separated the clothes so she could look at them in more details. Her face was red and she was green with envy. Slamming the wardrobe door shut, she could see a pair of red shoes sticking out from underneath the bed. She moved quickly towards them. Bending slowly she reached to grab one. Jane paused, her eyes focused on a box she could just about see from underneath the bed.

Curiosity got the better of her and she lay flat on the floor so she could grip it properly. She was huffing and puffing as her body tried to roll deeper under the bed. Jane's face was concentrating and her tongue was hanging from the side of her mouth. "Come here, you little bastard," she moaned. Sitting up on the floor she placed the box on her lap. She was a right nosey bitch and she couldn't wait to look inside it. Slowly she pulled the lid off it. Her brow was trickling with sweat. As she searched deep into the box, she pulled out some old photographs of Paddy and Nelly. Holding them out in front of her she giggled to herself. "Fucking hell Nelly, look at the size of you here, you must have eaten a few pies back in your day I can tell you." Her hands flicked through the old snaps and she was smirking. Suddenly her eyes fixed on a white card. This was John's business card with his number on it, just like the one he'd given her when he first started seeing her. Her nostrils flared and she closed her eyes. Slowly she squeezed the card together with all her might. "I fucking knew it, you conniving tart. Here's me believing that John is just helping you out, when it's quite obvious he's banging your brains out. What a fool

I've been, why didn't I see it? Kendal you slag, just you wait. I'll fix you for sure, just you wait and see."

Jane searched high and low in the box for more evidence that John was sleeping with her best friend, but there was nothing. Her mind was working overtime and she was putting two and two together and coming up with five. Her hormones were all over the place and she just wasn't thinking straight. Holding a diary in her hands, she let out a menacing laugh. "Well, you'll never know about your mother now, will you? You think you're smart learning to read and all that, well, you'll never read your mother's diary because I'm taking it with me. An eye for an eye and all that." Jane stood up and dug the book down the front of her baggy trousers; she was talking to herself as she paced about the bedroom. "Keep your friends close, but your enemies closer, that what they say isn't it? Well, just you watch Kendal Wilson you're going to come down to earth with a bang when I've finished with you. What a dick head I've been."

★

Kendal walked out of the classroom when the bell rang; it was time to pick Ella May up. Betty ran after her and touched her shoulder. "You've done great today, you're really coming along. Just think of all the doors this will open for you."

Kendal was shy, her cheeks blushing; she'd never been praised before. "I want to be an author one day Betty," she dipped her head low as if the dream was too big for her. She continued with a giggle in her talk. "Who knows, with your help I might even get there one day."

Betty rubbed her hands together with excitement. "The world is your oyster my dear. Go for your heart's

desires, anything is possible if you believe in yourself."
Kendal walked off and waved her hand over her shoulder.

"See you tomorrow Betty, get some nice biscuits
in for a change. Them 'Morning Coffee' ones taste like
cardboard," she joked. Betty disappeared back into her
office, her job was done for today.

Ella May was playing up and as soon as she got out
of playgroup she was moaning. Even walking home with
her was a struggle; the child kept sitting on the floor and
refusing to move. Kendal was at breaking point as she
scooped her up from the floor. A man was stood near the
bus stop in the distance and he was watching the goings
on, his neck was stretched. He was a good looking guy
and slightly older than Kendal. As Ella May finally got to
her feet he could see Kendal dragging her along by the
hood of her coat. The bus shelter was busy and people
raised their eyes as the child started whinging again. The
man stood near Ella May and started to make funny
faces at her, instantly Ella May stopped crying and began
giggling. Kendal followed her child's eyes and focused on
the man stood next to her. Her jaw dropped, he was eye
candy for sure. The male had raven black hair and a body
to die for. Kendal had to shake her head to stop gawping
at him, she was drooling.

"Is she tired? They're always like that when they need
a sleep. My sister's kids are always moody when they need
some shut eye." Kendal fidgeted about, this guy was too
good to be true, he even knew about childcare too. Ella
May took to him straight away and he was keeping her
amused. He introduced himself as Steve. The two of them
never stopped talking from the moment they met; it was
like they'd known each other for years. He had a wicked
sense of humour and he had Kendal in stitches laughing

with his one liners. The bus came and Steve helped Kendal board the bus with Ella May, he was being so helpful. Sitting next to each other on the bus you could see he was getting ready to ask a question, he looked agitated as he licked his dry lips.

"Do you want to go out for a drink?" Kendal wanted the ground to open up and swallow her. She'd not been on the dating scene for years, and she looked uncomfortable as she played with the cuff from her sleeve. He poked her in her waist with his slender finger. "Well, come on then. I need an answer; I have to get off the bus at the next stop." Kendal was bright red, and she was stuck for words. He pulled a white piece of paper from his pocket and quickly scribbled his phone number. As he passed it her he whispered. "Give me a ring tonight and we can get to know each other properly. I'm not a rapist or anything like that, so you don't need to worry." Steve stood to his feet and made his way along the moving bus, he kept twisting his head over his shoulder as he walked to the front of the vehicle, he was a player for sure. Ella May was shouting after him and he waved his hand back at her. He was gone.

Kendal held the phone number in her hand; her heart was beating faster than normal. Hearing, banging at the side of her head she turned to face the window. Steve was stood there and he was blowing kisses to her, everyone on the bus was watching her. "Ring me later," he shouted at the top of his voice. Kendal dipped her head low as the bus set off again. Ella May was crying after Steve as the bus left his side and she was doing her best to comfort her. Jane was never going to believe what had just happened, never in a million years.

Jane snarled as she heard the front door open. She sat

up straight in her chair and scooped her hair back from her face. Ella May came running in first, closely followed by Kendal. "You're never going to believe what's just happened, never," Kendal had Jane's attention.

"What, go on then, stop wasting time, just tell me you crank. You know I hate waiting," Jane hissed. Kendal plonked down on the arm of the chair and rubbed her hands together with excitement.

"A guy just hit on me at the bus stop. I swear, there I was just sorting out that mard arse over there," she pointed at Ella May who was playing with her doll on the floor. "And, this guy called Steve starting flirting with me. He was good looking as well." Jane raised her eyes to the ceiling. Kendal always kicked the arse out of any story she was telling and Jane just wanted her to get to the nitty gritty. "He give me his number, and he wants me to ring him tonight," she covered her face with her hands. Jane snatched the number from her fingers; she wanted to see it with her own two eyes before she believed her. Once she seen the name Steve on it she flung it back at her.

"Why are you getting chuffed about a guy giving you his number anyway? Are you that desperate for a man? It sounds to me like the guy's a crank. Don't tell me you're going to ring him? You don't know him from Adam. He could be a wrong un." Kendal let out a laboured breath; she was sick to death of her friend's negative outlook on life and told her straight.

"Listen here you, why are you being so off with me lately? I just don't mean now, you've been gunning for me for days. What's your problem?" Jane should have spat out what was troubling her, but she wasn't sure if she was right. She hunched her shoulders and grabbed the remote control from the table.

"Nothing's up with me, I'm just a bit fucked off lately. I mean, look at the state of me." Kendal stood to her feet and plonked down on the chair facing her.

"Well, you were the one who thought you knew it all. I told you not to have a baby didn't I, but oh no, Mrs know it all thought she knew better. It's your own fault you're feeling like this." Jane was fuming and sat cracking her knuckles, her temper was boiling. She waved her hand in front of her.

"Ring him then, I was just saying, that's all. Just don't come crying to me when he ends up being a fucking weirdo."

"Don't worry I won't," Kendal cursed. Jane reached for her mobile phone and rang John. He should have been there hours ago to pick her up, but he was late again. Kendal sniggered and thought she would give her a taste of her own medicine. "Is he not answering again?" she kept her eyes fixed on Jane waiting for an answer.

"No he's fucking not, so get off my case," she snapped.

Kendal stood up and placed her hand on her hips; she was ready for action she was ready to tell Jane some well needed home truths. "I don't blame him for not answering you. I tell you what Jane, you've changed. You're a miserable self-centred cow lately, where's the old Jane gone?"

With that, World War Three broke out and they were ready for scratching each other's eyeballs out. Jane sprang to her feet and ran at Kendal; she gripped her fingers in her hair and ragged her about like a rag doll, it was going off big time. "Get off me, will you Jane. I won't hit you while you're pregnant." Jane was like a woman possessed and all her anger was out in full force. She let go of Kendal's hair and stood tall, her breathing was struggled and she took a while to get her breath again.

"You think you've got it all worked out don't you Kendal? Well, mark my words you'll come down to earth with a bang one of these days you will and I for one hope I'm there to see you fall. You say I've changed?" she rolled her eyes as she continued. "Well, take a good look in the fucking mirror love, because it's you who's changed. You think you're better than me now that you're learning to read and write. Well, let's get that straight, you're fucking not. You'll always be fucked up Kendal Wilson no matter what." Kendal was raging and although she wouldn't raise her hands to Jane there was no way she was letting her get away with that, she retaliated.

"You've got room to talk. You'll always be second best to Jackie; if John was going to leave her he would have done it years ago. Admit it, go on; you're just a shag-bag who got knocked up by an old man." Ella May was screaming and she ran to her mother's side, she was scared. Jane backed off and looked for her coat. Turning her head slowly she walked to the living room door and darted her eyes at Kendal.

"I hope Scott finds you and deals with you proper. You deserve everything that's coming to you. You'll always be nothing Kendal, the sooner you realise it the better. I'm done with you for good." The front door banged shut and shook the house. Kendal paced the room and she was crying with temper, her teeth were gritted together.

"I'll show her, the daft bitch," she mumbled under her breath. "Just you wait and see Jane, you'll eat them words you will, just you wait and see."

Later, Kendal sat looking at Steve's phone number. Ella May was asleep in bed and she was bored. Slowly picking her phone up, she dialled his number. Her face cringed as she spoke to him. "Hi Steve, it's me Kendal, do you remember from the bus stop today?" She was giggling and within seconds she started to relax. The call lasted about half an hour and Steve was invited around to the house the following week. She knew this was all happening too quickly but she was lonely and needed some company. Jane was her best friend and after the last argument she knew their friendship was over for good.

A week later, Steve walked into the house holding two bottles of red wine and four cans of Stella. They'd been talking constantly on the phone all week. He pecked her on the cheek and sat down on the sofa. He was looking hotter than ever wearing a pair of stone-washed jeans and fitted black t-shirt. Kendal was hovering, she didn't know what to do; she'd never entertained a man before and this was all new to her. Running in the kitchen she searched for two glasses, she was frantic. Quickly checking her face in her reflection in the window she headed back. "Did you find my house okay, it's a bit of a nightmare to find isn't it," she was trying to make conversation.

"Yeah, my mate used to live up here so I'm quite familiar with these parts." His eyes were all over her and for a minute, she looked scared. "Come and park your arse then," he laughed. "I don't bite you know. Well, not unless you asked me to." Kendal sneaked in at the side of him and opened one of the bottles of wine, she needed something to steady her nerves, she was trembling inside. The wine trickled into the glasses and she couldn't wait to gulp her first mouthful. Starting to relax she kicked her shoes off and curled her feet up at the side of her. She hated her crusty feet and hid them away out of sight behind a pillow.

The two of them were getting on like a house on

fire and before long their first kiss began. Kendal was pissed and she was more than willing to have sex with him. Steve kissed her neck slowly and his mouth slid over her soft skin cherishing every touch of her flesh. This was nothing like the sex she'd had with Scott in the past, this was bang on and just like she'd seen on TV. Two bodies lay naked on the sofa and before long he was inside her. Kendal dug her fingernails deep into his back and you could see her face change as he slid in and out of her. Something strange was happening and without any warning she let out a sexual moan, she'd reached her first orgasm. Steve was gentle and his body tensed as he came too. Small beads of sweat were scattered all over his body and his face changed as he found heaven. Kendal's body was quivering and she felt like a real woman. If this was proper sex, than she was having more of it, that's for sure. She never imagined it could be as fulfilling as this. Scott was like a pig in a fit when they had sex and she never knew that an orgasm was part of the parcel during sex, she felt cheated.

Reaching over, she grabbed the cigs from the floor and passed one to Steve. They both lay smoking as their bodies came back to normality. Kendal was relaxed with him and spoke softly. "That's the best sex I've ever had." Steve patted her arm and held his head back.

"Yep, no doubt it was. I'm a lover not a fighter and I always make sure I look after my woman in the bedroom." Steve was so full of himself and to him Kendal was just another notch on his belt.

Kendal sunk her head low and hid her face away. "Was I any good, or was I just a waste of space? My ex-boyfriend said it was like shagging a wet lettuce when he was having sex with me, so I just wanted to know."

Steve sat up and gripped her face gently in his hands; his warm sweet breath tickled her face. "Your boyfriend was a prick then wasn't he? You're gorgeous Kendal, and sex with you is special." Her eyes welled up and she knew at that moment that Steve was a keeper, he was her saviour. The two of them spoke into the early hours and he asked her to be his girlfriend. Life for Kendal couldn't have got any better and all her problems seemed to fade away into the background. She knew one day soon she would have to face her fears, but for now, she was living for the moment.

Jane gave birth to a baby girl a week later. One of Kendal's friends told her all about it and she said Jane was in a right state after it. Apparently the father of the baby had left her and she was gunning for him big time. John Daley knew the two girls had fallen out and liked it that way. He was still going to see Kendal on a regular basis and loved being near her without Jane hogging the limelight.

Night-time fell and Kendal stood looking out from her bedroom window. Steve was asleep and his gentle snoring was making her smile. Looking at the moonlight she gripped her body tightly. The days to Scott's release date were ticking away fast and she knew he would be hot on her trail as soon as the prison gates opened. Steve knew about her abusive ex-partner but she'd never told him about the threats he'd made about her from inside the prison walls.

Creeping back to her bed, she spooned Steve and dug her head into the small of his back. He was her knight in shining armour; she just hoped he would slay the dragon that was Scott, when he made his move. It was only a matter of time before Scott reared his ugly head into her life again; the clock was ticking for sure.

CHAPTER TWELVE

Scott gazed out of his prison window; his hands gripped the cold iron bars as he inhaled the gentle breeze from outside. Today was the day he'd been waiting for, this was his release day. He'd served two and a half years in the notorious jail in Manchester called Strangeways. His face told you that his time there hadn't been easy. Deep creases in his skin formed around his mouth and his skin looked saggy due to the weight he'd lost; his hair looked a lot thinner. Turning his head slowly he looked at his worldly goods lying on the bed in front of him. The grey blanket spread across the bed looked old and sweaty and if it could have spoken it would have told you all about the tears this man had cried over the years.

Scott hurried back to his bed when he heard the rattling of keys outside his cell door. His body was shaking inside and he still couldn't believe his sentence was over. Scott had been in a single cell throughout his sentence and his social skills had left him a long time ago, he was a solitary prisoner. His head dipped low as he gripped the black sports bag from his bed, yanking it over his shoulder he headed out of the place he'd called home for the last few years. The screw smiled at him but Scott just growled and tried to avoid any eye contact with him. Conversation was non-existent as he trudged along the prison landing. A few of the inmates shouted over to him from across the landing, but Scott didn't answer them he just waved his hand above his head and carried on walking.

After all the paperwork had been completed Scott

stood waiting to leave the prison. A few other inmates were due to be released with him today and they stood bouncing about waiting for the main gates to open. The others cons were excited and they were cracking jokes to each other. "Oh, I can't wait to get me some pussy," the young inmate chuckled at the side of Scott. "Three years these babies haven't been emptied for," he scooped his nuts in his hands and swayed them about. "I swear I'm going to be like a stallion all night long. Who's coming to a brass gaff with me then?" Scott raised a smile. Sex was the last thing on his mind and he had bigger fish to fry.

"Nar mate, not me. I've got to get home. You go and enjoy yourself, give her one from me," he sniggered. The daylight hit the inmate's eyes and Scott held his hand over his forehead. The sun was bright and the weather was warm. Seeing a silver Astra car parked in the distance he walked towards it with a bounce in his steps. Mikey was stood on the pavement and he was holding a bottle of brandy out in his hands.

"Come on fucking "McVicar"; get this down your neck." The lads hugged each other and Scott got in the passenger side of the car. Scott twisted the gold top off the brandy bottle and swallowed a large mouthful.

"Take me home Mikey ay. I've got things to sort out today, my head's spinning I just need to get my head sorted out, my head's blowing up." Mikey smiled and turned the engine over. He knew more than anyone how weird it felt to be released from jail and obeyed his mate's order. The day has finally come for Scott to set the record straight. His face stared out of the window and he looked in a trance, he held a menacing look in his eyes.

★

Kendal sat looking through the newspaper, and she was really reading it now, not just looking at the pictures. Ella May was at school and Kendal was ready to go to work. Mrs Jackson had helped her to get a part-time teacher's assistant job in the school where she worked and she loved every day, that was her life now. Steve was working away on the railways and she was missing him madly, he wasn't due home for another week. If she was true to herself she knew he was a player and he'd lost interest in her a long time ago, but she just plodded along, happy with the whole set up. Locking the front door she turned her head over her shoulder, she thought somebody was watching her and she was edgy. Kendal knew Scott had been released from jail and she was always watching her back. Looking up above her head she blew a hard breath as she clocked she'd left the top bedroom window open. Checking her wristwatch she knew she was late for work already, so she left the window open and set off for work. As Kendal walked along the road she watched the passing cars, with each glimpse her body shook thinking she'd seen Scott. She started to run as she saw her bus approaching. Her heels clipped along the pavement. Sat on the bus she opened her bag and checked she'd brought everything she needed, she felt like she'd left something behind.

Jane sat watching the clock; John should have been there half an hour ago to give her some money for the baby. This was a regular occurrence in her life and he'd made it quite clear that he didn't want anything more to do with her. She'd tried to win him back, but after months of pleading with him Jane finally accepted that it was over.

The knock at the door made her spring up from her seat. Jane looked older as she walked to the door, her face was covered in make-up and her clothes were hanging from her waist, she'd lost so much weight. Jane's hands shook as she opened the front door. John stood there holding a brown envelope out in his hand. "Here, you scrounging cunt, get it before I change my mind." Jane snapped at him and made sure he could hear her.

"Who the fuck are you calling a scrounger? I bet your still bunging that slag Kendal money aren't you? Do you call her a scrounger, I bet not?" John had heard this a hundred times before and held his head back and chuckled.

"Do you want the money or what? Get over Kendal, will you? I've told you time and time again that there is nothing going on between us, just fucking deal with it." Jane clenched her fist tightly at the side of her, she was ready to strike. Eva, her daughter, walked into the hallway and ran to her dad.

"Daddy," she screamed. John picked her up in his arms and kissed her rosy red cheeks.

"I'll come and get you at weekend sweetheart, I'm busy today, but I promise I'll come and see you on Saturday." Jane held her back up against the wall and tried to put on a face in front of her daughter.

"See, I told you he still loved you. You can see him on Saturday." John backed off from the door. Keeping Eva a secret from Jackie had been hard over the years and the only reason he was bunging Jane money was to pay for her silence. Jane was a gobby cow and she'd told him straight that if he ever missed a payment for his daughter she would drop the kid on his doorstep. John knew she meant business too, and he always coughed up the cash. John waved his hand at Eva and blew a kiss in her direction.

"Have her ready on Saturday about twelve will you? I'll take her out for the day." Jane opened the envelope and she was counting the cash. Once she knew the money was all there she gave him a cunning smile.

"She'll be ready as always, don't be late for her because I've got a date this week and I don't want to be late." John looked her in the eyes, he knew she was lying about the date, she was always saying she'd met the man of her dreams and that she was over him, but the late night calls to his mobile phone from her told him she was still madly in love with him.

Jane sat down and hung her head between her legs, her face was sad. Tears streamed down her cheeks and she was sobbing. Reaching for her phone she dialled a number. "Hello Sheila, it's me Jane. Do you fancy going out tonight and getting rat-arsed. It's my treat," she gripped the cash John had just given her in her hands and fanned it out. "Yeah, ask your Marline to babysit for me, we can go to The Queens on Monsall, there's Karaoke on there tonight." Jane ended the phone call after a few minutes and flicked the TV on. Sat watching Eva playing in the corner of the room she shook her head. "What a fucked up life I've got. Where's my Prince Charming when I need him ay? Where the fuck is he?"

Later, Jane walked into the pub with her friend. Sheila looked like mutton dressed as lamb. Her micro pink mini-skirt barely covered the cheeks of her arse. Jane's friend was a loud mouthed hussy and the world and his wife would know when she'd arrived anywhere. Waving her hands above her head she walked into the bar and shouted at a punter stood there. "Ay Larry, line them Sambucas up love. If you play your cards right tonight, you might have a fuck buddy." The man at the bar rubbed his crotch and shouted back.

"Get your arse over here then, I'm lining them up as we speak. You're my kind of woman." Sheila nudged Jane in the waist.

"That's us sorted out for tonight. Fat Larry is wadded. So what if I have to sleep with him for a few drinks. I don't mind taking one for the team if he's paying for my night out." Jane flicked Sheila's ear.

"You're such a slapper you are, here, hold my bag while I go to the shitter." Jane strutted her stuff across the dance floor; she's already drunk half a bottle of vodka before she'd come out. From the corner of her eye she could see someone she knew. He was a blast from her past. Sneaking by him, she headed to the toilets keeping a low profile. Girls were in the mirror applying make-up to their bright red faces, they were caked in it. The noise was deafening as they yelled to each other from inside the cubicles. Standing next to one of them at the mirror Jane smiled as she watched her applying some bright pink lip-gloss to her lips. She nudged her in the waist. "Can I have a go of that lippy love; it's a lovely colour?" At first the girl frowned at her but after a few seconds she passed it over.

"Ay, you better not have any cold sores or owt, I don't want to be catching the mange from you." Jane giggled as she shaped her mouth in an oval shape in the mirror.

"You cheeky cow, I'm clean me. I'm not no dirt-bag like some of the girls in here." Jane passed the lipstick back to her and stood watching the girl examining it. She headed inside the toilet.

Jane checked herself one last time in the long mirror;

she was ready to go back out. Walking into the pub again, she giggled as she heard Sheila singing, "Girls just want to have fun" by Cyndi Lauper on the Karaoke. Standing watching her for a few seconds she decided to make her move. Walking to the side of the pub, she met a gang of men. She tapped one of them on the shoulder and waited for him to turn around. "When did you get out Scott, long time no see, ay?" Scott went white in the face; he looked like he'd seen a ghost. Jane knew that they'd never seen eye to eye in the past but she was hoping all that had changed since he'd got out of prison. She made conversation with him trying to break the ice. Scott was watching her like a hawk, this was Kendal's best màte and he was hoping she was with her. He played the waiting game well and refrained from asking her any questions for now. Jane knew what he was after and couldn't wait to tell him about the years that had passed. She never told him where her best friend was though; she kept that to herself for now. Jane was a right vindictive bitch.

"Are you getting me a drink or what?"

Scott shook his head. "I see you've still got more front than Blackpool, some things never change do they?" Jane followed him to the bar and her eyes were all over him like a rash. She fancied him and liked what she saw. Hitching her red skirt up a touch she told him she was going to sit down. As she walked away she could feel his eyes burning into the back of her head. Sheila was still hogging the microphone and nobody could get a sniff near it to sing a song. She was doing her usual medley of Karaoke hits.

Scott was pissed and his eyes were glazed over. He knew Jane could fill him in all on the missing pieces of the jigsaw; he just needed to get her talking. He could tell she was covering up for her friend, but hopefully after the load of drinks he'd lined up for her she would be singing like a budgie. Jane sat next to him and punched him in the arm playfully. "So, when did you get out? I hope you learnt your lesson you naughty boy," she squeezed the side of his cheeks together causing his mouth to hurt. Scott pulled away from her and he had to restrain himself from banging her out, he hated this girl with a passion and had to play the part of a friend.

"I've had a lot of time to sort my head out since being in jail Jane. I'm a changed man now." She smirked at him and she didn't know if he was winding her up. Reaching for her drink she gulped back a large mouthful, she needed it for what she was about to tell him next.

"I think John Daley's shagging Kendal. You know I've got a baby to him don't you?" Scott's face dropped to the floor, and he was gobsmacked, his jaw was swinging. He had his own insecurities about his ex-girlfriend with John, but Jane had just put his mind to rest, he'd been right all along. Scott tried to keep his cool and shook her last comment off, hoping she would carry on.

"Kendal means fuck all to me anymore Jane. She's old news, she's so yesterday I've got a new bird now and I'm happy," he was lying through his front teeth. Jane was like a loose cannon and she was spilling the beans on her best mate.

"I've not seen Kendal for time, I kicked her sorry arse to the kerb when she done the dirty on me with John. I mean, I was her best friend and she goes and does something like that." Scott placed his hand on her lap and tapped it slowly.

"I know love, its bad news that, she's a wrong un for sure. You should be glad you got away from her when you did if she's like that." Here it was the moment he was waiting for; he sat back and prepared himself, she was going to grass Kendal up.

"She's living in Middleton now; John set her up with a house and everything. She lives at the end house on Shelborn Street." Scott coughed to clear his throat, he was trying not to look interested but he was taking in every bit of information she was giving him. "Did you know she couldn't read or write?"

Scott looked confused and hunched his shoulders. "Nar did I fuck, she hid that well then."

Jane jumped in and spit was hanging from the corner of her mouth, she was pissed out of her head. "She hid a lot well Scott, she's a snidey bitch. You should have seen her when she started learning to read, she thought she was the dog's bollocks. I know I couldn't read or write too but I was better than her. I tell you now Scott, she changed. She was right up her own arse. She thought she was above me and all that." Scott kept the beer flowing all through the night, and by the end of it he knew everything he needed to know about his ex-girlfriend, more than anything he knew where she lived. Jane was slouching all over him now and she was doing his head in, he'd got what he needed from her and he wanted to get off. Pretending to go to the toilet he made a quick exit away from her. He zipped his coat up and pulled his hood over his head, he walked into the night like a man on a mission.

★

Kendal lay on her bed reading one of her "Quick Read" books that Betty had given her. They were only small books but they were right up her street. The words were easy to follow and the book only consisted of one hundred pages, so it didn't take forever to read it. Kendal had searched the house from top to bottom trying to find her mother's diary but had never found it. After months of crying she'd finally given up looking for it and came to terms with it, she would never read her mother's final thoughts. Tonight it was warm and sticky and the bedroom window was open fully. The curtain was rising with the small breeze flowing in from outside. Steve had been on the phone for the last hour and she'd only just said goodnight to him. Relaxing onto her pillow she prepared to read her book. Her face was concentrating as she studied the words. Reading was like a new world to her and even though she'd been reading for over a year now she was still struggling with some of the bigger words. Flicking the main light switch, she turned on her small pink lamp at the side of her bed. Before long she was drifting off to sleep with her book still resting in her hands.

The area was quiet and the moon shone brightly in the sky, it was a peaceful night. Across the road from Kendal's house the bushes were moving about, you could hear them rustling. Hidden away deep inside them a man sat watching the house. His face was smiling as he sat cracking his knuckles. "Payback time," he whispered under his breath.

John Daley sat across the road from Kendal's house in his car. He took a long deep drag from his cigarette and flicked the butt through the window. He knew Scott was out of jail now and he knew more than anyone what he was capable of, he was an evil bastard. He'd sorted a few guys out for him in the past and some of the stories he'd been told about them would have made your toes curl.

John looked at the shiny silver key in his hand. It was a spare key to Kendal's house. When he'd got the property for her he made sure he got himself a key cut too. He never used it, but it was there in case of emergencies. Seeing the light fade from inside the house he turned the engine over and crawled from the alleyway where he was parked. He had a gut feeling Scott was on the prowl and he wanted to make sure he was there if Kendal needed him.

Scott rubbed his hands together; this was a lot easier than he first thought. Jane spilling the beans on her best mate had saved him a lot of time and effort. He was ready to set the record straight. Creeping from his hideout he faded into the shadows of the night. He was plotting his revenge. His day had come.

CHAPTER THIRTEEN

Jane stood at the front door with a face like thunder. Eva was with her and she was restless, she kept tugging at her mother's cardigan. They were waiting for John to come and pick her up, he was late again. Jane kept stomping to the end of the garden fence and stretching her neck over it looking out for him. "Bastard," she mumbled under her breath. Marching back into the house she grabbed her coat from the banister, there was no way she was putting up with John's shit anymore, she'd had enough. He was always doing this to her daughter and she was sick to death of him. "Come on Eva, let's go and see what Daddy does when I take you to his house. That will teach him to fuck about with your feelings." She pulled the child by her hand and set off like a woman on a mission down the main road.

Kendal sat watching the TV. Ella May had stayed at her friend's home the night before and she had a bit of spare time before she went to pick her up. Feeling lethargic she made her way up the stairs for a bath, she was sure she was coming down with a cold or something her nose was blocked and her head was banging. Running the bath water she turned the radio on and she was singing a "Take . That" hit called "A Million Love Songs Later". Kendal sounded like a strangled cat but that never stopped her, she kept on singing. Peeling her pyjamas off she stepped into the bath and submerged her body deep underneath the warm water, she was relaxing and closing her eyes. Holding her head to the side she opened her eyes quickly. Kendal heard a loud bang from downstairs. Frozen for a second she carried on washing herself.

Still singing Kendal walked into the bedroom with a white towel hanging around her body. Her body was dripping wet and she looked cold, she ran to the window and slammed it shut. "Brrrrrr," she shivered. Stretching her body over the bed she lay staring at the ceiling enjoying the quality time she had left on her own. Her cheeks were blood red and she had red patches all over her body. There it was again, the noise from downstairs. She sat up and looked alert; she was chewing on the skin at the side of her thumb and debating her next move. Standing to her feet she crept to the door, she was edgy. Her face dropped and she hung her head over the landing trying to get a better look, she thought her mind was playing tricks on her again. Kendal couldn't see anything so she edged more forward. Her feet touched the first stair and she was in two minds whether or not to turn back, her hand gripped the banister tightly. Standing in the hallway, she could see the back door swinging open. Kendal felt relieved and walked towards it. The door was faulty and it was always opening on its own. She peeped outside in the garden and once she saw it was deserted she went back inside, with a relieved look on her face.

"You fucking nutter Kendal Wilson, "she said to herself. Her eyes shot to the living room, she was sure she'd seen someone running past the door. Holding her towel tightly around her body she walked inside with caution. She was angry with herself and hated that she was so jumpy. Her eyes shot to one of Ella May's old teddies swinging from the light fitting. It had a cardboard note hung from the front of it with black felt tip writing on it. Her eyes were all over the front room but she couldn't see anyone. Reading the note she sounded out the words. "Did you miss me?" Her heart was in her mouth, turning on her feet she got ready to phone the police. A hand gripped her back by her hair. Before she knew it she was lay flat on the floor with a man stood over her. Scott pulled his hood down and let out a menacing laugh.

"Payback time bitch," he grabbed something from his pockets and she could hear a buzzing noise. Scott pressed his knee deep into her chest bone and dragged her head up. Seeing the shaver in his hands she screamed out at the top of her voice. Kendal wriggled about but it was no good, she was kicking and screaming. Scott did what he'd set out to do, he shaved her hair off. Within a few minutes only a few stands were left and she looked like a cancer victim. Standing to his feet he swung his foot back and surged it deep inside her ribcage. Kendal double up in pain and hid her face away from him, she knew the worst was yet to come.

"Did you think I would forget about you ay?" He knelt down and gripped her face with his hands, he was squeezing it hard and she was gagging for breath, he was choking her. "You and fucking John Daley. I knew I was right all along, you slag." He spat into her face and stood up. Kendal felt warm liquid being sprinkled all over her body, he was pissing on her. With every inch of strength left inside her she reached for a cup off the side of the unit and launched it at his head. This man was quick and he was like a bullet firing from a gun. She never stood a chance. He let rip and beat her within an inch of her life, with every blow her head swung from side to side. Kendal was barely breathing when he'd finished, he stood over her and his nostrils were flaring. Sweat was dripping from his nose and his chest was rising with speed.

"Job's a good un. I told you I would be back for you didn't I?" There was no reply, Scott was gone.

There was hair all over the floor and blood was splattered all over the walls. You could see Kendal's eyelids flickering slowly. Her mobile phone was ringing constantly from her bag at the corner of the sofa.

Jane stood tall as she knocked on John Daley's front door. She was more than ready for action, she'd had enough. Looking at his house she growled and clenched her fists tightly together. There she was struggling to feed her child and here he was living like a king in his five bedroom house. No one answered the door at first and Jane stood kicking the bottom of it with her foot. Eva was pottering about the garden looking at the three gnomes sat on the side of the grass verge and she seemed oblivious to what was happening. The bright red door opened slowly and Jackie was stood there dripping wet through. She was dressed in black leggings and a pink top; she looked like she'd been working out. Her eyes shot to Jane. "Yes, what do you want love?" Jane's mouth was dry and she licked her lips, she was nervous.

"Is John in?" Jackie rested her hand on the doorframe and regained her breath; she wiped her forehead again and raised a smile.

"I've just been on the treadmill, sorry, who did you want again?" Jane inhaled and knew she was dicing with death, but she continued with a stroppy tone, she had to get it off her chest.

"It's john I want not you, is he in?" she took a

deep breath and you could see her swallowing hard. "I've brought his daughter to see him since he never turned up for her yet again." There was silence as Jackie digested the information. After a few seconds she gritted her teeth together and gripped Jane by the throat, she was clocking the area.

"Listen you scruffy tart, get your sweaty arse out of my garden before I rip your bastard head off." Jane was white in the face and she gasping for breath.

"Eva is John's daughter. I bet he's never told you about her has he?" she pulled away from her. "I was seeing him for months behind your back, and he told me he loved me." Jackie clenched her fists and swung it hard into Jane's face. There was no way she was taking this from a shag-bag. She ragged Jane down the garden path and kicked her up the arse.

"John doesn't have any kids, don't you be coming around here saying things like that. What is it ay? Are you after some money from him or something, you money grabbing bitch?" Eva ran out from the garden and Jackie stopped dead in her tracks when she saw her for the first time. The little girl was a ringer of her husband; she was the spit from his mouth. Jane saw her looking at Eva and ran and picked her up in her hands, she was shaking from head to toe.

"You know she's John's child, just look at her," she waved her hand about in front of Jackie's face. "Just deal with it will you and take your head from up your arse." Jane stood with her hand on her hip, she was giving it back now and she wasn't afraid. "Don't you worry though; he hasn't been with me for ages. He kicked me to the kerb a long time ago after I told him I was pregnant. It's Kendal Wilson who he loves; he's been seeing her for years. So she's the one you need to sort out not me."

Jackie ran at her, "What do you mean Kendal Wilson, that's his fucking daughter." Jane looked confused, and watched as Jackie covered her mouth with her hand.

"Did you just say Kendal was John's daughter?" Jackie ran back into the house and slammed the front door behind her.

Jane stood with Eva in her arms; the child was sobbing her eyes out, she was scared. The rain started falling and Jane wasn't sure what to do next. Cars on the road passed her at speed and she seemed in a world of her own. You could see Jackie Daley stood at her living room window watching her every move with evil eyes.

John Daley hammered on Kendal's front door, he looked frantic. Walking over to the front window he cupped his hands over his eyes and tried to look through the living room window. His jaw dropped when he saw her lying lifeless on the floor. Searching in his pocket he pulled out his spare key and ran inside the house in a panic. "Kendal!" he screamed at the top of his voice. For the first time ever John Daley fell to his knees and cried his eyes out. "Please don't be dead, please." His hands trembled as he rang the emergency services; his voice was frantic as he reported the crime. Lifting Kendal up softly in his hands he rested her head on his lap, he stroked her forehead slowly as his tears fell onto her face.

Sirens blaring outside made John alert, his body was weak and he couldn't move, it was like two iron bars were tied around his body. Two uniform officers came running into the front room closely followed by the medics. They looked at the state of the victim and knew this crime was serious. The ambulance man assessed Kendal and started to give her emergency treatment, she was in a bad way. Blood was seeping from the side of her head. The officers took John into another room and probed him for answers regarding the crime.

Within minutes the area was a crime scene. The forensic team were all about the front room dressed in white paper suits looking for any scrap of evidence as to what had happened. John wasn't grassing, no way; he wanted to keep Scott for himself. Sat with his hands on his head he gritted his teeth tightly together and stamped his feet, he was cracking up under the pressure.

Paddy was Kendal's next of kin and the only person she had left in her family. There was Molly of course but she was out of the picture, nobody had seen her for ages. Sitting around the hospital bed Paddy Wilson sobbed his heart out. His heart was breaking in two, and he was regretting everything he'd ever done to Kendal in the past. Watching the heart monitor at the side of the bed he broke down in tears. He pledged there and then that who'd ever done this to his family, he would kill them stone dead, they would never breathe again. Paddy looked fresh and clean, and he'd gained some weight. He looked like he was off the beer too, his complexion looked healthy. John Daley walked into the room and Paddy stood to his feet. "She's a mess mate, who the fuck would do this to her." John cradled Paddy in his arms and led him back to his seat. "I don't know pal, but the word is out, and as soon as I find out who's done this, they'll be a dead man walking." Police were hovering outside the room and they knew John Daley was keeping quiet about what he knew. John was known to the police and they knew more than anyone that he was keeping whatever he knew close to his chest.

Jane sat down and switched on the TV. Kendal's story was all over the news and as soon as she saw it she burst out crying. "Fucking hell, Jackie's done her in," she screamed. "Oh, my god, what have I done?" Pacing the floor she wrapped her hands around her trembling body and let out a scream like an injured animal. Grabbing her phone she tried to ring John's number. She was desperate and her hands were shaking. The phone was ringing but it kept going to voice mail. "Answer the bleeding phone John, just answer the bleeding phone."

Scott sat at Piccadilly Train station waiting to leave Manchester; he was getting on his toes. He knew the police would be hot on his trail and he wasn't sticking around to find out. Buying his train ticket he sat on the platform with his head bent low. Looking at his hands he could see speckles of red claret on his fingers. Popping them into his mouth he sucked at his ex-girlfriend's blood. "Revenge is sweet," he whispered.

Jane took Eva to her friends and asked her to watch her for a few hours. She was a walking wreck and her face was white. Running to the bus stop she headed to the brass gaff. John was always there at this time and she had to see him. Her heart was in her mouth as she sat on the bus heading towards Lady Jane's, this was such a mess and she regretted ever telling Jackie about Kendal.

★

Jackie turned the engine over on the car. She'd been trying to ring her husband all day but he hadn't answered. Sticking out from the top of her handbag was a silver pistol. John always had one knocking about the house; he said it was for emergencies. She screeched out from her driveway, she was driving like a mad woman. The music was pumping inside the car and she was frantic. Black tears rolled down her cheeks and she was constantly wiping them away. "Dirty no good bastard," she hissed. Her husband had done it this time, she was going to make him pay big time. Jackie knew he'd been unfaithful in the past but she'd just swept it under the carpet to keep the peace, not this time though, she was letting him have it. Punching her fist on the steering wheel she cursed under her breath as she waited for the lights to change.

Jane stood at the bus shelter; she could see John in the car park which was facing her. The dimly lit street light was the only lighting in the area, all the others were smashed. John was dragging at a woman's arm and she was going back at him with all guns blazing. Jane crept across the main road so she could see better. As she neared the car park she could hear shouting. Hid away behind an old white transit van she positioned herself so she could see what was going on. John had the woman by her throat and he was yelling into her face. "Listen you junkie, you've had your last penny from me. Did you think this would go on forever? I'll kill you if you ever come near me again." The frail woman was losing her balance and she gripped him to steady herself from falling.

"You said you loved me John, you said we would be together." John struck a blow to the woman's face and she fell to the floor like a dead weight. Checking the area he dragged her into the alleyway, he was panting for breath. Jane was on her tiptoes and she was chewing on her fingernails. She was alone and all she could hear were a few groans from the side street. John walked back into the light and he was ragging his fingers through his hair. Jane knew it was now or never, she watched him near his car and stepped out from the shadow of the night.

"John, I need to speak to you. It's all my fault. You never turned up for Eva and I just lost the plot." John looked over his shoulder and stood waiting for her to get nearer to him. His hands were shaking as he pulled his cigarettes out from his pocket.

"Listen, I don't need any shit from you. I was busy today that's all. I can see Eva tomorrow, now fuck off mithering me." Jane touched his hand softly; tears were streaming down her face.

"No John listen, I went to see Jackie. I've told her about Eva." There was silence – John chewed on his lips and you could see him closing his eyes.

"Are you right in the fucking head or what? What have you gone and done that for?" Jane dropped her head low and her bottom lip trembled.

"I think its Jackie who's done Kendal in."

John gripped her by the throat, "What do you mean by that, why would she be gunning for Kendal?" Jane tried breaking free; she knew he was going to hurt her.

"I said it in temper. I told her you loved Kendal." Within seconds Jane was on the floor with blood streaming from her nose. In the distance you could see the shadow of a figure leaving the alleyway. Jane sprang to her feet and started to run off. "I still love you John, please let's sort this out, if not for me then for Eva." John jumped into his car and locked the doors; you could see his head plonked on the steering wheel. Jane ran back at him and banged her clenched fists onto the glass. "John, please, I'm sorry." The car started up and the engine roared. His face focused on her and he reversed slowly. She was stood on some white gravel facing him. All she could see were the headlights in her eyes. Jane covered her eyes and stood with her hand held out towards him. "John, please," she begged. The car screeched towards her and she dived out of the way just in time. John was trying to kill her. Running at speed she scampered over a nearby wall and fell to the ground. The sound of her body crashing to the floor could be heard and you could see John skidding out from the car park.

★

Jackie stampeded inside Lady Jane's, she was gasping for breath. Her foot smashed at the reception door opening it with a swift kick. With eyes all over she snarled at the woman stood behind the sofa. "Where the fuck is he?" Jackie walked closer to her and growled with her teeth showing. "Don't be hiding him, tell me where he is now." Maddy was the head girl at the brothel and she kept the girls in line. Standing to her full height she pulled her red silk dressing gown tighter around her body.

"Listen Jackie, he's not here. Stop causing a commotion will you. We've got punters in you know, we have to earn a living so don't fuck it up."

"Do you think I give a flying fuck about anybody being here you daft bitch, I'm here for John, now tell me where the cunt is hiding before I blow your fucking brains out too." Maddy backed off; she knew more than anyone what this woman was capable of. She'd watched her in the past with one of the girls who was giving her trouble. Jackie was ruthless and she wouldn't think twice about striking a blow to her.

"Honest Jackie, he's not been in here tonight. He phoned me earlier and said he was on his way, but he never came. Just sit down and relax a minute love, what's up?" Jackie ran through the reception area and looked along the landing. In a wild frenzy she checked every room, John wasn't there. Walking back to reception she watched as a few of the girls sat together whispering.

"Ay you load of shag-bags, if you have anything to say, come and say it, don't be fucking whispering behind my back." None of the girls replied and you could have cut the atmosphere with a knife. Jackie searched her handbag and lit up a cig. Sitting by herself she stared at the wall facing her. Maddy walked over to her and tried to smooth things over, this was all she needed – a psychotic bitch sat in the waiting area.

"Do you want a drink? Come on, you need to calm down. John should be here soon and then you can sort it out whatever is troubling you." Jackie lifted her eyes and snarled.

"Not this time cock, he's done it this time, there's no going back." Maddy turned her head and raised her eyes to the two girls stood there. It was going to be a long night.

★

Jane held her broken body as she headed home, she was struggling to walk. The moon shining bright in the sky looked magical tonight. Hid away in the dark of the night she kept out of sight. Jane was coughing up blood and she knew John had hurt her bad.

John sat in his car watching his house. It was in darkness. He knew behind the front door that his wife would be waiting for him. Jackie was no pushover and he knew that the night was going to be long. Leaving his car on the driveway he prepared himself for the long hard battle that would probably last all night. Placing his key in the front door his face crumbled. "Jackie," he shouted, there was no reply.

CHAPTER FOURTEEN

Two weeks had passed and the police were hot on Scott's trail. His mug shot was all over the media and it was only a matter of time before they caught up with him. Kendal lay in her hospital bed and she was due to go home. She had a woollen hat over her head, her hair had started to grow back slowly, but she still hated it. Paddy was sat at the side of the bed and he was staring out of the window. "It's nice today, the sun's out for a change. What time did they say you are allowed to go home?" Kendal sat up straight in her bed, her body was still recovering and she was weak.

"The doctor is due around anytime now and he said if all my tests come back clear, I can go home today." Paddy played with the curtain but kept his face looking out of the window.

"Why, don't you and Ella May come home with me. I've loved having her about the house with me these last couple of weeks and I can look after her until you get yourself back on your feet?"

Kendal sat thinking, touching the corner of the blanket she sighed. "Granddad, I can't give my house up. Scott won't get near me again. Once the dibble get hold of him he'll be getting slammed in prison for a very long time, so I'll be fine."

Paddy walked back to her, his heart was low, he was lonely. "Well if that's what you want, so be it. You will come and see me though won't you?"

Kendal smiled, "Yeah of course I will. Without you I

have nobody. I know we've had our ups and downs but you were here when I needed you most. I'll never forget that." Paddy sat back down and sighed. Kendal and Ella May were all he had too.

The doctor was in the room and he was reading through Kendal's medical notes. "You can go home today. I'm happy with your test results and there is no reason for you to stay in hospital any longer. I want you to take it easy though," he looked at her with a serious face. "You've had some nasty injuries and you'll need time to mend." Paddy smiled and started to pack all Kendal's belongings together, he hated hospitals, it reminded him of death. The doctor left the room.

"Come on then, get ready. It's a lovely day today; you can get some fresh air." Kendal stretched her legs out of the bed, they were pale and hairy. As her feet touched the cold floor you could see the strain in her face as she tried to walk. Paddy passed her clothes and she headed to the room at the side of them to get ready.

★

Jackie sat watching her husband eating his breakfast; she was tapping her long red fingernails on the table. You could see bruises all over her face and arms from the last battle she'd had with John. The last few weeks had been a nightmare. Night after night the couple would fight until the early hours but still John denied that he had a baby to another woman. Jackie flicked her cigarette ash into the ashtray on the table, she was studying her husband. The radio was on low and it was the only noise in the room. She reached over and snatched the newspaper from his hands. "Listen, I want you to leave. I can't do this anymore. I don't believe a fucking word you're telling me.

That kid is yours, I'm not daft. I saw her with my own two eyes; she's the double of you." John opened his wallet and passed Jackie a wad of cash.

"I love you Jackie; no other woman has ever come close. Do you think I would risk losing you for some little scrubber chatting shit?" He could see her face melting with love for him. He knew he had her on side.

"Well, why did she say it? Come on John, I'm not that stupid. Give me some fucking credit please," she sank her head low.

"Just take the money and go shopping, get something nice to wear and we can go out tonight." John kept his eyes on her and stood up from his chair. Walking to the back of her he ran his fingers slowly through her hair and kissed the top of her head, goose pimples appeared on her arms. "Come on Jackie, I love you. Let's be friends. I hate it when we argue." She kept her head down, her head was spinning and she knew the old cunt was lying through his back teeth. She'd been through the same thing with him years ago when she'd found out he'd been sleeping with Mary Wilson, but he always denied that Kendal was his child. Slowly she pushed his hands from her body; he was making her skin crawl. If she was ever going to find out the truth she would have to catch him bang at it. Picking the money up from the table she shoved it down the front of her bra.

"I swear John; if you're lying to me, you can kiss my arse goodbye, because this time, I mean it, you'll be gone. You'll be out on your arse." John let out a laboured breath.

"Jackie, I swear to you, straight up, I'm telling you the truth." Watching her leave the room he picked up his mobile phone. His fingers moved quickly as he typed out a text message to Kendal. He was going to see her shortly.

Kendal lay on the sofa watching an old black and white film. She'd always watched them with Nelly when she was alive and she loved the storylines in them. She was a sucker for a love story. Pulling the duvet over her body she snuggled down to watch the film. The sound of the letterbox rattling filled the room. Kendal sighed and hated that she had to get up from her comfy seat. "Who the fuck is this now?" she cursed. Wearing black leggings and a green top she made her way to the front door. She'd lost a lot of weight and she looked extremely thin, Scott's attack on her had taken its toll on her.

"What do you want?" she growled as she opened the door.

Jane looked a mess and her body was quivering. "Please Kendal; just let me speak to you for a minute."

"Let you speak!" Kendal snapped. "You can fuck right off. Where were you when I needed you most ay?"

Jane held her arms out and tried to calm her down. "It was me who was jealous, I was wrong, I know that now. You know what I'm like when I get a bee in my bonnet. I'm sorry Kendal. Please can I come in and talk to you for a minute, please?"

Kendal walked inside the house and left the door swinging open. Jane followed her slowly. Shooting her eyes at the TV Jane smiled hoping to break the ice. "Don't tell me you're still watching these old granny films."

Kendal ignored her and sat down, there was no way she was getting around her that easy. Popping a cig into her mouth she crossed her legs and folded her arms. "Well, come on then, say what you've got to say, and then you can fuck off home."

Jane looked shocked, Kendal was always so laid back and this behaviour was so out character for her. "Fucking hell Kendal, just give me a chance will you? This is hard for me too you know."

Kendal chugged on her cig and blew a cloud of smoke out in front of her. "Like I'm arsed," she replied in a stroppy tone.

Jane took a deep breath before she began; she was sat cracking her knuckles, this wasn't going to be easy. "John never came to pick Eva up, and I just lost the plot. You know what I'm like when I see my arse?"

Kendal raised her eyes and blew her breath. "Don't I just," she said sarcastically.

"I just didn't know what else to do, so I went to see Jackie."

Kendal froze, her jaw dropped. John had never mentioned this to her and she was eager to hear more. "What, you took Eva to meet Jackie? Are you right in the head?"

Jane sat back in her chair and she started to relax. "Well, it wasn't to meet Jackie. I just wanted her to know what a cheating bastard her husband was."

Kendal covered her mouth with her hands and she kicked her feet up underneath her. "Jane you're a mad-head, what did she say?"

"I just told her straight that John was a wanker and that he'd been shagging me for months. She knew by looking at Eva that I was telling her the truth, you could see it in her eyes."

"Fuck me Jane, what did she say to that? She's a fucking barm-pot Jackie, you're lucky to be still breathing." Jane chuckled and she looked serious.

"I said to her, did she know that John had a daughter,

and do you know what she said?"

Kendal was on the edge of her seat, she loved a drama, and this was right up there with the best of them. "What did she say?"

Jane spoke slowly and every word seemed to go on forever. "She said, 'who do you mean Kendal?'" Silence, both of them sat staring at each other; you could have heard a pin drop. Kendal looked gobsmacked, she chewed on her fingernails.

"Why is she saying that? Why would John be my Dad? Is she right is the head, she's fucking tapped that woman?"

Jane came and sat by her side and touched her arm softly. "That's what I thought, but she seemed quite adamant that you were John's child. When I told her that Eva was John's daughter she fucking nearly choked me. Look at my neck; it's still black and blue."

Kendal sprang up from her seat and pushed her away. "Stop chatting shit Jane, stop fucking about. This is serious. Why do you always wind me up? Don't you think I've been through enough?"

Jane sat forward and held her hands between her legs. "On my life, that's what she said." She held her hands out in front of her and her eyes were wide open. "I swear it's true."

Kendal sat back down and shook her head. "No I don't believe you. You're lying again. You've always been jealous of John with me and this is your way of putting a spanner in the works. Just deal with it, he doesn't want you anymore."

Her words stabbed Jane right in her heart and you could see a lump forming in the back of her throat. "I told Scott where you lived," she blurted out. Tears ran down the side of her cheeks and Kendal was just stood gawping at her with her mouth wide open. Jane melted to the floor and Kendal ran at her. She gripped her by the hair and ragged her about the floor, she was fuming.

"You horrible jealous bitch, so it was you all along. I knew you were low, Jane, but this, this is in a league of its own. Get out of my house now. I never want to see your ugly mush around here again. Go on; fuck off back to the gutter where you belong."

Jane was hysterical and she was pleading with her. "I know what I've done was bad, but Kendal, my head was over the place and I wasn't thinking straight."

Kendal wasn't listening and she ran to the front door. Stood with it opened she shouted at her again. "Get the fuck out of here you rat."

Jane walked slowly towards her; she was rummaging in her coat pocket and her face was desperate. As she got to her friend's side she pulled out a small book. "This is yours, I stole it from you."

Kendal's eyes were fixed on the book in her grip. Grabbing it from her hands she realised it was her mother's diary. "So, it was you who had it all along. Oh my God Jane, you are so fucked up in the head. You need help. Go on, get out of my sight, you've got a screw loose, you have." Jane walked down the garden path, she never looked back.

Kendal was striding around the front room like a headless chicken. Her chest was rising and she was white in the face. "Bitch, bitch, bitch. How could she do that to me?" she cursed.

Sitting down slowly she held the diary out in front of her. Slowly she opened it and looked at the first page. Her eyes closed slowly and tears ran down the side of her cheeks. At last she could read her mother's last words. The letterbox was rapping and Kendal slammed the diary shut on the chair at the side of her. Peeping through the window she could see John Daley stood there. Jerking her head back quickly, she hid away from him. Her head was in bits and she didn't want to see anyone, especially John. Kendal could hear her name being shouted in the hallway, she ignored him. Sinking to the floor she brought her knees up to her chest and rested her head onto her lap.

★

That night after Ella May had gone to bed, Kendal climbed the stairs with a heavy heart. In her hands she held her mother's diary; she was planning to read it tonight. Kendal pushed the bedroom door open and she could see Ella May lay in her bed reading. "Goodnight sweetheart," she whispered as she pulled the bedroom door shut.

"Goodnight mummy," the child replied.

Kendal's body collapsed onto the bed and her eyes shut for a few seconds. Pulling the duvet over her body she opened the diary. Folding a pillow underneath her head she made herself comfortable. Kendal's reading was slow and you could see her lips moving as she sounded out the words inside the diary. Sat up in the bed her chin dropped and she held the book to her heart. Eager to read on she flicked the pages quickly; Mary's last moments were unfolding right in front of her eyes. Kendal lit a cigarette and stood up at the bedroom window. Her face was puzzled and she was thinking. All of a sudden she fell back onto the bed and her arms cradled around her body.

"No, no, please no."

Kendal dived out of her bed the following morning. She was rushing about and she was eager to get Ella May off to school. Her mind was all over the place and she was snapping at her daughter. "Ella May, will you hurry up. If you're not eating them bleeding cornflakes just leave them on the table."

Kendal ran up the stairs to get ready. Her mobile phone had been ringing constantly but she ignored it. "Fuck off," she screamed at it.

Kissing Ella May on her cheek she left her at the school gate. Usually she would have gone into the classroom with her, but today she was too busy. Pounding out of the school gates she headed towards Harpurhey with a frenzied look in her eyes.

Today was market day and all the shoppers were out in full force in the area. Kendal sat on a red brick wall not far from the superstore's entrance; she was watching it with eager eyes. Nobody could get past her without her seeing them first. Pulling her hood up over her head she tried to keep a low profile. The wind was picking up and it was cold, her lips were blue. Kendal still wore a woollen hat on her head and every now and then she would shove her finger underneath it and scratch at her scalp. Scott was lying heavily on her mind and there was still no sign of the police catching him, he was gone with the wind.

Kendal sparked a cigarette up and inhaled deeply. From the corner of her eyes she could see a gang of people walking towards the entrance. Each one of them looked rough and you could tell just by looking at them that they were drug-addicts. She sprang from the wall and dusted her jeans down. Dipping her head low she began to follow them.

The smack-heads were a regular sight around Harpurhey, they were the lowest of the low and they were shunned by the neighbourhood. It was well known that they would nick anything that wasn't bolted down, they were scum. Kendal looked at the scrawny junkie who was with them. She quickened her steps to reach her. When she was at her side she grabbed her by the arm. The drug-addict looked shocked and started to pull away from her, she thought Kendal was the dibble. "Take your hands off me you dick-head. I've got fuck all on me. Come on, search me if you want to you daft cow, I've got fuck all."

The woman was bouncing about with her hands held up in the air. Kendal panicked as a few people gathered around them watching the commotion. Keeping her voice low she spoke to the woman. "I'm not the police; I just want a quick word with you, that's all."

The female looked relieved and started to walk off.

"Nar, do one. I've got to earn some money; I've not got the time to be wasting it on you?"

Kendal dug deep in her coat pocket and pulled out a crumpled ten pound note. Holding it out in front of her she shouted after the woman. "I'll make it worth your while."

The addict stopped dead in her tracks, she waved her friends on in front of her. There was no way she was sharing the money with them. She was roasting her tits off and the money the woman was offering was just what she needed to score her next fix. The smack-head walked to her side, and tried to snatch the cash. "No, not yet. I need a word with you first," Kendal said. The crowd disappeared from around them and the show was over. Taking the junkie to a quiet area Kendal spoke to her in a low voice. "I'm looking for Molly Wilson, can you help me find her. She's my auntie." The woman's eyes were all over the place and small droplets of sweat were dripping from her forehead.

"Nar, I don't know her, where's she from?" Kendal folded the ten pound note in her hands and started to put it back in her pocket, she had to up her game if she was ever going to find Molly.

"You're no use to me then, sorry you're not getting a penny."

The woman licked her crusty lips and rubbed at her arms vigorously. "Hold on a minute, I think I know where she is?"

Kendal was hanging on her every word and urged her to continue. "You better not be having me over, otherwise you can kiss this tenner goodbye. Take me to her and I'll make it twenty quid."

The woman blew a hard breath. "Just let me score first. I'm roasting my tits off. I'll be rattling if I don't get a hit soon."

Kendal knew not to trust a bag-head. She stood tall and kept to her word. "No, take me to her first then I'll give you the money."

The woman marched off in front of Kendal, she shouted behind her. "Come on then love. I've not got all fucking day."

Kendal was hot on her trail; the woman seemed to be walking as if she'd shit herself. The cheeks of her arse were squeezed tightly together. "Wait up then," Kendal shouted after her. The two of them headed towards the Two Hundred Estate that wasn't far from the market. Kendal looked at the woman in more detail and realised she was only young. Her eyes held dark black circles underneath them and her skin looked yellow.

"How long have you known Molly for?" Kendal asked as they walked along. The woman kept walking and never looked at her as she replied.

"About five years. I met her at my mate's house in Gorton and we just became friends from there. Why are you looking for her anyway? I hope she's not in trouble because she'll go sick if she knows I've brought you here."

Kendal smiled and played along with her. "You can just leave me at the door; I won't say a word about how I found her. Her Dad is ill, and I don't think he's got long left, so I need to tell her to come and see him before he dies."

The junkie shook her head. "Well, I've done something good then for a change, if he's dying she needs to go and see him then doesn't she?" Kendal nodded. "Right its number three over there. It's the one with the red door. Just bang on the window hard. They won't open if you knock on the door. She's always there. I was with her last night, so don't let them have you over."

Kendal handed her the cash. "Thanks," she shouted as the junkie ran off into the distance.

The house looked full of poverty. Discoloured net curtains hung from the window and the front garden was overgrown with weeds. As she stood near the front door she could smell cat piss. Zipping her jacket up Kendal edged towards the kitchen window. Slowly she banged on the pane of glass with a rounded fist. Standing back from the house she searched for any sign of life, she'd stood in dog shit and she was scraping her foot on the grass verge. The front door opened with a creak and a man wearing only his boxer shorts stood gawping. Kendal knew she had to be quick and she shoved her foot inside the door. "Is Molly in?" The man seemed off his head and scratched at his ball-bag.

"Yeah she's in bed. Go up, second door on your right." Kendal watched him disappear into the front room. Looking around anxiously, she stepped onto the stairs. The house stank of weed and she covered her nose with her hand. Pressing down the door handle Kendal walked into a bedroom.

The curtains in the room were closed slightly and the daylight was just breaking through. Old syringes were all over the floor and burnt tinfoil was at the side of the bed. Kendal coughed and approached the figure in the bed with caution.

"Molly," she whispered. There was no reply. Slowly she shook the body in the bed. "Molly it's me Kendal wake up." A head appeared from under the crusty bed sheets and you could see a woman who looked like death warmed up. Kendal stood back and her mouth dropped. The female looked twice her age and her face was covered in bruises. Molly sat up and rubbed her knuckles into her eyes. She was trying to focus.

"Who the fuck are you, get the fuck out of my bedroom," she hissed.

Kendal took a deep breath and opened the curtains so she could see properly. " Molly, it's me Kendal, Mary's daughter."

Molly bolted up from the bed as if boiling water had been poured all over her, she was screaming at the top of her voice. "I'm not Molly, so fuck off out of here. I don't know who you are, so just piss off and leave me alone will you."

Kendal knew she had to up her game; there was no way she was walking away from her without getting some answers. She gripped the woman's bony arms and threw her to the floor. Standing over her she pressed her knee into her chest. "Oh yes you do know who I am Molly and you know why I'm here too don't you?"

Molly was wriggling about and she was desperate to break free. Kendal looked at her arms and she could see track marks all over them, they were black and blue. "Molly, I know what happened to my mother. I've worked it all out. I've read her diary and I know all about you and John Daley."

Molly covered her ears with her hands and rolled about on the floor. The truth was crippling her. Kendal released her grip and stood in front of the bedroom door. "You're going nowhere Molly until you tell me what really happened. You owe me that at least, I deserve to know the truth."

Suddenly, Molly smashed an empty bottle of vodka on the wall and ran at Kendal with the jagged edge of it. "I swear if you don't let me out of here, I'll slash you to fuck, now move out of my way." Kendal grabbed an iron bar from the floor. It looked like it had come from inside the wardrobe.

"Come on then let's have it. I swear Molly; I'm not budging from here until you tell me the truth, so you'll have to fight me to the death."

Molly stood back and she seemed to melt, she was sobbing. Dressed in only a vest and a pair of tracksuit bottoms she looked anorexic. Kendal watched her from the corner of her eyes, she knew she could strike at any minute and didn't trust her. Sliding down the door she sat facing Molly.

"Why did you leave me Molly?" Kendal asked. "I only had you left and you left me. Why Molly, why?"

Molly dragged her scrawny fingers through her thin greasy hair, she was desperate. "I had to go Kendal. I didn't leave you. It was him who made me do it. He told me if Mary was out of the picture then we could be together. He lied to me, he lied."

Kendal was holding the lower part of her stomach, she was going to be sick, her face was green. "Who lied to you Molly?"

There was silence and you could hear Molly snivelling. "John Daley. He was the one who fucked my life up." Kendal stood to her feet and spewed her ring up at the side of the room. Molly sat watching her as she rolled a cigarette up with shaking hands. "He's evil Kendal; you don't know the half of it. He's a mental case, he needs sectioning."

Kendal came to her side and touched the top of her head. "Molly, I need you. Please come home with me, please. We can get you some help and get you off the shit."

Molly looked her straight in the eyes. "I need heroin to block out what happened. I wish I was dead Kendal. I'm a bad person."

Molly rocked her body slowly on the cold wooden floorboards. "Will you tell me the full story Molly? Please, I need to know everything."

Kendal's auntie stood to her feet and grabbed a jumper from the side of the bed. "I will, but not here. I don't want you sat here in this shit-hole; it's a bad place to be. Come on, let's fuck off."

Kendal didn't know if she was having her over or not, she was watching her carefully. Creeping down the stairs Molly held her single finger up to her lips. "Be quiet, I owe Tony a tenner, if he hears me getting off, he'll go sick." Once they were out of the front door Kendal could see the full effects that heroin had had on her auntie. She must have only weighed six stone wet through.

"Come on follow me," Kendal said. "We'll go to my house."

★

After running her a bath Kendal passed Molly a clean towel. "Get a wash and that and I'll make you something to eat, you smell like shit. I can't believe that you would let yourself get this low Molly." Kendal's auntie took the pink towel and tried to raise a smile.

"That's drugs for you love, they just get deep under your skin and the rest is history." Kendal looked at Molly's brown broken teeth, most of them were missing and just a few decayed stumps were left behind.

"Hurry up; I'll make you a drink." Molly went into the bathroom with the clean clothes Kendal had sorted out for her.

Holding the cup close to her mouth Molly began. She kept blowing at her brew and slurping at it slowly. "Your mother was always the one who got the attention from the boys. I never got a second look when she was about, a proper tart she was," the corners of her mouth began to rise. Kendal smiled and played with her fingers. "When John first came to our house I was in love with him straightaway. I knew he was a lot older than me but he was fit as fuck. Me and our Mary was like flies around a camel's arsehole when he was about," Molly held her arms around her body as the hairs on the back of her neck stood on end, this was so hard for her. "I kissed him first you know, so by rights he was mine," her face was desperate. "Your mother was a ruthless bitch and she told me straight that she was having him no matter what. John was a pervert and he loved the attention he got from the young girls. We wasn't the first on the estate to have a bit of fun with him you know, he was shagging us all," Molly tilted her head to the side and her nostrils flared. "Mary got herself pregnant just to spite me. She knew I loved him and she loved rubbing salt in the wounds." Kendal looked horrified as the identity of her father bounced about in her head. Molly rolled a cig and popped it in the side of her mouth.

Kendal urged her to continue, she was hanging on her every word. "So who killed my mother?"

Molly choked up and her shoulders were shaking, she was cracking up. Kendal stood up and walked to her side, she run her fingers through her damp hair. Molly looked up at her niece and the truth was there in her eyes, she let out a scream like a crying banshee. "It was me Kendal, I killed my sister."

Kendal was suffocating and her face was as white as snow. Molly sank her head into her hands and for the first time ever she told the secret that she held deep in her heart for years. "I saw them together, I just flipped. After you were born John told me it was over between them. He promised me the world you know. He said we were running away together. I was young and vulnerable; I believed every word he told me." Kendal ran from the room and you could hear her retching into the kitchen sink. Molly followed her and rubbed the small of her back. "They were arguing in the park and John had hurt her bad. I saw him from where I was hid. He told me he hated her and she was just after his money. Seeing her running from him I knew that was my chance to get rid of her for good. Once John was gone I saw her on her hands and knees crawling from her hideout. I only hit her once at first, but before I knew it, the brick was smashing into her head and I lost control."

Kendal wiped her mouth. "So John knows you killed my mother?"

Molly froze; she backed off and stood with her back against the door. "No, he doesn't know it was me who finished her off. I told him I saw him in the park with her and he knew I saw the fight they had. He thinks he killed her."

Kendal dropped to the floor and sobbed. Slowly she lifted her head up. "So John Daley is my father then?"

Molly nodded her head. "Yes, he is your Dad."

Later that night, Kendal lay in her bed; her eyes staring at the moonlight, she seemed like she was in a trance. Molly was in the next room and she could hear her sobbing through the paper-thin walls. Holding her mother's diary in her hands she placed it on her chest. John Daley was going to pay for this mess, somehow, someway; he was going to get what he deserved. Kendal closed her eyes; she was drifting off to sleep.

CHAPTER FIFTEEN

Jackie Daley walked around the Manchester Arndale centre, she knew John had given her hush money and she hated that he thought he could buy her off. With a heavy heart she looked in the shop windows looking for something to wear, she was in no mood for shopping. The reflection in the shop window made her turn her head slightly. Jackie kept her head low and watched the child and her mother enter the toy shop next to her. It was Jane and Eva.

Jackie stared at the pair of them with a cunning look in her eyes. The corner of her mouth started to rise and she nodded her head slowly. "I'll teach you to lie to me John Daley, let's see who's laughing now then." Jackie followed Jane around the shopping centre, she was planning something you could see it in her eyes, she was ducking and diving. Eva ran out of the shop and you could see Jane paying for something at the till. Jackie was like a preying lioness and she knew she had to be quick. The exit was only a few seconds away from where she stood and she made her move without any further hesitation. Sprinting to the child's side she gripped her tightly and led her through the double doors. "Come on sweetheart, your Daddy wants to see you; he's got you some new toys." Eva smiled and walked away with the stranger, she was so trusting. Once Jackie was on Market Street, she mixed in with the crowd and she knew Jane would never find her, it was hammered with shoppers.

Eva was singing "Twinkle twinkle little star". Her

voice was low and she sounded sweet. The kid was cute
and she was prettily dressed in blue dungarees and a pink
t-shirt. "Where's my daddy? Is he coming to see me?"

Jackie was flustered and she was dragging the child
by her hand.

"Just be quiet will you, he'll be here in a minute."
Her car was parked not far from the shopping centre and
she knew in just a few more paces she would be safe. Eva
was getting worried and her feet stopped moving.

"I want my mummy," the child said as she started to
cry. Jackie didn't have any experience with children and
she was struggling to keep her occupied. Digging in her
bag she gripped a pink lip gloss.

"Here put some of that on, it's your Daddy's
favourite colour." The kid took hold of it and seemed
pleased with her new treasure.

"I love lipstick," she giggled.

Jackie clicked the seatbelt around the child and
started the engine. Checking her face in the mirror she
gave Eva's cheeks a friendly squeeze. "Your Daddy will
be so pleased to see you. You just sit there and be a good
girl, you'll see him soon enough." Jackie headed home;
she was speeding and nearly crashed a few times. It was
payback time…

Once she got back, Jackie Daley closed the curtains in
the front room and made sure all the doors were locked.
She piled sweets and biscuits high in front of Eva and
that seemed to keep her entertained for now. Gripping
her mobile phone she dialled her husband's number. "Hi
baby, I need you to come home now. I've got a surprise
for you." Her face was red and you could see that she
was under pressure. "Okay darling, see you soon." Jackie
was running about the front room and she was making

sure everything was in place for the next part of her plan. Gripping the silver pistol from the safe she shoved it down the front of her jeans. She was ready for action.

A car door slammed shut and Jackie was at the window checking who it was. John held a cocky look on his face as he bounced up the driveway, his arms was swinging at the side of him. "I'm going to wipe that smile right off your face, you lying bastard," Jackie whispered from her lookout position. Walking back into the front room you could hear whimpering from inside the small cupboard at the back of the room. Jackie turned the radio up to cover it up. Taking a deep breath she prepared to meet her husband. John walked into the living room and his eyes were all over.

"So, what's this big surprise then? It better be good Jackie, because you've just pulled me away from a right good earner. Some kid was selling leather jackets at rock bottom prices, and I've missed them now because of you."

Jackie poured two glasses of brandy and passed one to John. "Be patient my dear, be patient." Walking about the front room John's eyes followed her; he knew she was up to something. Sitting in his leather armchair he blew out his breath.

"Jackie, will you stop fucking about? I'm a busy man; I have to go back out."

She sat on the chair facing him; her eyes were dancing with madness. Tapping a cigarette on the table at the side of her she lit it slowly. "John, you do love me don't you?"

"Yes, for fuck's sake, yes. How many times do I have to say it? Don't tell me you've brought me home to ask me that?" Jackie chuckled.

"You would never lie to me would you?" John stood up and he was searching for his car keys.

"I tell you what, you're losing the plot. Fancy bringing me home, just to ask me that. Are you right in the bleeding head, you could have said that on the phone."

Jackie jumped from her seat, she snapped. "Sit back down wanker," she pulled the pistol from her waist and waved it at her husband. John's face dropped, he backed away from her.

"What the fuck are you doing with that you lunatic, go and put it back in the safe before someone gets hurt."

Jackie held her head back and giggled. "Oh, somebody is going to get hurt John, don't you worry about that." She fired a single shot into the wall and snarled at her husband. "I swear to you, you move one step closer to me and I'll shoot you. I mean it John; I'll blow your fucking brains out." John was sweating; he sat back down and loosened his collar. His chest was rising with speed. Edging back slowly Jackie never took her eyes off him. Her hand pressed the handle on the door and she grabbed the child from inside. Eva had black tape over her mouth and her hands were tied behind her. With a swift movement, Jackie pulled the tape from Eva's mouth.

"Daddy," she screamed when she saw John for the first time. Jackie stood tall and held the child back by her shoulders. John was white and lost for words, his lips were shaking. Walking closer to her husband Jackie waved the gun about in the air.

"Is this your child John? You've gone very quiet all of a sudden. I'll ask you again, is she your daughter?"

Jackie rammed the gun at the side of the child's head and he knew that in her state of mind she would have pulled the trigger at the drop of a hat. "Please Jackie, let Eva go. She's innocent in all of this. Look at her she's shaking."

Jackie ragged the kid about. "Does this face look like it gives a fuck? If she's not yours why are you arsed?" John knew he had to come clean; he couldn't risk his wife using the gun. Eva was hysterical and she was holding her hands towards her father.

"Daddy, I'm scared, make her stop please." John fell to his knees, his game was up. Lifting his head up slowly, he pleaded with his demented wife.

"She's mine Jackie. There you go, I've said it. Just let her go and we can sort this mess out. The police will be looking for her. You don't want to go to prison do you love?"

Jackie dragged her fingers through her hair, she was pacing the floor, she was a ticking bomb. "I fucking knew it, you dirty no good bastard. Why did I ever think you could be trusted?" Her body was in shock and she grabbed Eva in her arms. Pointing the gun at the side of the child's head she shot a look back to John.

"And what about Kendal Wilson, is she your child too?" John was taking no chances; he was edging towards his wife. As he stepped nearer to her she dragged the child away. "I said is Kendal yours too? I swear John, if you don't tell me; I'll kill this little fucker stone-dead. She means nothing to me, do you hear me, nothing."

John clenched his teeth tightly together; it was time to get it off his chest. "Yes, she's mine too."

Jackie's face creased and you could see the pain in her eyes. Sinking to her knees she let go of Eva. John grabbed the child with both hands and threw her to the corner of the room. Jackie held the gun in her hands and she was pointing it at John.

"Why, why John. I've given you the best years of my life and you go and do this." John knew he had to move fast, this woman was dangerous and it was only a matter of time before she pulled the trigger, he could see it in her eyes. Walking up and down the room he answered her.

"You couldn't give me a child, what did you want me to do? I wanted children, and you couldn't have them."

Jackie wiped her forehead with the sleeve of her blouse. "That wasn't my fault though was it John? Remember when I was sixteen and you made me have an abortion, that was the real reason I couldn't have kids, wasn't it you bastard! You sent me to some back street doctor who nearly killed me." John growled at her and edged closer. Jackie was hysterical. "Oh you've always liked the young girls haven't you John? The only reason you put a ring on my finger was because you knew my brothers would have cut your dick off otherwise. That's the truth isn't it, come on say it. I can take it." John pounced on her and grabbed the gun from her hand, he smashed it on the side of her head and she crashed to the floor like a lead weight. Her body shook for a few seconds and then she was lifeless. John sprinted to Eva's side.

"Ssshhh , Daddy's here with you now, everything going to be fine, sshhhh." He grabbed his car keys and ran with Eva to the car. Jackie's body lay on the floor and blood was seeping from the corner of her mouth, her breathing was shallow.

John nearly took the front gates from the hinges as he drove out of his driveway. Eva was still sobbing and he knew the police would be out in force looking for her. Picking up his phone in a panic he dialled Jane's number. He was shaking. "It's me John; I've got Eva with me. Are the police with you?" You could hear Jane screaming down the other end of the phone. "Please Jane get rid of them, just say you've made a mistake, please sort it out and we can be together again." The phone call ended after a long heated conversation and Jane said once she'd sorted it out with the police she would meet John at the Old Loom pub on Moston Lane. John reached over to the passenger side and stroked his daughter's hands. "Shall we take you to McDonald's? You love the chocolate milkshakes there don't you?" Eva snivelled and nodded her head.

★

Molly sat down with Kendal and her body was rattling for drugs. Sweat was rolling down her forehead and she looked grey. Holding the lower part of her stomach she stood to her feet. "I need to score Kendal. Have you got any money for me? I'm sorry, I can't do this anymore. I'm a drug addict, and I need a fix." Kendal stood up and wrapped her hands around Molly.

"Why did you ever get mixed up with heroin? You must have known how you'd end up." Molly sobbed.

"John gave it to me first; he said it would calm me down. Night after night he plied me with it, and then it was too late, I was addicted."

Kendal sank to the floor, her head rested in her hands. John Daley had fucked with her family for the last time. "I will come to the doctors with you Molly; we can go now if you want? Please for me, I just need you to be normal again." Molly stood shaking and spit hung from the corner of her mouth, her eyes were rolling to the back of her head, she was rattling.

"Just one last fix and I swear I will get clean. Please Kendal, just give me a tenner and I'll go and sort myself out. I'll be back before you know it. Please, I'm dying here." Kendal dug her hand into her bag and opened her purse. Holding the ten pound note out in her hand she watched Molly grab it with desperation.

"I'll be back soon. I promise," she said. In seconds the front door slammed shut, Molly was gone.

★

The police finally caught up with Scott and he was on remand at Strangeway's prison. An anonymous phone call had ended his freedom. His case was due in court the following week and he was looking at a heavy sentence. The police wanted Kendal to come and be a witness at the trial but her nerves were bad and she didn't think she could stand the ordeal of it all. Kendal told them she would think about it. Scott had pleaded not guilty to his crime and the case was set to run for three days at Manchester Crown Court. The story was all over the media.

Jane stood outside the pub on Moston Lane. Her hair was all over the show and she was pacing up and down like she'd lost the plot. Seeing John's car pulling up on the roadside she ran to it with speed. "What the fuck did you take her for? The police have gone ballistic at me for wasting police time. I had to say that I forgot you took her, do you know how that makes me look? I'll have social services knocking at my door first thing in the morning for sure."

"Get in the fucking car will you? I will tell you what's happened when you've calmed down," John ranted. Jane moved Eva to the back of the car and clicked her seatbelt around her. When she saw her face she realised she's been crying.

"What's up baby? Why are you upset?"

John screamed at the top of his voice, "Just close the car door and shut the fuck up." Jane obeyed him and sat in the passenger side of the car. She'd seen John in a temper before but this was in a league of its own, he was shaking from head to toe. The car pulled off and headed towards the motorway.

"Where are we going John? Are you going to tell me what's happened or what? You're scaring me." John wound his window down slowly and the cold air circulated around his face. Taking a deep breath he kept his eyes on the road.

"Jackie took Eva," before he could finish Jane was ramming her finger in his face.

"She's a crank her, I knew there was more to this than you were telling me. I tell you what, turn this car around. I'm going to see her. Who the fuck does she think she is taking my child. I swear to you, I'll rip her fucking head off."

"She's in a bad way," John said in a low voice. "I'm not sure if she's still alive."

Jane took a moment to digest what he'd just said and she looked in a trance, her mouth was moving but no words were coming out. Her hand gripped his arm. "John tell me you're lying, if you're not then please take me home. I don't want any part of this."

He banged his rounded fist on the dashboard. "I thought you loved me, if you do, then you'll keep your trap shut. We can move away together and start again. I thought that's what you wanted. Don't you want us to be a family, think about Eva."

Jane sat in silence her head was resting on the window. Nothing was ever straightforward in her life. Eva was asleep in the back of the car. John spoke in a low voice. "We can move to Blackpool, I've got a secret hideaway up there. Me and the lads used to use it back in the day when we needed to keep our heads down, so nobody would find us, we'll be safe there. I can go back home tomorrow and tell Jackie it's over." This was all too much for Jane to take in; she kept quiet and closed her eyes. John turned the music up and sped along the motorway.

CHAPTER SIXTEEN

Scott stood in the dock at Manchester Crown Court. His face was cocky and he showed no signs of remorse for the crime he'd committed. Molly stuck to her promise and she'd been free from drugs now for over a week. Her face looked different and the signs of improvement were visible already. Holding Kendal's hand she whispered into her ear. "It will all be over soon and then you can get on with your life. Scott will get what he deserves, trust me." Kendal sat in the courtroom and her body was trembling, she knew she would see her attacker for the first time since the assault. The police had offered her a room to give her evidence by video link, but she told them straight that she wanted to look her ex-boyfriend straight in his eyes when she gave her testimony. There was no way she was letting the bastard think she was scared of him. Kendal's hair had grown back now and she had it nicely styled. Her locks were still short but she suited her new look. She looked like a pixie.

The usher ordered everyone to stand up as the judge entered the courtroom, you could hear whispering inside the public gallery. Judge Byfield looked like he wasn't taking any crap today and he shot his eyes at the gallery for the people to remain quiet. Scott's eyes were all over the courtroom and he smiled at his sister Pat who was present. His jeans hung from his waist and you could see his shoulder blades sticking out from under his t-shirt. He face looked old; he wasn't coping with prison life at all.

The prosecutor stood to his feet and shuffled the

pieces of paper in front of him. Lifting a glass of water to his mouth he sipped on his refreshing drink. The trial was ready to begin. Pat leant over and whispered into Kendal's ear. "Please don't be a witness against him, look at him he's suffered enough, he can't hack another sentence, he'll string himself up, trust me."

Molly turned her head slowly; she was more than ready to bang this woman right out. Covering her mouth with her hand she stared at the woman. "Listen, Mother fucking Teresa. Your brother is getting slammed like it or not. Do you think we give a toss if he does himself in? My niece could have died, he left her for dead, are you forgetting that?"

Pat sank back down in her seat, she wasn't ready to give up, she grabbed Kendal's arm. "Just do it for me and the family, are you forgetting how I looked after you when you had nobody?"

Kendal pulled herself away. "Pat, I'm telling the truth. Why should I protect him? He's a low life?" Molly was ready for jumping over the seats to attack Pat, but Kendal held her back. The usher marched over to them now and warned them about the noise, she was fuming and made it clear that if there was any more noise they would be ejected from the courtroom.

The prosecution read out the details about the case and you could see people sneering at Scott. They were shaking their heads when the defence read out that he'd shaved his victim's hair off. Molly sat cracking her knuckles, coming off drugs was hard and she was finding it hard to concentrate, sweat was dripping from her forehead. A little later, the courtroom door opened and Paddy Wilson walked inside, he was dressed in a grey suit and looked smart. He dipped his head low as the judge looked at him. Paddy knew Molly was back on the scene but this was the first time he'd seen her. Sitting at the end of the front row he turned his head towards Kendal and nodded his head slowly. The trial was in full swing and it was soon Kendal's turn to take the stand.

Scott's barrister was a right smartarse and he was ready to pull Kendal apart, which was his job after all. She was sworn in by the court. The barrister was chomping on the bit to rip her apart on the stand. Walking slowly towards her he kept his head low and stuck one of his hands inside his trouser pocket casually. "Is Scott a violent man Kendal?" Her head was spinning and her throat was dry, she could feel the eyes of the courtroom on her, Kendal's cheeks were blushing.

"Yes, he is," she replied in a timid voice.

"Is it true to say that in the past, he was romantic and often bought you gifts to show his undying love?" Kendal was gripping the gold bar at the front of the dock her knuckles were turning white, she was trying to keep her cool but this man was winding her up. It was like she was on trial.

"He might have bought me the odd box of chocolates, but that was only after he'd beaten me up. I bet he never told you that did he?" She shot her eyes to the criminal and she could see him smirking, he was a lying bastard and he loved every minute of her pain. The barrister looked at her and told her to calm down; he was doing a great job of letting the courtroom see her temper.

"Did you let Scott inside your property on the night of the attack hoping that you would get back together?"

Kendal stood to her feet and waved her hands about in the air, she was ready to snap. "I don't know what he's told you, but he's lying. He broke into my house and attacked me," she pointed her finger at Scott. "Tell them Scott, tell them the truth. Don't be a nob-head all your life." Kendal was asked to sit down; she was like a wild woman. "No," she screamed. "You're listening to his pack of lies and believing him. Why am I being treated like the criminal when it's that prick sitting over there." Scott loved her outburst and smiled at his sister, he gave her a cheeky wink. Once Kendal had regained her composure she continued, her answers were blunt and she was answering yes and no to the questions she was asked. There was no way she was getting into another argument; it was just what Scott wanted. The case was adjourned until after dinner. Scott stood up from his seat and gave Kendal a cunning grin, he was so arrogant and she wanted to knock the smile right off his face.

The courtroom was buzzing as Judge Byfield left the room. Pat stood up and walked past Kendal in a strop, she had a face like a smacked arse. Molly was on her guard and made sure she couldn't get anywhere near her niece. Paddy walked slowly from the courtroom. Once Kendal was by his side he reached for her hand and squeezed it gently. "It's going to be fine love, don't let the cunt get to you. He's getting time shoved up his arse no matter what." Kendal carried on walking she was ready to burst into tears; it was all too much to take in. "Come here, let me give you a hug," Paddy said. Molly walked behind them and she knew the time had come to face her demons. Her father had banished her from the family house years before and she'd said some things in the past that she was ashamed of. She was treading on egg shells as she walked behind them.

The sun shone brightly outside the court. As soon as they stepped outside the three of them searched their pockets for their cigs, they were gasping. Standing huddled together a thick cloud of smoke circled over their heads. Molly looked at her father and her voice was low. "I'm sorry Dad, I've been a disgrace to this family and I deserved everything you said to me." Paddy was choked up and large lump formed in his throat, he wasn't ready to talk, he just couldn't do it yet. Molly touched the middle of his arm, and he was finding it hard to show her any kind of forgiveness, he pulled away from her slowly. "I was at my Mam's funeral you know, I was hid away so you couldn't see me. She had a good send off didn't she?" Paddy took a deep breath.

"She sure did, thanks to John Daley; he paid for all the cars and flowers you know?"

Molly's face changed and Kendal was sure she was going to tell her father all about his perverted mate. "He's a prick Dad; you don't know the half about him. Trust me he's a wrong un," Molly said. Kendal changed the conversation quickly and Paddy stood gawping at his daughter, he was trying to digest what she'd just said, you could see the puzzled look on his face, he wasn't letting it go.

"What do you mean by that Molly? Don't you be stirring up any shit. John has always been here for this family, so don't be badmouthing him, he's a good man."

Molly was chugging hard on her cigarette and nearly choked. "The guy's a sex-case, trust me," she whispered. Paddy was ready to dig deeper but Kendal made sure he was stopped.

"I'm starving, can we go and get something to eat before I faint, I feel weak." The three of them walked across the small road in front of the courts. None of them were speaking and you could see by Paddy's face that he was confused.

In a side street near the courts John Daley sat in his car. If Scott walked free from the courts today he wanted to see him with his own two eyes. If that was the case he was getting him done in for sure. There was no way in this world the crank was walking the streets again, not on his watch anyway.

John looked like he had the worries of the world on his shoulders; his cheekbones were prominent from his face. Jackie was nowhere to be seen, when he'd returned home she had disappeared, cleared out her clothes and left a note telling him it was over. Jackie's brothers were phoning him constantly as they were worried about her whereabouts. John made up a pack of lies and told them that she'd gone on a cruise to get away for a while. Jackie's brothers weren't daft and they knew something had gone on. But for now all they could do was sit and wait for their sister to get in touch with them. John screwed his eyes up as the sunshine hit his eyes. Gripping the steering wheel he concentrated on the figure he could see in front of him.

His jaw dropped when he saw Molly with Paddy and Kendal. "What the fuck is she doing here?" he snapped. "Fuck me, that's all I need. I tell you what Molly Wilson you raging bag-head, you're dicing with death. If you think you're making waves for me, you can think again. I'll sort you out good and proper this time trust me, you dirty fucking smack-head." John sat cracking his knuckles.

Kendal sat in a cafe munching on a tuna sandwich. Molly was scranning her food too and she ate like she'd been starved for months, she was nearly biting her fingers off. Paddy was quiet and he sat looking out of the window, something was playing heavy on his mind. Molly nudged

Kendal in the arm. "We don't have to stay at court now you've given your evidence, let's do one and go home." Kendal stopped eating, her face was serious.

"No, I want to see the prick's face when he gets sentenced. I'm not scared of him anymore, and he's going to see that when I laugh in his face when he gets years shoved up his arse." Molly backed down as Kendal's phone started ringing, it was Steve her boyfriend. Steve had still been in the background all along but something told Kendal he wasn't interested in her anymore, he was just her fuck buddy when he was home in Manchester. Even after her attack he'd only phoned her to make excuses why he couldn't come home. It was only a matter of time before she kicked him to the kerb. The relationship was over.

★

Jane stood with Eva at the train station. There was no way she was staying with John anymore, he made her skin crawl, he was a crank. Night after night she watched him pace the floor fighting with his conscience, he was ready to snap. "Mummy, where are we going," Eva asked. Jane gripped her hand tightly as they sat down on a bench.

"We're going home chicken. Daddy's a bad man, and we need to get away." Eva snivelled and sunk her head on Jane's lap. She was going to miss her daddy. Jane boarded the train to Manchester with Eva held close to her body.

★

Kendal and her family sat back down in the courtroom. This was the day for sentencing. Scott had been found guilty on all charges. Sitting in the dock he growled at Kendal and her family. Molly was grinding her teeth at him and he laughed in her face. The room was quiet and the moment had come for Scott to meet his fate. The judge summed up and looked at the criminal in the dock. "You are a danger to society young man, and I hope the time you spend in prison will help you to mend your ways." Scott was nodding his head slowly.

"Just get on with it you old cunt," he mumbled under his breath. The screw at the side of him warned him to keep his mouth shut. Kendal was sat on the edge of her seat and was chewing on her fingernails.

"I sentence you to six years imprisonment," Judge Byfield said in a loud firm voice.

Pat stood up from her seat and she was up in arms. "Are you having a laugh or what? Come on, fucking murderers don't get that long, you need to sort this out." The usher escorted her out from the public gallery, she was ranting and raving and it was clear she wasn't happy. Scott nodded his head slowly; walking to the front of the dock he made a gun with his fingers and pointed at the jurors.

"Don't worry you shower of shit. I'll be out soon and I've clocked each of your faces, so sleep tight wankers." The security grabbed him by the arms and he was led out of the courtroom before he could say another word. One member of the jury stood up and he was frantic.

"So, what are you going to do to protect us? You've just heard him saying he knows who we are, what protection are we going to get when he gets out." The judge tried to calm them down and asked them to come to his chambers to discuss the matter further.

A woman sprang up from her seat and she was white in the face, she was trembling. "I tell you what, I'll never sit on another jury again. I've got kids you know. How do you expect me to sleep knowing he could find out where I live?" The clerk of the court was calming the jurors down, but they were having none of it, they wanted answers. Kendal stood up from her seat once the judge had left the room. She seemed in a dream and nothing felt real.

Molly came to her side. "What a result ay? I told you the wanker was getting slammed."

Kendal rolled her eyes and turned her head slowly. "Six years is a shit and a shave for him, he'll do that on his fucking head. I wish he was dead then he could never come back. It's like the jurors said, he'll be out soon and then what happens? You don't know him like I do, he's dangerous, he's fucking tapped in the head."

Molly pulled her closer. "I'm here with you now, I would die for you, you know that? There is no way that cock will ever get near you again, trust me." Molly made sure nobody was listening and covered her mouth with her hand. "I can get the cunt done in. I know a few guys who will do it for a quick earner, I swear to you, he'll be gone forever." Kendal pushed her away and started walking out of the courts. As she stepped outside Pat was there waiting for her. Her face was red and you could see she wanted war. Pat stomped towards her with a face of fury.

"I hope you're happy now you daft bastard. You always have to go one better don't you. We could have worked this out, but oh no, you had to get the dibble involved. I'll tell you what Kendal, when he does get out, I'd hate to be in your shoes. You're going to get what you deserve, you grassing bitch." Molly ran at Pat and gripped her by the throat; she dragged her around the corner out of public view.

"Listen you fat cow, if your brother comes within a mile of my niece, I'll come looking for you, do you get me?" Pat wriggled free and spat in Molly's face.

"Do you think you scare me you fucking junkie? Get back where you belong in the gutter, you're nothing but scum." Molly dug her hand inside her jacket and pulled out a small penknife. Pointing it at Pat's face she clenched her teeth together.

"Like I said, I'll come looking for you." Kendal was at Molly's side and she dragged her away.

"Just leave her; she's not worth a charge sheet." Kendal looked over her shoulder as she walked away, she could see Pat on her mobile phone.

"Blood's thicker than water Kendal remember that," Molly whispered. "No matter what, family comes first."

Paddy stood waiting for them both; he'd been in the toilet and missed all the commotion. "Shall we go back to my house? I can make us something to eat. I can even make Corned beef hash just like my Nelly used to make if you want?" Molly was sold; she'd not had any home cooked food for years. Usually she lived on toffees and crisps and anything else that she could get her hands on to curb her sweet tooth. They all headed to the bus stop.

John Daley watched the family from his hideout. He had to get to Molly before she told anyone about his secret, he wasn't taking any chances. Turning the engine over he advanced slowly from the side street. Kendal saw a black car honking its horn in the distance. Paddy screwed his eyes up and sighed. "Come on its John, we can get a lift home. He's a saviour that man is. He's always there when I need him. He's our angel in disguise." Kendal and Molly shot a look to each other. Paddy was already walking towards the car. "Come on girls, hurry up, he's parked on double yellow lines."

Molly leant into Kendal's ear, "Right you, don't say a fucking word. Just get in the car and let's get home. John will get what's coming to him trust me, but for now keep your trap shut." Not a single word was spoken between them in the car. They both sat in the back of the car staring out of the window. Paddy was aware of the atmosphere; he was watching the girls from the wing mirror. John tried to make conversation with them both but they completely ignored him. John looked in his rear view mirror and Molly stared back at him and smirked. She loved that he was uneasy and she kept her cards close to her chest. Pulling up outside Paddy's house the girls jumped out of the car and headed inside, there were no goodbyes.

Paddy looked at his mate and he couldn't hold his tongue any longer. "What's going on with them two, have you fallen out with them or something?"

John chuckled and tried to sweep it under the carpet. "Not as far as I know Paddy. You know what women are like; they're probably on the blob or something." Paddy looked at John's face and knew he was hiding something.

"Cheers for the lift John, see you around pal." John watched Paddy walk away and banged his clenched fist on the window.

"Fuck, fuck, fuck." A mobile phone started ringing. "Hi Jane, I'll be home soon, I'm just in Manchester sorting out some business." His ear was pressed hard to the phone. "What do you mean you've left me? Jane where are you? Please I need you." The phone smashed against the dashboard. Taking a few minutes to regain his composure, John drove away.

"I couldn't even look at him Molly; I wanted to tell

him that I know all about him and my mother." Molly made sure Paddy was out of the room. She held her hands out in front of her.

"And then what? He's not going to say, oh, yes I'm your Dad is he? Think about it?"

Kendal stood up and looked at her face in the mirror, pulling her fringe back from her face she turned her head back around. "I look like him don't I? Why have I never seen it before?"

There was a noise from outside the door and Molly crept towards it with one finger held up to her mouth, she opened the door quickly and she could see Paddy going into the kitchen. Pressing the door firmly shut she sat back down on the sofa.

"We have to keep this to ourselves, no one must ever know." Kendal was white in the face.

"We should tell my Granddad you know. Why are you protecting John; he's ruined this family, and my life, we owe him nothing."

Molly was frantic, "Just keep a lid on it for now; I need to think this through. John will be gunning for me now he's seen me with you, he'll be crapping his pants." Paddy walked into the room holding two dishes in his hands, his face looked troubled.

"Here get that down your neck, it's just like my Nelly used to make. Go on have a taste, and see what you think?" Molly and Kendal started eating; they were dipping thick slices of bread into their food. Paddy sat twiddling his thumbs.

"Why aren't you having anything Granddad, it's nice."

"I've lost my appetite, I'll grab some later," he moaned. Paddy seemed edgy and he didn't stay long in the room. Popping his head back inside the living room you could see him holding his coat in his hands. "I'm going out for a walk."

Molly nodded her head and carried on eating her food. Paddy was gone.

CHAPTER SEVENTEEN

Betty Jackson sat with Kendal in the staff room, it was break time. "Put the kettle on love, I'm parched," Betty uttered. Kendal's mood was low and the events of the last few months had taken their toll on her. She looked tired and her spirits were low. Kendal loved her job as a teacher's assistant, but at the moment her mind wasn't on the job, she just couldn't concentrate. Betty walked to her side and bent her knees. "Kendal do you think you should take a bit of time off from work?"

"Why am I that bad Betty?" Kendal sighed.

Mrs Jackson stood up as the kettle boiled and finished making the two cups of tea; she left Kendal at the table. "You just seem," she paused. "Well, distant, not your old self."

Kendal wrapped her arms around her body; she knew she was right; her head was all over the place lately. "I think I might you know. I just need to relax. I swear to you Betty; I'm not getting to sleep until three in the morning. Every noise I hear, I'm up out of bed checking it out. I'm a nervous bloody wreck."

Betty walked back to her side with the two cups hanging from her fingers. "Quick grab one of them cups, it's burning my finger." Betty looked relieved when the mugs were on the table. "Have you tried reading your books to help relax you at night? You know the Quick read books I got you?"

Kendal shook her head and inhaled deeply. "No, I can't concentrate anymore Betty. I've tried, but I just seem to be reading the same page over and over again, but nothing's registering." Kendal picked her cup up and blew her breath at the top of it.

"I was thinking of trying to write a book," she cringed and closed her eyes tightly waiting for Betty's reaction. Mrs Jackson smiled at Kendal.

"Well, just give it a go then. You're more than capable you know. I can help you too. It might just be what you need to clear your head."

Kendal rubbed her hands together. "Really Betty, do you think I could do it?"

"I'm more than sure Kendal. You have a way with words and I know once you put them down onto paper people will love them."

"What could I write about though?" Her eyes looked around the room as she was tapping her finger on her front tooth, thinking.

"Write about what you know," Betty advised. "That's always a good place to start."

"But Betty my spelling is crap, and even though I can read and write now I'm still no star student, let's face it."

Betty passed her a biscuit from the tin on the table. "Self-belief sweetheart, that's all that you need." Kendal nodded her head.

"Do you know what Betty, I'm going to start writing tonight. God knows what I will write about, but ay, he who dares, and all that." Kendal's mood lifted and she was smiling. She was going to book some time off from work and try to sort her life out. This was just what she needed to get herself back on her feet again.

Betty coughed and cleared her throat she was watching Kendal from the corner of her eyes. "One of your friends came to see me today. She wants me to help her to read and write, Jane she was called, she's a lovely girl."

Kendal snarled and smashed her fist onto the table. "What, Jane came here to see you?"

"Yes, she's got her little girl in the blue nursery and she told me she knew how I helped you."

Kendal stood up and forgot who she was talking too. "Well fuck her off Betty, she's nothing but trouble, she was the one who told my ex- boyfriend where I lived. She's no friend of mine. I swear to you, she's got more front than Blackpool that one has, trust me."

Betty raised her eyes to the ceiling and pulled her glasses down over her nose, she peered over them and spoke in a firm tone. "Kendal, don't be bitter. Forgiveness is a part of life, its takes a better person to forgive someone you know."

"Yeah but."

Betty stopped her dead in her tracks. "No buts Kendal. Everyone deserves an education; surely you're not begrudging her that are you?" Kendal bit her tongue, there was so much that Betty didn't know about Jane, so she backed down.

"No Betty, you're right. It's nothing to do with me if the girl wants to learn to read and write. Who am I to stand in her way?"

Betty hugged Kendal. "There you go, you're learning already, forgiveness feels good doesn't it?" Kendal smiled and grabbed her coat. Betty was right, forgiveness did feel good.

★

Ella May sat at the dining table drawing. She had every

coloured felt-tip spread out in front of her and she seemed lost in a world of creativity. Molly was staying with Paddy for a few days, he was a bit under the weather lately and he needed her help. The sound of the clock ticking on the wall filled the room. Kendal tapped her fingers on the arm of the chair. Casting her eyes over to the pile of paper next to her daughter she sat twiddling her thumbs. "Can Mummy borrow some of your paper sweetheart?"

"Yes, are you drawing too Mummy, we can draw a princess castle if you want?"

Kendal picked up the white crisp pieces of paper and smiled at her daughter. "Not tonight love, I've got to do some work for school." Ella May carried on drawing; her tongue was sticking out slightly as she coloured in the lines of the castle she'd drawn. Kendal sank her head inside her bag searching for a pen, once she'd found one she sat on the sofa with her legs tucked up under her. Rolling the pen about in her fingers, she sat thinking. Nothing was happening. Standing to her feet she went into the kitchen and grabbed a biscuit. Ella May was singing from inside the other room and it made her smile, swinging her hips she walked back into the front room, she was singing too.

The pen seemed to have a mind of its own and as soon as it touched the paper it began the journey of writing a book. Kendal took her time writing the first page and you could see her mouth moving as she read over what she'd written. Paper was rolled up in balls at the side of her and every now and then she would snap and throw the pen at the wall. "I can't fucking do this."

When Ella May was tucked up in bed Kendal was still writing, it was one o'clock in the morning and she was lay flat on her stomach penning her book. Kendal was writing about what she knew, she was writing a book based on her own life, she'd changed the names of the characters but it was so near the bone it was untrue. The book was fiction and she still hadn't come up with a name for it yet. Looking out at the night sky her eyes looked peaceful, Betty was right yet again, writing did calm her down.

Molly sat with her father and listened to his chest rattling. He was sat in his chair and his eyes were closing. There was a knock at the door and her face looked puzzled. "Who the fuck is it at this time?" she mumbled. Walking slowly to the door she could see a shadow of a man stood at the front door. With caution her fingers turned the catch. John Daley was stood there with his hand resting on the doorframe.

"Good evening Molly, is Paddy in?" Molly knew that was just an excuse for him to come and see her and she tried to slam the door in his face but his size nine foot was stopping her from closing it.

"Fuck off John, he's not well. My father's asleep, so just piss off." His hand slowly stroked across her cheek, he was chuckling to himself.

"You're not asleep are you though; can we have a bit of a chat?" Molly froze, even after all these years John still made her heart leap about in her chest.

"Me and you chat? What's all this about John, don't fuck about with me. Just say what you have to say and go." John leant in to sink his lips on hers, she could smell the alcohol on his breath and she jerked out of the way quickly. There was no way she was trusting him in the house. Grabbing her coat from the banister she walked out into the garden. "We can talk out here; you're not stepping one foot inside this gaff?"

John wobbled back and nearly crashed to the floor.

Molly could see a few youths playing at the front of the garden and she felt safe. She knew he wouldn't touch her with them about, it wasn't his style. Molly jumped onto the garden wall and started to roll a cigarette.

"You look well Molly, pretty in fact." She lifted her head up slowly and shook her head.

"Are you having a laugh or what? Cut the crap John, just say what you have to say, then fuck off." He pushed himself between her legs and made them separate.

"You're just like me you are Molly Wilson, you're a fighter. You've kept my secret for years and I owe you." She pushed him away and inhaled on her cig, he was spooking her.

"Yeah, I kept your seedy secret quiet John and how did you repay me ay?" she poked her bony finger into his firm chest. "You gave me drugs and got me addicted to heroin. I'm clean now though John and you know what?" her eyes were wide open. "For the first time in my life I can see you for the arse-hole that you really are. I should have grassed you up straight away to the police and then my life might have been different."

John moved in closer and he kept his voice low. "But are you clean now Molly?" he dug his hand in his trouser pocket and pulled out three small bags of brown powder. "Once a smack-head, always a smack-head. Here have these for old times' sake." Molly looked horrified as her eyes fixed on the drugs; she licked her lips frantically and rocked about slowly. She jerked her head back and spat into his face.

"You're an evil twat John. What kind of man are you?" She wiped the sweat from her head and started to head back into the house. John ran after her.

"I'll give you ten grand, to fuck off. I mean it, never

to be seen around here again, easy money, think about it."
Molly froze, turning slowly she shot a look at him.

"Why do you want rid of me John? Are you scared that now I'm clean everyone will know the truth about you?"

John was nose to nose with her. His warm breath was in her face. "Like I said, bitch, ten grand to fuck off. It's not rocket science is it?"

Molly blew a laboured breath and buttoned her coat up, she was cold. "Stick your money right up your ring piece John. You don't control me anymore. You and your drugs are no longer part of my life. And, do you know what John?" she grinned and held her head to the side. "It feels so good to see you as the underdog for a change. It's not a nice feeling is it when someone controls your life. That's how you made me feel when I had to beg you for drugs. The drugs, you got me addicted to."

John was stuttering, he was clenching his fist at the side of him. Molly ran from his side and stood at the front door. "Revenge is sweet John. I suggest you take your money and run. You never know when you'll get that knock on your door. You can't buy my silence anymore." The front door slammed shut and John was left in the garden alone. Cupping his face in his hands he knew the game was up. Molly was right, he needed to move away.

★

Kendal stacked the pieces of paper high in front of her. After three months of hard work, she'd finally completed her first novel. Her fingers slid over every page and she loved that she'd finally finished it. "Missing pieces," was the name of the book. Ella May had coloured the front cover and it looked bright and pretty. Today was the day she was going to show it someone for the first time. Every day in work she'd told Betty about her book, and she said she was dying to get her hands on it to have a read.

Kendal looked inside Betty's office before she started work and her face dropped. She could see Jane sat at the table with Betty learning to read. Kendal's heart was thumping in her chest and she had to cover her mouth to stop the sound of her heavy breathing. Dipping her head forward she peeped at Jane again. She looked different and she seemed to have put a bit of weight on. A hand touched her shoulder from behind her and she nearly dropped down dead. It was one of the other teachers. "Bloody hell Jenny, I nearly had a bleeding heart attack then. Don't make me jump like that again. Look at the state of me now, I'm a wreck." Jenny apologised, and gave Kendal a hug.

"Is Betty in her office, I just wanted a quick word with her?" Before she could answer her Jenny walked into the office. Kendal stood watching the door and before she could move, she could see a pair of feet on the floor. Lifting her head up slowly she saw Jane for the first time in ages. Jane filled up and her eyes were watering. The few seconds that passed seemed like hours. Kendal twisted her hair around her fingers and remembered Betty's wise words about forgiveness.

"Hello Jane," Kendal stood nervously. Jane raised a smile. There were no words spoken as she gripped her in her arms.

"Kendal I'm so sorry," Kendal pulled her from her body and placed a single finger on Jane's lips.

"Be quiet, we both know what happened. It's time to move on. God knows I've made mistakes, just let's start again from now."

A single tear trickled down Jane's face. Kendal placed her fingers on her cheek and wiped it away with a swift movement. "We've cried enough tears Jane, let's be happy from now on?" The two women shared a moment and Betty hid herself away back in her office, she'd been hoping that the two of them would meet up soon, and her wish had been granted. Jane smirked and her cheeks blushed.

"I'm learning to read and write. I should have done it years ago, but you know me, stubborn arse aren't I?"

Kendal dug her finger into her waist and made her giggle. "You sure are Jane, you sure are." Jane and Kendal arranged to meet later on that evening; there was so much they had to catch up on. They were friends again.

Kendal walked into Betty's office at the end of the working day. She held a black bag at the side of her with her manuscript in it. "Betty, can I have a quick word if you're not busy?" Betty was on the phone and waved her inside the room. Once the phone call ended she looked at Kendal eagerly.

"What's up darling?" There was rustling as Kendal pulled out the sheets of paper from the bag and placed it neatly on Betty's desk. Patting her flat palm on the top of it she smiled.

"There you go Betty, one finished book." Betty flicked rapidly through the pages, her face was serious. She knew Kendal was writing a book but she never really expected her to finish it so soon. With her eyes on the paper Betty pushed her glasses up over her nose. Kendal was like a spare part and she stood fidgeting watching her. With a cough she brought Betty back into the conversation. "Will you read it for me Betty and see what you think. I know there will be loads of spelling mistakes in it and all that, but I've tried my best." Betty chewed down on her lips; this was a proud moment for her. She gripped Kendal's hands in hers and smiled.

"This is amazing; you don't know what you have done. Look at all the words you have used. You have put so many sentences together, Kendal you are so talented." Kendal was embarrassed and her cheeks were going beetroot.

"You won't be saying that when you've read it Betty," she chuckled. "Before you start it, I must warn you that it is full of swearing," she covered her eyes with her hands waiting for her mentor to open fire. Betty giggled.

"Listen, I might be a teacher, but I am human you know. I've got a good collection of my own swear words that I use when I'm rattled, so don't be silly, swearing is part of life." Kendal helped her put the book into a bag. "I'm going to start it tonight; I can't wait to get my teeth into it."

Kendal smiled from ear to ear. "I'm nervous Betty, say it's shit? Then I've wasted all this time for nothing."

Betty was annoyed. "Listen you, stop saying you've wasted your bleeding time. Rome wasn't built in a day. Authors take ages to find their feet. You've done so much already, please see that."

Kendal flicked her fringe from her eyes. "I know Betty, I know. It's just the way I am. I have to start believing in myself don't I?"

"You sure do honey, you sure do," Betty replied.

That night Jane brought Eva along with her to Kendal's house. She needed her as a comfort blanket. Jane held her child close to her body as she walked inside the house. The clinking of the bottles of wine in the plastic bag made Kendal smile; it was just like old times when they were younger. "I bet that's that cheap plonk we used to drink isn't it?"

Jane pulled the bottles out of the bag and looked embarrassed. "How did you know that?"

"Some things never change love, and your taste in wine is just one of them." Kendal laughed and took the wine. Walking into the kitchen she shouted behind her. "I'll order us a Kebab later on and then we're straight. I don't want you saying I'm a tight arse for not buying any beer." The clinking of the glasses filled the kitchen. Eva walked to Kendal's side and pulled at her leg.

"Can I have a drink too?" Kendal shot her eyes down to the child and she nearly stopped breathing, she held her hands on her chest. This was her half-sister, her own flesh and blood. Looking into her eyes she could see John's eyes staring back at her, she backed off. Taking deep breaths she held her body up against the wall. She had a big decision to make, should she tell Jane that truth about her father and that Eva was her sister? Jane came into the kitchen and picked Eva up in her arms.

"What's she after, is she asking for food again? I swear Kendal, she eats like a horse, she's never full, her belly is a bottomless pit." Kendal hid her face away and dipped her head into the fridge.

"Orr, leave her alone she only wanted a drink, she's fine." Kendal could feel Jane's eyes burning into the back of her head. She was taking time to compose herself. "There you go Eva, two milkshakes, one for you and one for Ella May. Do you want to give it her?" The kid grabbed the two plastic bottles from her hands and ran back into the front room. She was eager to make friends and ran to Ella May's side passing her one of the drinks.

The night was in full swing and the two kids were

fast asleep on the sofa. Kendal and Jane were listening to old tunes and reminiscing about the days gone by. "I've written a book," Kendal piped up.

Jane held her stomach and laughed. "Fuck me Kendal; you don't do things by halves do you? I mean, you go from one extreme to the other."

Kendal hunched her shoulders and fluttered her eyelashes. "I know, you're right. It's just something that I've always wanted to do. When I'm writing I feel free, if you know what I mean. I can just well," she paused. "Be who I want to be, I don't have to pretend."

Jane slurped the last bit of her wine from the glass. "You've had some hard times Kendal, you're a strong woman. I will never hurt you again. I promise you from this day forward I will be the best friend you deserve. No secrets, no nothings."

Kendal blew her breath, it was time to confess. She couldn't hold onto the truth any longer, the wine had seen to that. "Jane sit down, I need to tell you something." Jane was still humming some tune and she was giddy. She held a flat palm towards her and tilted her head to the side.

"Don't tell me you love me and you've missed me, I already know that," she held the lower part of her stomach and rolled about on the sofa giggling to herself. Kendal grabbed her arm and pulled her back up.

"No Jane, this is serious, you need to listen." Sitting up straight Jane popped a cig into her mouth and offered Kendal one. After the cigarettes were lit they both sat staring at each other.

"Come on then, spill the beans," Jane urged. Kendal swallowed hard and she was playing with the cuff off her blouse. Keeping her head low she started to confess all.

"John Daley is my father."

Jane punched her in the arm and placed her hands between her legs. "Orr stop it, I'm going to piss myself. I swear to you, ever since I've had a baby I can't stop pissing. I sneeze, I piss, I laugh, I piss, it's not funny you know."

Kendal's face was serious. "I'm not joking Jane. I'm telling you the truth."

Jane frowned and leant onto the arm of the chair with her head resting in her hands. "Come on stop fucking with me, how can John be your Dad?" Kendal left the room and came back holding her mother's diary in her hands. Jane sprang up from her seat. "Don't tell me you're bringing up the past again, I admitted I nicked it from you, but I gave it you back didn't I?"

"Just sit down, for fucks sake. And I'll explain." Kendal started to read from the diary. Jane was hanging on her every word and she rubbed at her arms as the hairs started to stand on end. Once Kendal read the facts about her mother and John Daley, Jane sat thinking, she wasn't happy, her face dropped.

"That doesn't prove anything. It just says your mother had a bit of a thing with John. Fuck me, Molly as well, the man is a predator. I will tell you something, I'm so glad I kissed his sorry arse goodbye, he's a bad man."

Kendal knew she would have to put all the pieces together for Jane; it wasn't sinking in. "Why do you think he was always looking out for me? The evidence is there right in front of you. Eva is my half-sister."

Jane paced the front room and she was holding her hands on her hips, she didn't believe her. "Why has he never claimed you then? Surely, if he was your father he would have told you?"

Kendal sank on the sofa and swigged a large mouthful of her wine. "Sit down, there's more to this story. You need to promise me though, that what's said in this room stays inside this room." Jane wasn't sure at first but she made the sign of the cross across her head and body and swore her vow to silence. "My Mam got pregnant by John to spite our Molly. Our Molly told me herself that my Mam only done it so she could fleece John for money. Anyway to cut a long story short, John tried to do her in and Molly saw him."

Jane's jaw dropped and she covered her mouth with her hand. "Is this for real, you're fucking with me right?" she asked.

Kendal continued, "No, straight up. My Mam's body was found in Queen's Park, do you remember me telling you?"

Jane nodded her head slowly. "Well, Molly followed them both on the night she was killed and she saw it all with her own two eyes. She saw John attacking my mother and he left her for dead." Jane chewed on her lips.

"Well, who killed her then, because you said he left her for dead, not that she was dead?"

Kendal reached over and held Jane's hands tightly. "It was our Molly. John told her if my Mam was out of the picture that they could be together forever. She was young Jane and she didn't know what she was doing." Jane ran into the kitchen and hung her head into the sink; she was spewing her guts up. Kendal carried on talking as she rubbed her back. "John thinks he killed her, and our Molly has been fleecing him for years to hold his secret. He was the one who got her on drugs you know. He told her it would help calm her down; he's a bastard isn't he?"

Jane wiped her mouth with her sleeve. Grabbing

a cold drink of water she wobbled back into the front room. "This is some fucked up shit Kendal. Here was me thinking that John had the hots for you, when all the time the fucking fossil was your Dad. This is too much to take in, it's bad Kendal. It's really bad."

Kendal nodded her head, she was holding her chest and she looked like she was going to pass out. "I know Jane, I know."

"Somebody needs to knock him down from his high horse then. If you live by the sword you die by the sword. He needs his comeuppance," Jane ranted.

Kendal nodded her head slowly. "He'll get it one day, don't you worry. It's just a matter of time; it all comes to those who wait."

CHAPTER EIGHTEEN

Molly looked agitated; she sat looking at the clock on the wall. She was stressed and she was snapping every time Paddy tried to make conversation with her. "Dad, will you just be quiet," she moaned. "I've got a banging headache and all you're doing is making it worse."

"I was only telling you about this jockey on the horse I've backed. Go and get back in bed if you feel rough. You were up until late last night wasn't you, because I heard you rummaging around in the middle of the night." Molly bolted up from her seat, she'd heard enough from her old man.

"Fuck me Dad, you should work for Crimewatch you should. I wasn't up all night for your information, I went to the bleeding toilet, so wind you're neck in before it gets you into trouble." She left the room and slammed the living room door shut behind her.

Molly tapped her finger on the screen of her mobile phone. Kendal had given it to her and it was just a cheap one from Asda. Spread across the bed she typed a text message and pressed the send button. Whoever she was texting was a secret because she was watching the bedroom door at all times, she was edgy. Seconds later there was a ringing tone and she gripped the phone in her hands as if her life depended on it. Molly was whispering and she was walking about the room. "Okay, meet me tonight at nine o'clock. And don't forget the money." The phone call ended and she plonked her body back on the bed, Molly lay staring at the ceiling. Clocking the mirror at the end of the bed she sat up facing it and ruffled her hair. Drugs were never far from her thoughts and even though she had been clean for months she still craved the rush of heroin through her veins.

Kendal walked to school and her head didn't seem her own. She tripped over a kerbstone that was sticking up on the path and nearly crashed to the floor. After Ella May had gone into her class room she walked into Betty's office hoping to see Jane there. She was always there on a Friday at this time. The door creaked open and she could see Betty stood at the sink at the back of the room. "I thought Jane was here today, is she late?" Betty look flustered.

"No, she phoned me early this morning and told me she wasn't coming in today, she said she had family problems." Kendal closed the door behind her and sat down, she was confused. Jane hadn't mentioned anything to her about any family problems, so she probed deeper.

"Did she say what kind of problems she was having Betty, or who with?"

"No, sweetheart, she did sound a bit upset though, come to think of it. She wasn't her normal bubbly self." Kendal pulled her phone from her jacket pocket and dialled Jane's number; you could just hear the phone ringing. Nobody picked up.

"That's strange Betty; she always has her phone to hand. I hope she's okay." Betty placed a comforting hand on her shoulder and squeezed at it softly.

"Jane's a fighter love, whatever she's going through she will bounce back, try not to worry." Kendal dipped her head low.

"Yeah you're right I suppose. I might call and see her after work just to make sure though." Betty rubbed her hands together and sat down at the table, she was bouncing about in her chair.

"Go on then ask me," she giggled.

Kendal lifted her head up and her face was blank. "Ask what?" Betty bent down underneath the table and grabbed a black bag. With strain in her fingers she pulled Kendal's book from it. Their eyes met and Kendal smiled. "Have you read it then?" she was nervous and fidgeting about. Betty's eyes filled up and she poked her finger inside her glasses to hold the tears back.

"It's bloody amazing. I can't believe you have written so much and so well." Betty placed her hand over her heart. "Promise me, you will take this somewhere and see if you can get it published," her face was serious.

"Are you joking with me Betty, come on it's not that good is it?"

The teacher sat back in her chair and her face was angry. "Why don't you ever take any praise Kendal Wilson? The book needs editing and a few tweak's here and there, but what you have here is the start of an amazing book."

Kendal raised a smile and looked at Betty in more detail, she wasn't lying. "I enjoyed writing it. What did you think about the storyline?"

Mrs Jackson held her arms around her body and she made sure they were alone. "It was bleeding brilliant. I felt every sentence and I was involved with the storyline from the first page. I felt like I knew all the characters personally," she stared at her longer than she needed to and sucked on her bottom lip.

Kendal was going bright red and she knew Betty knew that one of the characters was based on her own life. Taking a deep breath she replied to her. "Well, you did say write about what you know, and that's what I've done."

Betty patted the pile of paper in front of her, she was alive with excitement. "Right, if you want, I will edit the book to the best of my ability. But promise me once it's done, you'll start sending it out to some publishers."

Kendal chuckled; her eyes were dancing about. "Really Betty, I can't thank you enough. One day I will pay you back for this, you're a star."

Kendal left the room and her face was happy, she punched her clenched fist into the air and walked along the corridor. "Get in there you beauty," she chuckled.

★

Jane sat in her house alone. She seemed in deep thought. Eva was with her brother and she had the day to herself. Picking at her nails she stood up and paced the front room. With a quick glimpse at the time, she grabbed her coat and ran from the house, she was in a hurry.

Paddy was watching the horseracing on the TV, he was shouting and bawling at the screen. "Oh, you lazy bastard, whip its arse, it's a fucking donkey," he was screaming the house down. Flinging his betting slip at the TV he stood up and grabbed his coat. Just before he opened the front door he stopped dead in his tracks, he'd forgotten something. Turning quickly he dipped his head into the small cupboard and grabbed something from inside it.

★

Kendal hammered on Jane's front door. She bent her knees and placed her face up to the letterbox, cupping her hands around her mouth she shouted out. "Jane it's me Kendal, are you in." Eyes peering through the small gap she could see into the hallway. "Jane," she ranted again. After five minutes Kendal gave up and started to walk away from the house. As she left the garden she looked up at the windows looking for any sign of life, there was nobody about. Kendal was alone tonight and she could have done with the company. Ella May was staying at a friend's house and she hoping she could have spent some quality time with her friend. Walking away she swung the plastic bag at her side. She would have to drink the wine herself.

Molly stood near "Lady Jane's" her eyes were all over the place as she hid away in the shadows of the night. She had a black sports bag at the side of her and it weighed heavy. The wind was circling her body and she was shivering. Her decayed brown teeth were chattering together. Bending down slightly, she picked the bag up and started to walk onto the main road. A car honked its horn in the distance and she could see John Daley's car pulling into the car park behind her. With speed in her step she headed back towards him, she was fuming. "Fucking hell John, we said nine o'clock. What time do you call this?" He nodded his head slowly and smirked at her.

"Get your arse in the car and we can sort this shit out once and for all." Molly climbed inside and slammed the car door shut.

"Come on then don't piss me about. Just give me the money and I'm gone. We said ten grand, yes," she raised her eyebrows at him. John reached inside the glove compartment and pulled out a brown envelope. Before he gave it to her he sat back and sniggered in an evil manner, he was teasing her.

"So where are you off to then?" Molly snapped, she

was sweating and wanted to get the money from him as quickly as possible.

"Does it matter where I'm going? As long as I'm not around here, you don't have anything to worry about it, so just chill out." John swallowed hard and his chest was rising at speed.

"Be nice to me, are you forgetting who I am?" Molly held her head back and huffed, she was taking no shit from him.

"You're just an old man these days John. Maybe back in the day you had it all, but now you're just a coffin dodger."

Molly's head crashed against the window and John climbed from his driving seat to make sure he had a firm grip of her. "Listen you sweaty runt, I'm still the man around here. Men shake when my name's mentioned, I'm still the top dog and don't you fucking forget it."

Molly could never hold her tongue and she fought to break free. "You're a sex-case John Daley. You prey on young girls and ruin their lives." A loud banging noise caused them to both check the area, somebody was about. John opened his car door and scanned the car park. His eyes were all over the place. Nobody was there. Jumping back in the car he held the envelope out towards Molly.

"Suck me off and we're done. I'll give you the money and then you can go where ever it is you're going." Molly snarled and her nostrils flared, she was sweating.

"Go and fuck yourself. I'll tell you what; stick your money up your arse. I'm going to the police." John chuckled loudly and pressed the central locking on the car.

"Why don't we run away together, me and you, just like old times. You loved me then, you can love me again, can't you?" Molly ignored him and sat staring out of the window; she was testing him for sure. As she spoke she kept her face turned away from him.

"You killed my sister; you made me a heroin addict. Do you think I would ever get involved with you again?" John Daley seemed desperate; he stroked the back of her neck with his trembling fingers.

"Come on, think about it. We both have a past to run from. We could be happy." Molly turned her head and sniggered.

"Just open the door John, stick your money as far up your arse as it will go. I thought I could leave Manchester behind me, but do you know what?" she smirked at him. "I've faced my demons already, can you say the same?"

Molly reached over and pressed the button for the central locking. John was in some kind of daze and his eyes were just staring into space, his mind was somewhere else. Molly was quick and her hands grabbed the cash from the side of the seat, he didn't even realise it was gone. The car door slammed and Molly sprinted off into the night. John was alone.

John Daley sat tapping his fingers on the steering wheel. Molly was a ticking bomb and he knew he should have killed her when he had the chance. Jerking his body forward he got out of the car and locked it. The crunching sound of his feet along the gravel filled the air. He kept turning his head back over his shoulder as he was walking, he was aware that someone was following him. His footsteps quickened as he passed the alleyway. Before he knew it his body fell to the ground and a figure was on top of him thrusting a silver claw hammer deep into his body. Blood surged from his head and he didn't stand a chance. John Daley wasn't moving as his attacker ran into the night. You could hear their rapid breathing as they ran off into the shadows. John's cold body lay under the street lamp as the winds swept over his body.

John Daley was dead.

Kendal lay in her bed reading a book. She seemed lost in the words and whatever it was she was reading it was making her smile. She lay with her pillow folded in two and the duvet cover was tucked in tightly around her body. Flicking over the pages she rubbed her knuckles into her eyes. It was nearly two o'clock. Placing the book face down on the cabinet at the side of the bed she flicked the switch from the lamp. The room was dark and the only light was from the moon. Kendal's eyes stared out of the window and as she closed her eyes the corners of her mouth started to rise.

CHAPTER NINETEEN

Kendal knocked on Jane's door and this time she opened it. Kendal stormed in and she was upset. "So, what happened to you last night? I was ringing you for hours, why didn't you answer me?" Jane trudged inside the front room and plonked down on the sofa.

"I left my phone at home. I had to go around to my Mam's house, her and my Dad were nearly killing each other again. I swear, you would think at their age they would have calmed down by now." Kendal didn't believe a word she was saying and sighed loudly.

"Yeah, whatever Jane. You must have seen all the missed calls on your phone when you got home last night, why didn't you ring me back?" Kendal was waiting for an answer but Jane blanked her.

"Listen, I'm sorry. What was so important anyway that it couldn't wait?"

"It doesn't matter now, just forget about it," Kendal moaned. Jane stood up and walked towards the kitchen. Kendal noticed that she had bruises on her wrist.

"Do you want a brew; I'm making one for me so you may as well have one?"

"Go on then," Kendal said. Looking around the front room Kendal could see an empty bottle of vodka at the side of the chair. The ashtray was overflowing with cig dimps. Reaching over for the bottle she shouted into the kitchen.

"So, were you pissed last night then?"

"No, I haven't had a drink for days. I'm saving it

for my birthday next weekend," Jane answered. Kendal looked confused and placed the bottle back where it was. Jane was hiding something and she was going to do her best to get to the bottom of it.

"Quick grab one of these cups from me," Jane screamed out. Waving her fingers about in the air she hooked the other cup from her fingers. "I swear, I'm always doing that, it's a wonder I've not got third degree burns."

Kendal was amused and she was watching her every movement. "Did you say you didn't have a drink last night, did I hear you right?" There was no way she was letting this go.

"Yeah, are you going deaf or something. Der..... I told you I went to sort my Mam and Dad out." Kendal grabbed the empty bottle and held it up in front of her.

"Stop lying, what's this then?"

Jane went white and she swallowed hard, she was stuttering. "Well," Kendal urged. Jane chewed on her lips and sat cracking her knuckles, whatever she wanted to say was trapped on her tongue. Grabbing a fag from the packet on the table she lit it with shaking hands.

"You're not going to like what I'm going to say Kendal. It just happened, I swear to you he just turned up here out of the blue."

"Who did?" Kendal urged. Jane inhaled hard on her cigarette and blew a cloud of smoke from her mouth.

"John Daley," there was silence.

"Are you having a laugh or what? After what I told you? You're finished with me Jane. What a sell out you are." Kendal jumped up from her seat and headed for the door. Jane ran after her.

"Just hold your horses you crank, let me finish."

"No, Jane, if you're back with him then our friendship is over." Jane stood in front of the door.

"I'm not back with him trust me. He came here begging me to go back to Blackpool with him. He was pissed and just sat there feeling sorry for himself and telling me all about his problems. I told him I knew about Mary and Molly."

Kendal's mouth dropped. "Are you right in the head? That was our secret; you swore you wouldn't breathe a word."

"Fucking listen!" Jane screamed. "Look at my hands, the bastard tried to rape me. He knew there was no way I was going back with him and he started to get violent." Kendal clocked Jane's arms as she pulled her sleeves up and she could tell by her face that she wasn't lying.

"He's going to find us and deal with us now. There is no way he'll want us grassing to the police. Oh, fucking hell Jane what are we going to do?"

Jane seemed distant and spoke slowly. "He won't be coming near us again, don't you worry about that. I told him if anything happened to me you would go straight to the police." Kendal walked back to the sofa and sat back down; her head was resting in her hands.

"Get ready, you're not staying here on your own. You can come and stay with me, there's strength in numbers. Well, that's what my Nana used to say anyway." Jane agreed.

"Right, just let me pack some stuff up then. Come with me into the bedroom, I've been shitting myself all night. Look at me I'm a nervous wreck." The two girls hurried into the bedroom.

★

Molly sat behind her bedroom door. In her hands she held the money she'd stolen from John Daley. All night long she'd been awake and she was waiting for the knock at the door. Paddy was shouting her from downstairs, he'd just come in the house. "Molly, come down here quick." Sprinting to the bedroom window she searched for police outside. There was no one there. Hesitating she walked onto the landing and popped her head over the banister. "Dad, what do you want? I'm getting in the bath?"

Paddy walked into the hallway you could see his feet.

"Just come down here a minute, you're not going to believe it." Molly hurried down the stairs. Inhaling deeply she tried to calm herself down; her heart was beating ten to the dozen. Paddy was pacing the front room; he looked like he's seen a ghost.

"It's John Daley," Molly was about to turn and get on her toes but her father's words stopped her in her tracks. "He's dead."

Molly gulped and her eyes were wide open.

"How?"

Paddy sat down on his chair and he cupped his hands together. "He's been murdered. The police are all over the place searching for evidence. I've just seen them team-handed up near Lady Jane's brass gaff."

Molly ran to the living room window and lifted the net curtain up slowly, still no police.   "Do they know who killed him?"

Paddy shook his head slowly. "I don't think so. But I heard one of the officers saying it was a brutal attack."

Molly was sweating, her palms were hot and she kept wiping them on her faded jeans. "I bet it's something to do with drugs, he had his fingers in a few pies didn't he? So who knows? Personally, I'm glad. The man was a twat."

Paddy kept his head low, I'm sure he was smiling. Molly searched for her coat and put it on in a hurry. "I'm just nipping out, I'll be back soon." The front door slammed shut and Paddy turned the TV on.

Molly ran all the way to Lady Jane's. As she neared it she could see police vans parked up around the surrounding areas. Pulling her hood up over her head she crept towards the crowd of people who were gathered behind the yellow tape. "Someone must have had it in for him to leave him like that. It was a cold-blooded attack. The guy didn't stand a chance."

Molly was listening to a man talking at the side of her, she barged her way closer to him. "What's happened mate, is somebody dead?"

The onlooker loved sharing his information and he pulled her nearer to fill her in on all the gory details. Molly was gobsmacked, she was free at last. This man had ruled her life for as long as she could remember. Walking away slowly she whispered under her breath. "Fuck you John Daley; I hope you burn in hell." Molly skipped along the road and headed to the bus stop. In her pocket you could see the top of a brown envelope hanging out.

★

Kendal and Jane sat with Paddy. Once they'd heard the news about John's death they were both upset. Perhaps they were tears of joy but they put a good show on in front of Paddy. Molly came into the house and she was holding a plastic bag in her hands. "Fish and chips everybody? I've just bought us all some from down the road." The aroma from the chips filled the air. Kendal was starving and followed Molly into the kitchen to help her put the food onto plates.

"He's dead Molly, he's really dead." Molly kept her back to Kendal and kept her voice low.

"I know love. It was a cold-blooded attack; the police said he didn't stand a chance."

Kendal looked sad. "He was still my Dad you know, I do feel it a bit…"

Molly grabbed her by her arms and made sure the door was closed. "Don't you ever feel sorry for that prick. He was no Dad to you; he was an evil controlling bastard. Let's forget about him and get on with our lives." Kendal jerked the tears back as her auntie passed her a brown envelope. Opening it slowly her jaw dropped.

"It's money, bloody hell Molly where did you get it from?"

"Ask no questions, tell no lies," she chuckled. "It's for you Kendal, it's to help you get your book published. Let's say it's what I was owed from somebody." Kendal was about to speak, but Molly put her hand over her mouth and kept her quiet. "Like I said, it's for you. Now, come on, help me put this food out before it gets cold."

Kendal was puzzled and she kept looking at Molly with a concerned look on her face. Had Molly really killed John Daley?

★

Night time fell in the Wilson household. Jane and Kendal were staying there that night and they were all sat around the table drinking wine. Paddy was watching them all with a smile on his face. Molly was dancing and she had them all in stitches laughing, she had no rhythm at all, she was dancing like a pig in a fit. Paddy stood up and walked to Kendal's side. Leaning in to her he pecked her on the cheek. "Goodnight love." He did the same to Molly and

Jane; he'd definitely mellowed with age. Once he left the room Molly raised her glass and whispered softly. "Up yours John Daley." The other two girls smiled but you could see the sadness in their eyes, they both had the reasons to mourn John's death.

Kendal woke up the next morning and Molly's foot was sticking in her face from the other end of the bed. The three girls had all slept in the double bed. Kendal squirmed as she focused on the black toenails near her mouth. "Bleeding hell, them toenails need cutting Molly, they're like hooves." There was movement from the other end of the bed. Jane sat up slowly and her eyes were small. Stretching her hands above her head she yawned.

"What time is it? I need to go and get Eva from our kid's." Molly rolled over and dragged the duvet over her head.

"Sssshhh will you. Some of us have a hangover." Kendal kicked her with her foot and you could see Molly wasn't impressed. "Turn it in Kendal. I swear my heads going to burst, if you carry on like that. Just leave me alone will you?" Jumping out of the bed Kendal pulled at Jane's hands.

"Come on I'll make us some breakfast. I will cook us some bacon and eggs and mushrooms." Jane heard the word food and she was up out of the bed. They both headed down stairs. Molly shouted after them.

"Do me some too; it might be what I need to sort this hangover out."

"Get your bony arse out of bed then, come on, get up," Kendal shouted back at her.

Paddy was nursing his cup of tea; you could see the steam rising up from it. "I'm making some breakfast if you want some Granddad?" Kendal asked.

"Not for me chicken, my stomach's a bit off at the moment, I'll grab something later."

The letterbox rattled, it was the post. Kendal walked into the hallway and she could see a few letters, one of them stood out because it was handwritten. Her eyes were all over it, she could see it was a prison letter. Her heart was banging inside her chest, she held her back up against the wall. Checking no one was watching her she shoved the letter deep inside her housecoat.

"Jane you start the breakfast, I'm just nipping to the toilet." Jane nodded and walked into the kitchen, you could hear pots and pans banging together.

Bolting the toilet door behind her Kendal sat on the toilet seat. Slowly she ripped the envelope open. She recognised Scott's writing straight away and panicked. "What the fuck do you want?" she cursed under her breath. Her eyes hit the paper and her jaw dropped. This man was a head-case for sure. Even from the prison walls he was still trying to rule her life. He'd made threats to her in the letter and told her straight that he would never stop looking for her when he finally was released from prison. Folding the letter she rammed it into her pocket. She flushed the toilet and headed back downstairs, she was fuming.

Jane was stood at the cooker and the bacon was under the grill, the aroma from it made her mouth water. "What's up with your face," Jane enquired. Kendal sighed and brought out the letter from her pocket.

"It's that nob again chatting shit to me. He said he's never going to stop looking for me." Jane snatched the letter from her hands and started reading it.

"What a prick he is. I'll tell you what, get on the blower to the prison and tell them what's going on. They can stop any letters from him to you. Plus, he's going to get fucked because this is a threatening letter. He's going to get more bird now for sure. Go on, phone the prison now, I'll do the breakfast, you need this sorting as soon as, the man is a crank."

Kendal rolled her eyes, "Yeah, I'll do it in a bit. He's just put me on a right downer now though. Who the hell does he think he is?"

Paddy sat watching the TV. John's death was all over the news and the police were no nearer catching his killer. Kendal coughed hard to get Jane's attention when a spokesman for the Greater Manchester Police read out his statement on the TV searching for any witnesses. Paddy sat forward in his seat and he was in a world of his own as he listened to the news carefully. Molly stood behind her father's chair and her hands were gripping the cushion on it, her knuckles were white. Jane and Kendal sat next to each other and both of them seemed uneasy. Paddy stood up and shook his head. "What a world ay? Nobody is safe anymore." No one answered him as they all sat around the table eating their breakfast. Paddy went upstairs.

CHAPTER TWENTY

"Kendal it's here, come and see. The van's just pulled up outside," Molly screamed. Kendal ran to the window and pulled back the net curtains so she could get a full view. A man carrying a large brown box entered the garden, his face was strained and whatever he was holding seemed heavy.

"Open the bleeding door then," Paddy yelled. "We've been waiting for this day for ages. Go on, quick move your arse before the poor man keels over." Kendal headed to the door at speed. Taking a deep breath she opened the front door. Three boxes were piled high and the delivery man looked exhausted.

"Can you sign for this lot love? I tell you what they weigh a bleeding ton whatever is inside them." Kendal was smiling and her body stood tall.

"It's my new novel, these are the first copies."

"So you are an author then?" the man asked. Feeling her face burning up she had to think about the question again.

"Yes, I suppose you could say that," she giggled. The man helped bring the boxes into the front room and he left.

Their eyes were all on Kendal and Jane was dancing around the place as if she'd won the lottery. "Open the box then, come on let's have a look at this piece of art," Jane shouted.

Kendal bent her knees and slowly she pulled the brown tape from the top of the box, she could see the top of her books. Her hands moved at speed and finally she held her book in her hands for the first time. Jane grabbed a copy to and passed one to Paddy and Molly. Everyone was speechless; Jane choked up and found it hard to hold back any emotions. "I'll be able to read this soon. My reading is almost there Kendal, I can't wait." Kendal closed her eyes and held the glossy book cover to her chest.

"This is for you Nana," she whispered. Paddy was illiterate and had never wanted to read, this was the only time in his life that he regretted his illiteracy. Molly walked to his side and placed her hand on his shoulder.

"Don't worry Dad, I'll read it to you." He sank his head low and blushed. Kendal opened the book and her eyes filled up.

This was her first novel called "Missing Pieces." Turning each page slowly she remembered writing every single word on the page. Betty had done what she said and her editing skills had made the book a work of art. Molly came to her niece's side and popped her head over her shoulder. Reading the acknowledgements she choked back the tears. It said, "To the mother I never knew Mary Wilson, I hope this makes you smile." The credits were endless and Betty had got the mention she deserved. Kendal checked the time.

"Oh, I better get a move on. I'm doing the book signing in an hour." Betty had arranged it with the local book shop, she was as proud as punch of her pupil and she wanted the world and his wife to know all about this girl's amazing achievements.

Kendal sat in the taxi staring out of the window; she was going to the book shop first to meet Betty. Jane and Molly were making their own way there. Driving down Moston Lane Kendal put her hands on the driver's shoulder. Can we just go into the cemetery first? The man looked frustrated.

"My clock will still be ticking love, so make it quick." Kendal nodded and guided him to the grave she wanted to visit. Thick black mud was all over her shoes as she walked along the grass verge to the graveside. Once she was there she pulled her novel from her bag. Wiping her mother's name and her Grandmother's slowly, she cleared the dirt from the headstone.

"Look you two. This is for you both. I hope I've made you proud. It's called 'Missing Pieces' it's my first novel." Kendal wiped the tears from her eyes and spoke in a low voice. "I know the truth now mother and I can put it to bed. This time is for me and Ella May now and I'm going to show her that with a bit of self-belief, you can do anything. There are still secrets in this family, and I suppose I'll never know all of them, but for now mother, I'm at peace." Kendal made the sign of the cross and placed the book on the grave. Walking back to the taxi she smiled and raised her eyes to the sky.

Paddy lay in his bed. His health had suddenly deteriorated and he was finding it difficult to breathe. Dragging his body up from the bed he smiled at the chair facing him. "Nelly is that you?" His face seemed alive and he seemed to have a second wind of energy. Paddy was holding his hands out towards the chair and you could see his fingers curling at the end of his hands. His eyes closed slowly and he smiled softly.

Jackie Daley pulled up at Manchester airport. Her two elder brothers were close by her side. Before she went inside the airport she hugged them both tightly. "Thanks for sorting John out for me. He deserved everything he got the no good bastard." Simon her eldest brother gripped her face and nodded slowly. "Nobody fucks with my sister. Go on catch your plane. We'll be over to see you soon." Jackie walked off holding her suitcases. With a quick wave over her shoulder she headed off to start her new life.

Kendal sat at the table in the book shop and a crowd of people stood in front of her eager to get their book signed. Jane and Molly were stood at either side of her and they looked like they were protecting her. Betty was buzzing around like a bumble bee and she looked at her wit's end, it was so exciting. The first woman stood at the table and passed Kendal a book. The black pen was shaking in her hand and she was unsure of what to write. Betty saved the day. She whispered into Kendal's ear. "Just say thank you for your support and sign your name." Kendal scribbled her message and passed it to the fan. Within seconds she was signing books left right and centre. Kendal Wilson was now an author and her books would be sold worldwide.

When asked by the press what had made her write a book she giggled and spoke clearly. "Life gave me the words to write my books. Education gave me the tools, and I gave myself self-belief by writing them, that was all I needed." The press snapped photographs of Kendal Wilson in the book shop and this time the smile she carried on her face was real, she was no longer covering up.

THE END

Other Books by Karen Woods

Broken Youth
Black Tears
Northern Girls Love Gravy
Bagheads
Teabags & Tears
The Visitors
Sleepless in Manchester

To order any of these titles visit:
www.empire-uk.com